I0523345

OUR KISS

A NOVEL

J. A. Alldredge

This book is a work of fiction. The characters, incidents, and dialogue drawn from the author's imagination included in this book are not to be construed as real persons, incidents, communications, or actual events. Any resemblance to actual persons, living or dead, is entirely incidental.

Our Kiss. Copyright © 2015 by Joseph A. Alldredge

ALL RIGHTS RESERVED. Printed in the United States of America. No part of this book may be used, reproduced, or transmitted in any manner or form or by any means, electronic or mechanical, including photocopying, recording, or by any information storage and retrieval system, without prior permission in writing from the publisher and author, except in the case of a brief quotation(s) embodied in critical articles and reviews.

Our Kiss may be purchased for educational, business, or sales promotional use. For information please write: Joseph A. Alldredge Publishing, P.O. Box 1555, Santa Rosa Beach, Florida, 32459.

First Edition

ISBN # 978-0-9963274-0-4 (paperback)

ISBN # 978-0-9963274-1-1 (ebook)

for my Say Jay
My friend, my love, my inspiration

1

I T WAS SUPPOSED to be just another typical Wednesday morning. The day on the calendar read June 3, 1987. I rolled out of bed to the sound of my crying alarm clock, showered, put on my face, threw a few curls in my over the shoulder blonde hair, and dressed myself in my navy pinstripe suite-jacket with a matching pencil skirt—all before the sun peeked above the horizon. Everything unplugged and put away. I take one last quick peek at my hastily applied makeup, especially around my pale-blue eyes before turning off the bathroom light.

The house was still and dark, all quiet, except for the faint sounds of snoring rumbling behind my parents' bedroom door. Switching off my bedroom light, I tiptoed down the hallway and down around the winding wooden staircase. My four-inch heels clicked softly on the foyer tile as I crept towards the front door. Breakfast wasn't an option as usual, since I already felt rushed to get out before anyone else.

The air was so thick, warm, and sticky as I stepped outside. It was going to be the hottest day of the summer so far. Atlanta can get so humid this time of year, even when the sun is still down. A steamy cloud of mist swallowed me up. My hair was already going flat before I could even reach the car.

As my engine fired-up, I glanced up through the windshield to see my father's bedroom light flicking on. His curtain moved slightly as he took a quick look outside to see my headlights coming on. It had almost become a game between us, to see who was at the office first each morning. An unspoken bet had been created between us, with the prize being a matter of pride. A tiny little ammunition to prick the other with as you boasted about how productive you were today, or to be used as a shield whenever the other attacked with the accusation that one of you was being too lazy. It was just a small part of a long history of prideful competition between us, starting from when I was still in grade school. And Patrick S. Morgan did not like to lose to anyone—especially to me—his one and only daughter and continual disappointment, Emma Morgan.

To give you some idea of just how competitive he was, his middle initial stood for *Stone*, as in *Stonewall*. He was named after Stonewall Jackson, a notoriously fierce General for the Confederate Army that stood against the Northern Army like a *stone wall*. Stone, was also his nickname—one that he truly relished. It was always a reminder for him to never be a pushover! And he always did his best to live up to his namesake.

Even now at twenty-six, after finishing my second year of law school, I forced myself to keep up the pretense that I enjoyed our little games of jousting. Pretending that I was still his little girl who enjoyed whatever it was we were still doing. Ultimately, it was just too hard to disappoint him.

I understood it wasn't his fault that he turned out the way he is.

You see, my father was from a long line of strong Southern men, going all the way back to the American Revolutionary War. From settlers, to slave owning plantation owners, his family eventually amassed a small enough fortune to allow them to move on into big business and politics. A large portrait of his favorite great-grandfather is hanging above the mantle in the living room as a testament to our powerful heritage (replacing the family portrait of the four of us pretending to smile warmly). In his most austere and domineering pose, Grandfather William Morgan maintains his watchful gaze over his descendants. To me, granddad is more like a ghost that won't ever leave. Unfortunately you can't simply use an exorcism to rid yourself from the past. Like a pesky ghost, his looming forceful presence has in many ways possessed my father. In many ways, he has haunted my own life—through my father.

Grandfather Morgan even made a run for Governor of Georgia once. He lost, but only because the other candidate was a no-good, cheating, scallywag carpetbagger—as my father had explained in far too much detail, on far too many occasions. Somehow, that seemingly inconsequential political defeat way back when, got wedged deeply in my father's craw. In the back of his mind it still pricks at him for some reason. Even to this very day, that one long-ago painful defeat seems to drive him every day to work harder than the above average man.

That's especially so with me and my older brother Jonathon. Being two years older than me, with more time in the trenches with my father, poor Jonathon has not fared as well.

Jon, as I call him, wasn't blessed at birth with the extra layer of skin. I somehow did inherit that quality from my father. He apparently was gifted with my mother's softer side. Some would even say he had acquired *a more delicate nature.* It should have been more apparent to my father that Jon was a homosexual, but those types of things were easier for my father to ignore, rather than accept.

The problem for Jon wasn't that he couldn't best my father, since he certainly could, if he had too. He was always much better at finding ways to avoid those situations than I ever was. But when he had to compete with father, Jon didn't hold back at all. I think mother and I were the only ones who noticed the thinly hidden gloating smile on Jon's face every time he humiliated father at golf, snow skiing, chess, the arts, or even historical trivia. Whatever Jon had to master he managed to pull it off somehow, with their epic showdowns nearly always ending with father being utterly embarrassed.

Slowly, over the years, it became obvious to everyone in the family that my father was turning his attentions to me. More than likely he was just seeking an easier challenge. Of course I let him win—most of the time. But sadly this tactic only seemed to encourage him. I came to know exactly why Jon always fought his hardest to win against father. Clearly being the smartest one of us all, Jon quickly realized that if he lost, father would only keep coming back for more. But if he always won big, always, father would whimper off like a whipped dog—hopefully never to return for another humiliating beating.

We all still live at home, suffering under the same roof, with all the same pressures that come with that slow-cooker of a situation. My only release valve was the bright light shining at the end of the tunnel up ahead—finally getting my law degree, passing the bar, getting paid as a first year associate at my father's law firm, Donaldson and Morgan— and then immediately getting the hell out! But poor Jon seemed destined for a little more tenderizing. He was floundering in design school. The economy was stagnating with high unemployment. So he was resigned to sticking it out at home for now. At least he managed to escape out into the carriage house above the garage. Lucky for him, the carriage house was much better than any place I could afford for the next couple of years.

My mother, Evelynn, or just Eve, provided a protective cover for Jon until he could finally fly from the nest, as mothers usually do for their favorite children. She was his biggest blessing and most fearsome curse all sewn up into one big patchwork baby-blanket. The one that he could never seem to now unwrap himself from, or ever leave behind to finally grow up into an adult. It was just so warm, comfy, and protective, even if it was getting old, tattered, and a little clingy. They made the perfect pair. More like codependents really. They were forced together in many ways by father—at least he became one of their favorite excuses.

Of course I was jealous. But Jon needed mother in those ways that I didn't. So it worked for them.

I will admit that it was a guilty pleasure of mine, at times, to watch poor Jon getting batted about between them. Like a scurrying mouse trying to squirm out of their grasps, mother and father played him back and forth between them in a sadistic cat and mouse game. "He's going to take golf lessons and that's final," father would thrust. "But that won't work, since I've already signed him up for tennis classes with me," mother would parry. It went on and on, back and forth, day after day. Best of all, it left them with less time to focus on me. But Jon did his utmost best to get them to see me, along with my shortcomings. Or, to get them to lump me in with him on everything they forced him into. But what about Emma…why doesn't she have to go too?

Mother did her utmost best to protect Jon. She understood him in ways that father and I never could, or would. Always the cliché' Southern wall-flower—a gladiolus, only blooming in the moonlight, soft and subtle, knowing just when to reveal her true self or when to stay hidden. It was hard for her to be confrontational with father, even when she was absolutely right. Most things she let go, especially anything to do with money or his family. Anything having to do with Jon however was different, completely different, and she never shied away from stepping in-between them when necessary, whenever Jon had reached his breaking point. At those times, she was no wilting flower. She was the growling momma bear standing tall up on her hind legs with her long sharp teeth and claws bared.

Again, I was sometimes jealous of her absolute loyalty to Jon. Perhaps I wasn't the bad-girl that deserved that type of protection. It just wasn't in me to find out.

Liberal amounts of white wine often seemed to draw mother out of the domestic shadows, especially when we least expected it. As we got older it got worse and worse. The strains of life took her to that point—to where she just needed a little more in each glass. We've all been there. We've all seen it happen to someone we know, but that doesn't make it any easier. On occasion, when they would have company over, mother would blossom a bit more than father could stand. His red face would glow as brightly as the sun whenever he was upset with her, or when he became embarrassed. He always held his composure like the *stone* that he was, never letting on. Displaying emotion was strictly reserved for the weaker sex. He couldn't even allow himself to shed a tear at his mother's funeral a few years back. It really hadn't donned on me until this day, that I had never seen him cry. Always the stoic gentleman—he held his tongue until he and my mother were finally alone.

At least he thought they were.

Jon and I heard most of the *more heated* arguments. Sadly, we agreed with both of them—to a point. It's like an old recording that you hate to hear play again. "All you do is work," mother thrust, "You're never around anymore…never at home." Father would inevitably parry with, "Isn't this lavish lifestyle what you wanted?" Mother would counter, "The children need you around more." Father blocked with, "I have obligations that you just can't understand," before throwing a low blow, "All you do now is drink and play cards with your friends down at the club, or tennis, or shopping, or whatever it is you find to do all day while spending my money!" Then the gloves would come off, and the bare-knuckled punches would fly. Mother would jab, "Lousy Bastard!" Father would go for a knockout, "You're nothing but a lazy drunk!"

And that's the point where we tuned them out—the best we could anyway. Somehow, despite my best efforts, their arguing voices return to haunt me nearly every time I leave home.

I can barely hear their faint echoing screams bouncing around in the far-back recessed canyons of my mind—just like this morning—as I put my soft-top Mustang in reverse and rev up the engine. Backing this little gem up, making a sharp swing to turn around in the driveway, they remind me of just how lucky I am. This sleek, sickeningly cute, baby-blue, two-door roadster with a sparkly vanity plate that reads, *All Ems,* was given to me as a college graduation present by both of my parents. Not that they saw it the same way. "She's getting spoiled rotten. Why don't you just get her one of those new Hondas like the one we gave to Jonathon?" Mother snipped. "It's my money," father groaned back, "I worked hard for it. I'll decide how to reward my daughter for her hard work." Here we go again. "Jon never got a car like that!"

"That's because Jon never deserved one like it!"

"Bastard!"

"Bitch!"

The long winding driveway was way too long—since it gave me way too much time to remember it all. Waiting for the electric gate at the end to slowly swing open didn't help either. It was just a little more time to try and not think about it, as I looked around the estate, waiving politely to the groundskeeper who was already at work, getting a jump on the sun, but already dripping with sweat.

Father had picked out this four acre plot to build his enormous home on. Having heard about it through a friend, he had to snatch it up quickly before anyone else found out it was available. It was one of only a few large forested pieces of property left that close to downtown Atlanta.

Then, starting with some ancient logs pulled from a riverbed, he used them to frame our six bedroom seven bath rich man's wet dream of a home. No expense was spared for his masterpiece to lavish living. Italian marble, tile, and granite covered every surface as far as the eye could see. Glistening etched glass and crystal, freshly polished by our daily maid service, dazzled in every room. Upstairs was a full spa with a hot tub, a dry sauna, *and* a steam-room. Downstairs we had the very first in-home eight seat theatre room in the neighborhood. Everything else was either imported or handmade. Every hedge was trimmed even. Each blade of grass snipped as fine as any PGA putting green. Finished off by this audacious hand-laid red brick herring-bone driveway—the one I get to closely inspect every morning while waiting for the damn electric gate to slowly swing open. The one we don't really need, but father believed it made us seem more important—more imposing.

As I try to finally force my parents screaming voices out of my head, I dropped the clutch and stomped on the gas—spinning my smoking tires like a dragster. With a big devilish grin, I left behind a long black skid-mark blemish on the driveway as I peeled away.

Check that out dad!

2

BESTING FATHER WASN'T the only reason I had for getting up and leaving the house early. That was just a tasty sweet cherry on top. I had my own, other selfish reasons.

I could jump onto Highway 19 and speed straight down Peachtree Street into Midtown. It was only about nine miles from home to work. That would get me to the fourteen story office building where father's law firm was located well before most of the other *Atlantians* clogged it up with traffic. But instead, I like to use my head-start for a few moments of alone time. The only peace and quiet I would have for the rest of the day. So, as usual, I take a left turn, and head a few blocks over to Piedmont Park.

All the parking spaces are still empty. The 186 acre park is nearly empty. It's so quiet. Only a few joggers drift by far off in the foggy distance. Walkways take me that short distance to the edge of the lake, to where my bench is patiently waiting for me to arrive like an old friend. My initials are carved into the wooden bench, right next to my first *real* boyfriend's initials, with a silly plus sign between them. Ethan is his name. Tall and thin for his age back then, he was a few years older than me, but not as smart, yep, I could tell even then. Sometimes, on days like today, I daydream we are sitting together again, watching the sunrise, holding hands, and making plans for the future like we used to do in the summer when we would meet here—secretly. Jon knew about us, but he kept it quiet, at least until we finally broke up when school started back.

Maybe someday, the daydream always begins—

I take my seat on the wooden bench and look out across the park. Lake Clara Meer is a dark mirror reflecting the morning light. As usual, the harsh reality of being all alone inevitably takes hold. My thoughts eventually begin to sink lower than the murky water at my feet. I feel as though I'm drifting down a hopeless well, knowing that Ethan would have to remain an elusive day-dream, for now.

Forcing myself back to the surface, I try and lighten the mood.

Sunlight begins to filter through the tallest magnolia and oak trees on the other side of the lake. With the softness of starlight the tiny waves on the lake begin to twinkle. The water-heavy air rises like an apparition being beckoned home by the warming rays streaming down from above. A cloud almost forms, with a hazy fog clinging to the top of the water. Soon it will give in to the sunlight, slowly lifting up into the brightening blue sky. As the light spills through the disappearing mist, all of the colors blossom at once. Everything begins to brighten. At that precise moment, it all comes together just like a sublime painting, with all the softness and anticipation of a fairy tale coming to life. The hazy air shades a harsh reality, where the pink hydrangea, purple wisteria, white dogwood, cherry and magnolia blossoms.

There are flowers in shades of blues, yellows, and reds, all surrounded by every shade of green—with drooping weeping willow branches bending down to where they can gently touch the top of the dark shimmering water. I paint with my imagination the rest of what I want to see—thousands of sprouting reeds, all reaching up out of the water, bending over slightly as they lilt over flowering water-lilies, as if they are paying homage to the splendor.

An amazing spectacle of life erupted before my eyes. It was a scene that I had witnessed many times over before. But this day was different. And with my romantic reminiscing and fanciful fantasizing about all of the *what-ifs,* and the, *if onlys,* I had let my emotions get too close to the surface. My emotions suddenly got the best of me as I thought of what I'd missed out on. On all that I'd sacrificed, missed out on, or given up on. Teardrops appeared on my eyelids as I fought back the urge to cry. Looking over at the empty park bench next to me, I imagined that David was sitting there next to me, seeing the same spectacle—with the same shimmering teardrops clinging to his eyelids—feeling how he would have felt at this very moment.

If you were as passionate about impressionist art as I am, especially *The Water Lilies* by Monet, then you would understand completely. David understood why. Ever since I was the tiniest of little girls I can remember loving those hypnotically sensual scenes of water, clouds, lilies, reeds, and trees—all looking like they were floating in some fantastical dream. It was a place I could escape the moment and just be me. Staring into those dreamscapes I was transported to another dimension, to where life seemed simpler, even more real somehow. A place that drew me out of myself, to where

I could feel everything—every emotion. A place I never wanted to leave.

As I stared teary eyed over Lake Clara, I imagined that Monet must have felt the same exact way—fighting back the same emotional tears as he painted.

It was his work, and those like it, that first inspired me to become an artist. With mothers' encouragement I joined the art club at school, staying in it from fourth-grade all the way up through high school. Father didn't discourage it, just as long as my academics didn't suffer. Not a chance of that. My grades remained top-notch, straight A's, top ten in my graduating class. I excelled at the reading, writing, and arithmetic stuff, but art was always my true passion.

Father had always been a local philanthropist, patron of the arts, community big-wig, for as long as I could remember. It wasn't that he was truly personally invested in the arts—being as far from an art connoisseur as one can actually get. He was obviously driven by a passion to obtain power, wealth, and status. His ultimate goal was to be nominated as a Federal Judge. Now it was right at his fingertips, and he was grasping desperately for it. Getting a lifetime tenure position, with all the power of a small kingdom at his hands, almost made father mad with desire. So instead of embracing the art world, he just took advantage of it. He got himself appointed to the Board of Directors for the High Museum of Art. "That'll look wonderful on my resume'," I remember him explaining to mother; even though I was still too young to really understand.

It paid-off for me later however. Starting in my freshman year of high school father used his influence to land me a summer intern position working inside the museum. Even during school months I spent as much time as I could hanging-out there, helping out whenever and however I could. "This'll look great on your college application," he squawked constantly like some insipid parrot—as if *that's why* I was doing it.

His attitude changed when I actually did apply to Emory University as an art major. Father nearly fainted when I broke the news to him. It was almost frightening the way his face turned so red, with his eyes bulging out along with the veins in his neck. "This isn't going to get you into a good law school," he groaned, as he looked over the application at the dinner table. It seemed like the best time to break the news to him. While I would have someone there to back me up. I could see the torment on his face. As thoughts of me wasting years of my life, along with my wasting many thousands of his dollars, raced through his anguished mind. "This isn't what we planned for," he pointed out, "now you're going to end up just like your brother…a penniless wannabe artist… worthless!"

The look in Jon's eyes as he got up to leave the table was heartbreaking. Mother kept her eyes down, mostly, nervously stirring and picking at her vegetables. "She's not like her brother," she added. "She'll do fine…just as she always does." I knew what she was really saying, without really saying it, in her mother coded language. She was saying let her do it, since she'll just eventually marry some well-to-do and live like I do. Yes, she'll do fine, because she's pretty enough to marry well.

I had never felt more alone. It turned into the longest dinner of our lives. Neither of us was willing to give in. Not until the money thing came up—as it nearly always does with father. "I'm not sure I can agree with allowing you to throw my money away on this little adventure of yours dear," he begrudgingly said, sounding like a businessman at a boardroom table negotiating a contract. "How about, you agree to major in something else, apply to law school, and at least attempt it…and I'll agree to fund everything for you till then. Sound good?"

I finally compromised with him. As I was expected to do—just like every other time we disagreed about something important to me. After agreeing that I would major in English, with a minor in art history, I excused myself and left the table, without eating a single bite.

We never spoke about it again. Not until today.

3

I T WAS HARD to leave the park bench. The sun was above the treetops now. My impressionistic dreamscape was destroyed by the brightness of the direct sunlight now hitting me in the face. Remembering my unwanted compromise with father to get his money had ruined all of the emotion anyway. My eyes were as dry as bones in the desert sun again as I peeled myself away and turned to walk back to the car.

Walking towards the parking lot was not easy. Like most days, I felt as if a strong wind was blowing into me, pushing me back towards the bench, the lake, and my lost serenity. By going to that office building down on Peachtree Street, to a place I didn't really want to be, to do a job that I really didn't enjoy—every day was another compromise to please father all over again. My feet dragged over the grass. My legs felt heavy and numb as I lumbered over a small hill. My heart felt nothing. It no longer mattered if I got there first since I was going to be the loser anyway.

By the time I reached the car I was back to being the person I despised deep down inside. It was me, the person that learned to hide the fact that she had been slowly manipulated into one compromise after another until fully giving in to the will of her father. There was always a big friendly smile on my face when I got to the office—armed with a firm handshake for a greeting, an impeccable wardrobe, an insightful quip at the ready. I was now the perfect law partner's daughter, just like he always wanted. It made me cringe every time he introduced me to someone with his cheesy proud smile. "This is the daughter I told you about...soon to be our newest partner." They would just look at me with a glazed-over, feigned, polite smile—the one I've seen appear on a thousand uncaring faces. Like I was some admired prized pony at the fair that he had groomed to be put on display. *Isn't she just precious!*

It was a short drive to the fourteen story office building. Our firm occupied all of the twelfth, thirteenth, and fourteenth floors. Father's office was in the corner of the fourteenth, with a full wall of windows that let him look down on Peachtree Street. I'm sure it made him feel important to look so far down on the little people below. My office was directly opposite his, catty-corner, on the twelfth floor, small, in the back, right next to the closed-file storage rooms and the janitor's closet. Perfect. Far enough away to almost ensure that I wouldn't get many pop-in visits—just to check in on me.

"Hold the elevator," Carly yelled across the foyer to me as the doors began to shut. With the swiftness of a ninja I swung my arm in-between them just in the nick-of-time, forcing them back open. "Thanks," she said breathlessly as she rushed inside. Carly was a first year associate and the only person I could call a real friend here at the firm. Unless you include my boyfriend Thomas—definitely not Tom, since he hates it when I slip up and call him that. It makes him fell less important, diminished somehow, as if I was comparing him to the "Tom" in the "Tom and Jerry" cartoons. And I really couldn't honestly put him in the *friend* category—either. Not since we started sharing toothbrushes, on occasion.

Carly blew back a swath of hair that had fallen over her face. Her barely combed through brownish tangles were sticking out every-which-way. Her wrinkled dress looked slept in. "Long night again," I groaned with sympathy. "Oh yea," she moaned back, as she wrestled to get an armful of files under control. She had taken them home with her (as she usually did) to try and get caught up with some work. In a law firm billable hours are everything—everything! They are the mother's milk, the life-blood, the sun moon and stars all wrapped up together forming the essence of life. It is how the firm gets paid, for every minute each attorney can say they worked on a case. And, "every associate had better be spending every waking moment working on a case if you want to make partner," father reiterated the gospel doctrine of lawyering on a daily basis, reminding everyone to keep up the "good work."

Carly couldn't stop herself from glancing down at my finger. "He didn't ask," she whispered while giving me that pouty look. I hate that look. That, *oh you poor thing…I'm sure he'll ask you to marry him someday,* look.

Carly couldn't keep her mouth shut—not for anything. Very verbal from a small age she tells me. Reminding me often of how she was from a very large family from out in the boonies, where they had to fight for whatever they could get, including a seat at the dinner table close enough to grab some leftovers after her big brothers, sisters, mother, and father were all done. Holding one's tongue was not a good thing where she was from. It's actually one of the many reasons I liked her. She didn't put herself through a State University waiting tables, get into law school on a small scholarship, and graduate at the top of her class, without being a bit on the aggressive side. That's what convinced my father to hire her, but I didn't hold that against her. Luckily, she didn't hold it against me that I didn't have to do those things to get ahead.

Her frumpy attire and street fighter attitude were the other of the top three reasons we were friends. For one, she would stand up for when the others attacked me behind my back. And secondly, her mismatched outdated clothes got most of the attention—keeping the office gossip topic on her instead of directed at me. Carly kept me safe any way you looked at it. Otherwise, we had absolutely nothing in common—which was the third, and probably the biggest reason we became friends. I fed off of her spunky take no prisoners attitude towards life, and she got some styling tips along with some borrowed clothes, from me.

I didn't mind Carly asking me about Tom, since I knew she was just looking out for me.

Tom and I went out over the weekend to celebrate our third year anniversary together since we became an item; a real, *committed, exclusively dating* couple. Carly knew he was taking me back to the place where we had first met for our special anniversary dinner. We both thought it would be *the* night—that special unforgettably romantic night to never forget. Down on one knee, nervous, gooey-eyed proposal night.

Only, it was none of those things, and it was *very* forgettable.

"Thomas said it wasn't the right time right now...not

yet," I replied, remorsefully. "He wants to make partner first, on his own terms, not as the boss's son-in-law. You understand how that would look…right?"

Carly shook her head, letting me know that she understood the reason—without agreeing with him. "Not like he needs any help," she mumbled, as if talking to herself.

I huffed and pouted, knowing full well she was right. Hearing the truth did sting a little more coming from her. Most people would sugar coat his reluctance to marry me, or try and give it some rational explanation—just like I had been trying to do before Carly stated the truth so bluntly. I desperately wanted to keep believing that he was just older, wiser, and didn't make mistakes. He was far too smart for that.

But as usual, Carly had cut right through that tortured logic like a hot knife through butter. Thomas never needed any help getting anything he ever wanted, including me apparently. A partnership at my father's law firm was a given. It was his for the taking, even from the day of his first interview with my father. As far as I could tell father probably even gave him his blessing to marry me on that day too! Tom walked on water around these halls, and everyone seemed to be bowing down before him, as if he were some prince who was next in line to a throne.

Sadly, obviously, Tom was holding out for someone better—*after* he was made partner. After he was out from underneath my father's thumb. It all fit together like pieces of an imaginary puzzle coming together inside my head. *Was his reason for not wanting to get married just some elaborate lie? Was he using me…trying to get me to pressure father into speeding things up for him…so that he could be made a partner sooner? DUH!*

Carly was now staring up at me like a puzzled poodle, with her head cocked to one side. It must have been obvious what I was thinking. She must have bit down hard on her lip to keep herself from butting in. She actually kept her mouth shut—letting me puzzle it all out before the elevator doors opened up on the twelfth floor where we would have to part ways.

That bastard! I was beginning to fume, as I ran through the evidence supporting my suspicions.

Tom, that's right, Tom—he was team captain of his chess club in high school. He loved to brag about being sent to compete at the national championships. I know he was an academic All-American student. A "who's who" listed leader. He was the student body president at Yale University, *and* a Summa Cum Laude graduate and associate editor of the Yale Law Review. His resume was so impressive that he may have actually been *Captain America* for all I knew?

It was undeniable. The evidence was overwhelming. And it took Carly finally pointing it out in her own brutally blunt way—to get it to finally sink inside my hard head. Of course Tom *was* using me.

The real question was—was I going to let him?

Tom is as physically appealing as he is smart. Tall and slender, in a very muscular way like a European soccer player, sporting thick wavy hair along with a sharp-edged jaw line leading down to a strong smoothly shaven oh-so-cute dimpled chin. His friendly smile and sweet maple brown eyes made all of the women in the office swoon like vapid airheads.

Bastard! It's not a fair fight. He is too perfect. Maybe I should urge father to speed things along. So what if I'm married to a partner at my father's law firm? Let them gossip. None of that matters since he'll be mine, along with everything else I've earned.

"Oh, I'm *sure* Tom will make partner *real soon*," Carly said sarcastically, giving me a playful little jab with her elbow. "And *then* he'll pop the question." I glanced at her as she gave me a little wink. It was almost as if she was reading my mind. And she was looking at me with such a know-it-all grin, as if she really could.

Blood rushed to my face. My blood pressure spiked and my stomach suddenly felt like it was falling faster than the elevator was rising. The tiny space was shrinking even smaller. It was getting very warm. We seemed to be slowing down as we passed by each floor—9, 10, 11—with each floor feeling like an eternity.

I wanted to be angry. I wanted to say something mean, something rude, something brutally honest that would put her right back in her place. But that was impossible. She could just read me too well. The whole situation was all so embarrassing, that's all. It wasn't her fault.

As I started to say something to change the subject, the chime sounded, announcing our arrival to the twelfth floor. The doors parted. A janitor quickly stepped inside, parting us. I glanced over his shoulder to give Carly a half-hearted smile before quickly stepping out as the doors started closing. My moment to say something, anything, had passed. "See you later…and say hello to your father for me," she attempted to say, with her voice getting muffled behind the doors as they shut.

The halls were still empty. It was a pleasant feeling finding myself alone. I slinked through the dark cubicles where the secretaries sat. All the computers and phones sat silently on the desks waiting for everyone to arrive. The place would soon be like a chaotic beehive. It was my one chance to get to the break room alone. All I wanted to do was get some coffee, maybe even one of those leftover stale bagels or donuts, and then hide away in my little office—before everyone else swarmed into the narrow halls.

4

MY CUP WAS tipped way up, so I could get to my last drops of coffee, when there was an unexpected knock on my office door. The doorknob was turned and my door was cracking open by the time I was able swallow and mutter, "Mm...come on in." In stepped my father. He was cleanly shaven and sharply dressed in a pinstripe suite with a perfectly matching designer tie that all together cost nearly as much as my car. His sparkling shoes had a fresh waxy shine—impeccable as always. Perfectly trimmed charcoal black hair was now turning grey, especially along his sideburns.

"You busy?" he asked politely as he stepped all the way inside and closed the door behind him.

"No, oh no, of course not...come on in...sit down," I mumbled, nearly gagging on my coffee. Not only was it completely shocking that father would just pop by so early in the morning—he also had the strangest look on his face—looking like some overly eager young boy holding back an urgent secret that he desperately wanted to share.

My cup nearly fell from the edge of my desk as I nervously put it down, while I was pushing my stack of papers and files over to one side. Whisking away the crumbs from my bagel off the cleared desk I noticed some of them were clinging to my blouse that I briskly swatted away too.

The pile of files and documents covering my desk were not there by accident. It was a clever way to keep more of them away from me. That's one of the first things I learned working here—the more work you get done, the more they shovel your way. Keeping my desk full of unfinished projects helped to keep new ones from appearing, so I always kept my desk stacked high with unfinished work. "I can see you're busy," he said, looking over my cluttered, coffee drip stained, crumb covered mess. "Already hard at work...now that's my girl," he grinned with pride. "I won't keep you long." It was working perfectly. "No problem...what is it?" I replied with a forced smile.

"Nothing important really...I was just hoping to steal you away for lunch...like we used to do," he suggested. The sincerity warming his voice was hard to ignore. We hadn't been to lunch together for quite some time. It was apparently his way of reaching out to me again.

"Well...I suppose I could sneak out for an hour or so." My eyes intentionally scanned over the scattered files, let-ting him believe that it was a tough decision. Really, I just needed an *out,* some way to leave gracefully if things went bad. Nearly every lunch date we ever had ended in us get-ting into a heated argument, to where one of us stormed off. Needing to get back to the office, back to my heavy case load, was about the only excuse father would ever accept—from anyone.

His eyes rolled a little, I think. He may have been on to me? Apparently father could read me too well—just like

Carly. "Let's meet at the *1280* around noon. I have some Board business to attend to over at the museum this morning...so we could meet there after I'm done." The *Table 1280 Restaurant* is a part of the museum, located at 1280 Peachtree Street—hence the name.

I leaned back, sitting straight up in my chair, glaring at him with a furrowed brow. "You want to meet at the *cake?*" The *cake* was my nick-name for the High Museum. The metallic all white building, with three levels that reduce in size as you go up—looks just like an enormous multilayered wedding cake, all covered in smooth white frosting. To me, the museum has always been *the cake.*

Father rubbed his hands together, something he did when he was worried. It bothered him that he had an obvious, *tell.* That's why he always tried to keep an ink-pen in his hands when he was in court, or during a high-stakes settlement conference, or even worse, when he was playing high-stakes poker with his buddies. When he realized what he was doing he dropped his hands to his sides, and locked his eyes with mine. It was time to get serious. Something he was more comfortable with. "That's right...I want us to have lunch over at the High...as we once did...before all that trouble got started."

My eyes thinned as I stared him down. He could see the emotion building inside of me as his words tumbled around in my head. *Trouble! How could he dare refer to David as trouble!* I could feel my heart racing and my blood pressure rising—and we hadn't even made it to lunch yet.

Clearly he had said the wrong thing, in a very wrong way, and lunch with him was going to be out of the question—if he didn't say something fast. "There's a new exhibit going on display…one that I believe you will *really* want to see," he quickly suggested. His voice was warm and inviting again. His eyes softened, almost begging, looking like an old dog needing attention. It was sincere—and it was undeniable. "Please come with me Emma," he asked sweetly, to seal the deal.

I was still his only daughter—so how could I ever say no?

5

FATHER LEFT MY office door cracked open as he left. I popped up to shut it behind him to keep any more unwanted surprises from getting in. Then I thought a little more coffee would be nice—maybe one more bagel too?

The halls were still sparse and quiet. The other employees were slowly dragging in to begin another day of work. That's when I heard a familiar sounding voice wafting over the tops of the cubicles that formed a maze on the interior of the office floor, where all the secretaries were clustered. It was out of the way, but I couldn't resist. Taking a sharp left turn I wandered into the maze of thinly walled half boxes with attached desks. As I got closer, his voice got clearer and clearer, until it was most definitely clear that it was Tom. He was giggling and laughing—sounding like he did when he was with me—while flirting.

"Good morning," I said as I popped around the corner. My voice must have startled them, by the looks on their faces. It wasn't a coincidence. I sounded just like my father, with a restrained yet domineering tone that let other people know who was in control. As when a general enters into the mess hall at chow time, or the barracks when the soldiers are all relaxed, and snapping them to attention. It was one of the very few *good* qualities I picked up from him. Their giggling chatter ceased instantly. It was all nervous smiles now. A tense silence as they wondered how I was going to react.

"Oh…morning Emma," Tom finally replied. He wasn't prone to blushing—he was way too cool for that. That's how I knew he was up to something. First, his face flushed a ghostly white, just before flashing a soft pink color like some sea creature using a genetic camouflaging technique for protection from being eaten. "I was just about to head to your office…and I ran into Christina here…she's new…and I was showing her around…and—"

"Hello," Christina interjected with an outstretched hand for a handshake as Tom continued fumbling over his words, still searching for some *believable* explanation.

Tom had mentioned her at lunch a few days ago. I knew she was coming to work here, but he didn't say exactly when. It was now obvious why he was sparse with details about her. She had just turned twenty. Tom had personally selected to hire her right out of community college after she completed an Associate Degree in Paralegal Studies (something fairly new for Atlanta in the 80's). By the sound of his flirting voice, it wasn't her education that inspired him to offer her employment. Tall, she had the look of a runway super model right out of the pages of Vogue. Her long, thin legs, propped-up on higher-than-high heels, made her appear to be even taller *and* skinnier. It was hard to tell how she could keep herself upright with the enormously developed breasts she was carrying around.

Everything about her made me dislike her—instantly!

His office was up on the thirteenth floor. There was no

real reason for him to be down on my floor, other than to see me. Smart move on his part—putting her so close to my office was his attempt at a clever cover. It was his first excuse after all, but that is what blew it for him. Plus, it was just so poorly executed, with his bumbling and fumbling, *"Oh...I was just...just coming to see you...at your office...blah, blah, blah."*

He had better get better at slinging bullshit on the fly if he wants to be a courtroom litigator! My face must have been screaming at him, what I was actually thinking. *Right...like I'm buying that line of B.S.?*

Sadly, that was another trait I picked up from my father—don't trust anyone, especially other attorneys.

"I was just on my way to get some more coffee, and I heard your voices, so I came over," I said calmly. Not letting them know how steaming hot I was on the inside. I felt like I was hosting a television morning show, where I was being forced to show the camera a friendly smile—when I really just wanted to smash it over the head with my coffee mug. "Nice to meet you," I said with a relaxed smile that was as cold and empty as my mug that I was clutching between my squeezing fingers. *If only it was her lovely, long, thin, delicate little neck, between my fingers*, is what I was feeling. It was a miracle that my mug didn't shatter.

"Same here," she replied with a sheepish grin. Her voice was hesitant, as if she could feel what I was imagining. "I'm sure we'll see each other around."

Moving briskly through the maze, I marched off toward the break room without even a glance at Tom. "Wait up, I'll come with," he blurted out as I disappeared around a corner.

His voice was apologetic. But I was having none of that—not today—not after last night.

I was already pouring steaming hot coffee into my mug by the time he came rushing into the room. "I bumped into your father in the elevator on my way up," he mumbled nonchalantly, trying to get a conversation started. Completely ignoring what just happened. "He seemed to be in a good mood for a change," he snickered, wanting to flirt. His hands ran around my waist and he pushed himself up against me, squeezing me while pressing me up against the counter. His chin swept back my hair as his lips nibbled softly over my neck. His tongue fluttered on my soft skin, tickling me all over. It felt amazing—yet incredibly frustrating—all at the same time.

"Christina is *quite* the looker," I whispered. "She's the perfect choice for you." He would've had to have been completely brain dead, to not hear the disdain in my voice. It wasn't the first time I'd caught him with another woman, or the second, or the third, or the fourth. Nor would it be the last time, I'm sure. It was only a matter of coming to terms with that's just the type of man he is. The price I'd have to pay to be with such a man of perfection.

"She's just temporary," he whispered back, while flicking my earlobe with the tip of his slippery tongue, "till I get my new office upstairs."

"You mean, until you make partner?" There was no flirting in my voice. It was time to end his little charade. Put it all out on the table—get it all out in the open. "Just like us you mean?" I spun around locking eyes with him, to say, "it's all just temporary…you, me…everything is just temporary till you make partner…is that it?"

His puppy-dog pouting eyes were priceless as he started to plead with me to forget about everything that mattered to me, "you know I just need a little more time to get us to where we need to be…before I can fully commit…we just need a little more time…."

All I could hear was him blathering, babbling on about needing more time and all the other usual excuses—that was all just sounding like more *blah, blah, blah*. It was more than I could stand to listen to right now. "You're not answering me…again," I snapped back at him. The deep scowl on my face should have told him how serious I was this time. "Why can't you ever just give me a straight-up answer about where we are going with this relationship? Am I just another Christina for you to string along until you've gotten everything you want out of me?" My hands pushed him back away from me, just as forcefully as my question had. "I'm not your little toy to play around with until you get bored."

Shock, that's how I'd describe the look on his face at that moment. It was the first time a woman had spoken to him with that defiant tone before. Well, at least not since his mother last jerked a knot in him for throwing a tantrum when he was a little bratty boy, I imagine. "I had no idea you felt so strongly about all this…about what we are doing… what we are trying to become someday…," he tried to say, in just the right way. Just like a lawyer. But he just couldn't quite get out the right words. Not in the right way. Not without compromising his position. Not without committing himself fully to what was "*us*". That would require him giving himself up, completely, just to me.

"About *us* Tom," I jumped in. "Yes…I feel that strongly

about you… about you and me…about *us*. Is that what you are trying to say?"

Tom pulled me close to him. His long arms wrapped around me and pulled me in, to where it felt warm and safe. As hard as a rock could be, his muscles seemed to be caressing me as we pressed together. Pressing his soft lips on my forehead, he squeezed me tightly, while whispering, "sweetheart…let's not get into that again…not right now. You know how much I feel about you…about us." I could feel my body going soft—as I began melting against his hard and hot body, like a stick of butter placed on top of a very hot oven. My eyes moved up, as his lips moved down, to where we found one another, embracing in a passionate kiss—that lingered a little bit too long.

"Oh, sorry, didn't realize you were still in here…," Christina stammered, after she walked in on us. She spun around like a scared cat and scampered back out, before we could even unlock our lips.

"I better get upstairs," Tom snickered.

"Right…we better get back to work," I added playfully. Inside I was begging for more—for just a little more time with him. We were breaking such good ground right then, and it hurt, being forced to stop way too soon. We were getting so close to a breakthrough. All I needed was a few more minutes alone with him, I was telling myself. He was about to fully commit to me, maybe even a marriage proposal— until she had to barge in and ruined it all. *Stupid Slut!*

I lingered by the coffee maker, thinking. Tom moved slowly for the door. He turned at the last moment, with a thought of his own, to ask, "You want to catch some lunch with me, later on?" An excited shiver went up my spine.

Apparently he wanted to continue our conversation about us, and our future together. Perhaps, he finally really does want to tell me how he truly feels—that he loves me.

My lips started to tell him, *of course I do*, when I suddenly remembered that I already agreed to meet father for lunch. "No, sorry, I already have a lunch date," I replied with a flirtatious wink. Running my tongue up over my top lip, tasting what was left of him, I wanted to leave him with a slutty wet-lipped smile.

"Your loss," he said with a devilish little grin, as if to call me a liar. He didn't believe me. He thought I was toying with him. So, I let him leave with the idea that I was going to be meeting him for lunch, just for fun. I could be a naughty flirt too, when I wanted to be.

Plus, I couldn't wait to get to see Tom's cringing face, when he arrived at our table for lunch, only to find my father sitting there waiting for him. It would be so easy to tell father about how I caught him sneaking around behind my back with the new girl, flirting, hurting my feelings. Playing it up, with tear filled eyes, until father was red-faced, burning with anger, and ready to rip his head off. Since Tom deserved a good, hard, kick in the balls right about now—just for making me so upset!

Tom deserved it—especially today.

6

OWNING ANOTHER CUP of coffee did the trick. Time sped by, and before I realized it, everyone was scurrying past my office on their way to lunch. "Oh hell," I murmured with a glance at the clock. Father hated to be kept waiting, saying it made him feel unimportant, which was the worst kind of insult to him. That's probably why I always left early, hating to be late for even the most trivial of planned activities—feeling it would be rude to arrive even a second too late.

Before I could straighten up the file I was working on and get to the door, Carly came busting in without even a simple knock. "You too busy for lunch?" She asked with a giddy chuckle. It was her attempt at friendly sarcasm—so annoying. Only because it was mostly true that I was never too busy for anything, including lunch. But she didn't have to point it out so effortlessly.

"I'm meeting father at the Table 1280...and I'm already late," I muttered as I tried to push past her and join the throngs of office workers stampeding to the only elevator. Carly didn't take the hint and fell in line right behind me, following me closely, asking, "Sounds good...mind if I tag along?" No response was needed, since she was pressing herself up against me as we sardined ourselves inside the packed elevator. We may as well have been Siamese twins, with her attached to my hip. "Just thought you could use some company…with it being today and all," she announced a little too loudly as we sucked in a deep breath, squeezing ourselves together to where the doors could finally shut. "David should be here instead of me," Carly whispered sympathetically in my ear. An actual whisper!

I looked down at her resolutely, to whisper back, "he is."

The doors sprang open and we all spilled out like inmates getting released from a long stint inside solitary confinement. We all simultaneously took in another deep breath of fresh air. Warm air was flowing inside the building through the many doors being propped open to let us all escape onto the busy Atlanta streets. Looking like thousands of spawning salmon heading upstream, the throngs of city workers bustled in the directions of the few available eateries. It was important to arrive before the hordes invaded every restaurant, to get served quickly in order to be able to make it back to work on time. Only two blocks to the High Museum, and Table 1280 Restaurant, but it felt like an eternity as we zigzagged through the stampeding masses.

It was easier to just skip lunch rather than fight this crowd everyday—exactly what I had planned to do today. But there I was, beading up with sweat walking down a hot sidewalk, getting anxious, bumping shoulders with strangers, going to the last place I wanted to be today, with Carly nipping at my heels. It was turning into one of *those* days—the *one* that never seems to end.

"Wasn't this the day they were supposed to put some of

David's works on display?" Carly bluntly asked, knowing full well that this *was, the* day. "It didn't work out for him," I replied. My voice was intentionally distant and cold. So cold that it could have dropped the temperature outside by a few degrees, but I don't think Carly would even notice. "Father made certain of that," I added. Carly already knew that, but it felt good to remind her of how I was feeling. It sometimes took such a hard verbal punch in the face in order to get her attention—to remind her of how other people were feeling in certain emotionally fragile situations.

By the time we arrived at the museum entrance our hair was wet with sweat, and our blouses were sticking to us in spots. Making a beeline for a little known side entrance— bypassing the small crowd that had gathered around a bronze sculpture called, *The Shade,* by Auguste Rodin. The size of a very large man, the grotesquely bent over statue was a gift to Atlanta from the Country of France. Placed on this memorial site in 1968, it stood as a stark reminder of a tragic plane crash that occurred at the Orly Airport in Paris on today's date, back in 1962.

We rushed inside the museum and panted under the air duct that was blowing down a pleasant stream of cooling air. Taking a moment to fan ourselves dry, we both noticed a small group of people gathering on the far side of the expansive main hall. They appeared to be admiring a newly placed piece of art—a large marble statue of some sort. "Let's take a look," Carly prodded me. I glanced at my watch. "C'mon we have time," she insisted with a push on my back. "Your father can wait."

It began to feel almost like we were walking into some solemn ceremony, like being inside a church on Sunday, as we stepped closer to the large grouping of people. No one seemed to be moving. Every eye was gazing intently at the marble sculpture. It was eerily quiet—too quiet. As Carly pushed her way through, forcing people to step aside, I followed her up to get a closer look at what all the fuss was about. Before we made it all the way to the very front, I noticed a familiar face in the crowd. Off to one side, standing still like the others, gazing up with tear filled eyes—it was father! He glanced in my direction, just as a single tear found a way to fall. It trickled down his quivering cheek, as if moving in slow motion. As his eyes connected with mine, I noticed another tear, trickling from the other eye. Both of his eyes suddenly swelled with overflowing tears. It was too much for him and he turned away.

When I swung my eyes back in the direction of the sculpture, I could see the top of Carly's head moving around it, as she slowly started to circle around. That's when I felt a hundred eyes falling on me—as heavy as bricks—as everyone turned to look straight at me. They all seemed somewhat shocked, as if seeing a celebrity in the crowd. People standing in front of me shuffled back, moving out of my way. There was a clear path for me to walk right up to the base of the sculpture. It was a carving of a man and a woman, naked from head to toe, sitting together on a tree stump. The woman was reclined slightly, supported by the man with his left arm wrapping around her subtle back. Her right leg was draped gently over his left knee—forcing his legs apart slightly. His right hand placed delicately on her waist. They were gazing deeply into one another's eyes—at the moment their lips touched together, ever so slightly, for a passionate kiss.

It was my favorite piece of sculpture in the whole world, a rendition of *The Kiss*, by Rodin. I had seen many different versions of his original before. They are displayed in famous museums around the world. However, none of them could compare to this work. This recreation was by far the most alluring. David had carved a true masterpiece. I was staring at a moment of true lover's passion, perfectly captured in stone. This was the most alluring thing I had ever experienced before, in my entire life.

A small golden plaque attached at the base had the name of the piece inscribed on it. It was named, *Our Kiss*.

After drifting through many art history courses at the University, looking at works of art had become almost a mundane experience. Everything was becoming an amalgamated blur at times, just another realism piece with stiff life-like features, a twisted contemporary expression, or a melodramatic renaissance portrait of another master artist, with nothing stirring any emotions. It took something exceptional to actually get my complete attention again. When my eyes fell on this work of passion it took my breath away. I felt like a child, in awe.

Before I even realized what I was doing, my fingertips reached out to touch the smooth, cool marble. As if I were all alone, I let myself feel the muscles carved into his body, running my fingers up from his rigid toes, up over his sinfully muscular calves, over the knee, all the way up to his hard rippling thighs. My fingertips paused at his bulging groin— breathing out a heavy sigh. I suddenly felt weak, wanting to be up there, held up in his arms, gazing deeply into his eyes again—waiting for his lips to touch mine.

"Looks just like you," Carly bellowed, sounding even

louder, as her voice echoed through the chamber hall. It popped me out of my momentary spell. I could feel all of those eyes on me again. There was a rush of murmuring whispers sounding like rushing water. Pulling my hands back, I peeled myself away from the sculpture. I stepped away, blushing, feeling utterly embarrassed. "She really does," Carly pointed out again, before adding, "and that must definitely be your David…I'd recognize those sexy legs and abs anywhere, by the way you described them."

A steady hand pushed up against my back, as support. I turned to find my father standing beside me. "I did this for you," he whispered softly, "I wanted to try and make up for what happened." Those were not my father's eyes I was staring into. This had to be another man—a changed man. Tears welled-up in his watering eyes. Falling into his arms, we wept together, without shame.

The people around us drifted away, with a tear forming in every eye. They glanced back at us, to join in our emotion. "He did it for me…for us," I mumbled in father's ear. "I was wrong," father replied softly, as tears fell as a soft cleansing rain.

"Is everything alright?" I heard Tom say softly. He had walked up to us without us noticing. This was not the surprise I had planned for him, but the situation he had wandered into was even more uncomfortable for him. When I turned to look at him with strained, tear-filled eyes, he had the expression of a lost child. I smiled, softly.

"No Tom…everything is not all right. Everything is all wrong," I replied. "I need some time to be alone."

Tom's face grew even more lost, as if he were in a dark forest as the sun was setting, with the last bit of light slowly fading away. "I don't understand?" he murmured. Pulling myself away from father's arms, I stepped over to him and stared up into his troubled gaze, to say, "That's why it's all wrong. That's why you're all wrong for me." He couldn't respond, with his eyes getting wider as he scrunched his forehead like he was trying to solve an unsolvable math problem.

"Goodbye Tom," I said calmly, before striding away towards the exit. Turning to watch me leave him, he asked, "well, are you going back to the office…do you want me to come with you?"

With my back to him, without slowing down, in a sternly determined voice, I answered him, "I'm never going back to that office *and* I never want to see you again."

There was a heavy silence in the exhibit hall as I walked out the exit door. Father was wiping his tears as he circled the marble statue. Tom wandered off towards the restaurant to eat his lunch, all alone. Carly was smiling with the biggest grin she had ever made. Walking over next to father, staring up at the kissing couple carved in marble, she was thinking; *Way to go David!*

7

WHAT I SAID to Tom as I walked out of the museum was true, even more than I actually realized in the heat of the moment. Having your entire life upended in the space of a single moment can be dizzying, downright disorienting. It would take some time to figure out what I was doing, where I was going, and why.

Stepping out the door under the wilting noon-day sun, the concrete sidewalk was as hot as a stove-top. My already spinning head wasn't prepared to face the intense heat so quickly. I felt faint. The closest seat was the dark marble bench built underneath the bronze statute. *The Shade,* as it is named, didn't provide any shade from the sun at all, but the bench was a pleasant relief. I plopped down to think about what had just happened, and what I had just done.

I turned my eyes upward to look at the strange naked man looming over me. His bronze casted body was almost black, as if blackened by the burning sunlight. It gave me a melting feeling. I could feel him wilting under the beating down heat, getting hotter and hotter inside, with his outsides melting like the wax of a burning candle. Drooping over, his elongated neck can barely hold up his burdened head that almost rests on his falling shoulder. The sweltering heat is a heavy burden to bear, apparently, even for a man of made out of metal. At the end of his dangling arm, it takes everything he has left to lift up his finger, to point down, down to where I am sitting.

That's when I remember the phrase that inspired Rodin to create this melting metal man in the first place. This was one of the giants standing guard at the gates of hell, letting everyone know that when they entered, *they must abandon all hope*. A slipping feeling swept over me—a sickening helpless churning in my stomach—that feeling you get when you walk up to the edge of a dangerously high cliff, slide your foot over to the very edge as you cautiously lean over to take a look down—and someone pushes you from behind.

I was already walking on the razor's edge. My own dangerously emotionally high ledge, where I tiptoed along a tightrope trying to keep from falling over as the winds blew harder with each agonizing inch. Every day was a struggle, forcing myself out of bed to go do something I merely tolerated, seeing people I couldn't stand to be around—all-the-while—forcing myself to continue dating someone who was constantly betraying me in so many ways.

It took seeing David's masterpiece a moment ago to finally give me that shove I needed—to push me over.

I could feel myself dangling, precariously, wanting to fall off the cliff, filled with a fear of what will happen if I do, second guessing myself until my stomach is churning and my head is spinning—desperately wanting to hold onto what was here for me now, what I knew, what I could touch and feel and understand, and not have to worry about.

Was David right about me all along? Of course he was right. I was just too afraid to face the realities of it, until now.

He was right about many things he showed me, what he taught me, how he inspired me. Showing me how art can reach across time and touch people in ways they never thought possible, making them feel things they never believed they could. He found a way to open my eyes today, with his passion. I couldn't deny him. I couldn't deny myself—not any longer.

Am I really going over this cliff? Can I let go? I wondered, feeling myself starting to let go, and fall. Can I defy father once and for all and refuse to finish law school, refuse to become a lawyer like he always wanted, and refuse to go along with all of his little plans he has devised for me? Can I survive without his money? Will I finally become who I want to be, and do what I really want to do with my life?

I've never had the courage to defy them before today. Courage like David had. Not the biblical David from the *David versus Goliath* story—my David—the real life giant slayer that wanted to save *me*.

❧

My eyes drifted down to the marble pedestal supporting the bronze statute. Slowly, I looked over the names etched into the speckled stone. This was a memorial for the victims of the Orly Airport plane crash that happened outside of Paris, in 1962. A few years later the French Ambassador had presented this Rodin sculpture to the people of Atlanta in honor of the victims killed in that disaster. All of their names are now memorialized here, along with David's mother. *His name should be here too*, I thought. *He's as much a victim of that crash as anyone.*

My heart jumped a beat with the return of a fond memory. This is where I first remember catching sight of David.

Right here, beneath this statue. My mind returned to him, to David, and that first glimpse of him.

It all came rushing back to me, everything we had been through. And I knew, right then, that my life was beginning all over again, right here, right now, in this very moment—all thanks to David, and *Our Kiss*.

Feeling resolved, relieved, even a little bit happy, my thoughts stayed with him, reliving those fateful moments we shared—all over again. Beginning with that special day when we first saw one another....

❧

It was June, 1968. I didn't understand the significance of the event at the time, but there was a large gathering of people here, myself and father included. He had brought me and Jon with him to be present as the French Ambassador presented this Rodin sculpture to the people of Atlanta. Most of the notable dignitaries of the City at that time were in attendance. It was a hallmark occasion. Father was newly appointed to the museum board of directors and it was his first real opportunity to stretch his politically ambitious legs.

My tiny six year old brain certainly couldn't comprehend what it was all about, or why we needed to even be there. All I knew at the time was that it was stinking hot, just like today, and I wanted to get back home and jump in the cold pool with my friends. It was my first experience with attending a wake, or funeral, or something of that solemn nature since it had that sort of feeling. Everyone seemed to be sad for some reason, with red, tear filled eyes, dabbing handkerchiefs and blowing noses and all, as if someone had died. Little did I know at the time that they really had, many of them, most of them were connected to the museum, real patrons of the arts, people who were working to grow the art culture in Atlanta.

I wish I could say that being at the memorial was part of my first memories of being at the museum, or, at least a memory with a little more noble intent—something that could leave me with a feeling of pride. But it wasn't. My actual first memories of being here are of when Jon and I were hanging out in one of the galleries, as usual, waiting for father to return.

It couldn't have been more than a few months before that day, a year tops. It was after hours, and the museum had closed for the night. Everyone had departed except for a few lingering employees in the back rooms. Father was in some meeting or something, and we were trying to fill the time like children do, playing hide-and-seek, furiously chasing each other down the long corridors desperately wanting to tag the other. It was all a dizzying blur until that very moment when it happened. When Jon was looking back at me, as I reached out to touch him, his feet moving fast without looking at where he was heading—straight into a pedestal holding a marble bust. Wham! Little Jon bounced off the stone pillar like a bug, but the weight of him crashing into it, forcing the tall thin pedestal to tip slightly. The heavy bust rocked back and forth—until wham—it crashed down to the floor, nearly crushing us.

We stood there, frozen, for what felt like forever. Jon sprang to the other side of the bust to where he could tilt it slightly, enough to get a look at the back of its head that was pressed against the tiled floor. His eyes were wide and he inhaled a deep breath. Looking up at me, his face turned as white as the face of the man carved into the bust. I scampered around to see the damage. A large chip had broken free. A piece of his hair on the back of his head about the size of my fist had broken off and slid against the wall. "What do we do?" Jon whimpered. We knew far too well that father would murder us both if he found out what we had done.

Together, we propped up the bust on the floor, getting him upright at least. I can still feel the weight of it in my hands as we strained with all of our might to lift the stone off the floor, getting it about an inch up, before giving up and letting it back down. Jon's face turned almost purple as he strained every tiny muscle he had to lift it back onto the pedestal. "It's no use…it's too heavy for us…we can't lift it back all the way up there," Jon muttered, out of breath. His head barely cleared the top of it, and we probably would have been crushed to death had we actually lifted the bust up that high anyway. Taking turns, we scampered up and down the semi-darkened hallway, peeking around corners and listening for the sounds of anyone else coming in our direction. It was as silent as a graveyard at midnight. No one came to investigate. So, we carefully slid the upright bust against the wall, with the back of his head hidden from direct view, before slinking like cats back out to the foyer where father had left us.

Jon and I swore oaths of secrecy to one another of course. Father came out to find us patiently waiting for him in our seats. Not a word of it was ever spoken of again after that night. If father did ever find out anything about the broken bust, he never mentioned it to us.

Come to think of it; the only other person I ever told about the broken bust, was David.

I didn't know it at the time, but David was about ten years old when I first laid eyes on him at that presentation outside the museum. Father was doing his thing, drifting from dignitary to other important person, getting acquainted and brown-nosing, as usual. Mother was there, but she was one of the first to escape the heat by disappearing inside the museum as the final applause was still fading. Glaring down, she scolded me with her threatening eyes, saying clearly, "you had better not get your dress stained in the grass," before she left. She knew I would anyways. I remember playing on the grassy hill in front of the museum entrance, ignoring mother, rolling around and running back and forth, moving in and out of the shade when it got too hot. Watching as the finely dressed adults slowly began to disperse, as if they were leaving a church service, shaking hands and saying their good-byes. I just wanted father to hurry-up. Of course he didn't. He was always the last person to leave anything.

Not this time.

Once the crowd had dwindled down to just a few, I noticed him lingering over by the statute. It was David, just much younger. Sporting the look of a tiny California surfer, he was different from all the other boys I knew. Milky white skin turned a golden brown from a being out in the hot summer sun. Boyish freckles lightly speckling his nose and cheeks, long curling blonde hair that needed combing, dressed uncomfortably in a new suite and tie just for this occasion. He looked completely lost and alone in the middle of all of the adults surrounding him. They smiled warmly down at him and said encouraging things, kind gestures, trying to be extra nice to *him* for some reason. They weren't looking at me that way, or saying nice things to me—only the normal looks of annoyance and the finger over the lips telling me to *shush*, whenever I would get a little to playful or loud at the wrong time.

I couldn't understand why he was over there, and not over here by me, playing on the grass. Instead, he clung to the statute's dangling fingers for a little while, then, he gently rubbed his fingers over the names on the marble memorial, staying over there, with all of the other adults, looking just as sad as the rest of them—why? It even looked as though he started crying at times, wiping away the occasional tears that forced their way out. His gloomy eyes kept looking up at the statute in a way I couldn't understand at all. As if he was looking for something. Searching for something that no one else could see.

A lone man stood close by, while keeping his distance. He was watching David as if he were concerned for him, but didn't want to interfere. Father eventually made his way over to this man. They shook hands and chatted, occasionally glancing over at David and the statute. Father's face began to look like the other man's face—with a look of concern. They stayed there watching him for a long time, even for father. They talked for a while, long after everyone else had left. Finally mother poked her head out of one of the doors and called to him. Father seemed reluctant to leave the man, but he did, giving him a long handshake with a soft reassuring pat on his arm. Far too friendly for father, so I assumed it must have been some distant relative or old friend he had bumped into.

As father walked up and took my hand to take me inside to join mother, his eyes were puffy and red like he very close to tearing up. Must have been the heat and sunlight, I imagined. "Who was that?" mother asked him somberly, after getting a look at his bloodshot eyes. "I'll tell you later," is all father could mutter—sniffling back his tears. Later, he blamed his allergies and the horrible pollen for his condition.

I knew better—even then.

8

I T WAS ANOTHER scorcher of an afternoon the next time I saw David. About four or five years later as best I can recall. I was nearly ten years old. He must have been about fourteen. We were in the same place. It was around the same time of year. From what I can recall it was near the end of school and we were on our very last field trip. I was inside the museum again, wandering aimlessly around looking at the same stuff I had seen thousands of times. If the teacher had let me, I could have taken the whole class on a guided tour, showing them hidden details that only I had discovered while trapped in here so many times before. My best-friend at the time, Lisa, trailed right behind, following me around as we wandered through the exhibits with our classmates.

It had been a very long and stressful school year. One of those years that seemed to never end. Lisa and I were feeling more than a little restless. I couldn't believe they had brought me back here—again! The boredom was becoming overwhelming. Something had to give. Breaking away from the pack, while trying to appear to be still interested in the displays, I scooted us across the room to get us away from the rest of them. Lisa must have been wondering where I was taking her. The look in my mischievous eyes must have told her that it definitely wasn't someplace we were supposed to be going. Seeing that no one else was watching us, we made a run for it.

As the class shuffled towards the next room, I tugged on Lisa's skirt, directing her around a corner, motioning down a long hallway towards a wall of windows. Tempting sunlight was streaming inside, beckoning for us to come outside. There was an exit door waiting for us—the one that was rarely used. One of the little secrets I knew about. It exited out of the side of the building, onto the lawn where the memorial was located.

I just needed a little break. It was cold in there. The warm sun would feel so good. The way out was just a few feet away. A few quick steps and we would be free. "Let's go," I whispered anxiously to Lisa, nodding my head at the door. A sinister smile appeared on her face, letting me know she would follow me out the door. That's why we were friends I suppose—we thought the same way about things.

That's also why they tried to keep us separated back at school. Trouble makers, they called us. Luckily for us, we were both far too cute to punish severely. Plus, our families had a lot of political pull at the school. Getting into trouble for us wasn't a real concern.

Scampering over to the glass door like a couple of escaping convicts, we couldn't help but giggle a little with the rush of anticipation. I went head first, wanting to rush out the door before anyone saw us leaving. Lisa was now nervously laughing, pushing on me to hurry. Wham! My face pancaked onto the glass. Lisa slammed into me and fell back onto her butt. The door was locked this time. Someone must have tipped them off?

It didn't really hurt—not real bad. My embarrassment was worse than the pain could ever be. There he was, looking straight at me through the door—it was David—with his bright blue piercing eyes staring directly at me. He was standing over at the memorial. From outside it must have sounded like a bird had flown into the window. Glancing up at the sound of a hard vibrating thud, his eyes caught mine for just an agonizingly long few seconds. Until my face warmed to a scarlet red and I stepped back, away from the glass, to where he couldn't see who it was behind the glare.

His eyes dropped back down to the names on the memorial. Nothing about his expression changed at all—looking solemn and sad, almost angry. My eyes stayed glued on him as they tried to refocus. I felt like I was caught-up in a fantasy, with my head dazed slightly by the blow. Time slowed for a moment. I was transfixed on him.

Lisa was sprawled out on the floor, laughing hysterically, with her arms and legs sticking straight out. The white stockings on her calves were sagging down to the tops of her shoes, where her shoelaces were coming undone. She had to grab her tummy she was starting to laugh so hard.

I wasn't hearing anything.

I remember feeling a little weird seeing him again. A tickling feeling swept over me, one that was exciting in a way. It reminded me of being on a swing when you go up too high and feel yourself lifting up off the seat, floating in mid-air, detached and momentarily weightless. I wasn't sure if it was it the knock to my head, or something else making me to feel this way?

How I even recognized him at all was the real mystery. That wasn't the same cute innocent boy that I wanted to roll around in the grass with. His hair was much longer, now a sandy-brown, with wispy curls that were wild looking, like on some wannabe rock star. He looked nothing like the boys at my school. They wouldn't have even let him through the front door for that matter, with his tattered blue jeans full of torn-out holes, his tattered and faded black T-shirt from some long-ago rock concert, and his silly braded leather necklace with a sharks tooth pendant and semi-matching wrist bands. Hardly the person I remember. *Ugh, what a weirdo maniac he'd become?*

So then, *why* can't I stop looking at *him*—I wondered?

Lisa grabbed the bottom of my tartan skirt and pulled down—trying to get me to help her up. "Stop it," I groaned and swatted her hand away. I didn't want to turn away from the glass door, not yet. All I wanted to do was keep watching him. To keep feeling that inexplicably strange feeling that was feeling so good, like when I ate too much chocolate really fast. "Help me," Lisa cackled, while I continued to ignore her. "C'mon Em," she giggled, begging for me to help. She reached up and grabbed onto my skirt again— this time tugging even harder. My skirt slid down my waist, almost coming all the way down. The bottom of my blouse was barely covering the frilly trim of my white panties. My fingers snatched the tops of my skirt back up—just in the nick-of-time. David glanced back up just as I was pulling my skirt back in to place. Lisa was now laughing even harder, to the point of nearly crying. My face must have been a bright red, even visible through the window, as I tried to step back, only to catch my heels on Lisa and tumble down over her onto the floor.

We both erupted into teary, gut-busting, uncontrollable laughter. Until the teacher's scowling face appeared above us. We had never seen her look more fearsome, and that was saying a lot. Everyone believed that she was once a nun sent from some far away monastery—after they kicked her out for being too mean and cruel to the poor orphans that she was supposed to be caring for. That's what we started calling her, the *evil nun*, whether the story was true or not. She certainly dressed the part, hair tied up and hidden behind a scarf, a black dress like something out of an old cowboy movie from the 1800's that covered every inch of her body—no matter how hot it was outside. Dry and wrinkled, without a stitch of makeup, her face appeared to be just as old. "Get up off the floor this instant," she growled, straining to restrain her voice to avoid getting noticed by the museum staff. "Just what in tarnation do you two think you're doing…you're making a spectacle!"

Lisa and I jumped to our feet and busily straightened our clothes, tucking in and smoothing out our blouses as we tugged our skirts back in place. The teacher's laser beam eyes were burning holes all the way into our souls. "Get back over with the rest of the class," she instructed, pointing with her bony finger. She stormed off, expecting us to follow right behind her. Lisa did, with her head bowed in humble submission.

I hesitated. My eyes were pulled back towards the window. Even the fear of getting another nasty chastening from the *evil nun* couldn't stop me from taking another peek at David. Before I could think about the consequences I turned back to the door, to peer out. He was still there. Along with that man who nearly brought my father to tears.

The man placed his hand on David's shoulder lightly, as if telling him his time was up. Shrugging his shoulder, David pulled away, saying no, I'm not ready to leave. The man lingered for a moment, before he turned and sauntered away. David's eyes flowed up over the marble memorial with the etched names of the airplane crash victims. As if seeing something new, his eyes went up to the statute. Suddenly he took a step and leaped up onto the pedestal and grabbed-hold around the statute's waist. Rubbing his hands slowly over the bronze man's metal skin, he was feeling every intricately carved contour of his rippling skin.

My face pressed up against the glass, as I watched him. It was his passion—such a powerful sensation—pulling me to him through the window. It wasn't the bump on my head this time, putting me into a trance—it was only David. I was so caught up in the moment that I didn't hear Lisa rushing up from behind. "What are you doing?" She whispered, "You are going to get us killed." Her fingers dug into my rigid body and pulled back, but I wasn't about to move. That's when she realized that I was transfixed on whatever it was I was looking at through the window. "What are you looking at?" she whispered in my ear, as she looked out too.

There was a long silent pause, before she gave up a deep sigh. Her fingers relaxed on my waist. "Oh, that's what," she giggled softly. She couldn't say anything else, as she began to notice what I was seeing. The same passion subdued her as well. Mesmerized, we stood like two marble statues on display, as we watched David with *The Shade*. It was as if he was connecting with it in a deeper sense, knowing it, becoming a part of it.

Lisa and I were perfectly still, our noses almost touching against the glass. We could feel the rhythmic beating of our hearts in our chests. We could hear our sighing breaths. Two small circles of condensation formed on the window in front of us—where our mouths hung open.

"What did I just tell you girls!?" The *evil nun* roared out from right behind us. We nearly jumped out of our skin. Scampering across the room we joined the rest of the class and finished the tour.

I don't really remember much about the rest of that day. All I could imagine was David. Nothing else inside the museum was as captivating or inspiring. Not even close. After that experience with David, everything else was almost down-right dull.

The look on Lisa's face told me she was feeling the same way—staring off to nowhere with a far-away dreamy gaze and a giddy smile, like she had sneaked some of her parents' liquor.

I wouldn't feel that same way for a few years after that. Not until I happened to bump into him again at the High Museum of Art—yet again.

9

I HAD JUST FINISHED my freshman year of high school. Father arranged for me to start an internship at the museum. He knew I was extremely fond of the art world. It was the perfect fit. We had talked about my working here as a summer intern as far back as I can remember. It was a good way to polish-up my resume, keep me out of trouble, learn some valuable life skills, and all that. Plus, it was also an easy way for him to keep tabs on me—since he was there at least a couple times of week for Board meetings.

They kept me pretty busy in the back doing inventory, moving stuff around, packing and unpacking deliveries, along with prepping new displays. Nothing like the ideas I had for working there. It was supposed to be glamorous and trendy, getting to rub shoulders with the high fashion, champagne, glitz and glam crowd. Jon was jealous at first. It was his dream to get the drop on all the newest fashions before they hit the racks. Nothing could be further from the truth of what I was actually doing. After a few hours stuck down in the basement rooms sorting through box after boring box of the weirdest contemporary art one can imagine—I was ready to scream. Jon wouldn't have lasted an hour working here.

His creative nervous energy would have had him crawling up the walls and jumping off.

Laura and Marcus, my supervisors, were both just as thrilling to be around. She was your typical run of the mill drama teacher types who was so emotionally dramatic about the tiniest of things—it was downright scary at times. She could be a different person every other day, and never even realize it. Wearing knitted sweaters one day, camouflage the next, a frizzy hairdo with strange handmade ribbons holding it all back in a makeshift pony-tail, all the time, she was a rollercoaster ride of a person. Walking on tip-toes over egg-shells around her was your only option.

"Just whatever you do, don't do anything that might set her off," Marcus confided as he tore open another cardboard box. With long straight greasy hair and mangy whiskers, he was more like a rehashed hippy left over from the sixties. A pudgy, pasty, mellow mushroom type of guy, nothing seemed to bother him—except not getting to have his smoke break. Wanting to be an art instructor, he spent years in college, without ever actually graduating. Year after year, course after course, bong toke after bond toke, his life had drifted aimlessly along—until the day they refused give him another cent on his student loans. His day of reckoning, a harsh reality, had finally arrived. He had to get a real job.

The two of them had been working here for a few years before I arrived. Marcus and I were getting a new piece of sculpture ready for display. On loan from the Louvre in Paris, it was very valuable. We had no idea how important a piece it was. For us, right now, it was just another *thing* that had to be unboxed and carted upstairs and placed *just so*, before the doors opened up for the general public the following morning. "Get the door," he muttered, struggling to tilt back the heavy marble statue on the padded two wheeled dolly. With a grunt, his mushy, almost useless muscles, heaved and pushed until it was rolling forward. "Need any help," I asked with a snicker, chiding him a little bit. "Oh no my princess...you've been so much help already," he chortled, giving it right back.

Marcus rolled the dolly into the service elevator and I hit the button for floor number three. Up we went, ding, the doors sprang open, I held the button until he rolled the dolly out again. Down a hallway, around a corner, I followed him until we reached the right spot. A scent of clove and tobacco wafted in the air behind him. It was his own mixture that he rolled into cigarettes by hand. It was an ever-present scent that clung to him. With another grunt, Marcus lowered it back down, swiveling it on its base a little, to get it in just the right spot.

"Perfect," I announced with relief. With a half-hearted grin and with a little shake of his furry head, he let me know exactly how he felt about my assistance. He was right about me—in that—I wasn't much help. I really wasn't needed at all.

As we turned to return to the elevator, my eye caught sight of a man lingering at the other end of the wing. It was after closing, and there shouldn't have been anyone else up on the third floor. I watched him as shifted over to look at another painting on the wall. Tall and slender, yet very muscular, golden toned skin and softly curling sandy-blonde hair touching the top of his collared shirt—round and firm in his tight blue-jeans—even from behind I could tell almost instantly who it was. But after so many years I wanted to be sure. "Who's that?" I asked Marcus who was already hitting the down button. Tilting his head, letting his hair fall away, he eyed the man carefully, before nonchalantly replying, "that's just David…he'll be gone soon."

"Who's David?" I asked. My voice was quivering with excitement—and nervousness—anticipating the answer I wanted to hear. Marcus thought for a few seconds. Short-term memory wasn't his best attribute. With a blank stare, he realized he really didn't know. "Don't really know his last name." Turning back to the opening elevator doors, he mumbled, "Everyone just calls him David. He's been coming here for years…as long as I've been working here. He shows up every summer around this time."

"Should he be up here after closing," I asked softly, trying to act and sound casual, uninterested, just kind of concerned, really. "Should I tell him to leave…or something?"

Marcus rolled his eyes over at me. Rolling the dolly inside the elevator and punching the button for the basement, he called back to me through the closing doors, "that's a great idea princess…why don't you go tell him to leave…or something." The last thing I heard as the doors came together, was Marcus starting to chuckle—mocking me in his own special way.

Suddenly it was so quiet. I was alone, on the third floor, with him—that person I only knew as David. Someone that I had never actually met, but felt like there was some passionate connection, in a secret admirer, star-struck groupie, kind of way. Then I realized my heart was racing, and it was getting harder to keep breathing normally, or to even think clearly. This was all new to me then. Love was still make-believe. Something mystical that happened between the princess and prince in some fairytale land—not with me and some cute guy in reality—not in the right here and now. The only other person I could barely relate to as my boyfriend would have been Ethan, from a year ago, before he moved away. We had planned on dating after we turned sixteen, when our parents would allow it, but as fate goes, it wasn't meant to be.

Staring across the room at David, stirring up a strong flurry of butterflies inside my stomach, reminded me of my overwhelming virginity, not just with sex, but with every-thing to do with the male species. I had not even had a real first kiss from anyone, including Ethan, who was overly well mannered to the point of being a bore at times. I was com-pletely unprepared for doing what should have been so sim-ple—to just meet him—to just talk to him.

David shifted over to another piece hanging on the wall. Fighting through my nerves, I started to take a step in his direction. It was too late. He turned to look straight at me with those bright blue eyes of his. They were like two glaring spotlights. And I was a deer caught in them—staring dumb-founded back at him. Nearly stumbling, I kept moving, even though I felt like I may be tripping over my own feet. For some reason my mind wanted to look down at my shoes to direct them on how to walk properly, while at the same time screaming at me to look confident and calm. Really, I had never felt this nervous about anything before. *Stand up straight and push your chest out,* I told myself, wanting to look older and more mature, someone closer to his age. My eyes must have been as big as silver dollar coins. It was a miracle my feet didn't tangle together—when he looked up at me, and smiled like a fairy-tale prince charming.

"You must be one of the new interns," he said calmly, as

if he had done this many times before. He was so full of the confidence that I was lacking. Not a hint of being nervous. It caught me even more off guard. Suddenly I didn't know how to react.

"What gives you that impression?" I replied smugly, with a nervous grin. My feet stopped, without tripping, a few feet away from him. Sticking my chin out, with my hands planted on my hips, I struck a confident pose. I wanted to come off as mature and intellectual, yet casual and quirky, while still being seductively captivating in the feminine way—just like a princess. I was doing my utmost best to try and hide the fact that my heart was pounding and my head was swimming.

"You going tell me I have to leave or something," he said almost jokingly. The casual smirk on his face said it all. He definitely had no interest in me, not as a possible girlfriend. My stomach fell straight down through the floor. I cringed inside, realizing that he was actually looking at me like I was some bratty, annoying, little kid that was bothering him. He didn't even want to know my name. Nothing could have been more painful, or so I thought. I couldn't even respond with a cogent thought, before he hit me with another unexpected low blow.

"You certainly aren't a security guard," he pointed out, looking me slowly up and down with another cocky half-smile. "You're way too tiny for that," he snickered dismissively, "probably still a freshman, right?"

My head was now spinning. What was up was now down, and I was turned all around. My mind was telling me to yell at him—*to get out!* Another part of me was desperately wanting me to plead with him to reconsider, pleading with him to stay; *oh no, don't go, please stay as long as you would like. I will even hang out with you—if you would like?*

This split-personality battle was ragging inside of me until *she* appeared right out of nowhere—slithering up beside him.

"Who's this David?" She asked coldly, while staring me down. She was intimidatingly tall, perched way up on her spiked high heels, with a pencil width skinny body that made her look even taller. She was about the same age as David, and just as good-looking. Quickly clasping ahold of his hand, her fingers entwined with his, letting me know that they were *together*. Her bugged-out hazel eyes glared—letting me know that I had intruded on some private moment between, *them.*

At least she wanted to know who *I was*—sounding almost jealous!

"No one is supposed to be up here after closing," I grumbled, trying to keep my voice firm—trying my best to hide my bitter disappointment. To them, I must have sounded just like the timid freshman that David thought I was.

"No problem…we're on our way out anyways," David said with a sweet smile. Just for a moment, he must have felt some pity for me. The despair in my eyes must have been too much to hide. "I was just showing her around," he said softly, "maybe I'll see you around the next time."

As they turned to leave, David glanced back over his shoulder to shoot me a secretive flirty wink. His bitchy girlfriend was none the wiser. My lips curled up with a giggly smile as the butterflies returned to tickle my insides some more.

Oh yes, I will see you again, next time—I sighed.

10

THERE WAS NO next time, not for a very long time. The next few years past like all the ones before them. School, work, play—mostly school, with homework taking up as much of my evenings as classes did my daytime. There was little time for boys, dating, and all that. I was lucky just to find time for making a female friend or two.

Lisa remained as my closest friend all the way up through high school, for good reason. Playful and carefree, she was a feather floating on the wind, compared to my led filled shoe life, where everything was planned out for me. A true Gemini if there ever was one, Lisa never seemed to be down about much of anything. If she ever was, she didn't let me know about it—not often. Only the time her parents almost divorced after a trial separation, did she seem to be constantly on edge, a little worried about things. Other than that she was utterly happy and carefree.

Unlike me, since I became even more moody, sullen, and withdrawn over the years.

With stringy brown hair, braces tracking over her awkwardly bent teeth, and unusually large dark freckles, Lisa certainly wasn't in the supermodel category. Her dumpy misshapen boyish body made her even less attractive. It didn't seem to bother her not being the prettiest girl in the room, class, or school, or even all of Atlanta. She used me to meet cute boys. Egging me on, getting me to flirt with everyone, so she would get a little attention by being in my company. In reality, it was Lisa that was getting all the attention. I was just the honey drawing them to us, but she was the life of the party, keeping them entertained and happily buzzing around us.

Wish I could say the same for myself. Even with the boys giving me a lot of attention, according to Lisa who noticed, I simply ignored them for the most part, treating them more like annoying pests—which they actually were, while we were in high school. A latest of the late bloomers, boys weren't really on my radar until after I got to college, then I took notice in a big way. Still, I kept my distance.

David was always lingering in the back of my mind. For some reason, in my fantasy filled daydreaming mind, I had built this image around him, as if I knew him, really. He was the model, the prototype of the perfect man, where I used my made-up version of him to carve out the ultimate male creature. He was my imaginary *Prince Charming* that I would wait for *patiently* until he appeared just in the nick of time to sweep me off my feet and take me away from here—to a life where I could be completely filled with never ending glee and oh-so-happy with everything—*forever*.

Huge mistake! Since no guy could ever live up to that false image, and no one ever would. Poor Thomas, even he couldn't get there—even though he was about as perfect as guys can get—if you looked past all of the imperfections.

College was altogether different.

Father stuck to his promise and kept his bargain with me. I pursued a major in art history and minored in English Literature. He managed to pretend to be pleased with my perfect grades, holding back the taunts and jeers, but I knew what he was actually thinking; *big deal, it's easy to get perfect scores in such easy courses.* Being top academic student in all of my classes wasn't good enough for him. He wanted me to be in advanced biology, business, computer science, or chemistry, something far more challenging and intellectually demanding—all for the benefit of *his* ego of course. But I was happy, even if it was all still leading to what he wanted in the end, my admission into law school.

Lisa blossomed in a major way. Like popcorn popping, everything about her changed almost overnight it seemed. By the time we were in our junior year at Emory University, Lisa had morphed nearly into that super model that she wanted to become. Growing a few inches taller than the rest of us, she stretched up into a long-legged diva, with sumptuously thick wavy hair, punctuated by a pair of swollen sweet melons on her chest—what a knockout!

Now she was the one getting all the attention, and I was the tagalong third wheel, which was fine with me, most of the time.

Her carefree attitude combined with her newfound attractiveness took her in a completely new different direction—away from me in many respects. Our friendship was strained when she was asked to pledge with the Kappa Alpha Theta Sorority. Widely considered to have the best looking members, some even believe it was a condition of being allowed to join.

I'll have to admit that I was somewhat—strike that—more

like extremely disappointed—when I didn't get the same invitation. My head was stuck in the books for so long that I let my looks tarnish, and my personality wasn't exactly shining either. But it hurt just the same when Lisa giddily accepted and moved into their palatial house on campus—away from me still living with my parents in our old neighborhood. I had never felt more like a nerdy homebound child more than the day she moved out. With her bags stuffed inside her car, standing in her family's driveway, we said our farewells. "We'll always be best friends," she gushed, looking down at me with pitying eyes. She bent down to kiss me on the cheek.

"Of course we will," I whispered back, knowing it wasn't true.

We waived to each other on accession, when we would pass each other on our way to and from classes. Once in a while, not very often, we would meet for a quick lunch to catch up on things; the neighborhood, high school friends, family, and whatever else was new with us. Mostly new with her, since my life was a repeating episode of the same boring melodrama wherein I played the *plain Jane* role—with nothing really changing for me other than the days on the calendar.

Of course I was jealous—as hell!

Lisa was now the beautiful campus debutant, surrounded by all of the hottest guys, attending all the best parties, hanging out with the cheerleaders and jocks. While I spent my days in the library studying for another exam, or in the museum basement moving around pieces of art with the other interns. She was exploring and experiencing life—while I was dating, debating, wondering about what my life may be like, someday.

That's why I was so shocked when Lisa called me straight

out of the blue and invited me to accompany her on a week-long snow skiing trip with a few of her sorority sisters. Her sister friend Gabriel was engaged, soon to wed, and everyone was taking off on a last minute getaway to Breckenridge Colorado, for a girls trip/bachelorette bash over spring break. Everyone else was heading to the beach, so it would just be our small group of six girls. "C'mon, it'll be such a blast," she nearly screamed at me over the phone, loud enough that mother overheard—from all the way on the other side of the kitchen. Lisa was speaking fast as she excitedly filled me in, "if you go, the flight is covered and all you need to pay for is your share of the room, lift tickets, and for food and extra stuff."

"Go on, go, you need a break," mother whispered with an almost sinister looking smile appearing on her somewhat inebriated lips. "You've been studying so hard…you've earned it." Clenching down on the stem of her half-full wine glass, mother sighed deeply with the thought of getting her own break. A far off gaze came over her as her eyes glazed over. Lost in thought she suddenly looked so happy. I could tell she was reliving one of her own girls only trips filled with debauchery, back when she was in college—well before she starting dating father of course. I tried not to think about what she was remembering for fear it would become far too graphic for my own virgin brain to handle. "Oh yes, you should definitely go," she sighed again, speaking with a distantly soft voice, that sounded almost like she was getting sexually aroused.

With mother's fond endorsement, and encouragement, what choice did I really have? "Sure I'll go with," I replied eagerly, "finals are not for a few weeks, and I'm all caught up."

"Wow, you're still such a goody two-shoes," Lisa snickered. "Just be packed and at the airport by eight Friday morning…you won't regret it." Her voice was gleefully happy, and just as sincere I remembered. "She's going," I heard her saying, with some of the other girls were chatting and giggling in the background as she hung up the phone.

It wasn't until we started boarding the flight to Denver that I happened to overhear one of the sorority sisters mentioning to someone, that; "Deb couldn't go with, and none of the other sisters wanted to go skiing instead of the going down to Florida, so Lisa got her rich friend Emma to use her ticket *and* cover Deb's portion of the other expenses."

She didn't know I was close enough to overhear her conversation, standing a few feet away, hidden behind Lisa. I was a little heartbroken. But so what, I was used to being the tagalong girl by then. It didn't ruin the entire trip. Lisa was still the fun-loving friend she used to be. She may have turned into a super model on the outside, but she was still that goofy, lighthearted, freckle-faced-girl on the inside. She heard the gossip too, and she jabbed me in the ribs and snickered like she used to do in junior high. My spirits immediately jumped back up and I giggled like we were *that young* again. "So, I'm the spoiled little rich girl that you used to pay for your trip," I murmured, playing like I was upset. "Damn right," Lisa laughed, poking me some more—forcing me to laugh out loud to where everyone could hear.

As it turned out, mother was right, and I did need a break from my rut of a life—even if it meant almost losing it!

11

W E TOUCHED DOWN in Denver, found our luggage in the carousel, and climbed into a shuttle bus that would take us up into the mountains—all the way to the front door of our small mansion turned Bed and Breakfast. It looked like a Swiss mountain chalet, with wooden beams and a tiled roof. There was even a tiny ceramic gnome on the porch to welcome us.

The mountains were high and the blue air was crisp and dry. "Not much snow lately…the runs are hard packed and icy," the innkeeper grumbled out as a warning. He looked like he was in his eighties and had weathered many long harsh winters up here. His dry cracking skin and gray hairs sticking out with the appearance of some mad scientist made us all giggle and laugh—to his utter annoyance. "You girls better take it easy on the slopes," he snarled, looking us over cautiously. "Not the ideal conditions for amateurs right now…you'd be best to keep your wits about you while you're out." He was talking more about the boozing he expected us to be doing, more than his concern over the icy ski runs. We laughed even harder knowing that he had us pegged.

"Don't worry, we are experts at going down," Lisa snickered

in the background. The old man didn't seem to get it, and he handed out our keys to our two rooms with a stern uncaring sneer. "Rooms 400 and 401, fourth floor, no elevator, only stairs over there," He said, pointing across the living room decked out lobby. We all jostled past the fireplace to the far wall, formed a single line, and pulled our bags slowly up the four flights until we reached the right floor. There would be four of us to each room. Lisa and I would have to bunk together in a queen bed.

"I'm glad you decided to come along," Lisa said as she flopped down on the down mattress to give it a try. I flopped down right next to her to try out my side. It was terribly lumpy and in need of a long overdue flipping over. At least the pillow was nice and soft, in just the right ways. "You don't wish Deb was here instead," I whispered back, as we settled in and relaxed for a moment, taking in the rustic mountain cottage ambiance. "Definitely not," she whispered back. When she looked over at me, it was just as if we were those little girls again—just two best friends—on a sleepover.

The other girls were busily unpacking clothes and fixing themselves up for a night out. A wine bottle popped as a corked got pulled. Lisa smiled and said, "C'mon, let's go have some fun." She leaped from the bed and grabbed my arms to help pull me up out of the hole in the mattress that I was stuck in.

Popping open our bursting suitcases, we started going through our wardrobes piece by piece. Lisa turned to me with an exacerbated frown, and said remorsefully, "looks like was have some shopping to do first." We had absolutely nothing suitable for the frigid mountain air, or for skiing. A constant shivering had gripped all of us as soon as we left the airport exit. By the time we got inside the hotel, we were absolutely frozen to the bone. Everything we had brought was now looking thinner, feeling lighter, and was actually far less flesh covering than we had imagined it to be when we packed. All we had imagined was frolicking in skimpy outfits to the delight of all the hot guys. No need to dress like an Eskimo, since their hot bodies would keep us warm. And besides, Atlanta is no place to shop for winter wear. Of course my clothes were a little bit thicker and warmer than the rest of the ladies, but still no match for what we were facing. "We won't last five minutes out there," I groaned.

"I didn't bring enough money for that," Lisa moaned. Her family wasn't doing very well financially, and she had been getting by lately mostly on her student loans—that were about tapped out. Her father's business was faltering and heading into bankruptcy at any moment. It was a secret that she wouldn't dare share with the other sisters.

"Don't worry," I whispered, "father lent me a credit card, for emergencies." We shared a smile as I pointed out, "and this is an emergency."

The rest of the week was kind of a blur. Daytime shopping sprees, beers for lunch, sliding down bunny slopes with hot ski instructors, hot-tubs, food, followed by binge drinking fueled nights, dancing, more hot-tubing, before passing out—then waking up to do it all over again. It dawned on us a few days in, that we didn't need extra clothes, since we wound up stripping mid-morning after a few beers anyway. We almost felt hot and sweaty by lunchtime. Perhaps, it was just the hot ski instructors who were holding us in their arms and helping us stay upright or falling over on top of us— when we eventually fell-face-flat, or backwards down on our asses. Anyway it happened, the snow and ice was melting fast as we heated things up.

On the morning of our last day of skiing, Lisa was getting brave. It may have been all the alcohol building up in her bloodstream. Right after breakfast we all headed over to the lounge in the ski lodge for a, "going back home cheers". By the time she had finished her third mimosa that morning at the bar she was getting way too light headed, even for the ultra-thin atmosphere way up in the super high altitude. She may have even fallen on her head one too many times. Whatever it was, she was getting nuts. "Let's do something we will remember forever," she gushed with a scary looking maniacal smile. Everyone stopped chatting to glance over at her, skeptically.

"What exactly do you have in mind," Sara asked with her own devilish smile. We were all thinking; an impromptu skinny dipping party in the hot tub with ski instructors, skinny skiing with skin instructors, anything to do with getting drunk and naked with those hunky ski instructors!

"I'm going all the way up to the top," Lisa announced heroically, sounding like some explorer who was about to embark on a quest. To everyone else, she just sounded like a drunken frat girl who was about to do something very stupid—something she would forever regret.

All the sisters busted out laughing. I chimed in, saying, "That's definitely something you will never forget...if you survive?"

Before we even realized what she was doing, Lisa was headed out the door. We all followed her outside, champagne glasses in hand. With jittery laughter we watched as she pulled her boots on and clamped on her skis. Almost everyone was silent when she finally strapped on her helmet and awkwardly glided away, heading toward the lift. "She's actually going to do it," I heard someone say. "Should we let her go alone?" Someone else asked nervously. Lisa had almost fallen a few times before she even got to her place in line to wait for a seat. "Oh shit, that's the black diamond line," Sara murmured. "She's really going to do it."

There was a spontaneous gasp. The sign above Lisa's lift showed that it was a double black diamond, with a large E and X printed inside each diamond—extreme terrain! Only the most expert skiers would even dare to tackle that run, even sober ones. No one could take a single breath, and we watched open-mouthed, until she finally took a seat on the lift and was whisked away up the steep mountainside. "Isn't someone going with her?" A voice asked from the middle of the group. The trip had all seemed to be like a dream coming true—up until that point—now it was a nightmare.

"I'll go after her," I muttered, reluctantly. My voice was quivering, and not from the cold. The thought of being all the way up there at the top, let alone coming down, made my entire body quiver. A few of the other girls had taken to the slopes. They were pretty good skiers compared to me. I had stuck to the bunny slopes with the beginners and small children, fearing to even get close to the higher, more difficult runs.

"I'll go too," Sara said boldly, before I finished getting my boots on. She was one of the better skiers of the group. Her family was one of those that took annual ski trips since her parents were avid skiers. She tagged along and became pretty good herself, but certainly not a pro by any stretch of the imagination. Having spent most of her time flirting with the boys and hanging out in the shops, she wasn't much better than the rest of us really. Her skills were still rusty on this trip and she had only managed to get halfway up the mountain—on a dare. There was a noticeable fearful trembling in her voice.

We strapped on our gear and slid off towards the lift. The others gave us some parting words of encouragement, but I couldn't even rationalize what it was they were saying, being almost in a state of mental shock. I wasn't even thinking about what was happening until the lift swooshed us up and whisked us away. It was more like falling, and I felt a little sick to my stomach. I kept my eyes open until we got up a little too high—then I clenched them shut. "It's beautiful up here," Sara muttered through her shivering lips, trying to make the best of it. Up and up we rose like frightened angels ascending into heaven, or hell, depending on how you wanted to look at it. My fingers gripped down on the lap bar until they went numb inside my gloves. I peeked out to see what she was talking about. Turned out, she was right, it was a little bit better than hell.

Wispy white clouds drifted like cotton balls across the crisp blue sky above us. It was absolutely silent except for the whirring of the moving metal ski lift that was humming along. A soft wind tickled at our ears, noses, and eyelashes. Below us, the pine trees were nearly covered up completely by fresh snow. "Wow, we're not really all that far up from the ground now," Sara pointed out. We had no idea that while we were sleeping off another night of heavy drinking last night, a storm front had unleashed an unseasonably thick layer of deep sticky white powder. A few feet of snow had been deposited on the slopes below us. It wasn't apparent until we had gotten so far up.

The locals, along with the other avid skiers, were all streaming up the freshly plowed roadways to take advantage of the pristine ski conditions. The news was letting everyone know about how a storm of the decade had left the mountains buried in snow—a few more feet deep—ready for some of the most awesome ski run *shredding* in years. Only, they forgot to mention the avalanche threat that came along with the fresh snowfall. Not that we would have noticed the warnings anyway, or cared.

Along with the avid skiers heading up top, an elite search and rescue team had been dispatched to ward off an imminent avalanche threat. They were already scouring the area, searching the rugged backcountry terrain for areas blanketed with an unstable snowpack. As we neared the summit, we could see a couple of them with orange and red vests and helmets. One even had a red cross on his back. We had no idea what those skiers were doing zigzagging through the trees, making winding tracks way off the beaten paths, heading away from the other skiers.

"Wonder what that's all about?" I stammered to Sara. But she wasn't listening. Her eyes were glued to the imaginary point where we had to jump off—or get knocked off.

"Ready," she said loudly, yet thick with nervous fear. Her hands shifted and pushed the lap bar above our heads—while I was still pulling it down. "Let go," she yelled as she forced it all the way up and out of our way. "Ready for...?" I started to ask as she pushed herself off the seat, planting her skis firmly in the snow and gently sliding away down the hill over to where the run starts. "Wait!" I yelled to her frantically trying to push myself off right behind her. With my skis crossing in front of me, I landed awkwardly, my skis popped off, and I was flung face forward to where I face-planted onto the icy-hard packed snow. My body slid like a toboggan until slamming into some snow piled up against a few trees. My skis slid past me, tauntingly, gliding away in opposite directions.

Sara was laughing hard as she went off to retrieve them for me. "Should've been *more* ready," she chuckled. Lifting up my face, it was covered with stickily clinging snow that I tried to blow and swat off. By the time I got back up and preened all the snow away from my goggles, bib, scarf and hat, Sara was gliding up next to me with *my* skis in hand. Tossing them down in front of me she giggled, "There's no time for making snow angels…let's go."

If only I had been smart enough to stop then. I could have begged the lift operator for a pity ride back down. But luckily, fate had something better in store for me.

Sara didn't stick around to watch me struggling to get my skis back on. Huffing and flailing around like I had had a stroke. It was nearly impossible. But I finally managed to put them on *the right way*. The only good thing at that moment was that my heart was pounding and my body was getting hot—to the point of sweating inside my thick ski garb that I paid way too much for on a whim. It was the colors that sold me on them. I'm a sucker for anything in baby blue, and it was the last one in my size. Thank the lord for father's emergency credit card. As fate would have it—my clothing wouldn't be the last of the very expensive emergency expenditures charged to him on this trip.

"Wait up!" I cried out as Sara disappeared down the mountain. Turning my skis to point in her direction, I pushed off, and started down. She was gone in a flash and never even looked back. I seriously doubt she could have heard me anyway. That was the only ski run down, and she knew Lisa would have gone that way. I would just have to try and keep up, or catch up. Both were impossible.

By the time I reached the first fork in the run I couldn't see anyone, let alone Lisa or Sara. It was hard enough just staying upright. There was no way I could navigate and manage to follow their tracks in the snow. Turning right was about all I could do. Turning left wasn't my strong suit. Not wanting to fall I plowed straight on, with just enough of a slight right lean to get me to go in that direction. Within seconds, the trail seemed to be dropping out from beneath me, going almost straight down—with a sharp turn to the left coming up fast. Before I knew what was happening I was screaming straight down the steepening slope until I was completely out of control.

In a flash I found myself whizzing off the trial into the trees—where there was no trail. I managed to swerve around one tree, a true miracle, before heading straight at another larger one. Throwing my body to the right, my skis twisted crossways and I plowed face first into the pine tree with a glancing blow that didn't even slow me down much. The impact just knocked the air out of my lungs and blurred my vision. Unfortunately I was still alert enough to see the edge of the cliff—that I was about to go over! I felt massive shockwaves battering me as I slammed up against some knee-high boulders hidden beneath the snow. I pitched forward and flew through the air like some circus acrobat—flying over the edge.

There was no real sensation that I could remember feeling

as I crashed down into the soft pillow of deep snow at the bottom of the thirty-foot, or so, ravine. Falling through the air for what seemed to be an eternity, before landing in, and being swallowed up within, the thick pillow of snow again, was such a surreal out of body experience. I would have to say now that it was actually kind of fun. It was like landing in a cloud up in the sky. So soft and quiet, with everything seeming to be almost heavenly, downright peaceful—right before my head struck that rock, and everything went black as I was knocked unconscious.

12

WAKING BACK UP was just as surreal, and just as heavenly. It was all white again, the best I can remember. Like an angel had opened up a doorway to let me back out of a tiny pitch black room. Slowly the light grew brighter, from the softness of a single candle glow, to the sharp brightness of a beam of noonday light piercing into my squinting eyes.

It was not just any angel opening my door to let me out—it was David. I couldn't see his face at first, but I knew his voice.

"Try not to move," he called down to me, from up above, just like an angel. He was laying on the surface of the snow-pack. Sunlight was streamed down through a small tunnel that he had burrowed down to where I was, buried beneath a few feet of packed snow from the small avalanche I managed to get started as I hit the boulders.

When I first saw him looking down, he didn't look like the David I remembered. But his voice was cold and con-fident, as fiercely determined as the frozen air surrounding us. Instantly I felt safe, even though I was far from it. His face was covered by a thick grizzly-man type beard. Some wilderness hardened mountain man, who hadn't come down out of the mountains in years, was my initial impression. "Can you breathe?" He called down to me, with his eyes staring directly into mine, searching for signs of conscious life. It was at that moment, that I felt fully alive again—as if I had broken the surface, rising up from beneath a deep dark body of water, opening up my mouth to refill my lungs with fresh air again.

"Yes…I can breathe," I muttered, straining to get my weak voice all the way up to him. My mouth was nearly frozen in place, just like the rest of my body. As I breathed my mind reawakened along with the rest of me. A shiver turned into a body shaking painful spasm as my nerves returned to normal, sending out pangs of wrenching pain up to my semiconscious brain. Then I could feel the full weight of the snowpack pressing down on my chest. It was getting harder and harder to catch my breath and everything started spinning and blurring like I was inside the eye of a tornado, looking up at a pinprick of light at the very top—and the light was dimming fast. "Help me—," I tried to say, before blacking out once more.

"Hang on…just keep breathing," I thought I heard David calling down to me as everything went black again. He had frantically ripped the snow away with his bare hands to relieve the pressure. His buddy arrived just in the nick of time with a shovel and they had managed to dig down and pull me free before I completely succumbed and passed away. David's lips pressed against mine, and he breathed a life-saving breath back inside of me.

When I opened my eyes again, he was there, right beside me. I was laid out on a stretcher-board, strapped down and being prepped for the ride down the mountain. David was kneeling down next to me with his warming fingertips gently pressed against my wrist, keeping an eye on my vitals, and told me to, "Just look at me…look here…keep looking into my eyes". My eyes locked with his and I tried to focus on him. A blurry happy smile appeared on his scruffy face, "You're going to be just fine," he whispered some encouragement. There were ice crystals dangling off his whiskers looking like tiny little icicles. They shimmered and sparkled as he spoke. His hands were busily lashing black nylon straps tightly into place around my numb body, securing me onto a flat red rescue sled.

I smiled too, and whispered out his name, as if I were dreaming, "David?"

A puzzled look came over him and he leaned back. Dropping the last strap, his eyes widened and he stared intently at my face. He was clearly surprised that I knew his name. It was obvious that he didn't have a clue who I was, or how I could possibly know him. With my thick coat and high collar up to my ears, scarf wrapped around my neck, hair matted down with ice crystals and my skin having turned nearly blue, I wasn't looking like myself at the moment—so it was O.K. if he couldn't recognize me. Leaning back over me, he gazed deeply into my hazy eyes, while trying to puzzle it out. "Emma?" He softly mumbled, unsure of himself.

He knows my name! I was screaming inside—and I think I was smiling—even though I couldn't feel my lips.

Just then the emergency sled that I was strapped onto lurched forward. His hand slipped out of mine as his paramedic partner pulled me away from him. The sled was harnessed to his partner who had the job of skiing me down off the dangerous mountainside. David had finished doing his job—of finding me buried in the snow, pulling me out, and getting me stabilized, and ready to be brought back down. I wrenched my head around as far as I could to look back. It felt like leaving him was more painful than my sprained ankles and all the bruises all over my body.

Well, it did, until I thawed out, then the injuries turned out to be way more painful. By the time we got all the way back down to the lodge, I was feeling every agonizing aching bruise and sprain.

All the girls were waiting for us, including Lisa and Sara. They had made it down just fine, with a few falls and spills now and then, but nothing life threatening. It was certainly one of the most embarrassing moments—ever! They acted concerned at first, of course, until they learned that nothing was broken; no fractures, no concussions, no internal injuries, nothing severe at all. The tiny medical clinic discharged me within the hour and advised me to use crutches to help support my sprained ankles. They even gave me a couple of free ice packs to put on the worst of my bruises. I was just another amateur skier, going home with the typical wounds.

Those pains didn't even compare to the intense pain I felt when father opened up his credit card bill the next month.

By the time I got back to the B and B, the other girls were already packed and lugging their luggage down to the lobby. All concern for me had vanished. My accident, the rescue from off the mountain, and my trip to the medical clinic had taken up the entire day. "We're never going to make it in time now," one of the sisters snipped from across the room. Now, all anyone cared about was getting to the airport in time to catch the flight back to Atlanta. We had about a two hour ride in the shuttle bus and there wasn't a second to lose. Thankfully Lisa had been thoughtful enough to pack my things and tug my bags down to the shuttle.

A couple of the girls fell asleep on the drive to Denver. The others pouted, arms crossed and grimacing while giving me the stink-eye, as if it was *all-my-fault*. Especially Sara, who was murmuring to the others that, "I never should have gone up there to begin with."

Lisa was torn. She was sympathetic with both sides. I felt like she sided way more with her sisters. "I really didn't need any help," she kept reminding everybody and rubbing it in at the same time, "got down the mountain just fine on my own and nobody needed to come to my rescue." That hurt deeper than those bruises covering my shins. It turned out to be one of those thorny things that get stuck down deep inside of you, that you have to carry around with you—for the rest of your life. She could've at least apologized for doing something so stupid that forced me to follow her up there in the first place. At least she thanked me for caring about her, enough to risk my life for her. It hurts just the same.

Thanks for a great trip Lisa!

Luckily we made it to our gate just in time for final boarding, and everyone was finally able to relax. They didn't say so, but I felt a little bit of forgiveness from the sisters. The snide glances disappeared and the friendly chatter returned. Lisa was sitting next to me on the isle. She let me have the window seat. It wasn't long before she asked about, "what happened up there," and, "how did they find you". So, I started telling her of my harrowing adventure on the mountain, and all about how I nearly met my death underneath a frozen deep blanket of avalanched white death. When at the last second I was ripped from certain death by a burly young guy with enormous muscles, furry beard, and sweet eyes. Not to mention his luscious lifesaving lips.

All the sisters sighed—imagining the hunky woodsman pulling me free from the snowy coffin saving me from certain death. Holding me tightly within his strong arms, warming me up with the heat of his body, he planted his lips on me—melting me completely. The air inside the cabin rose a few degrees as the girls began panting with anticipation.

That's just how I wanted them to believe it happened.

"So, did you get his name?" Lisa gushed, squirming in her seat like a giddy tween.

"David," I responded, letting his name pass my wanting lips—without thinking. All of the girls stopped chatting—instantly. It was suddenly so quiet inside the airplane cabin. All of their eyes turned to look directly at me. There was only the low roar of the engines, as they waited to hear more.

"David?" Lisa asked, "David who?"

Oops, I had said too much. All those romantic exaggerations didn't help at all either. There was no way I was going to tell them all about David. How I had a secret crush on him since seeing him through the window at the museum when I was a young girl. How I somehow remembered everything about him, secretly fantasizing about him for years, without ever actually getting to know him. Hell, I still don't even know what his last name is. How in the world could I possibly explain that one without seeming like a complete psycho? These girls would think I was imagining it all, had gone insane, or had really cracked my head open on a rock up there. They never would believe it was actually my imaginary prince charming that came to my rescue—some fairy tale that became reality.

I can hardly believe it happened. Maybe it was some blissful delusion. Hitting my head could have made me believe it was all real. Maybe I was just knocked silly? Or maybe I was delusional and seeing things due to a lack of oxygen? I was under the snow for quite a while before they dug me out. Who knows!?

"Well, who was he?" Lisa demanded, jabbing me with her elbow.

"You know what…I'm not really sure…I think maybe he said his name was David?" I nervously backtracked. "No telling…it was really all just a blur after I hit my head on that tree. I can't really remember what he said…if anything."

Lisa was staring at me like I really was delusional. She was disappointed, along with the rest of them. With a sinking heart my eyes fell away from Lisa, down to the floor, along with my thoughts. She didn't notice the longing expression coming over me. I suddenly felt that I had abandoned him— the one person who had just saved me.

Everyone instantly lost interest in my story. The low roar of the engines was gone again as the airplane cabin erupted with loud incoherent chatter. "She's so full of it," one of the sisters muttered beneath her breath, thinking I couldn't hear her over the other blathering girls sitting all around me. "Such a drama queen," another one whispered. I slumped all the way down in my seat and pretended to fall asleep—with my longing thoughts of David as my only company.

If only he could save me from this long flight home with all of these annoying bitches.

13

I'LL ADMIT IT—I was becoming a bit obsessed. By the time we set foot back inside the Atlanta terminal, all I could think about was finding out if that really was David who pulled me out of that snowy grave up on the mountain. Maybe I just wanted to prove all of those stupid bitches wrong. How else could I save face? Besides, it couldn't have been *just* a *mere* coincidence? There was not a snowballs chance in hell (with me being the snowball) that he *just* happened to be up there on that mountain, *just* in time to find me and rescue me from certain death, *just* at that *precise moment* in time—for *absolutely* no other reason at all.

It just had to be fate!

Completely ignoring Lisa and the other girls on the long car ride through downtown heading back to Buckhead, I began wracking my brain for every detail that I could remember about him, his name (the most generic American name in history other than perhaps Joe), his height, his approximate weight, the details of his face (dreamy beyond measure), and of course his hair and eye color (brown and blue). But that was about it.

THAT WAS IT! That's all I could think of. Nothing else about him came to mind? I WAS CLUELESS!

My family thought I was still suffering from the blow to my head since I seemed to be so out-of-it. My mind was just preoccupied. Hardly saying a word to anyone I headed straight up to my room. I didn't really need my crutches that they forced me to take with me when I left the clinic, but they sure came in handy when it came to convincing my family to give me some space—just little peace of mind to let me wrack my brain for a while. Haphazardly clanking my way up the stairs like some science fiction project gone awry, I played it up. Mother was all too happy to shoo everyone away for me, telling them, "Go on and leave her alone. Give her some peace and quiet. She needs time to heal." Pulling my bedcovers back and fluffing my pillows, she snickered, "You need to get some rest dear after such an exciting trip." She was reminded of herself of course—stumbling back home, all bruised, battered, and worn completely out, after going on one of her girlfriend's bachelorette parties in Vegas or some other cities full of tantalizing debaucheries. I flopped down on the mushy soft mattress with a gleeful sigh. "Looks like someone had a little too much fun," she giggled with delight. She gave me a sinful wink before shutting my bedroom door.

The following Monday morning, as soon as I got back on campus at Emory, I headed to the library to pour over the phone books for Atlanta, Breckenridge, and even Denver. I didn't have any other ideas about how to contact him, so I started calling nearly every David listed. I must have called a thousand men named "David". At least it felt that way. Worst few hours of my life. It wasn't until I got yelled at one too many times that I decided to finally give that up. *This is a stupid waste of time*, I realized, with a man screaming in my ear through the receiver, "Why are you bothering me right now…how can you be so stupid!"

The next couple of months I spent more time at the High Museum, offering to help out even when I wasn't needed for anything, or just lingering, meandering aimlessly through the exhibits, not paying any attention to anything. I had already memorized every detail about—everything. If someone asked where some piece of obscure art was located, not only could I provide them with precise, step by footstep directions to where it was, I could most likely recite the artist who created it, when, where, and how it was done, without even forcing myself to think. It was all there in my brain now, stored there like information in a computer data base, just waiting for someone to type in the query to get me to spit it back out at them.

Nearly every day I would wind up wandering over to the window, to where I first saw him. Walking up to the cold glass, pressing my lips close up, my warm breath would fog it up, just as it had done on that day. Before leaving, my hand would wipe away the wet spot—after I had run my finger through it, so at least I could see his name appear:

David.

It was the only thing I really knew about him. At least I had that, along with my fading memories.

The last time I wrote his name on the fogged up glass I was beginning to give up on finding him. Then, with one of those Earth shaking, stunning moments, I remembered why he was out there by the memorial in the first place—duh! His parents or some other close relative must have passed away on that flight that crashed in Orly France. That man, one of his relatives, must have been bringing him up here to the view the memorial, to remember them. *His relative's names must be on the memorial, including his last name.*

Busting through the glass door I skipped over to the marble memorial with the etched names of the crash victims. The looming bronze statue, "Old Shady", with his head bent over his grossly long neck, seemed to be looking down with me. It almost seemed like even he was doing what he could to help me find my clue. With his drooping arm, his limply pointing fingertips showed me where to look. My eyes carefully scanned every detail trying to find something, anything, the tiniest of tiny tidbits that would help me narrow it down to who I was looking for.

Was he named after someone? Probably not, since there wasn't a David Senior, or a Junior, or a David the First, or a Second, or even a Third. There were a few David's however. That was at least a start. But how could I possibly contact these families—after all these years—with some sobbing little love story. How pathetic I would appear. *What a psychotic stalker I would look like.*

But I wouldn't let that stop me—never had before. I just needed a better plan. The library just may have the answer. There, I managed to locate a book about the Orly crash that included a few stories about the victims. All the names were there along with some vital clues about their extended families. Well, it was a starting point. But not much of one— since I was right back where I started; flipping through the pages of another phone book, with a receiver shaking in my hand, my index finger nervously poised to start punching out a phone number, a number to a stranger, someone that would most likely be just another dead end, and ending up with me getting yelled at through the receiver—again.

"Why in the hell are you calling me you crazy bitch stalker!?" I could hear it now. My head was beginning to hurt before I had even touched the keypad. My finger wouldn't go down. I couldn't push the button on the phone.

So I needed an *even better* plan. It took some time to come up with one.

My internship at the High Museum was over. Since I was nearing graduation and polishing my application for Law School, father wanted me to move on to more important things. My doing things for the community, to prove that I was a good, honest, respectable citizen, was all over. It was time to get down to real-life business. A few weeks later, I started my part-time summer pre legal internship at father's law office

Since I wasn't officially in law school yet, even though it was already a given and all lined up for me to attend— since father had even forced me to meet with the Dean and a couple of my future professors to grease the skids. My summer job at the firm was more or less a glorified reception-ist, mail and court runner, and the get me some more coffee girl. Father paid me more than anyone else in that position. Not because he wanted to, but because he wanted me to pay back the all the money I had run-up on his credit card. I was supposed to be learning how to act like a lawyer too. That was not a hard thing to learn—just act like you know it all, and dress nice. The second part just forced me to run up his credit card bill even more forcing me work even more hours—such a vicious cycle!

While sitting at my confining receptionist desk, completely bored out of my mind after several mind-numbing hours of transferring phone calls—I was struck with an idea. *What if I used one of the firm's investigators to help me find David?*

It was actually Mitch's call coming in that put the idea in my head. He was calling in to speak with one of the attorneys about a case he was working on. Mitchell, or Mitch as everyone around the office called him, was our go-to investigator for tracking down hard to find leads. Having retired from law enforcement a few years back, he was a well-seasoned human blood hound of sorts, with a body worn down by time without dampening his spirit for the chase. He was just having trouble keeping up with the times. We just recently got him to stop wearing his fedora hat and tattered old overcoat. "You stick out like a sore thumb…he must have spotted you coming a mile away," we overheard father scolding him a few months ago after having his cover blown while out snooping on a personal injury claimant that was believed to be faking his injuries. "How the hell do you expect to sneak up on people nowadays looking like some old-timey F.B.I. agent right out of some ancient black and white movie? Now get rid of that hat and coat before I get rid of you once and for all."

Taking off his hat revealed a balding scalp with age spots dotting his skin. All of his once dark hairs are now fading to gray. The men's hair dyes wouldn't even hide it anymore. Beneath his coat he was always dressed sharply—if only out of style in most respects. Wingtip shoes polished with a shining reflection, a tight crease in his trousers, a vest or a sweater with a freshly dry cleaned elbow-patched sport coat or pinstriped suit. Always ready with a quick witty remark or a captivating story to tell, it was never a boring moment with Mitch in the room. Everyone seemed to like having him around, if only to remind them of someone special they had lost, a father, uncle, or grandfather. He was a real man's man type from a bygone era.

It's a little bit embarrassing, but I have to confess, that sometimes, when he's talking to me with that happy twinkle in his eye, I try to envision him as he was in his younger days—still sporting his slick-backed jet-black hair, a lean and chiseled muscular physique, big strong hands and squared jaw, sharply dressed, with a sincerely sweet smile above his chiseled manly chin. He could have given Clark Gable a run for his money back in his day. I actually start to get a little aroused whenever I think about him, back then. That is when I have to quickly force those images out of my mind, reminding myself of just how old he is, and how those thoughts are so disgusting.

Just stop it right now—you sicko!

It was the sound of his salty streetwise voice on the phone that put the idea in my head. *If Mitch can't find him, then nobody can.*

"Can you put me through to Anthony," he asked without even saying hello, not knowing that I was the one answering the phone. He didn't have to say who was calling since everyone instantly recognized his voice. "Who may I say is calling sir," I replied sternly, fighting to hold back a welling-up giggle.

"You serious?" he groaned back, "who is this?"

I couldn't stop myself from having a little fun with him. With my sweetest, southern-girl, flirtatious voice, trying my best to sound just like some *"Gone With the Wind"* character; I replied, "Why it's Emma Morgan of course, you old bag of bones. Certainly you should have recognized my sweet young voice, you old scoundrel you? Now Mitch, have you gone completely senile, or are you just going deaf now too?"

"O hell…I shoulda' known it was you short cakes," he chortled, before giving it right back to me—exactly where he knew it would hurt most. "Your father has got you chained to a desk already? You poor thing…he's such a nickel pinching slave driver…guess you really never had a chance? When you see him, tell old *Stoney* I said hello, won't you sweetheart?"

I let out that giggle, sounding like the little girl he still thought of me as. "Of course I will Mitch, but hey, while I have you on the phone, there's something I needed to ask you." My mind was wracking itself trying to quickly conceive of some reasons for asking him to get on David's trail and track him down for me. "Speaking of father, uh, he wanted me to ask you to help him out with something."

"That's what I get paid for doll…let's hear it."

"Well, he's got me working on one of his cases," my head was spinning a webby tale faster than my mouth was talking, "it's a probate case…with a missing relative someplace…that needs to be found…a beneficiary, his name is David, lives in Colorado possibly, that's all we know really, but he must be found in order to distribute what's left in the estate, so father can finally close the case, that's all it is."

"Stoney got you working cases now too?" He asked. I could hear the skepticism in his deep voice that slowed down to a more serious tone. It was an actual case now, not just some silly bantering back-and-forth with the receptionist on the phone.

"That's right…just this one thing for right now…to get my feet wet," I replied calmly. No more joking around.

"Alright then toots…put the details in a memo and leave

it on my desk and I'll get on it as soon as I can. Now can you put me through?"

"Thanks Mitch," I said before transferring his call.

As soon as I hung up the phone I was picking up a memo sheet to start typing out the investigation request:

MEMO

TO: Mitchell; please locate the following estate beneficiary

Name: David, last name unknown.

Description: white male, mid-twenties, brown hair, blue eyes, approximately 6' tall, 200 pounds, perfect build.

Address: unknown, last known location was Breckenridge, Colorado. Known to have resided in Atlanta area prior to Colorado, and possible surviving relative of the 1962 Orly crash, Atlanta Arts Assoc. (check cases worked for other surviving relatives, may be some potential leads).

Occupation: ski rescue, EMT.

I slipped the request into a manila envelope marked for internal office delivery, rushed upstairs one story and slipped into his office, where I set the envelope on his desk just as he instructed. It was right in front of this chair—top of the stack. It was a bit exciting, straight out of a spy novel, doing something so sneaky. A shiver of anticipation tingled over my entire body as I rushed back to my receptionist desk, jumping back into my little swivel chair and start punching the blinking phone lines, before being missed, "Donaldson and Morgan, how may I help you?"

14

THE WEEKS WENT by so slowly, without getting any word back from Mitch on how the search was progressing. Not even a call or scribbled note—nothing! My anticipation was turning to nerve wracking anxiousness. It was all I could think about everyday—all day. He had called in several times, and I would put all of his calls through to him, but while he was on the phone being all flirty, as normal, he would never even mention the case, or David. There was almost a palpable sensation that he was completely avoiding the subject altogether.

"So how are things…heard anything new Mitch?" I dared to ask him one time before transferring his call.

"No time to chat doll, can you put me through," he grumbled. There was no playing around—it was all serious, working, no time to chat.

I couldn't take it anymore—it was time for a confrontation!

Mitch was calling from his office this time, so I put through his call, stood up and marched up the back stairs to his office, where I knew he would be still on the phone. His door was cracked open, so I pushed my way in and slinked up to his desk and sat down in one of his side-chairs. There was an outdated, broken, wooden hat rack holding his favorite fedora, along with his dusty overcoat—the one that he was now neglecting. With an unbuttoned collar, loosened-up tie, he sat up straight when I entered the room. Reclining back in his chair he watched me sitting down. His right eye shot me a wink. Yet, the look on his face was definitely not a friendly invitation to sit down and chat—anything but. His voice remained calm as he finished up his phone conversation. Then he reluctantly hung up the phone. "What can I do for you sweetie?" He asked coldly, sounding like I was disturbing him. A detectibly nervous twinge was in his voice. He already knew what I was doing there, and what I wanted to know.

"How's it going finding that beneficiary for my father?" I asked in a professional voice, wanting to sound like just one of the other attorney's needing information on a case.

"Remind me…which one was that again toots…I got so many cases going right now?" He was playing coy, pretending he didn't remember my memo.

That was my specialty—it wasn't working for one second on me.

"I know you got my memo about finding David," I growled, actually sounding just like a pissed off attorney, surprising me a little. Pointing at his stack of paperwork piled up in front of him, I reminded him that, "I put it right there in front of you…right on top."

His face went blank. A learned behavior he had mastered, over the many years of avoiding answering questions put to him. Especially the ones that caused him trouble. Glancing around the room he swiveled in his creaking old office chair as if he was searching for something. Another learned avoidance technique he had mastered—not looking directly into my glaring eyes that were demanding answers. "I must have misplaced it someplace here," he murmured while nervously shuffling his stack of papers around.

"David," I blurted out angrily, "his name was David…from Colorado…you must remember trying to locate a beneficiary named David? It was a simple task. It should've taken you just a few minutes to find him?"

The swiveling stopped. His hands went still. His face went flush. His voice sounded like a criminal that had been caught red handed, about to confess his crimes, as he muttered out, "Oh yes, David…that guy you were looking for, living out in Colorado…yes…I found him alright." Reaching below the top of his desk he pulled open the small pencil drawer. As if showing me the smoking gun evidence, he reluctantly pulled out a single piece of paper, and stated, "Here it is… my report. I must have just misplaced it?"

My eyes stretched wide, along with a smile. "Well, did you find him then?" I asked excitedly.

Reclining back in his chair again he held up the report to where he could read it clearly. "Oh yes, I found your David from Colorado alright." Then he stopped reading and looked up at me with steely eyes, as if wanting me to stop searching for more—to just let it go.

"Yes, good…go on, tell me what you found," I pressed him.

Rattling the paper in his fingertips, his eyes fell back down to the words on the report, before he continued reading aloud. He read slowly and softly, sounding like he was reading from an obituary; "I found him living out there… up in Breckenridge…along with his young wife Victoria…

and their two little children, Jimmy and Kaitlin, ages two, and four."

My eyes fell flat, along with my smile.

"You want me to go on reading sweetheart…or would you prefer that I just pass this report along to your father?"

The remorse in his voice was crushing my heart. I hadn't felt that way since my grandmother's funeral a few years back. All the worse, I had never felt more like a complete idiot than I did at that very moment. It was now painfully obvious that Mitch knew I was the one lying the entire time. Mitch knew exactly why I was really looking for David.

He had been trying to protect me from embarrassing myself—again!

I had to get out of his office before bursting into tears. "I'll take it up to him…it's my responsibility," I muttered, fighting to maintain some composure. Taking the report from his fingers while shading my face, I headed straight for the door.

"Hope that information helps with the case," Mitch said reassuringly as I opened up the door.

Glancing back at him, holding back tears, I let him know it did, by saying, "you're the best Mitch."

On the way back to my desk, without looking at the paper with Mitch's report on it, I tossed it into the shredder box—along with my stupid fantasies about David—where they belonged.

Over the next few weeks I passed through the usual moods—anger, mostly at myself, remorse, for not getting what I wanted most, fear, of not ever finding what I wanted most, despair, as every day seemed to be telling me what I feared was coming true, and then finally, depression, since I eventually convinced myself that I was right and would never find my *Mr. Right*. Slowly, the days seemed to be drifting by, as if I was only existing within the spinning celluloid frames of a silent black and white movie—a very solemn, dreary, sad kind of movie where the old spinster never marries, or ever finds true love.

That's when father introduced me to Thomas, on a rainy day a couple of months later, in June. It was so cold and bleak outside, much like the way I was feeling on the inside. Father had noticed me moping about the office. He rarely saw me at home anymore, since I was confining myself to my room more than ever. He believed it would be a great idea, a way to pick up my spirits again.

Wow—I really know how to throw a pity-party!

While Thomas was in town interviewing for his legal internship position, father suggested to him, "How would you like it if, I have my daughter Emma show you around the office?"

"I would love to meet your daughter Mr. Morgan," Tom must have replied with his most sincere smile. I can see it so clearly now. That was the same smile he used on me when we first laid eyes on each other in the hallway—probably the same smile the serpent used on Eve when he enticed her over to the tree of *Knowledge of Good and Evil* to taste one of its delicious fruits. It worked on me in the same way. Nothing brings out the sinful side of you like a good bout of deep depression. Those whispering sinfully delicious ideas sound so good right about then. A date with the devil appeared to be exactly the cure for what was bringing me down. And Thomas, with his tall, dark, and handsome routine, filled the bill perfectly.

"Emma," father caught my attention in the middle of the hallway as I was leaving my receptionist post to deliver a message, "I want you to meet Thomas…he's one of our new associate interns."

Glancing up at his smile, my knees nearly buckled, as I started to melt. Thomas was standing right in front of me, right next to my father. He was dressed in a new black Armani suit, accented by a crisply fashioned tie (in my favorite shade of blue) sporty wingtip shoes with a fresh shine, silver cuf-flinks, with a glisteningly new Rolex wrapped around his wrist that he received as a graduation gift. He was absolutely to die for, literally. I could just picture his long lanky torso beneath his clothing, thin yet muscular, with the look of a soccer player or tennis pro, or matador. It was easy to imagine running into him somewhere in Italy, or Spain, while sipping a latte outside at a café—just a casual tryst that quickly erupts into a stormy romance. "Hello Thomas," I tried to say calmly, while gripping his strong hand for a firm handshake, "it's so nice to meet you." My face blushed as a sudden rush of warmth swept over me. I was actually feeling light headed.

Calm down! I screamed at myself, my heart thumping.

"It's such a pleasure to meet you Emma," Thomas replied softly, looking confidently into my eyes while holding onto my hand like a true gentleman—gazing into my eyes in a way that stopped time for a moment, the way it does whenever your heart skips a beat, and you can't catch your breath.

Father lingered silently, watching his matchmaking plan unfold before him. It must have given him so much pleasure to watch me swooning like that. His little girl, getting swept off her feet by a knight in shining Armani! To finish me off, he asked me for a tiny little favor. "Hey Em…would you mind showing Thomas around the office for me…I have a meeting to get to right now…and—"

Catching my breath again, I didn't even give father time to finish with his excuse before gushing, "of course I would love to show him around." Without letting go of Tom's hand, I pulled him away from there—*to show him around.*

Damn that serpent and his sumptuously tempting apples! Well, so much for my pity party.

15

MY FANTASIES ABOUT David faded—in the same way that my warm breath used to fade from off the glass, along with his name, as it evaporated away. Only a small invisible trace of him was left behind, that could never be completely erased from my memory.

Thomas did his best to remove any idea of even thinking about other men, past, or present. Not that there were so many, or those that were so very memorable and hard to forget about. Love was never matched up with my life in that way, so I never had a love-life to speak of. After Ethan, David was as close to real love as I had gotten. That was only because it was all imagined. Real guys always managed to destroy any pretense of being a love interest before the introductions were even over. I'm just a stuck-up bitch when it comes to dating. At least I have high standards—which inevitably leaves me with few options.

Do you hear a tiny violin playing? Moving on....

Getting up before the sun and racing down to the office was not such a bad thing after getting introduced to Thomas. My mood lightened a little more each time our eyes met. There was a tickle in my stomach when he touched me that made me giggle inside—every time. I tried my best to hide it, but I would almost always shiver, get goose bumps galore, make a silly grin and start nervously tugging or twirling on a strand of my hair. Doing everything I shouldn't do, giving him every indication that I was just a pile of melting putty in his hands.

While I didn't like the idea of being toyed with, I definitely enjoyed being his toy, and being played with. Does that make sense? It seemed to make perfect sense at the time, so I fell for him, hook, line, and sinker.

Thomas was absolutely perfect—too perfect. After that first meeting he managed to keep his distance for a few months, which only heightened my passions for him. Nothing seems to make someone fantasize more about wanting something, when that person isn't getting what they believe they want most of all. It was almost as if he instinctively was aware of that fact. The way he would slink around the office, tomcatting through the hallways, giving attention to anyone who would stroke him the right way. Getting scratches behind the ears from the ladies really made him purr. That always pumped up his ego. At some time during the day he would eventually show up at my door, or in the break-room, or law library, or at the elevator, running up to catch the door so we could ride it down together.

It was the way he always looked at me, with that smile. There had to be something more? He had to have an interest in me—romantically? I thought there would be more to it, and sooner. But, he kept his distance. Weeks turned into months as I was going nuts. No matter how hard I wracked my brain, I just couldn't figure it out? My frustrations forced me to turn to the only other females in the office that I thought would relate to my situation. "Is he trying to be some perfect gentleman?" I quizzed the secretaries over coffee in the break room. "Or, is he just too afraid of upsetting father to ask me out?"

After saying the words out loud, as the room suddenly became quiet, with every one of them turning to look at me strangely. That's when it hit me like a pie in the face—realizing that they must have all been thinking the same thing; *did it ever occur to you that, perhaps, just maybe, he just isn't interested in dating a spoiled brat like you?*

Oh no, that's not it—they are jealous!

It couldn't have been more obvious by their expressions that they were having the same fantasies about Thomas. The same desires were burning them up—every time he slinked passed them with that oh so sweet smile of his. Many times I had witnessed, first hand, as a few of them even sniffed the air he left behind, desperately wanting to catch a whiff of his heavenly scent. Not to mention them bending over to check him out—if you know what I mean.

We were all so pathetic!

As my question sunk in, they're expressions changed, as they all started to look at me as if I was an innocent naïve little child. "Just ask him out...before I do," Gladys perked up, shattering the silence and giving them all a good reason to cackle like a bunch of jealous hens, at my expense. Before the laughing died down, she added, "get with the times sister...we don't have to wear white gloves and panty-hose anymore...all prim and proper...waiting for them to ask us to dance at some debutante' ball. We can dance to our own grooves now, with, or without them." With that, they scurried out the door, chatting and giggling, heading back to their cubicles and offices, while I stood there silently, alone, sipping on my hot cup of stale coffee—contemplating.

Gladys was way older than me and had experienced the sexual revolution of the sixties. She was even from California I think? We had nothing in common at all, especially our sense of politics, style, and what was considered appropriate social etiquette for courting. Before that moment, the thought of asking him for a date would have been a repulsive idea. I had been telling myself that for months now; *why, I'm a Southern Belle, and I would never stoop so low as to have to ask out a man—how utterly embarrassing. If word got out that I had to ask him out on our first date, my reputation would be ruined forever.*

With her chiding voice still echoing around inside my brain, along with the demeaning cackling laughter of the other ladies, I started to change my attitude, completely. *Courting? I'm a southern Belle? Oh Lord, listen to me…courting…really!? Gladys is so right…I have to get with times! I'll ask him out for lunch the very next time I run into each other. Nobody needs to know it was my idea. Hopefully he won't mention it to anyone else. But it'll be better, to be getting a little embarrassed, rather than a lot of, all alone.*

Not wanting to waist my surging energy, I put my cup into the sink and headed straight for the elevator. He should be getting ready to head downstairs for lunch soon. Traipsing down his hallway the debate in my head raged on—until he stepped around a corner and we nearly ran straight into one another. "Hey, fancy running into you here," I blurted out with a cheesy grin. The look on his face was priceless—he couldn't decide if I had lost my mind and he should run, or if he should reach out and pat the top of my head, thinking; *silly girl, go on back to your receptionist desk now, playtime is over.* My nerves got the best of me and I asked him, "going to lunch?" We both noticed that I was speaking way faster than normal.

"Well...I...," he tried to say before I blurted out the question I came to ask.

"Mind if I join you?"

"Why not," he replied with a big sincere smile. His whole entire body relaxed at once. It seemed that he must have thought I was coming to tell him some bad news or something. Looking back on it, to him, maybe I was?

That lunch was probably—no, definitely was—the highlight of our entire three year relationship. At least we had a mediocre conversation to get us started in the right direction. Unfortunately, we pretty much polished off every topic of mutual interest within the span of that hour. Where we grew up, where we went to school, how much we tried to tolerate our insane control freak parents who thought they knew what was best for us, how much law school sucked. Other than that, there was little red meat to our discussions. Lacking enthusiasm would be a fair way to put it.

To my surprise, and dismay, nothing in my life seemed to be changing as our relationship blossomed. Even when I was with Thomas, I still felt like I was all alone. He always appeared to be distracted by something that was clearly more interesting than *me*.

You ever been in a relationship that was a flat-liner from the get-go? He definitely got my motor running, don't get me wrong, but that was about it. My accelerator never got pushed down to rev-up the engine. No sparks flew on our first kiss. No fireworks. My tachometer revved up a little bit, but not much past idle speed. Things never heated up like I expected, and wanted. And when we did have sex—cue the trombone sound effect—there was a less than optimal outcome.

Nothing about our relationship made sense. Every woman wanted him, and maybe, just maybe, that was the entire problem. He was all show—a prime thoroughbred race horse stallion on the outside—while being all ASS on the inside. It wasn't until we got to know each other that I could see what all the other women couldn't.

He was that guy that watches the waitress walking away for a *very long* time—as if his eyes somehow got glued onto her backside. It's a miracle that his eyes didn't pop out of their sockets they were being strained so hard to see. It was like being with a cartoon character when their eyes get stretched out before snapping back into their head like rubber. In fact, every attractive woman in Atlanta must have been fitted with an irresistible tractor beam that would suck his face towards them. If he was wasn't twisting his neck while ogling another woman; he was playing with his Rolex, or his phone, or video games, or talking about his last round of golf, the one outdoor activity he was obsessed with.

Oh, and did I mention that I absolutely hate golf!

Hearing that tiny violin again? Me too!

Later on, I finally took my concerns about our relationship, or lack of it, to Carly—to get a dose of her keen and harshly direct insight. We met and discussed it over lunch. "Tom doesn't seem to be in love with me," I tried to explain so that she would understand, "it's like he's not ready for a real commitment."

I'll have to admit that I wasn't prepared for her somewhat cold and very detached analysis—even coming from her—since I thought we were friends? She didn't try one whit to protect my feelings.

"Just go with it for now," she mumbled with a deadpan attitude. She didn't even stop chewing on her turkey-club sandwich between words. No emotion or sympathy. Cutting right down the middle she wouldn't take sides. That's what made her an excellent attorney for dishing out bad news to clients in difficult situations, mainly in divorces, that just happened to be her specialty. "You're not going to change, and, he's obviously not going to change....so stop trying to change him. Either get whatever it is you can get from him. Or move on."

Was I really trying to change him? I pondered, struck by Carly's dry assessment of us. Thomas was exactly what I wanted, so I believed, until getting to know him better. Everyone gave us the thumbs up as the perfect couple. *Was everything I was made to believe in, what I was supposed to look for in a man, all completely wrong?*

While staring at Carly's mouth chewing like a cow with cud—I ran over my mental checklist. Thomas and I are both from well to do wealthy old money families with far reaching social and political ties. His father was a prominent Wall Street firm attorney that once had a U.S. president, and several heads of major corporations as clients. His mother was an industrialist heiress and had inherited an embarrassingly large fortune. From boarding to school to prep school, Thomas was one of the best educated, properly groomed, mannered, gentlemanly molded man, who ever graced the very tippy-top of high society.

"It's just that simple to you isn't it…just that cut and dry?" I attempted in a feeble way to challenge her.

"You asked me what I thought and so I'm telling you," she shot back, as if I wasn't getting it, "just learn to live with him the way he is. You guys are the perfect power couple, who are about to become two young successful attorneys in one of the biggest law firms in Atlanta. Soon you'll be partners, live in a huge mansion, drive the most expensive cars, take amazing trips around the world, and if things are perfect, you'll have a preciously cute boy *and* girl—perfection."

Ouch! She may as well throw in there, "and won't your father be so proud of you!" It was that simple and straight forward. Reality can be a real bitch. Time I faced the reality of what I was getting myself into. But those were not good enough reasons to stick it out with Thomas. She could see I wasn't satisfied by the forlorn look on my face.

"Hell Emma, every woman in this city would love to be dating Thomas, including me," she pointed out the obvious—still not helping me with my concerns, not one bit. As if I was just another woman like all the rest, standing in a long line of thousands waiting for my turn with him, and I should be so grateful.

"So you think I'm being stupid…that I should be happy with the way things are?" I pressed her to explain her logic. My simmering blood was now bubbling close to a boil, but I maintained. "What if what I'm wanting is the real thing from him? You know love…that old fairytale thing? Is that too much to hope for?"

Carly looked up from her half eaten lunch, looking

directly at me with that same exact expression that Gladys had scolded me with, back in the break room. She was saying with her face—what she wanted to scream at me. *What in the hell are you thinking? You can't be that much of a naïve little girl…that is love!*

She didn't have to say anything else. My shoulders drooped and I went limp in my chair. I gave up. Carly was right. Moving my salad around with my fork, since I'd lost my appetite, I just stared down, stewing in my own sad hopelessness. It was so hard accepting that Tom was the best man for me, but I had to just accept it—he was it.

"Give it a few more months," Carly whispered over the table. Now she was sympathizing with me, now that she had won. "He may come around eventually."

That was the rub of it—I wasn't sure if I cared anymore?

I gave Carly a half-hearted smile. "Alright, I'll give him a little-bit more time to figure out what he wants."

16

I T WAS LESS than a year ago. Law school classes, study groups, and late night cramming, was taking up all my free time. Fully entrenched in my legal internship with father's firm took up the rest. There was barely any time left for sleeping. My life was becoming a blur, with the days beginning and ending without anything changing other than the clothes I put on and the numbers on the calendar. I felt like I was on a speeding train that was racing down straight steel tracks that disappeared way off up ahead—into a black unforeseen future where I wasn't sure I wanted to go. But there was no possible way to slow down, or to get off.

I still found a little time to work at the High Museum now and again. It pulled at me, like a yearning, a deeply felt feeling, something I couldn't really explain. Like being with a lifelong friend that always could make you forget about the rest of the world, making you feel better for those few precious moments together. It was a tiny peaceful momentary break from my hectic life, a selfish moment all for me. An intimate time to reflect on what was most beautiful about life—the art—letting it sink in to refresh my soul.

The museum staff was getting me involved with more

important matters. Time permitting that is. Moving art in and out of the basement, sweeping up or taking out the trash was work for the high school kids and temps. They now kept me busy at the receptions desk, or leading tours for elementary school children, senior citizen groups, or tour groups from other countries. It was easy for me since I knew every inch of the place forwards and backwards and could give the tours blindfolded, if that was required for some strange reason.

Father managed to swindle me into being more involved with the Board of Directors of the museum, after hours of course, taking up more of my precious little time. He had me attending meetings, keeping track of minutes, taking care of incidental paperwork, running errands, making phone calls and scheduling appointments for him—basically being his unpaid personal assistant. Now I know what Mitch was talking about when he referred to him as that *nickel pinching cheap bastard!*

At least it gave me more time at the museum, one of the few places where I still felt a small semblance of sanity.

It felt good being so grown up and responsible, still, whenever I passed by the window where I first saw David, I struggled to put it out of my mind. With a heavy sigh, I forced the images of my younger innocent self, out of my mind—wiping the image out of my head, just the way I used to wipe his name off the glass.

Now it had become just a passing glance, out through the clear glass.

Little did I know that acting as father's assistant for Board business was going to be the thing that would throw a huge wrench directly into my life. The thing that would cause a crack in the rails, sending my speeding locomotive of a life off the tracks, causing my whole entire life to come crashing down around me in a ball of twisted steel and rubble—turning out to be the one thing that saved me, from me.

It was on a Friday evening, and I was busily scribbling notations trying to keep up with the business that was at hand during a Board of Directors meeting. My eyes were bloodshot and the lines were getting blurry. My head was throbbing from all the reading and writing I had endured over the past several hours. I had to keep yelling at myself to stay focused on what everyone was saying, as they kept talking quickly over one another, shifting from one subject to another without warning. Having spent the earlier part of the day jotting down bits of information doled out by my acutely boring law school professors, all of whom were so pompous and high and mighty that they made me want to puke—*pay attention*!

"Let's take up the new matter…number four on the agenda…awarding recognition and display of donated works of art for the Orly memorial," father announced from his formal seat as chairman of this committee. He was seated at the top of a long rectangular conference room table, along with eight other Board members, four seated along each side. I was sitting behind him at a small table with a note-pad, my red eyelids nodding as they droned on with mundane museum issues. Looking over at me with frustrated disdain, letting me know that I had better be paying attention, as he went on saying, "it appears that we have three applicants this year that have some real potential…and we need to take a vote on which of the three artists will get their work displayed." I perked up and dutifully scratched down my notes.

This was not the full Board, only a smaller group making up a select committee for special business, like this memorial recognition award. Father passed around to each of the other Board members photographs of artwork that was being considered for the display. They would be selecting from one of the three artists. Each of the artists was supposed to be from a group of surviving relatives, or close family friends, of one of the persons who perished in the 1962 Orly airport airline crash. Their work of art would be displayed as a memorial for the victims. It was an annual event. "Let's take a look at what we received this year before we take a vote," father instructed the Board members.

For the past few years I had assisted in putting it out on the museum floor. I was relied upon to find the perfect location, if it was a sculpture, vase, or twisted pop-art metal contraption of some kind, or, I would point out the place to hang it on the wall, if it turned out to be a painting, collage, print, or tapestry. I always found the spot, whatever it turned out to be. All I hoped was that it was something of true artistic value—not something created by an amateur, a gaudy looking piece of art, selected purely for political or sympathetic reasons. So far, everything I had put out for display had been truly lovely, touching, perhaps even artistically captivating. *Let's keep it that way*, I was musing as they silently inspected the glossy photos.

I strained my neck to try and see what father was seeing. The three eight-by-ten photographs were all laying side by side on the table top in front of him. The rest of the Board members bent their heads over to examine their own sets. From my seat I could only make out the vague image of a vivid expressionistic acrylic painting done by some obscure artist from California. *Pretty nice*, I gave that one my approval. Father's shoulder was blocking my view of the other two. After carefully reviewing each photo, he shuffled in his chair, looking around the table, before saying, "let's take a vote shall we? By show of hands we'll take them one at a time starting with the painting by Mr. Floyd Downing from Irvine California. Are there any votes for that submission?"

"Shouldn't there be some discussion first?" Loretta piped up from the end of the table.

Father huffed and lifted his hands up slightly off the table, the way he does when he's tired and fed-up. "This isn't a popular vote kind of thing Loretta…we've been over this before…it's the same every year…it's merely a vote for what you like the best…in a personal way…there's no need to try and persuade the others to like what you like."

"We're voting on something that is going to represent the museum," Loretta huffed back, not willing to let it go again this year, by pointing out, "this art is going to be reflective on the entire museum…that's something to take personal isn't it?"

The back of father's neck turned a bright red. His head would be spewing up like a geyser, with steaming wavy swirls of hot air rising up—if he was a cartoon character. It was the same routine every year. It never failed. Loretta had picked out the one submission that she wanted to be displayed, now, she desperately wanted to have her say, to try and convince the others to vote her way.

Loretta was in her mid-eighties and had was the oldest of the Board members—all of them. Her involvement with the High Museum, and the local Atlanta Arts Association went all the way back to when everything was run by the original

Women's Committee. That's how they would have done it back then—the vote that is. It wasn't going to change now, not for some uppity know-it-all lawyer who was trying to take over and change everything around to suit him. You could see it on her grimacing wrinkled face. They were going to do it her way, or else.

Loretta had a lot of political power in town. Lots of family, old money folks, with lots of close knit friends in very high places—places father wanted to climb up to. She had built up an enormous stockpile of favors over her many years of societal hob-nobbery, along with her sizeable monetary fortune. It was her intent to use both now, to get everything else she wanted in life. And today, right now, at this moment, it was that acrylic painting.

Loretta and father locked eyes in an epic stare-down, for just a tense moment, locking her glaring eyes with father through the top half of her bifocals, those old-timey glasses that have the little slender chain running from the ear around the back of the neck. She bristled beneath thick strands of silver chains, dangling from her neck and wrists, strung with glimmering jewels of all colors. Her age-spotted fingers fidgeting with a ring that held a sparkling solitaire diamond bigger than her boney knuckle, it alone being worth more money than father could make all year—a very good year. Four of her other fingers were adorned with similarly ornate and expensive rings.

Then it happened. It was the first time I ever saw my father blink first. He actually backed down. It was as if I could hear the sound of a great cracking noise as old *Stoney* caved in—with a hole being busted right through his stone wall exterior. His stone wall was no match for the old fortress that was Loretta. She battered him with her superior political good-will and finances.

I understood that father was just being a good general, using his tactical legal skills of negotiation, retreating to higher ground, waiting for reinforcements and allowing time to rebalance the scales in his favor—before he would continue with the war. Besides, keeping her on his side for now was the best way to *not* get completely obliterated. It was a much better strategy to keep her as a friendly ally, for now. "Fine Loretta, what is it that you would like to say," he said, capitulating to her demands.

Loretta made her pitch for the acrylic painting—making some very sound points. She was a shrewd debater, with a keen understanding of fine art. After being a student of the arts, with the opportunity to view, and own, most of the most revered works of art throughout the world, she would have picked up a few things. Having taught lessons, part time, with the Arts Association, she was no slouch of an artist in her own right. Two of her works made the memorial award in years past (when she wasn't a voting committee member of course). It was more than personal to her—the award reflected on her as an artist—something she would fight like a lioness for.

I just had to see what all the fuss was about, so I stood up to take a closer look at the photographs arrayed in front of father. Loretta was right, the painting was very nice indeed— very professionally done—yet, somewhat lacking in emotional appeal. I've stared at enough paintings to know when I get that telling, *meh, nothing special, seen that before,* feeling.

Then my eyes moved over to the second photo of a marble sculpture. A nearly three foot tall statuette that was absolutely sublime. A tingling shiver ran up my spine—something that rarely happens any more—as I stared down at the white marble delight. Reminiscent of ancient Greece, the toga draped young goddess with one breast exposed, is dangling her femininely slender arm down to gently touch the top of her child's head, a cupid of an infant naked boy standing at her side, playfully pudgy with a rounded belly and curly locks of hair, looking up at his mother with eyes filled with adoring wonderment. A truly sweet delight for the senses, it was a piece ripe with emotionally tantalizing beauty. It was an expressive work that made me want to believe that; *this is what life is for, the wonder of love.*

I was almost repulsed by the third photograph. *How did that get in there with the other two?* More like junk than art, it was some bent metal with splattered spots of paint all over it. *Now that's my nightmare!*

My eyes darted back to Loretta, trying to gage her reaction, wondering why she was so emotionally invested in the outcome of the vote. Her eyes were not angry at father. They were shielding her. And her hands were not fidgeting out of being upset with him—she was desperately trying to hide her anxiety. She was nervous about something. That acrylic is not as good as she's making it out to be. It definitely can't compare to the statuette. What's she up too, I had to wonder? All the tiny hairs covering my body rose up, as if they were little radar type scanners—all of them searching for something fishy.

That's it!

That bitch! Either that painting is by one of her friends, or even worse, it's actually her painting, and she has submitted it through some fake person's name. She's already told everyone that this is her last term on the Board, and this would most likely be her last chance to get another piece of her art displayed at the museum. That sneaky old bitch!

I wanted to scream out—stop the vote! But it was too late.

To my amazement however; when the first vote was finally tallied, it was split right down the middle. Half went for the acrylic painting—with the other four Board members raising their hands in favor of the exquisite marble sculpture. Luckily the Board had some artistic taste after all, and there were no votes cast for the ghastly metal attempt at pop art.

Father, as the Director, wasn't permitted to vote unless there was an impasse. This was according to the Board rules. "So, it's between these two then. Let's have another vote," he instructed them, "all those in favor of the acrylic painting raise your hands…and now, all those in favor of the marble sculpture."

The second vote turned out the same—as did the third, fourth, and fifth vote. By the time they lowered their hands for the last time, Loretta was glaring fiery darts directly at father. From my vantage point, sitting behind his broad shoulder, I could actually feel the stinging heat streaming up from where Loretta was fuming. "Well, I guess it's up to you this time Mr. Morgan," she snarled, grinding her dentures. Throbbing veins bulged out on her forehead and neck.

With all the lip biting, hand rubbing, eye rolling, eyebrow lifting, amongst all the other fretting gestures from all the other committee members, it was very obvious that they were getting a little thrill out of this sticky situation. Some of them anxious, some nervous, with a couple of them a little thrilled. Father was in the hot seat. They could all sit back and watch him squirm as the heat was getting turned up to the max. But one thing was certain about all of us—we were all wondering; *damn, how in the world is old Stoney going to get out of this predicament!?*

The tension grew as he stewed over his decision. It was killing him inside to let her win. I want to believe that he actually recognized how amazingly beautiful the statuette was—such a priceless gem that would be the perfect memorial display the museum had ever been graced with. But, probably not—he just didn't want to cave. Two bulls locking horns. The biggest ego would eventually win. Loretta's of course.

Father started to cast his vote in favor of the acrylic, "You win Loretta, I—," before I cut him off.

"Wait, father, before you vote," I announced boldly, as if I had something important to add. There was an audible gasp from the others. Instead of making some speech as they probably expected, I leaned over fathers back to whisper into his ear. Thankfully, his broad shoulders sagged down, relaxing, confirming that he approved of my suggestion. Turning his head slightly, he quickly shot me an approving little wink, telling me; *that's my girl.*

Turning calmly back to the group, he stated, "Emma has reminded me of something important…that I think should be addressed before we proceed with this vote."

Everyone was staring at father, expectantly. All except for Loretta, who was now fidgeting so violently it appeared that she was about to have a stroke. Her anxious eyelids batted up and down as she looked around the room, oh so innocently.

"Emma has kindly reminded me of what happened a few years back." A palpable tension filled the room as father went on about, "that time when an unknown artist who did not meet the qualifications for submission, attempted to get their piece slipped through this committee. It almost got to be displayed—improperly." Their eyes stretched open wide with frightful remembrance, as they recalled that upsetting moment in time—considered by some to be the lowest of low points in the museum's otherwise impeccable history. Father, as a master of persuasion, added reluctantly, "I don't want to jeopardize this institution's reputation again…not one tiny bit. I don't see how I could possibly cast a deciding vote right now…not without a thorough background check of these artists first. I won't stake any of your upstanding reputations on my meager, uninformed vote." He was so convincingly concerned for the museum, and them, at that very moment, they could feel the warmth of his burning compassion—making it impossible for them to refuse.

"Of course we remember that Stoney," Mr. Cartwright groaned, reminding them that, "it was very embarrassing for us all."

Stoking the flames he got started, father kept it up, saying, "We caught that mistake just in the nick of time, remember? There was barely enough time to get a proper piece put out before everyone in the community found out about it."

"Would have been quite the embarrassing scandal indeed," Mrs. Phillips chimed in. "So, what are you proposing Stone?"

"Let's have Emma go and check out these submitting artists," father stated emphatically, "just to make sure everything is on the up-and-up this time."

For some reason I couldn't stop myself—and my eyes looked over at Loretta who was now staring daggers into me.

If she could have ripped my head off and thrown it through the window right then, she would have. *Thanks dad!*

Ms. Murdoch leaned forward with a fiery passion in her eyes, to say to everyone. "That sounds like a wonderful idea Stone…we all think highly of your daughter…she'll do us a fine job."

The others mumbled in agreement, grinning and nodding to one another, all pleased with the suggestion of an investigation first. Loretta sat scowling, looking like a spoiled child who was being left out.

Feeling the room swinging in his favor, father pounced swiftly to close the deal, "Let's take a vote on it," father announced, without allowing Loretta time to even think this time—let alone say anything in opposition.

Seven hands shot up into the air.

Loretta's hands remained down on the table top, both of them, clenched together tightly. "Silly waste of time," she muttered with contempt.

17

N O GOOD DEED goes unpunished, as they say. I was about to find out the hard way.

With the committees work concluded for now, they all silted out the door with the sounds of chairs being slid on the tile, chattering and gossiping. Father was busy shoving the photographs and submission applications back inside his manila envelope—to hand over to me. "You've got until Monday to find out what you can," he told me like I was his old stalwart secretary, the stuffed shirt one with the tiny glasses who stuck to his side waiting for her cue to jump—the one who was always one step ahead of him like some trained dog that was able to anticipate his every move.

All I heard was *c'mon girl, go fetch.*

I reluctantly snatched the envelope from his hands, while pleading for some relief, "but I have finals coming up in a couple of weeks…can't it wait?" With my most pitifully sad puppy dog eyes I begged him. Unfortunately, they had no effect on him whatsoever. That hadn't worked since junior high school.

He just responded with that sympathetic smile, the one he uses when he gives me bad news. "Sorry to have to throw you under the buss…I really do appreciate you helping out dear. But you know this memorial has to be in place by the first week of June. Just find out whatever you can and let me know what you find out by Monday afternoon…please dear…do this for your old man and I'll make it up to you…I promise."

There's that smile again!

"Fine," I groaned, "I'll see what I can do."

Instead of heading straight home to study as I had planned, now, I was plodding my way back over to the office to get to work on my newest pet project. That's what I get for opening my damn mouth. *What a sucker!* The only good thing I could make of this situation was that maybe, just maybe, I could get to reveal Loretta as the conniving sneaky old hag that she was.

My head was filled with sinister images of me exposing Loretta before the entire Board, going over the evidence in dramatic fashion, like a really good fake attorney, methodical and relentless, like the ones you watch on television legal dramas. Street lamps shone down on me making the scene even more dramatic. I was about to finish presenting my amazingly polished closing argument to the astonished jury, all but damning her to eternal hellfire—when a black BMW went screaming past. There was very little traffic since it was way past rush hour. With darkly tinted windows it had screeched around the corner coming from our office parking garage, heading someplace in a hurry. Turning to look as it flew past me on Peachtree Street, I thought I could see Thomas' profile through the passenger window. *Was that him leaving with Megan, one of the associate attorneys?*

Now I had something else to torment me, by taking up

more of thinking power that I needed to focus on my exams. I don't need that in my head right now.

I tried to forget about Tom as I tore open the front door, stomped across the foyer and boarded the elevator, all alone. Most everyone else had left for the day. Like ghosts, the cleaning crews were quietly filtering through the lonely half-lit hallways, getting the trash, vacuuming, and wiping down the desks. A few attorneys stayed late to finish up some overdue paperwork or research some issues that had to be dealt with by yesterday, but there were not many. I could only see a couple of office lights still on as I stormed along my hall. Flicking on my light, I joined them.

Only I was merely doing some menial task that my father would refuse to do himself. I wasn't busily preparing for some exciting courtroom drama, as I pretended the other attorneys were actually doing. In reality, there work was just as tedious and boring, and probably even less worthy of mention than my little task. They were most likely holed-up inside their offices searching for some finely-printed loophole in a phone book sized contract, hoping to help some big corporation or absurdly rich asshole get out of paying for something they should have to pay for, after injuring or swindling some gray haired old granny—*great job!*

With my angry blood pumping hard, I was ready for a good-ole confrontation. Ripping open the manila envelope I yanked out the photos along with the applications. There it was, a submission form for a Mr. Floyd Downing; *if that is your real name?* Ooh, it was going to feel so good to vent out some of my pent up rage on that unsuspecting jerk! What a low-life scum-bucket, to try and help Loretta get her way by pretending to be an artist—for a memorial display no less.

Finding his phone number on the sheet, I started dialing. *How low can a person get!?* My utterly damning trial summation started playing in my head again—right where I left off, as the phone began to ring in Irvine California. *This should be good!*

"Hello…this is Floyd speaking," an elderly man answered the phone. His voice was shaky, yet sweet, sounding very much like my grandfather did, just before he passed away. He sounded to be about the same age as Loretta, just much worse for the wear.

"Is this the Floyd Downing…the one that lives in Irvine California?" I muttered softly, being caught somewhat off guard. I hesitated, losing my train of thought. Wasn't I a furious beast bearing my fangs and claws just a moment ago? What happened to that brash, on the attack, take no prisoners attorney? I sounded more like a lost child.

"That's right young lady," he answered me cautiously, "what can I do for you…everything alright?"

Suddenly, somehow, I was feeling bad, a little shameful. How could I possibly try to beat the truth out an elderly man, who probably wasn't even aware of Loretta's scheming tricks? "Oh yes, yes sir, everything is just fine," I stammered, trying to refocus. "I just needed to ask you a few questions… if that's alright with you Mr. Downing?"

"Alright, but I've told you folks over and over that I don't have the money to spend on those—," he started to explain, before I cut him off.

"No sir, it's not about buying anything…I just need to find out some things from you."

"Did Gloria tell you to check up on me again?"

"No sir, I need to find out if you submitted a painting to

the High Museum in Atlanta for the Orly memorial exhibit this year, or not?"

"Oh no ma'am, that wasn't me…not that I can recall… I'm not much of a painter, not any more. It's been quite some time since I painted."

Ah hah! My heart started to race a little—now there was some blood in the water, and I was moving in like the shark I envisioned myself to be. "And do you happen to know a Loretta from Atlanta?"

"Oh yes, Loretta…known her for many years. How is the old bird?" He asked kindly, completely ignorant of the fact that I was moving in for the kill.

That old bird is about to get plucked!

"So, you didn't submit an acrylic painting to the museum recently for the 1962 Orly memorial display, here in Atlanta Mr. Downing?" I felt like Perry Mason with a witness that about to confess to the murder—right there on the stand before the judge and jury—with me standing straight and tall in the middle of the courtroom, sporting a big winning smile.

"May have been my sister though? Yes, that's right, now I remember her talking about sending in one of my paintings I did years back."

I could hear my heart hitting the floor—flump! *Damn it!*

"Oh, I see, so your sister submitted a painting for you?" A cold brush of air swept over me, chilling my skin. It was hard to tell if it was the air conditioner kicking on and blowing down from the vent, or, if my heart had stopped. Either way I was dying inside.

"That's right," Floyd said, confirming it, "my other sister, the younger one, Maggie, she sent it in. I told her it was a damn waste of time since my paintings aren't worth a second look, but she insisted and sent it anyway."

Keep your wits, I braced myself, *witnesses can say things that throw you off track. Stay focused. Loretta may still have done something underhanded, since they know each other and all. Don't let up till you get the truth.*

"Then Loretta must have put your sister up to submitting your painting, right Mr. Downing? She must really like your work, right?"

"No, not really…haven't spoken to Loretta in over thirty years now. Maggie never met Loretta, since she's from out here. Me and Loretta, we did take some art classes at the Art Association together, back when I lived back East. Moved out here to California not long before my older sister Gracie perished in that horrible accident in Paris. Flying contraptions…I told her not to go you know?"

"I see…that right…you don't say…interesting story," is all I could mutter into the phone as he went on explaining. I think I could actually hear the sound of a heavy wooden gavel being slammed down on the bench—bang, bang, bang—as the judge found in favor of Loretta. Case dismissed!

18

MY STOMACH WAS churning as I placed the phone receiver back down. Looking over at the photograph of the marble statuette, I felt almost nauseated. There was no way I was calling another innocent person who was caught up in between my father's giant ego and Loretta. They could do the calling if it meant that much to them. Father was about to vote for the painting anyway. It was over. Loretta had won.

It's my own damn fault. Why the hell did I get involved?

As my eyes drifted over the silky white dreamlike image carved into that marble—my answer came to me. It was somewhat startling to realize the truth about myself. I wasn't saving my father from embarrassment, or to trying to protect his childish, selfish, unnatural fixation on winning everything. No, that wasn't it at all. I got involved because I absolutely cherish this exquisite piece of art. That's all it is. I can't ignore it any longer. It's in me. Art has become a part of me.

I had to accept the fact that this wasn't a fight between father and Loretta at all. It was a battle between me and Loretta—and I was fighting for artistic integrity!

Way to go me?

Ugh, I reminded myself that I have more important things to be doing right now. *Guess I should just get this over with?* I pressed on. *Besides, father is still counting on me.*

Flipping through the submission form for the statuette I located the applicant's name and phone number. It was an in-state number this time. Dialing the number I mused over his name. *Zachariah D. Laurent, wow, OK, now this guy sounds so old. He's probably even older than the guy from California. Hope he can at least remember sending in the submission this time?* The phone rang, and rang, and rang, for what seemed like an eternity—with no answer. Not even an answering machine.

Great, now what do I do?

Should I try and go over to his house? Checking his listed address on the form, it shows that he lives on Old Mill Road, way up north of Atlanta someplace, all the way up past Alpharetta. Pulling out a Georgia State map from my desk drawer, I ran my finger up the northbound highways, following along the roadways that were shrinking as my finger went up the map. He's way out there, farther than I thought, out in the boonies close to the Appalachian Trail up above Dawsonville. That would take me close to two hours just to get up there. There's only farmhouses out there, spread out on dirt roads, separated by acres and acres of farmland. Almost no street lights, no maps, nothing I'm familiar with. It could take another hour or so just to find his tiny farmhouse way out there in the dark. I wouldn't make it back home in Buckhead till way late at night. Plus—that sounds scary. I'm not a big sissy or anything like that, but wandering around in the dark on lonely back-country roads, all alone, is not a good option.

Besides, if Zachariah turns out to be anything like that ancient Cartwright—he's most likely dead already anyway. Even if I did find his house it would be too late. I could see myself turning his tarnished doorknob, standing alone in the dark on his windswept rickety front porch, cracking open the squeaking and creaking old front door, to find his decomposing corpse, seated there in his favorite rocking chair, flashing a skeleton smile up at me. The idea alone made me shiver.

That's when my office door began to slowly swing open. I slammed the receiver down and shot upright in my chair. "Who's there?" I called out, sounding a little frightened.

"Hello…it's just me," an older man said as he pushed open the door and walked inside. He was pulling a large plastic trash bin that was fitted with tiny wheels. "Excuse me… just cleaning up ma'am. Can I get your trash?" He asked politely. The name tag sewn onto his plain tan shirt read, "George". As he pulled the rustling plastic bag from my waist basket, he mumbled, "kind of late for you to still be working, isn't it?"

I couldn't tell if he was asking me a serious question, or if he was suggesting in a polite kind of way; "hey, here's an idea, why don't you get the hell out of the office so that I can do my job now?"

Now the pressure was really mounting. *But he's totally right*, I tell myself, no matter how he meant it.

It's Friday night. It's getting late. I should be already at home and out of this damn office. I have exams to study for. I'm late getting that motion to dismiss and supporting legal brief prepared for attorney Jenkins. Mother wants me to go shopping this weekend out in the countryside—off someplace way up in the foothills. Jon is expecting me to look over his portfolio of clothing designs he's submitting to some men's attire company. What am I supposed to do? There's absolutely no time left for me to go chasing down some unknown amateur artist this late at night. No time!

Shoving the photos and applications back inside the manila envelope, I make my escape—taking my usual route to the house, to my room, to my bed—without needing to think as I retrace my steps back home in a foggy, brain-dead haze.

Somehow I managed to undress before I flopped down as a semiconscious ragdoll onto the mattress. I know, because when I woke up the next morning, my clothes were lying right there in a messy pile, at the side of the bed, right where they fell the night before. "Oh-my-gosh, there's no way that's the right time," I grumbled with drool running out of my mouth. My bloodshot eyes had opened just long enough to glance over at the clock, with my head still mushed down into my pillow. "There is no way I slept in that long?" It was way past nine already. It was the first time in a long time, that I was the last person in the house crawling out of bed.

Father had no doubt already left the house. He had planned on leaving early to drive over to Augusta with a couple of buddies to play golf. It was something they had planned for a few weeks. They would be gone all weekend, returning late Sunday night. *Maybe he will have completely forgotten about the whole memorial art vote thingy while having an incredible time with his friends,* I mused, knowing I was kidding myself, *he'll come back bragging about his hole-in-one on the eighteenth green...and he'll never ask about what I found out...right...as if I could be that lucky?*

Sadly, that was the first thing to pop into my mind—before I could even swish back the covers to crawl out of bed.

But that leaves both mother and Jon home alone, each wanting my company. Numbly pulling on my pajamas and a robe, I make my slumbering journey downstairs knowing exactly what is awaiting me. Jon is seated on the sofa. Mother is seated next to him. They are eagerly going over his newest portfolios; stuffed catalogues filled with his own designs for men's apparel, both fine and casual wear, suites, ties, straight and bow, slacks, sweaters, shorts and shirts, pullover and button down, along with all of the requisite accessories, scarfs, socks, belts, and even suspenders. Everything a man of wealth and prestige would need for a jaunt to the club, or a business meeting with the company CEO, with all of it coming across as very elegant, much in the same fashion as Jon is as a person.

All I could see was how thick the portfolios were—all four of them—stuffed with thick page after big page with well over a few hundred separate designs he wanted us to review. Argh, there's no time!

By the way mother was dressed I could tell instantly that she was planning a day on the road. She even had a large daybag jammed with what she would need for a long day out in the backcountry, in search of the elusive, perfect nick-knack or antique; a vase, lamp, book, painting or vintage collectable, anything *cute* that struck her fancy. Whatever she ended up buying, it was typically something that made me want to gag. *Art, hah, more like junk?* I would always scoff behind her back. *They should call this place "Art and Junk" instead of an antique store.*

In the back of my mind I was tracing along the normal lifecycle of the *antique* she would eventually pay way too much for. First, she would lug it home and attempt to find just the perfect spot to place it. Second, not finding the perfect spot, she would settle for setting it out of the way in some obscure place in the house where no one could really see it. Third, after a few months she would replace it with something else she liked a little-bit better—something more suitable for that spot *right there*. Fourth, it would go into storage, into a closet, or up in the attic, anyplace with room enough for it, out of sight. Fifth, it would, at some point in the not-so-distant future, be discovered by mother as she rearranged some things, did some spring cleaning, or started to remodel again. Lastly, having been rediscovered, and with no suitable place for it—it would be either tossed into the trash bin or dropped off at a donation center where it would eventually be sold to someone else for far less money—to then repeat the cycle.

Yes, I'm kind-of a bitch. You haven't figured that out by now? Get over it! But can you blame me for not wanting to get dragged from one tiny North Georgia town, to another backwoods, po-dunk, time forgotten hick-a-billie town, while being forced to scavenge through rundown old shacks turned into what they call stores—all of them filled with the same dust covered estate sale rejects that have already been passed over by about a million other bored suburban housewives with their zombie like sons and daughters in tow. Exactly!

19

I T WAS CLOSING in on noon before we hit the road. Mother was in an exceptionally good mood—most likely because father was gone all weekend. "Let's grab some lunch in Milton before we get ourselves lost way up in *them thar hills*," she said, doing her best impression of a grizzled old mountain prospector. Then she giggled in a way she hadn't in a very long time—in a sincerely happy way. That actually put I smile on my face. Not the words she spoke, since that was actually pretty annoying. It was instead her giddy disposition that was beginning to rub off on me. "Yes, let's do that," I replied with a cheery little smile, in spite of her goofy prospector routine.

The day passed quickly to my delight. We managed to hit more stores than ever on this trip. Mother was finding all kinds of overpriced treasures to drag back home. Imagining the look on father's face when he found out how much money she had spent on this stuff kept that smile on my face all day long. Mother had no idea, and she would happily smile back at me as we browsed those dusty isles.

As the sun was setting over the looming mountains, we started our journey back home. Mother was tired, and wanted me to make the drive down through the heavier Atlanta traffic, so I gladly took the wheel. Getting home was going to take a lot less time—if you know what I mean. Settling back deep into my seat, I punched the gas, sending us speeding down the winding Cumming Highway. Our sleek white coupe was zipping past the turn of the century wooden farmhouses with their nostalgic split-rail fences running along the roadway. Those beamed barriers would lead up to large rustic gates that were topped with the carved out emblems and names of the farm or ranch. There was the "Big 'O' groves", the "Dawson Farms", and the "Rocking 'A' Ranch" to name a few. I snickered reading them. The blurry images and names faded away from my memory faster than we were racing past them.

Suddenly a beaten-up road sign came into view. What I thought I saw wrenched my head around to try and make sure I was reading it correctly. I asked mother, "Did that sign say, "Old Mill Road?"

"What's that dear?" She mumbled. Her eyes were closed as she started to nod off. Did I mention that we had stopped by a couple of family run wineries along the way? She ended up sipping on the homemade wild-berry wines. Those oh-so-sweet kinds of booze that often have very high octane levels, but you can't tell because they taste too good. Most of them should have three X's across the label because they have a kick that's more like moonshine. I tasted and spit—while she savored and swallowed, every last drop. I had to drag her away from the last place.

Now, the effects of the long day of driving and shopping, combined with a few glasses of soothing wine, had finally caught up with her. "Sorry sweetie," she slurred out the words, "can't keep my eyes open." Slumping forward, her head dangled, bobbing with the bumps in the road. Her seatbelt strapped across her shoulder was the only thing keeping her upright.

"You're a lot of help mom…not," I whispered.

Hitting the brakes I swerved into a dirt driveway. Throwing the car in reverse I spun us around beneath one of those large farmhouse gates. I didn't catch the name on that one, since my focus was solely on that tiny sign we passed. Heading back the other way, it came into view. Tilted over as if it was about to fall into the grass. It was sad and neglected. Bent, rusted, splattered with dry mud, with worn letters that were hard to make out. "That is it…right there…I can't believe it?" I murmured excitedly as I turned down the slender dirt road. "It really is—Old Mill Road."

There was no large gate with a name or emblem marking the territory. *I wouldn't want anyone to know this was my place either*, were thoughts that came to mind while driving slowly up the potholed littered road. The surrounding property was in poor condition, overgrown, neglected, appearing to have been abandoned. Bouncing around in our seats, we rolled over the rocks, holes, roots and deep ruts. Mother's eyelids lifted and dropped like window blinds, but she didn't fully awaken.

It was getting darker the further down the road I drove. Large trees as thick as a rainforest swallowed us up, making it seem like we were heading inside a deep cave. I love a good drive up in the countryside, but not when I'm feeling completely lost. The only signs of life were tire tracks on the road. Since I'm no seasoned tracker I had no idea how old they could be. *Somebody's been driving up this road…I think?*

And that's about all I could see at that point, since the sun had dipped completely down behind the hills. My eyes were glued to the road at the point where my headlights landed on the ground. *Well, even if someone's been up here*, I started silently debating, on whether or not to keep going, *there's definitely no big farm or ranch up this road. May not be any house at all? I doubt very seriously that old Zachariah Laurent even lives up here either? Hell…this is exactly how headlines get written—"Mother and daughter found dead on deserted road".*

I had started searching for a place to turn around, when I saw a mailbox up ahead. Covered in a thick layer of dust, it was dented and rusting, with its little door hanging half way open. It was fitting, since it seemed as lonely and abandoned as the road it was on. I'll turn around in that driveway, I considered. Pulling into the drive I threw the car into reverse—and for some reason paused. All I could imagine was father's disappointed face, looking at me with those ferocious eyes, knowing that I had failed him. I could hear him lecturing me already, saying, "So, you were right there, at his house, and you didn't bother to get out of the car? That's the daughter I raised you to be?"

Forced to do something, I decided to check the mailbox—to see if that was even the right house. Not having the application with me I couldn't compare the house numbers. There didn't appear to be any names or numbers on the mailbox anyway, nothing to show an actual street address. Popping the door open I scurried over to the mailbox and peeked inside. There was a stack of envelopes. They had to have been in there for months from the looks of them. Letters had been stuffed inside until there wasn't any more room to shove anything else in there. *Yep, I knew it, he's long dead,* I surmised, *why else wouldn't he be picking up his mail?*

There was only one way to be certain—I had to check the names on the envelopes. Carefully pinching with my fingertips the top letter, I slowly pulled. Expecting something to come scurrying out at me, I was nervously quivering, until the letter was all the way out. *Phew!* Luckily nothing flew or crawled out along with it.

There it was—his name. Well, his last name at least—Laurent. Only the letter was for a Pierre Laurent, not a Zachariah. Taking out another envelope, it was addressed to the same Pierre. Another envelope was addressed to a lady by the name of Melissa Meyer—what? Now I was terribly confused. Must have been delivered to the wrong house? Shoving the letters back inside the neglected mailbox I jumped back inside the car that was still running. Mother was still snoozing.

Now what?

Either I had to go all the way up to the house, or, I would have to drive back home to face father, and give him the bad news. He would be forced to vote for the painting then, since I couldn't verify the veracity of the sculptor. I couldn't even say if the guy was alive or not at this point. *The longer I wait, the darker it's going get,* I spurned myself to act. *And, the later you will get back home. And, don't forget, you still have to study for finals next week!* Throwing the car into drive, I spun the tires in the dirt and thundered up the long winding driveway. *I'll just verify that he's dead, moved, or whatever, and get my ass home.*

Cutting through a thick grove of trees and shrubs a small house appeared in my headlights. A ramshackle rancher built back in the 1940's. Its wood siding was peeling off layers of decades old paint like a snake shedding its skin. Cobwebs filled up the corners and spaces between the rafters. No real yard to speak of, more of a cleared space that was now filled with overgrown weeds, vines, saplings, and bushes. No car in sight either.

The curtain filled windows were all darkened. No light inside, and none outside. Not even a porch light. It looked like no one had lived in the house for years. Pulling up to the front of the porch, I let the headlights beam inside. If some-one was in there, surely they would notice the lights outside? Idling, waiting there, watching for movement—it was still, it was dark, no signs of life at all—nothing.

Popping open my car door, the interior light came on. Mother stirred in her seat without opening her eyes. "Are we home already?" She mumbled.

"Just stopped for gas," I replied softly, "stay in the car." Not wanting to arouse her I took the keys from the ignition and gently closed the door. She would've been frightened and forced us to leave immediately—exactly what a smarter person would have done. Reclining her seat back even more, she quickly nodded right back off to sleep.

The headlights were left on, shining on the front door. Floorboards creaked on the porch as I stepped closer. A gentle breeze tossed my hair around. I raised my fist to rap my knuckles on the wooden door, while thinking, what the hell am I doing? I knocked. No response. I knocked some more—still nothing. I called out, "hello, is anyone home… Mr. Laurent…you in there?" No answer.

He's dead alright. This was exactly what I had imagined—and there was no way in hell I was opening up that door to find his decaying corpse sitting in there smiling up at me! Spinning around I headed straight for the car. I couldn't get out of there fast enough. I was satisfied now. I knew that; *I did all I could do to find out what father needed to know. He would just have to vote for the painting after all—oh well.*

It was at that very moment that I heard a strange sound. It stopped me cold in my tracks.

20

FOR A MOMENT I was caught, unable to move, with the glare of my headlights nearly blinding me. From behind the house I could hear hinges creaking, followed by the distinctive thud of a large door being swung open till it bumped up against a wall. My heart jumped. I took a step towards the car. Then another sound reached my ears—the recognizable sounds of one of my favorite songs—"She don't know me", by Jon Bon Jovi.

My heart skipped a beat, as my lips mimed my thoughts—*no way?*"

Mother was still passed out in her seat. I watched her for a moment through the dirt and dead bug covered windshield. Her hair was swooped over her face making a makeshift fuzzy blanket. It would have been a shame to wake her up, so I turned and headed for the source of the music.

Circling around behind the house, I followed a gravely footpath that had been etched into the dirt. It took me into the back yard to where I could vaguely see the silhouette of a very large barn off in the distance. A hazy fog had settled over the area, in the cool of the foothills at dusk. The cloud thick air hung around what appeared to be a small orchard of apple and cherry trees. Beyond them, taller, fatter trees blocked a clear view. Stepping along the path I made my way past the orchard over to the healthy walnut and oak trees, until I was close to the enormous barn. A four-story brown building made completely out of old sawmill planks and beams—it was just like the Amish buildings I had seen on vacations up around Pennsylvania. One of the huge double doors was pushed open, with bright light spilling out. Bon Jovi was singing louder as some tantalizing siren, the closer I got to the open doorway.

At least he's not dead in his chair, smiling, I snickered inside. It was a relief finally finding someone—anyone. Stepping out from behind the last tree, I could almost see inside the barn. I started to call out, "Hello—," but my mouth was gagged by the sight of a naked man—standing over at the corner of the barn. My eyes popped open wide as I did a double-take. On the edge of the shadows, the outline of his body was clearly visible. Sneaking a look before quickly glancing away—only to take another peek—I so wanted to keep look-ing, but couldn't. *That can't be a real—*I told myself, dying to take him all in. Forcing my eyes to stare directly at him, I needed to be sure. My eyes had not deceived me.

There is a naked man over there!

I held my breath. He was most definitely there, right there, facing away from me. His bare bottom took my full attention; round cheeks, plump, smooth and hard as if they were sculpted onto him. Standing to what appeared to be over six-feet tall. He was slender yet very muscular. From what was visible, he had a nearly perfect male physique, like a statute of a Greek God. The pale white marble man looked like all the ones I've so admired in the museum—for many reasons. He was surrounded by a heavenly light blue haze, glowing in the soft moonlight. My immediate impression was; *that's got to be a statute of David…Michelangelo's sculpture of David? It looks like an exact replica. Well, I am looking for a sculptor…so that would make sense,* I finally concluded.

I turned my attention back to the music—turning my head to look inside the barn door.

I called out, "Hello…is somebody in there?" No one answered, so I called out a second time, only a little louder, "My name is Emma and I'm trying to find Mr. Laurent… is he here?" The music at the door was so loud that I could barely hear myself yelling. I leaned in, staring through the door, hoping to see someone moving around inside. No one was inside. Lifting my foot to take a step inside, I saw something moving out of the corner of my eye—it was the naked man in the shadows. Spinning my head back around to see— he was actually moving!?

Bending down to the ground, the naked statue man picked up a water-gushing garden hose. Standing back up, he held the water spewing hose above his head, letting the water spill down on him, running over his hair, face, shoulders, and torso.

I turned to watch—in stunned silence.

A milky white liquid ran down, starting at the top of his head and flowing down his entire body as if he were melting. As it moved through his hair, the white washed out to reveal his curly sandy-brown locks. *He's covered in body paint,* I realized—with relief. Mesmerized, I continued to watch as the water washed down his rock-hard body. Like a magic liquid that could turn cold marble into living warm flesh, his sensuous skin came to life as the water washed him clean. In a dreamlike state, my eyes flowed down over him with the cascading water—watching intently as he slowly let the water wash away the white body paint.

With every inch he moved the paint down, my heart beat faster with eagerly growing anticipation. Moving silkily down, over his shoulders, over his back, all the way down to where his muscular thighs melted into his thin waist and hips—down, washing over his stomach, revealing a patch of dark hair, down over his—.

Of course, that's just when he turned to face me. Right when my eyes were bulging out of their sockets. I gulped. Our eyes locked. He's gorgeously naked. Standing there, watering himself like some bronze demi-god statue in one of the fountains on the grounds of the Palace of Versailles. All I can think is, *well, whoever he is…he's definitely alive.*

He smiled at me, as if he knew me. And that's when I recognized him—*oh, that cannot be him…is that really David?* From the way he was smiling back at me—he seemed to have recognized me too. He kept the hose on his body, moving it down along his lower legs now. I got the sincere impression that he was very comfortable with me watching. My eyes drifted over him, along with the water, as he continued to bathe himself, until nearly all of the white body paint was washed away, even from his toes. David didn't seem to mind me checking him out. He certainly had nothing to be embarrassed about—nothing at all.

Pulling my eyes away like tearing surgical tape from a hairy arm—it hurt—I forced myself to turn away. Drifting inside the barn with a giddy head, feeling buzzed similar to having just having guzzled down a bottle of that strong berry wine. My body was swooning with passion. Almost lilting, I numbly walked across the bare concrete floor, following the sound of the music to guide me over to the stereo. I had only been intoxicated enough to black-out once before, and this is exactly what it felt like. Steadying myself, I dizzily turned down the music, so I could try and focus. My head was swimming from all of the water still splashing around in my thoughts up there—amongst other things. All I could see was him. "Oh, my…goodness me," I mumbled, with his perfect, wet body, standing firm, refusing to leave my mind. The whole entire bathing scene replayed in my unfocused head. Trembling a little, my legs felt weak. Turning around, I leaned back against the table holding the stereo—to brace myself.

Taking in deep breaths, I tried to stay calm. Pounding thumps wanted to bust through my chest. *He's coming in here. OK, just relax. You don't want to seem too anxious…not like some stalking weirdo creeper*—I scolded myself, while repeating—*just relax.* To take my mind off of his sumptuous nakedness, I glanced around the insides of the barn, taking in even deeper breaths.

It was a cavernous space. And bright, very bright, with flood lamps set up all around. There was a couple of black umbrella looking things to reflect the light around. It was all set up like a photographer's studio, with everything focused down on a round marble pedestal in the center of the room. Yep, there it was. A camera, on a tripod, set up and focused right on the pedestal. With a long black lens, it looked extremely expensive. The one's that only professional photographers would use. Situated around the room where several marble sculptures, different sizes and shaped, all in varying stages of completion. Draping sheets and tarps covered some of the works, either finished or not. A dusting of ground marble blanketed most of the room. The thick white powder was concentrated primarily around the bases of the marble statutes that were in the process of being carved. Next to one of the uncovered statues was a clipboard sitting on an easel, holding various black-and-white photographs of naked models. They were painted-up with the same white body paint that David was covered in. They were posed in tantalizing positions, as models.

David stepped into the doorway. Dripping wet, his long hair hung in strings of wet curls. The grizzly mountain-man beard and mustache were gone, replaced with a day old shadow of short whiskers. With both hands over his crotch, he sheepishly smiled, asking, "Mind if I get dressed?" His eyes motioned over to a table where he had left his pants and shirt. My eyes dropped to his hands, to see what it was he was hiding—lingering there, just long enough to notice that he wasn't wearing a wedding ring.

With a restrained smile, I responded, "No, I don't mind. You can put your clothes on." In my head I was saying, *yes, I do mind—very much*!

He started slinking towards the pile of clothes, while keeping his eyes and his front, to me. I turned away from him, pretending to be concerned about modesty. Not turning my face all the way, I kept his body in the corner of my eye, where I could watch as he started to get dressed. Within seconds he had toweled down, drying himself off. There was a half-inch scar running down his back from just beneath his shoulder blade all the way down to the top of his hip-bone. No underwear, he pulled his tight jeans up over his firm buttocks. After slipping his feet into some sandals, he pulled on his short sleeved button up shirt—leaving it half-way undone so that I could see most of his chest. There was another visible scar. About six-inches long, jagged, it ran across the middle of his ribcage.

Well, he's not made of stone. He's real, soft, tender, flesh and bone.

Moving slowly, almost cautiously, David sauntered across the room, staying on the other side, away from me. His careful eyes seemed to be searching me, sizing me up, while waiting for an explanation. "I've told them I won't be coming back anymore. They don't have to worry about catching me in there again," he said somberly, as if to apologize for something he'd done.

"I'm sorry...I don't understand?" I responded with a furrowed brow—looking lost.

"Didn't the museum people send you out here to tell me to stay away?" David asked, seemingly just as lost.

"So, you do remember me?" I smiled warmly.

"Yea, you're Stoney's daughter. You used to be an intern at the museum, right?" He wasn't smiling anymore. It was as if he were making an accusation against me—calling me out.

Shit! The last thing I wanted was for him to lump me in with my father. "That's right," I answered softly. My head was completely cleared up now. No more giddy swooning. My feet were planted firmly on the hard concrete slab, as I stiffened up. This isn't how I wanted to feel, not at all. "But that's not why I'm here to—," I started to explain, when he rudely cut me off.

"Go tell your asshole father and those other bastard people running the museum that I won't be back in there...never again!" There was a fierce anger welling up in his eyes. It was obvious he was suffering from something they had done to him. An emotional injury, felt deep and painful. For some reason, my presence was tearing away his protective scab, reopening this deep emotional wound.

His anger refocused my mind, to where I felt like that lawyer person again—cold and calculating. I glared back at him with my own fierceness, to get his attention. "Look David, I'm here looking for a Mr. Zachariah Laurent. Now, do you know him or not?"

David's expression went blank—stunned. Staring at me like I was some ghost, with a humble voice, he said, "My mother was the only person that ever called me David. Everyone else calls me Zach."

21

MY MIND HADN'T even processed the fact that I was staring into the eyes of the sculptor that I was looking for, Zachariah *David* Laurent—when mother suddenly stepped through the open doorway. Her nerves were frazzled and on edge, having woken up inside the car all alone, forced to wander up to the barn through the darkness searching for me. She asked, "Everything alright in here?" She was justifiably concerned, having just overheard our simmering exchange before she walked in. Seeing me, that I was there, and OK, she anxiously glanced around the barn—over at David—then back to me, as if still unsure. It must have been easy to read us both since she instantly started to relax now, knowing that her baby was fine.

Then a giddy smile appeared on her smeared lipstick lips. Staring at David a little too long, her still inebriated admiring eyes took him all in—bare chest and all. "Guess this is a full-service gas station," she quipped, shooting us a flirtatious wink. Unfortunately for mother he wasn't giving her the same flirty attention that she was flashing his way. Her hair was sticking out in all directions, like someone would, who had just spent the night sleeping inside of a car. The gray hairs poked up the most, frizzled tinsel, in all directions. I almost laughed, but that would have been too embarrassing for her, so I bit my lip.

David must have thought she had just escaped from a mental hospital down the road after receiving electro-shock therapy that way he was looking over at her. He ran his hand up over his forehead, pulling back his hair with his fingers, revealing a small scar running along his hair-line. The furrowed lines on his forehead deepened as mother began sauntering across the room in his direction, as if she were in a bar, primed, and ready to make her best cougar style moves. I couldn't tell if he was getting a migraine headache, or about to run.

"So what's your name…since I don't believe we've met?" mother asked him seductively—making me want to gag. Extending her hand to take his, she swooped down on him like a bird of prey, using her boney talons to take whatever she could.

"David," he answered nervously, letting her shimmy up to his side to take his hand, and arm, and waist, as she wrapped her arm around him and pressed up against his body.

I had never seen her act this way—ever! Was there something in the air, the moon, the water? No. Of course, it was that wine!

"Seriously mother?" I burst out, unable to restrain myself for another nauseating second, "we're in the middle of something."

"Oh, don't let me interfere with your business," she mumbled, as her hands continued rubbing over David's muscular arms and back. Her daring eyes took in even more.

"Mother!" I barked, to break her spellbound trance. She

finally backed off and drifted away, giving him a little space to breath. Moving towards the edge of the room, she turned her attention to the various marble carvings. I stepped closer to David to regain his full attention, since mother's intrusion had juggled his thoughts a bit—naturally. "You sent in the application for a submission for the memorial art exhibit this year, isn't that right…David?"

His eyes wandered back and forth between me and mother, not wanting to let her out of his sight. "Memorial… submitted an application?" he muttered, as his thoughts started to refocus on the here and now. I think the disturbing images of mother wrapping herself around him like a python, smothering him up while hissing out her alcohol infused breath in his ear, was fogging up his head.

"A statuette…of a woman and child," I stated forcefully, to help him focus—to remember. "Wasn't that your photograph of your marble statue you sent in to the High Museum for the memorial exhibit?"

His eyes caught mine, as he remembered more clearly, replying, "No, that wasn't my sculpture."

My heart sank. I so wanted it to be his, for many reasons, mostly the selfish kind.

"Is this the one?" mother suddenly called to us from the back of the room. She had wandered all the way out of site to where she found a covered piece, situated back in the dark recesses, away from the bright studio lights. There she had discovered a lone statuette draped with a plain white sheet. Snooping, she had pulled away the cover while still listening to us. "It's gorgeous," she gushed. Clearly, she wasn't that drunk after all.

David and I moved in mother's direction. As the statuette

came into view, he revealed to me in a solemn voice, that, "It's not actually mine. I can't take credit for it. That's my mother's piece—her last."

Mother was rubbing her hands over the silky white stone, admiring in the same way she had with David's body. Darkened by the shadows, the carving had more of an effect. The loving way the angelic woman's eyes gazed down upon the tiny boy's head, with a gentle mother's touch, she let the infant know that she was there—hovering above him—as he looked down, while innocently playing in a field of flowers. "Absolutely gorgeous," mother whispered again, completely memorized by its compelling beauty. This time mother was free to have her way, exploring every inch of it with her hands. I even wanted to join in, but I stayed back, enjoying the scene from a distance, where I could take it all in.

"So, you did submit it for the memorial exhibit?" I asked excitedly, with an expectant smile.

"Yes," David replied sheepishly, as if expecting some bad news. "That's probably breaking some rules or something, right?"

"I don't think so," I told him, "I'll have to look into that. But we just had to verify who made it, and that it was authentic piece, before we could display it, you know how that goes?" I tried to play it down, not wanting him to think we had some hidden agenda. This was all seeming creepy enough as it was. He nodded his head saying that he understood.

"What else can we find in here?" mother blurted out as she wandered off into the dark again. "Any more master-pieces we can get a look at?" She bellowed, with her loud voice echoing throughout the barn. "How about some wine to go with this art show?" Sounds of loud banging and the clattering erupted as she began searching through drawers and cabinets looking for a bottle, of anything alcoholic.

Nope, I was wrong. She is still drunk!

Forcing myself to stay on subject, I asked him, "If you submitted the work for the memorial, then, someone you know, a relative, or someone close to you, they must have perished in the Orly crash, is that right?"

David's head sagged. His eyes dropped and traced the dusty floor, before he got up the nerve to answer—fighting back the obvious pain. "My mother," he whispered reverently, glancing over at the statue.

"That's you isn't it…the little boy?" I asked him softly. His head nodded again. I didn't need him to say anymore. His dewy eyes said it all. That was a carving of his mother. She had finished when he was still a small child—something she wanted to leave for him. So that he would always remember her as an angel watching over him.

"It was the last thing she finished before leaving for that trip back to Europe," he muttered through quivering lips, while dabbing away the teardrop with the back of his hand—hoping I wouldn't notice.

I started to reach out to give him a comforting hug, but hesitated. Idiot! Don't ever waist a sincere moment. You may never get another one. Those were the times I wished I was more like my mother. She wouldn't have stopped herself, drunk or sober.

And right on cue!

"Ah-hah!" my own mother crassly interrupted, having finally found what she was searching for—an open bottle of bourbon. "I knew I would find you in here." It was almost empty, but that didn't stop her. The tinkling of glasses soon followed as she started pouring out two spilling over the rim shots. "Let's have a drink shall we?"

David shot me a disturbed look—pleading with his eyes—*please tell me that she is just kidding?*

We both grinned, nearly laughing. "That's my mother," I choked out—trying not to bust out. "I better get her outa here before she breaks something."

Unfortunately it was too late to try and stop her. Tipping back her glass she sucked down her entire shot before we could even get across the room. We could only watch and giggle as she poured herself another round as she waited on us to arrive. "Cheers," she yelled, holding out her glass for me to join in. I reluctantly took mine and eyed David. He shook his head to let me know that he wouldn't be joining-in with us. "Haven't touched the stuff in a few years," he mumbled apologetically.

"Cheers," I mumbled, to not leave mother hanging, before downing my throat burning shot.

"Cheers," David responded, with less enthusiasm, as mother and I gagged on the strong whisky. We made that squishy face that says, *wow that's nasty harsh, yet, somehow it feels and tastes so damn good!* Until the next morning, that is.

After three more rounds, I surprised myself and broke the ice further by reciting an amusing attorney joke Carly had shared with me at the office. I was amazed that I told it right, and they laughed. Mother and David chimed in with a couple of funny anecdotal stories about themselves. We almost rolled on the ground with our sides splitting as mother turned the bottle up and guzzled down the rest of the whiskey—about four shots worth.

After close to an hour had passed, just when everyone was starting to loosen up and have some fun, mother managed to throw a wet rag over us again, putting a damper on the party—the one that she had started. A mere mention by mother that I was in law school completely fouled my mood. Ugh, why did she have to say that! After that—that's all I could think about. That's when mother started stumbling around the floor trying to peek under the other sheets and tarps hiding the other carvings. "Hope this one's a hot naked man with a big—," she blathered on, pulling off the coverings one by one. Tugging on a big blue tarp thrown over the largest block of marble, bigger than all of us, she lost her balance and fell back against a smaller statue, nearly knocking it over before I was lucky enough to steady her, and the statue—before they both crashed down on the concrete floor. David's face cringed as he leapt over to help out. Mother was getting completely out of control. "So what's under there anyways?" she demanded to know what was hidden beneath the large tarp.

"Something special...I've been working on it for years... but it's not finished yet," David started to explain.

"Let's see it...I want to...just a tiny peak," mother slurred, while trying to lift up the bottom—swaying on her feet.

David was shaking his head—*uh please don't.*

We had worn out our welcome for the night. "I'm sorry David, but we really have to get going, since I have finals coming up and I'm way behind on my cramming," I reluctantly announced. Taking mother by the arm I forced her to move toward the door.

David gave me a sideways glance. Like the one he gave

me that night at the museum, when he glanced back at me behind his girlfriend's back as they were leaving. This time, he was sincerely sad to realize that I was the one leaving. "There's room for everyone here if you aren't safe to drive?" He suggested coyly. Mother giggled and perked up. Swinging her head around, she stared at him passionately, and was starting to say something suggestively naughty back to him—seriously considering his offer. Fortunately, the booze had slowed down her thought processes enough to give me time to cut her off.

I jumped in to save him in the nick of time, saying, "No, sorry, that's very sweet of you to offer, but I really have to get home. I have to be up early to study all day long."

Mother huffed and pouted like a spoiled rotten child who didn't want to leave the playground. "Fine…with me… you go…I'll stay…right here," she stammered her objection. Wobbling as she tried to put her arms around David's neck, I snatched ahold of the back of her arm, squeezing hard, like she used to do to me when I was the little spoiled brat. My firm grip on her forearm probably left bruises as I tugged her out the door. She deserved it, since I had to endure her drunken ramblings on all the way back to the car. "Why are we leaving? It's just getting interesting. You're no fun. Didn't you get a look at the ass on that? How the hell did I raise such a prude?"

David was kind enough to escort us out. He guided us back down the dark trail. Mother was passing out by the time we reached the car. We looked at each other, grinning, wanting to laugh, every time mother spouted off some silly garbled gibberish.

But I could sense that there was something more,

something deeper, every time we looked into each other's eyes. There was a desire, wanting more, a silently spoken yearning conversation that was felt more than it was understood. If there was such a thing as extra-sensory perception, I think we were feeling it? A connection of thoughts and feelings, of mutual understanding, unlike anything I had felt before.

Luckily, once mother was strapped back into her seat, she promptly passed out. It was much easier to try and ignore her snoring, rather than endure her drunken inane rantings for the entire two hour drive back home.

22

I T WAS PAST midnight by the time we passed through the gate along our driveway. The house was brooding, dark, and silent. Jon was dreaming in his happy bed—about who knows what—something to do with clothes, or half-naked, or men taking off their clothes that he designed, or something just like that, I'm sure. Mother was tossing in her seat next to me, intermittently snoring, with sticky drool running from the corner of her mouth. With her whisky stinking breath wafting over, making me want to jump out into oncoming traffic. Several times I had to gently push her face away after she flopped in my direction landing on my side of the car after a swerve in road.

Finally, we arrived home, and I couldn't have been more frustrated.

All the way back, my tired eyes drifted along the winding roadway, watching for signs, passing slower cars, seeing things—but not really seeing them. My body was on cruise control the entire way, moving the steering wheel, pushing the pedals, while my mind lived out dreamy fantasies with my own naked man, named David. The image of him washing away the body paint, slowly undressing his rock-hard sexy body—was almost more than I could take.

I'd never been so horny in all my life! But, pulling mother from the passenger seat, struggling with her up the stairs, coaxing her into her bed, smelling her putrid burping breath all the way as drool got in my hair—all cured me of that problem. Any thoughts of a sexual nature had disappeared by the time I put my pajamas on, removed my makeup and got a good look at myself in the mirror while brushing my teeth—wondering the whole time what David must think of me and my sot of a mother. I was so tired that I waited until the morning to shower, deciding to go to bed leaving her drying whiskey infused saliva caked in my hair.

Now that's tired!

Getting up early to study was my biggest concern. But thoughts of David had a way of trumping even that. As soon as my head hit the pillow, the dreamy images of his naked body returned. *Stop it...quit thinking about him...I need to get some sleep*, I pleaded with myself to no avail. Slipping in and out of consciousness, he was right there, on the edge of every imagination. Sometimes when I was waking up, or falling back asleep, I couldn't tell the difference between what was a dream, or really mine. It didn't matter if I was dreaming or not, just as long as he was there.

Stop it...and please just go to sleep.

Naturally I was the first one up. Without even leaving my room I hit the books first thing. There was a small coffee maker inside my bathroom for just those occasions, when there was not enough time to care about anything other than studying. Sipping down cup after cup with my face stuck between the pages of my Real Property Casebook, I crammed the morning away. The front door slammed, letting me know that Jon was up and out for the day. Mother was still passed-out in her bed—for the rest of the day. Lunchtime slipped by without my noticing, thanks to all the caffeine. It was another couple of hours before my stomach began to roar for some attention. I managed to ignore my hunger till nearly two—before I convinced myself to take a break for some much needed sustenance and some aspirin for a headache that was certain to arrive shortly.

Trotting down the stairs still wearing my pajamas, father strode through the door. Not a happy camper. Throwing his suitcase down, he headed straight for the minibar as a man on a mission. "You're back early, what's up?" I asked.

"Rained out," he grumbled, telling me that, "there's a big storm blowing in off the coast." Pouring up some bourbon on the rocks and taking a swig—making me gag. I didn't need to see that so soon, with that foul, day old stale whisky taste still lingering in my mouth.

"Sorry to hear," I pretended to care, thinking, *great, now he's going to be such an asshole all next week…even more than usual.*

He looked me over skeptically, noticing my pajamas, before glancing over at the clock on the wall. "Where's your mother?" he asked, as if he already knew the answer.

"Still in bed I imagine," I replied flippantly. "We had a very long day…and night." There was a long pause as he imagined the worst—mother getting drunk and forcing me to driver her downtown to some late-night male strip club, where she threw money at the dancers, along with her clothes, until being tackled and dragged out by the burly bouncers. Taking another long tug on his whisky, his face grimaced with lewd imaginings starting to run wild. Probably some things he had first-hand experience with. "Too much of that extremely potent country wine," I finally added, getting her off the hook. "She drank too much of it before we headed back from our antiquing trip in the hills."

Daddy smiled, in a sinister way. "She never learns," he muttered.

Prying open the refrigerator I quickly surveyed the interior, in search of some edible leftovers. Nothing looked good. Only moldy spaghetti next to some days of Chinese takeout, that nobody wanted to eat in the first place. My best choice was the yogurt and granola. But, I took a slice of the cold pepperoni pizza instead. Father caught me mid-bite with his jaw dropping question.

Staring right at me, he asked in his overly stern office voice, "So, what did you find out about those memorial submissions…anything interesting?" His weekend was ruined so his head was already back to work.

My mouth was full, chewing the gummy old pizza dough, which was a good thing, since it gave me few agonizing seconds to think. Not rational thinking—more like a panic. *Shit! I can't tell him about David. If he realizes I am secretly in love with him…wait a second…love…did I actually just use the word love…that's crazy! Why else was he giving me those looks then? How could I possibly be in love…we really just met for the first time last night? That's lust, you little slut, not love…?"* With my racing thoughts going a million miles an hour, I must have giggled a little, with pizza crumbs flying from my wise-cracking lips.

"Well…what did you find out?" father demanded with a low growl, now staring at me with snarling tiger eyes. He didn't tolerate such flippant behavior, especially not when he was in serious mode, and most definitely not when he was in a foul mood from having his weekend of golf rained out.

More crumbs flew out, as I spit out a mumbled explanation, between chews, "everything is on the up and up… uh…both pieces checked out…uh…they seem to be genuine artists."

In response, he glared back at me to let me know that he was not pleased with my rude behavior, of trying to talk to him with my mouth full. Grabbing the half-gallon jug of milk from the open fridge, I chugged it down, guzzling the silky milk to wash the sticky pizza from my mouth. As the jug fell, our eyes met again, and now he was glaring at me with an even angrier stare—at the very end of his fraying short rope—with his, *I'm about to explode,* stare. I immediately replaced the cap on the jug and put it back on the shelf.

"The painting has nothing to do with Loretta's vote then?" he began his interrogation, never one to rely on a simple answer. Tearing away the factual flesh down to the bone of everything was how *Stoney* treated every situation, no matter how trivial. "The artist has no personal connection with her?"

"No, not really," I attempted to satisfy him, if that was even possible. "He's some silly old man…sounds to be over a hundred years old…an amateur painter that lives way out in California. Said he hadn't even talked to Loretta in decades. He submitted the painting in honor of his sister that died in the crash…it all checked out…no connection to Loretta that I could find."

I could see the wheels spinning in father's head—rolling it all around up there—as he fact-checked my story for discrepancies. It must have all made sense for him. Taking another sip on his whisky, he asked bluntly, "What about the sculptor…same story?"

Oh shit—here goes!

I spun around to pretend like I was looking for something else to nibble on in the fridge, so he couldn't see my eyes. From the day I was born he could read me like an open book. Lying to him always got me into trouble—because I nearly always got caught, before making my full confession. Like the time I styled Jon's hair, for the first time, cutting jagged tuffs down to the scalp till he looked like a goofy Chucky-doll Halloween costume gone wrong. Hiding the clippers and the sprigs of black hairs didn't help—neither did smiling like an innocent princess. It wasn't ever a fair fight at all. My heart was too tender and he was too much of a snake.

How do you lie to a human lie detector?

"He's just some guy that lives up north of here…up past Milton…out in the foothills," I replied calmly—my first mistake.

Father swirled his whisky glass, clinking the ice against the glass, as he mumbled, "Oh really…is that right?"

Getting nervous, I started tossing some plastic tubs around, crinkling plastic wrap, clanking casserole pans together—trying anything to cover my tracks. I even started making a silly humming sound as if I was thinking of a favorite song. Turns out, it was that Bon Jovi song from the barn—making me more nervous. I could feel that princess smile coming on.

Ah—here I go again!

Father cleared his throat. Not good. "You talked to him in person then…right?" His eyes were on my back—I could feel the pressure of him watching me—as he impatiently waited for my answer.

"Yes…that's right," I replied, as cool as the air inside the refrigerator. "His name is David…lives alone…seems like a real nice guy to me." A weight suddenly hit me square in the jaw, feeling like getting punched by a professional boxer, reminding me of what father told me many times before while preparing for trials; *idiot! Don't adlib, that's how they catch you in a lie. The more you say, the more ammunition they have to attack you with.*

"What's his full name?" father pounced with a sense of urgency.

Great, I said too much, I realized. *But now I had to answer him.* "Zach, or Zachary, or something like that…all I remember for sure was David…Zachary David Laurent…I think?"

"Lives all alone?"

"Yes…at least that's what he told me."

"He's not married…with no children?"

"Don't think so?"

"No other family around?"

"He didn't mention any…we really didn't get into all that."

"Is he a good looking fella?"

I ignored the question—pretending to be indignant—with a huff.

"How old is this David?" Father asked loudly, with the low roar of a lion, making sure I couldn't avoid another answer. Now, he was sounding more intrigued, rather than skeptical. "I've never seen any of his work before. Strange, since he's obviously very talented."

Taking out a gallon jug of ice-tea, I spun around to face him, feeling a little bolder. "Oh, he's about thirty I would guess?" These were questions that I didn't have to try and manipulate to my advantage. And the tension seemed to have passed. Sounding somewhat sassy, I stated, "The carving was not done by him…it was made by his mother…for him."

"Certainly you spoke to his mother…to verify that?"

"Can't do that…since she's the one that died in the plane crash…and David submitted it on her behalf…in her honor." Instead of the princess smile, I would use the sad girl face—flashing my eyelashes while showing him my drooping frown. Didn't want to resort to such a harsh tactic, but he forced me to go there. But it seemed to be working, so I casually began to pour myself a tall glass of refreshing sweet tea. "Such a sweet gesture," I moaned as the glass filled to the rim—pouring it on. Pity can be so disarming, and I intended on using it to my full advantage.

Unfortunately, he wasn't done with me. "Didn't you and your mother just get back from a trip up there…up there in the hills…up around where David lives at?" father inquired, in his eloquently charming, oh so disarming, trial attorney voice. The one he uses to close his case—right before the verdict.

Tea spilled over the top of the glass as I froze. "Yes…that's right," is all I could reply. Holding my eyes down, not wanting to look at him. Even my tepid response sounded weak and desperate. I suddenly felt like a cornered rabbit with no place to hide, coaxed into a corner, eye-to-eye with the serpent that was slithered up to devour his delicious meal.

At least I didn't adlib!

Not wanting to push us into an inevitable fight or flight situation—knowing that I was about to take flight—father finally relented, turning his intent gaze away from me. Staring down at the ice in his glass, his tense shoulders dropped, and he said softly, "Well then, I guess that makes casting my vote all that much easier."

I looked up at him with a half-hearted smile, unsure of what he meant by that. I assumed that he was telling me that he intended to cast his tie-breaking vote for David.

He just smiled back, without telling me more.

Mother appeared at the top of the stairs looking like a zombie who had just managed to dig herself out of from her grave. Hair sticking out everywhere, with her padded eye-shades dangling down on the side of her head, after having gotten tangled up in her hair. Smeared mascara, dried and caked on makeup that she didn't remove, made her face all the more dead and decaying looking. Bloodshot eyes radiated between her sagging eyelids. Dehydrated and parched, she was smacking her lips and tongue trying to find a few drops of saliva. The moaning sounds she was making completed her zombie routine—perfectly.

Father instantly tensed up again. Shaking his clinking glass his shoulders raised back up. His face blushed as his blood started to boil.

That was my cue to make my escape. Sauntering past her on my way up to my room to study, I gave her a good-morning kiss. Not wanting to miss an opportunity to poke her, for a tiny taste of revenge, I whispered gleefully in her ear, "Oh, look who's back home already, its daddy."

23

OTHER AND FATHER were kind enough to wait until I was inside my room before they launched into their tirades. With all the banging and yelling there was no way I was going to be able to concentrate on memorizing case law. It was boring enough as is. And it was absolutely impossible to read with the slightest of distractions, let alone with two screeching banshees tearing the house apart downstairs. In the moods they're both in, it would go on all night, until they either kill each other, or pass out. Right now, I'm hoping for the first option.

Even if they weren't fighting I don't believe I could have concentrated. Not with those pesky images of David still swimming around up there. *Alright, need to concentrate*, I instructed myself. I managed to read down a few paragraphs, until, someone got in the shower. Then, all I could hear was the running water, splashing and running down—David's amazingly sexy body.

Stop it! Concentrate. I can't!

Slamming my case law book shut, I ran into the bathroom and jumped into my own shower. Getting cleaned up and dressed—provocatively, yet subdued, and mature, in a nice summery cotton dress that was perfect for a country stroll—I made my escape.

"Where you going young lady?" father asked as I opened the front door. He was fuming, needing to find someone to vent out his frustrations on. Mother had barricaded herself upstairs in her room, unwilling to spend another agonizing second with him.

"Out," is all I replied before slamming the door shut.

It felt good getting out of the city. The country air was fresher, sweeter. Driving as if I wasn't going anyplace in particular, strangely, I wound up right back where I was the night before. Time passed far faster this trip, as I wound my way up into the foothills. Wow, this looks so familiar for some strange reason I snickered, turning up David's driveway. With the bright sunlight it was easier to find the house. It all looked pretty much the same way, except now there was a Fat Boy Harley Davidson motorcycle parked out front, leaned over on its peg. Parking next to the hog, I got out, and walked up to the door—with my heart pounding and my palms all wet. I had to pause. It was hard to breath for some reason. *Why am I so nervous?* I had to ask myself.

Just knock already, I yelled inside, before pounding hard on the door. I wanted to at least sound like I was confident. Just like the night before, it was silent, with no answer. Peeking into the partially shaded windows, there was no movement inside. It looked to be abandoned. I pounded on the door some more with the same result, nothing.

He must be out back, in the barn?

Heading around the house, following the trail once more, I made my way back to where the barn was. Both doors were swung open wide this time. The closer I got—the louder a hammering noise got—with the sound of his mallet striking the top of his chisel. At the opening of the door, I paused. My heart was pounding even harder, my palms soaking wet, my mind racing, wondering if I should go in. *Was this the right thing to do?*

The chiseling stopped. Suddenly it was so quiet. There was only the pounding of my beating heart. It was now throbbing inside my chest.

"Who's there?" David called out.

How did he know I was there? That's when I noticed my dark outline on the floor. Of course, he could see my shadow cast on the floor through the open doorway. "It's just me," I called back softly, not wanting to upset him. "Is this a bad time…am I interfering with your work?" Stepping inside the door, to where I could see him. David was seated next to a block of marble that he was carving. The featureless stone was nearly as tall as he was, and same size round. No shirt or shoes. He was only wearing some old tattered blue-jeans, full of holes. Beads of sweat glistened on his skin. White powder dusted him as if someone had thrown flour all over him. A wooden mallet and metal chisel were in his hands.

My breath was stolen away in that moment—as everything stopped.

He smiled with his sumptuously dimpled chin. Shaking his golden locks of hair, fine particles of marble dust flew all around him in the air. There was a little laugher as he slung the white powder away. "C'mon in," he chuckled, as if playing a game, "if you dare?" A cloud of dust lingered around him, shading him for a moment, before settling down on the dust covered floor. All of his chiseled hard body reappeared—all for me, to behold.

Oh—I dare!

I walked inside. We stared at each other for a moment, seemingly lost for words. "You ever do any sculpting Emma?" he finally asked me, motioning me closer, as if wanting me to join in. "You must be an artist since you work at the museum, and all?"

"Not really…I mean, I've done some stuff with clay before…ceramics…stuff like that," I replied, with a giggly high-pitched twang, sounding goofy. Darn nerves.

David stood up and patted down his jeans, slapping away puffs of white powder from his thighs. Retrieving another stool close by he gestured for me to take a seat, right next to him. I moved over and used my hand to brush away the dust clinging to the stool. David snickered at my prissiness. "This is a nice dress…if you hadn't noticed," I jokingly pointed out.

"It won't be for much longer," he replied with a devilish grin. "Now take the mallet and chisel." I followed his eyes down to the tools waiting for me where he had laid them at the foot of the marble block.

"I don't want to mess up your piece," I pointed out.

"I'm just getting started on removing the outer edges. There's no detail involved…no way to screw anything up, just yet. You'd be doing me a favor by doing some of the work for me," He replied. His hands eagerly offered up the tools. Taking the mallet in my right hand and the chisel in my left, I held them up striking a silly pose—as if I really was about to start wildly hammering away. "Let me show you," he whispered, leaning in behind me. Pressing his chest to my back he reached around with his arms to touch each of my hands.

As he touched me—I shuddered.

He must have felt my trembling as he pressed his flesh firmly against mine, making us one person. Moving my hands into the correct position, working my arms like a marionette, he placed the chisel on the stone and struck it with the mallet. So very soft at first, then a little bit harder, then harder still—until I could feel my own hands taking control. With the flow of the weight going up and down and the pulse of the pounding, I forced the chisel into the hard marble. Chips flew away as sparks in the night sky—thrilling me to the bone. My heart was racing as I continued pounding harder and harder on the chisel. "I think I've got the feel of it now…It feels so right," I moaned as he let go, letting me pound away at the stone until I could feel a trickle of sweat running down between my heaving breasts. "Oh my God… that feels so good," I nearly screamed.

"I believe you're a natural," he spoke softly into my ear as I fought to catch my breath. My limp arms wilted to my sides. His calloused, hardened hands caught the mallet and chisel as they started to slip out of my weakened fingers. The barn was hot—getting steamy hot. "Let me help," he whispered, pressing himself harder up against me, with our misty skin sticking together. My dress clung to me a little more. Marble dust clung to us. The heat from our bodies pressing together sent a trickle of sweat along the back of my neck, tickling as it ran down my lower back. He dropped the mallet and chisel to the floor. Running his hands up my thigh, pulling up my dress—I could feel his other hardened tool, hidden within his pants, that was now ready for some pounding of its own.

"Uh, that was interesting," I gushed, slipping out of his grasp. I stood up and moved around to the other side of the chipped marble block. Over to where I was out of his frustrated reach—momentarily. David would have to wait—if he wanted to get a chance to use his *tool* to sculpt on *this* body. Our eyes were seducing each other just fine as it was for now. No need to rush it. "So, how is it that you remembered me last night?" I toyed with him, playfully blowing a tiny dust cloud off the block, directly at his face. "How did you ever remember my name?"

With a wide smile, blowing back the dust, he replied, "I asked. I wanted to know who the cute girl was that was throwing me out of the museum…in case we ran into each other again."

"So, why didn't I ever see you again?"

He raised a brow, as if worried, to say, "Because they also let me know who your father was…that I had better stay far away from you. That's why."

I could feel my pressure building, making me steam, imagining father's stupid meddling face. "Well, there's absolutely no need to worry about him…not at all. He's just a big teddy-bear really," I tried to play it cool.

David's eyes drooped down, as he revealed, "it wasn't just him…it was the others too." Glancing up, he looked just as steamed. "Mostly it was that old hag Loretta."

Jolting upright, my surprised eyes popped out. "What does she have to do with anything?"

There was a scorching fire lit in his eyes as he answered, "She's the one that got me banned from the museum, forever."

"Banned…for what…because of me…when I asked you to leave for staying too long?" My heart was pounding again. My mind anxiously racing—*oh great, what did I do now?*

Standing up, David turned away, sauntering across the room with a drooping face. "It wasn't just you. It's a long story," he muttered. His body became rigid. The anger was melting away. His voice sounded solemn, hurt deeply. "That's in the past now. No need to reopen those old wounds now."

"But she's the one stopping the Board from selecting your mother's statute for the memorial display," I murmured hesitantly, not sure if I should reveal that to him right now.

David swung his face around, glaring angrily at me. With trembling lips, he fought back the spite-filled filthy words he wanted to spew out—right into her face—like a venom spitting cobra. If he could, he would be gouging out her eyes right now with his mallet and chisel.

"My father is making the final decision however," I let him know, hoping to calm him. "I believe he's going to choose your submission. He definitely prefers it over that painting Loretta was forcing on everyone."

Picking up the mallet and chisel from off the ground, David sat back down on his stool and began slamming down hard—sending large chips of marble in all directions. A thick plume of marble dust swept through the air, getting thicker with each heavy blow.

Wanting to quickly change the subject, I asked him sweetly, "So, why did your mother call you David?"

Heavy beads of sweat were trickling down his forehead with his chest heaving, as he abruptly stopped chiseling— to look up at me. A relaxed smile returned to his face. "I love carving marble this way," he said very softly, as if finding a moment of Zen. "Everything else just disappears when I'm carving." His mind cleared out the anger he was fostering for Loretta. Staring at the scared white rock, a peace fell over him as he filled his mind with memories of his mother. "She wanted to name me after her favorite work of art—Michelangelo's famous statue of *David* in Florence."

"I definitely see the resemblance," I said, while moving my roving eyes up and down his body like a naughty flirt.

David laughed and blew marble dust off the chiseled block. Grabbing my hand he pulled me towards him, to where we met face to face inside the swirling cloud of white.

24

STARING INTO HIS eyes, the moment was too intense. Our bodies were sticky wet. White powder dust painted us all over. He leaned in to me, and I pulled away—as our lips were about to touch. *He doesn't even know me*, I thought as I stepped away from him. *But I desperately want him too.*

My being torn was easy for David to see on my face. Hopefully, it would be as easy for him to understand my feelings.

"At least you can't kick me out of here," he said sarcastically, letting my hand fall away from his. I walked meekly around the block of marble like a fragile virgin. His eyes followed me. He was letting me go—for now.

My dress was ruined. And I could care less.

"Now, why would I ever want to do *that* David?" I kidded with him. Thinking; *I finally have you right where I always wanted you to be…right here with me.*

"Well, why did you do *that*, the last time?"

I shot him a snarky look, telling him how I felt. "That wasn't at all what I was doing. I was actually coming over to meet you…if you must know. But you already had someone else with you," I reminded him, asking, "Or, have you for-gotten about *her?*"

He probably forgets all of their names—love'em and leave'em, right?

"That's right," David's face lit up as he recalled, "I was with Julie that night. She wasn't very happy with you…I def-initely remember that."

Oh great—he remembers her name too!

"So sorry to ruin your hot date," I snidely remarked—at the same time shooting him a wink that said; *I'm really not sorry at all.*

A dreamy look came over his face, as he fondly remem-bered that night. "Didn't turn out all that bad as I recall," he taunted.

Time to change the subject!

"Then how am I to blame for you getting permanently banned from the museum?" My eyes trained on him like a hawk as he started to gather his thoughts. This time I wanted a real answer. No more dodging. I didn't want him to blame me at all.

"It wasn't you. It wasn't even that night," he replied glibly. "Those problems got started way back before I was even born. That night was merely the final excuse for Loretta to drop the hammer on me…for good."

Whew…thank you!

"Why would Loretta have it out for you?" I persisted, now more curious than ever.

"She and my mother had a falling out way back when… years before that…before she died." Glancing at me distrust-fully, biting his lip, he was holding back. "Like I said…it's a long and complicated story…and I don't want to bore you with it right now."

Of course I couldn't let it go—not me! The lawyer in me took over and I started searching for clues. Perhaps I could use my skills to coax some information out of him. Looking around the barn, I noticed some unique details that may be of interest. I prodded him to tell me more. "This is all of your mother's work…this was her studio…isn't it?" The place had a woman's desire filling it, still, long after her death—a persistent passion.

David sat back down on the stool—positioning his mallet and chisel for another strike at the jagged marble block. As stoic as the hard stone, he stared into it deeply, as if searching for its inner being. "That's right," he replied in a reserved voice, as he readied the chisel point. "This was my parent's home. This was her studio."

Skirting around behind David, I surveyed the room some more, admiring the different statues, in their variety of forms. A few were finished, finely polished to a smooth surface. Others were ruffed-out blocks showing half-hewn images that were just beginning to emerge from the stone. "Are all of these your mother's carvings?" I asked distantly.

David returned to his work in progress, pounding on the chisel as we spoke—speaking between strikes. "Some. Not all. Some are mine. Some…I'm finishing…for her…and then there's one…that I'm just getting started on finishing… for me."

"Your mother knew Loretta down at the museum then?"

"That's right. They were both on the Women's Committee."

"Yes, I heard of them," I let him know, "they ran things before the new Board, right?"

"That's right," David grunted, landing another hard strike. They also taught art lessons together for the Atlanta Arts Association."

My eyes felt the curves of a lovely nude. With half my mind, I asked, "Is that how your mother wound up going on that flight to Paris?"

With one last hard hit on the chisel, David suddenly stopped. For a long moment he was caught—in a deep thought. A somber moment, he reflected on her memory, before answering, "Yes, that's exactly right." Lifting the chisel back to the point of attack, he whacked it again— even harder.

I could feel the trembling vibrations all the way across the room. I stopped talking, to listen.

"Loretta was supposed to be on that trip too," he explained, "but, for some reason she didn't make the flight." Another blow landed hard—sending out another shivering vibration across the floor. The statue next to me shook. A fresh cloud of white dust was stirring in the air. "My mother took her place, at the last minute." Wham! The entire barn shimmied, with dust filtering through the beams and falling down around us like snow.

"Is that why Loretta dislikes you now?" I had to ask. "Does she feel some remorse...guilt over what happened to your mother?"

David dropped his arms and looked over at me, questioning my sanity, with cocked-up eyebrows. "Loretta doesn't feel remorse...not for anything."

"Then what is the reason? Did something happen with her and your father?"

David turned back to face the cold stone, his face just as

hard, to say, "Loretta hated my parents for many reasons… well before that trip was planned." His shoulders drooped. All of his muscles softened. The tools dangled in his loose grip. Everything about him appeared worn down, fragile.

Where was the gallant soldier facing Goliath? The true David was not made of marble. He was only human after all.

"Did your father perish on that flight too?" I asked solemnly.

"You could say that," he replied in a withdrawn voice, sounding angry. "He was gone, all the same."

It seemed that David had been alone with himself for a very long time. Attempting to escape, withdrawing, hidden all alone in here. With no one else to listen to him, about what had happened to his mother. There was no one who cared to know, about him. I shuffled quietly over next to David, placing a reassuring hand on his shoulder, listening to what he needed to say.

"What happened, David?" I whispered into his ear.

He stared desperately into my eyes. Like two mirrors we reflected off one another for a few moments, each wanting to reach out to the other, looking to find something deeper. There was so much there for him to tell me. It was almost overwhelming—so many layers upon layers. He was lost in a funhouse of mirrors, and all I could see was him searching for so many answers reflected back at him with each direction he turned to look. He was lost. He didn't know how to begin to tell me.

I reached out and ran my fingers through his hair. We stared deeper into one another's eyes as my hand drifted down his neck, over his shoulders, and down his sides. My fingertips reached the top of the rough edges of his long jagged scar. It was running up his back, sloping across his side. He winced at my touching it, as if he were afraid to let me feel his pain. Turning away, he whispered, "It's a very long story."

Our shadows cast on the floor were getting very long and dark. The sky outside was turning a glowing orange and yellow, with soft pinks painting the clouds as sunset approached. "I'll have to be going soon," I said to him softly, running my fingers into his thick hair again, gently tugging to move his face towards mine. Finding his eyes again, I impressed upon him with my longing gaze, that; *it was all OK and that I was there for him, anytime he wanted to tell me his very long story.*

Hey, at least I tried to reach out. I'm not a professionally trained therapist after all.

"You get these scars from wrecking your motorcycle," I asked, to change the subject. Moving my finger from his hair to his forehead I ran it along the thinly imprinted pinkish line. The almost invisible scar felt like a raised bump that ran along his hairline. It seemed like the most plausible reason for having those types of injuries.

"Only a couple," he said straight faced, "but not these… those are all internal…brain damage mostly."

We studied each other's faces for a moment—waiting for some reaction. *Is he serious?* I pondered, watching his eyes and mouth, with him staring back at me, stone faced. Then, there it was, he couldn't control it any longer, and a thin curl appeared on his lips. Our faces broke into grins together, before I punched him in the arm and tugged on his hair again—hard—as we started laughing. "You're so gullible," he chuckled, twisting his eyes crossed, and draping his tongue out of a gapping mouth, to look like damaged goods.

"No, seriously," I demanded, forcing him to erase that silly expression, and behave. "What's up with all the scars?"

Calming down, he looked down at his side, saying, "these are from a fall I had a few years ago."

"Fall...a fall from what?" I gasped.

"I took a nasty fall from a rock face when I was doing some free climbing...tumbled about a hundred feet or more...bounced off some jagged outcroppings on the way down. But it was worth it, now."

"Where were you?" I gushed with a rush of adrenaline.

"Way off in the backcountry of Colorado."

"So, you spend a lot of time out there...in Colorado?" I asked, playing stupid. No way was I about to let him know that I had been stalking him, trying to find out where he lived. Plus, I wanted to know if he was really the person that saved me from my skiing accident?

"Yea...spent most of my life out there living with my uncle...after my mother died. He owns a Bed and Breakfast up near Breckenridge. My parents left me this place to live in, if I wanted."

"So, you're uncle raised you out in Colorado?" I asked softly. Running my fingernails down his back and shoulders I tried to help him relax—and to keep him talking.

"Pretty much he did. Once I got older, I would spend my winters out there going to school and working for my uncle, and most of my summers back here. Nowadays I've been staying here a lot more, to work more on my sculpting.

"You must be an amazing skier then...getting to spend so much time on the slopes?"

"Used to...before it all became work," David said with his voice dropping, becoming thick with annoyed agitation.

"I spent most of my time up in the mountains pulling half-frozen tourists out of the snow…having to risk my own neck just to rescue them. People can be such idiots…getting themselves into dangerous situations up there…not having a clue."

"Wow…those idiots!" I chimed in, shaking my head in disgust.

Oh no, please don't remember me!

"Do you ski?" David asked excitedly, staring right at me.

"Oh no…you kidding…a Southern girl like me?" I smirked dismissively. Adding, "Not a chance of me getting up in those mountains…up on skis….out in the snow….no way…hell no." Using what I had picked up in Junior High School Drama Class, I played it up to the hilt.

David shot me a skeptical frown. *Too much, play it down!*

"Too bad," he replied, "I certainly miss being up there."

"Maybe I need the right teacher," I snickered, giving him back a playfully skeptical squinty eyed stare of my own. Then I asked the fateful questions, and braced for his answers. "Well, if we did go to Colorado together, would I have to face a pissed-off wife that you failed to mention?"

David shook his head slowly, to say—*uh, no.*

"Have to be confronted by a crazy ex-wife then?"

He was still shaking his head—*definitely not*—with a wide, giddy smile.

"Have to babysit your illegitimate children?"

Shaking his head fast—*hell no*—before busting out laughing at me, and saying, "not a chance, no way, an adrenaline junky, living on the fly bachelor guy like me…getting hitched and tied down with kids…hell no! I was only engaged once, for about a minute, before we broke up. So damn jealous, she couldn't handle letting me out of her sight for two-seconds. She really was crazy."

Whew!

"Maybe you just need the right teacher too?" I said, playfully pulling his hair back to make him say that to my face.

We froze there—as my words lingered. A spirit of emotion swept over us, pushing us together, wanting us to kiss. With our eyes locked together, breathing in unison, we moved closer together, slowly, to where our lips almost met. Tasting our mixing breath, my heart was pounding—my mind racing—forcing me to a sad realization. *No, we can't get romantically involved...not until after the memorial exhibit vote is decided. I won't give Loretta any ammunition to hurt David with again.*

"It's getting late and I have to prepare for my finals," I whispered desperately, while pushing him back. It was enough for now, to see the longing in his eyes as I moved away. David stood and walked behind me. Stopping, he watched me leaving while standing inside the doorway of the barn. His shirtless body glowed gloriously in the warm setting sunlight. No spoken goodbyes. Exchanging departing smiles, this time, we knew there *would* be a next time—this time.

25

ANOTHER MONDAY MORNING and I strolled into the office, without my typical solemn demeanor. It may have frightened a few people in the hallways, seeing my friendly smile—on a Monday—how unnerving. It was even scaring me a little. Fighting against my smile, I kept my head down so my hair would fall over my face, shading my unnatural enthusiasm, not wanting to draw attention to how I was feeling.

Someone might start asking questions about my sanity?

There was no time to stop at the park this morning, since I was hurrying to get organized and everything situated for when I made my surprise visit on father. I would have to come up with a believable excuse before barging into his office unannounced, since I can't tip my hand about knowing David—not just yet. That would be such terrible timing and could blow the whole thing up. Especially knowing what a foul mood father was bound to be in since he didn't get to finish his golfing adventure with his buds. But that wouldn't deter me in the least little bit. My nerves were crawling with electrified excitement, wanting to hear the good news that David was getting the memorial exhibit.

Plus, that would give me the perfect excuse to pay that sumptuously sexy budding artist another unexpected visit that afternoon, to deliver the awesome news.

He may even be doing one of his naked modeling poses—BONUS!

Getting situated in my office I poured over the case files searching for some reason to bother father. Then, there it was jumping right out at me—the Foreman file. It was a simple landlord tenant issue, but it involved one of the business owners currently renting a small snack-foods-concessions space adjacent to the High Museum—bingo. I'll get father's take on the legal issues, since he is such a genius legal scholar, getting me through the door, while I pick his brain about the memorial exhibit vote.

Whispering to father's secretary outside his office door, I let her know I was just popping in for a short visit—not that unusual—and she waived me in without interrupting her phone conversation. As the door swung open I could see that someone else had already beaten me to the punch. Shit! It was Thomas, seated in a side-chair discussing something unimportant like golf, I'm sure. They were chuckling about something boyish, hushing up as I cleared my throat to let them know I was coming in. "Am I interrupting something?" I pretended to care, knowing they were just goofing off.

Father sat back in his chair, leaning way back to where he was looking up at me. "No, c'mon in sweetheart," father smiled big, motioning for me to sit down next to Tom. Apparently Thomas had managed to lighten up his mood.

Glad someone had finally managed to figure out how to accomplish the impossible!

Tom stood half-way up and kissed me lightly on the

cheek. "Hello darling," he whispered sweetly. His cologne wafted in the air, smelling divine as usual. Dressed in a sharp pinstripe suite that was fit for a gangster, everything about him was nearly too perfect. My excited nerves began to crawl around with the heebie-jeebies. All I could imagine was him up on some megachurch podium, with his perfectly coiffed hair, all gleaming with a sparkling smile and caring bright eyes, calling out to the adoring masses, to all join in with him—in worshiping him.

"What can I help you with dear," father asked in *that* voice, as if already dismissing me. That's the way he speaks to the other associates when he really doesn't want to be bothered with work. He was saying, make it fast, because I have more important matters to attend to—namely discussing his weekend, and golf, with Tom.

Tom sat silent, returning his attention to a magazine he was perusing before I showed up. Golf Digest—ugh!

"I wanted to get your opinion on that Foreman lease issue…that's all," I stated, trying to sound just as businesslike.

"What's the problem now?" Father murmured, dropping his smile.

"Foreman refuses to comply with the lease terms…he's deliberately breaking the terms of the lease agreement, and now the museum director wants to start eviction proceedings against him…and I was hoping—."

"Hoping what?" Father interrupted. "Hoping that I would intervene and get things sorted out for you?"

"Well no—I." I tried to explain before he cut me off again.

"That's your job now missy," father growled. "It's your case.

You have to deal with Foreman and get him to comply, or throw his noncompliant ass out!"

His curt response let me know very clearly that he didn't have time for such mundane matters. That case wouldn't even show up on his radar, let alone get his attention. Wow, did I ever choose the wrong excuse. This was his fatherly way of telling me to grow up and start taking charge of things—like a real attorney. That day had to come eventually, but I didn't expect it to be so soon, or to be so harsh—ouch! And right in front of Thomas no less.

Talk about a *wake-up* slap across the face.

That's when Tom chose to chime in, to point out an advertisement for the newest top-of-the-line BMW's. Looking identical to the one I saw him racing down the street in, it was all black, with racing tires, alloy rims, full leather, sporting the most powerful engine they make. "I'm thinking about getting one of these," he muttered, leaning over to let me see the photograph, adding, "Check it out babe? I would look pretty smoking in this sweet ride…don't you think?"

Tom's completely oblivious. Fuming doesn't even begin to describe how I was feeling at that moment!

"So, what about the memorial exhibit vote?" I blurted out, not caring what either of them thought anymore. "Have you made your decision yet?" Father's eyes dropped to his paperwork spread out on the top of his desk, avoiding mine. That was my answer, but I needed to hear it from his lips. "Well—have you?"

Leaning back in his chair, he stared me down again— unsuccessfully this time. His bullying wasn't scaring me off this time. It was too important for me. "Look—," he started to say, when I cut him off.

"You chose the painting didn't you?" Now he was the one afraid to say anything more.

"That's right…that was my choice," he mumbled, keeping his eyes on me, playing it cool, as if he could care less. My eyes were now glowing red, getting hotter, as he tried to explain himself, "I know you preferred the sculpture thingy, but, there was no need to upset the apple cart over this memorial exhibit thing."

"By apple cart you mean Loretta, *right?*" My voice was quivering with restrained anger. "You mean, you couldn't think of a reason good enough to upset Loretta right now… because you need her support for your federal judgeship, *right?*"

Father leaned forward and folded his hands, glaring at me across his desk, with bulging-out-eyes that were saying; *don't force me into a political corner, not right here, not right now, making me look bad in front of Tom*—who was finally starting to pay attention.

My voice was raised high enough, that even *he* couldn't ignore me any longer. Pushing the pages of the magazine closed, he casually asked, "What about a sculpture and a memorial…a vote…did I miss something?"

You missed everything! I was screaming inside—as I ignored him—glaring back at father.

Tom nervously looked back and forth between us, as we stared each other down like a bull and matador, squaring off in a ring, with only one of us coming out alive. "Should I wait outside…let you two finish your conversation?" He muttered, starting to get up.

"Stay put Tom," father said sharply, like ordering his pet dog to *stay*. Then he said to me, "We're done talking. Go take care of that Foley eviction," as his way of dismissing me from his office.

"Foreman, not Foley," I snapped. Jumping up out of my chair—I stomped my way out. I could hear Tom snickering as I left. "What about lunch?" he called to me as the door shut. I kept on walking.

Assholes!

Passing by the secretary's desk on my way out, I couldn't help but notice the letter on her desk—all typed out on our law firm letterhead—informing David that the museum Board appreciated his efforts, but had made the hard decision to reject his memorial submission. I couldn't stomach reading every infuriating word of it. But I'm certain it let him know that there were so many impressive works of art to choose from, and his was very impressive too, making the decision oh so difficult for them. Father just needed to review it and sign the signature line to make it all official, before she would seal it up and mail it to him. It took everything in me to stop my trembling hands from snatching-it-up and tearing it to shreds.

26

I T TOOK A couple of hours to calm down after my meeting with father. Thomas showed up right on time to take me to lunch, as usual. Seeing him at least gave me the opportunity to vent off some steam. And since it was Tom I could really let loose and get it all out—almost all of it. He pretended to be interested through most of my cathartic ranting. Sometimes he would even give me some good pointers on how to deal with it, showing that he was actually paying attention to me.

Of course I didn't mention David. I'm not an idiot.

Thomas listened and nodded his head, smiling sweetly now and then, as I told him the entire sorted story. About the memorial exhibit, the committee voting, and how Loretta was making such a stink about getting her way. Describing the works of art, I was very persuasive, even passionate at certain moments. How the sculpture was so elegantly carved, created with such artistic integrity, making it one of the most moving works of art I had ever experienced. Thomas was so moved by my description that even he agreed with how I reacted, standing up for what was right and trying to get father to side with me. Even he would have chosen Mr. Zachariah Laurent's sculpture.

Only because I left out the parts about finding out who the sculptor really was, and how I felt about him.

The rest of the week I put David and the memorial fiasco out of my preoccupied mind. Cramming for finals became my entire existence. The courses were terrifyingly difficult, so it was taking every neuron getting fired-up to digest all of the material. There must have been thousands of details in hundreds of cases I was attempting to memorize. Father even let me take the rest of the week off, more-or-less. I was still coming into the office but was using all of my time to study. My office door stayed closed—and locked.

The only other person that could get in to see me was Thomas. For some reason he was being extra sweet. Flowers got delivered, food for lunch appeared, fresh cups of coffee, back and shoulder rubs just when I got stressed to the max, not to mention the near orgasms after some hot sweaty passionate work off some built-up stress sex to help me focus. He was the perfect boyfriend.

Did I just think that?

Having Thomas around to help cram came in handy too. Not only was he drop-dead handsome, he was also a naturally gifted legal genius. Graduating at the top of his law school class wasn't for the feeble minded. Getting chosen to be on the law review was even more impressive. Those were two things I had not accomplished, to father's dismay. Father wouldn't have even kept me around his office if I wasn't his daughter. Thomas understood that, and never once let on. I should give him credit for that, at least. Being my study buddy he really helped, showing me critical details that I routinely missed. He even taught me some study tricks that he had been shown by some of his professors—tiny things that only they would look for on the exams—earning me a few extra points.

And every point counted since we would be graded on a curve, against some of the smarted students in the World.

But no matter how hard I crammed, or how sweet Thomas was, I just could not get David out of my head—not completely. That letter being sent from father was eating at me. It was so business like, so soulless. He deserved a better explanation than that. Especially since I essentially assured him that he would be getting father's deciding vote.

I finally decided that I would have to go back up there and tell him the news, personally, since it was now a personal matter. After my last exam on the next Friday I would go straight to David's house. He probably wouldn't have read the letter anyway since the mailman couldn't have stuffed it inside the already stuffed mailbox. It didn't appear that he was checking the mail, so there was good chance that I would be able to break the sad news to him, in a better way.

By the time exams were over, my feelings were scrambled-up. Thomas had been the perfect gentleman. Everything went well, and I was feeling beyond confident about my performance. These should be the best grades I have gotten yet—all thanks to Thomas. Things between us had really turned around by the time Friday afternoon rolled around, and I strolled out of my last test feeling amazing.

I may be giving David more bad news than I had prepared for.

The drive up was agonizing. I didn't tell Thomas were I was going, of course, and we were planning on meeting up later that night to celebrate. David had no clue I was coming up there, and part of me was hoping that he would not be home. *Maybe his getting the letter would be best*, I mused. *Maybe he never felt the same way about me anyways? Would never seeing him again be such a bad thing?*

But I kept going—unsure of everything. *Maybe just seeing him will clear-up everything, in that moment?*

Stopping at the mailbox I scoured through the letters. It wasn't there. So, I headed up to the house. David answered the door with an overly exuberant happy smile, the kind they paint on clowns. He looked like he had just won the lottery. I'm certainly not that hot—that he would ever be that happy to see me—no way? And, after reading the letter from father, he should be weeping right about now, or at least a little upset.

I couldn't hold back and I came right out with it, saying to him, "David I've got some bad news." My face was drooping, with the saddest frown ever, like the sad clown.

David kept smiling, like what I said didn't register. So, I continued.

"I'm so sorry David, but my father decided to not vote for your mother's sculpture."

The news didn't faze him at all—he kept on smiling.

"What's with the super happy face?" I asked shyly, now starting to wonder if he had lost his marbles and was about to chop me into tiny pieces.

"I've got some awesome news Emma," he gushed, as giddy as a boy on Christmas morning. "I sold a sculpture." His eyes were as wide as saucers, smiling so wide I could see all of his gleaming white teeth.

"So?" I replied, needing more info. Still wondering why he was so excited.

"It's more money than I could have made in five years working for my uncle."

"Which piece?" I blurted out nervously, now hoping against hope.

"The one I submitted for the memorial," he replied gleefully. "A man showed up here yesterday, wanting to buy it."

"How did he know about it? Was he from the High Museum?"

David thought for a moment, before replying, "No, don't think so? He was older like your father. Wore a weird hat and he said he was representing a buyer that wanted to remain anonymous."

Mitch!? This must be father's doing?

I stepped into the house and shut the door. David could read the concern on my face as I prodded him for more information. "Who else could have known about it? Did you do any advertising to try and sell it…tell anyone else it was for sale…anything like that?"

"No, that was the only time I ever let anyone else see it," he answered softly, while finally losing his smile. "Why? What does that matter?"

It seemed that he was more worried about possibly losing out on a sale, rather than getting shafted on the memorial.

"Well, that was your mother's piece…for one thing," I murmured. "You're going to let somebody on that Board take advantage of you…some pathetic politician like Loretta? Don't you want your mother's art to mean something special?"

David turned away to hide how I had hurt him. "The

man said it would be in a private collection…with someone who was truly inspired by it…that it would be cherished," he replied softly. "That's what meant something to my mother… not some petty squabble between pretentious museum Board members…using art as a pawn on some chess game…using it for some political clout. Anyone who would offer that kind of money really appreciates what my mother created."

His passionately inspired words struck me—emotionally knocking me off my high horse. *How could I argue with that?*

Then, David's wide smile returned again, as he said, "besides, I'm carving a duplicate right now."

"What?"

A look of smug satisfaction came over him—and he winked as he said, "I would never sell my mother's sculpture…not for anything."

"You bastard…you had me going," I groaned, punching him playfully in the arm. "So, what are you going to do with all that money?" Sticking it to father would be the icing on the cake. And, if he was the *anonymous buyer*, I wanted a taste of the action.

"They paid me a sizeable down payment, with the rest to be paid on delivery. I figured that I could put them off long enough to finish the copy. I've been working on one for a couple of years now, and it will only take a few more weeks to finish it up."

Kidding with him, I started naming off all the expensive things he spend his money on—"a new car, fancy watches, definitely a new wardrobe, remodel this old house—."

He cut me off mid-imaginary-purchase to announce, "I'm taking a trip to Europe."

"What—why?" I paused. That exuberantly happy clown face was back on him.

"It's something I've always wanted to do before…but never had the money to do it," he replied happily.

"When are you going?"

"Next week."

"So soon…but why?"

"It's something I have to do."

"Why?"

David paused in reflective thought, almost reverent. His eyes and smile softened, as he decided to tell me. "You know that larger piece out in the barn under the blue tarp…the one you wanted to see."

"Yes, I remember it," I replied. I had thought about it many times since. Not getting to get even a peak upped my curiosity level to the extreme.

"That was a piece my mother worked on for many, many, years, without ever finishing it. It became an obsession for her. She was sculpting it for my father…for *them*. It was to be *their* memorial…for *their* enduring love."

"What does that have to do with you going to Europe?"

"My uncle told me of how she seemed to lose the passion for sculpting. Over the passing years she lost the passion for life itself. She was hoping to find it again back in Paris, where she and my father first met. Now I want to finish that trip for her. And when I get back…filled with that passion she was searching for…I'll finish that sculpture for her."

I have to admit it—I was swooning at the romantic gesture.

My lighter than air head was trying to take it all

in—when—David took my hands in his, staring deep into my eyes, to say, "I want you to come with me."

Now my light head was now spinning like a Whirling Dervish making me dizzy. I wanted to say yes—oh yes. But thoughts of Thomas, father, plans and prior commitments, all kept flashing in there, getting my thoughts all discombobulated. *Is that really a word?* It fits—because that's exactly how I was feeling. Reeling, I stammered back, "Well… David…I would love to…go….but I…uh—."

"Don't answer yet," David stopped me from coming up with an excuse. "Just think about it, alright?"

I nodded. *Oh yes, I will definitely think about it.*

David eagerly started to tell me the story of how his mother and father met, but I glanced down at my watch and realized that if I was going to meet Thomas at the restaurant I would have to leave that minute. "I understand…you've had a big day…with prior plans…I understand completely," David said sweetly, before giving me a kiss on my cheek, letting me know, *it's alright, I'll tell you later.*

27

IT WAS TWENTY minutes past seven before I made it back to midtown Atlanta, found a parking space, and made the walk up to the restaurant where we were supposed to meet for my little end-of-testing celebration. Thomas had planned the whole thing. I would have preferred to get home and finally catch up on some much needed sleep. He invited Carly to meet us at the Vortex, my favorite quirky place to grab a bite to eat or happy-hour drink. I mentioned it to Lisa in passing and she took that as an invitation, most enthusiastically, to join in the fun. She was feeling the same testing anxiety and wanted to blow-off some end-of-semester-tension as well. And since I was running late, they should have been inside already waiting for me to arrive.

I was never late. Oops.

Pacing up Peachtree Street it was getting dark, with the tall buildings blocking last rays of sunlight. People were turning a dark grey as the shadows fell. The street lamps buzzed to life. Florescent bulbs hummed and beamed in ultra-bright colors as the businesses lining the street prepared for the night. Circling around the block coming from the other direction, a black BMW rolled into view. Traffic had lightened up considerably as rush hour died down. With half a block left to go, I stopped walking—to watch.

The black BMW rolled to a stop across from the Vortex, just pausing long enough for a man to get out from the passenger side. He didn't take a moment to say goodbye to whoever was driving. I assume he had done that while still inside. He merrily skipped across the street heading quickly for the Vortex entrance. My feet started moving, faster, pacing faster until I was close to a jog without being obvious. I needed to see who it was before he made it inside the restaurant. He opened the door and started to step inside, but was pushed back by a party of four who were exiting. Holding the door for all of them, such a gentleman, he lingered until the entrance was clear. Making it up to where I could get a good look before he stepped through the open door. And there he was—Thomas.

Bastard!

By the time I had caught up to him, he was at our table. Carly was greeting him with big hugs, smiles, and giddy laughter. Lisa was there too. And she brought a friend. It had to be Sara.

Thomas stole a smooch on my neck. As he kissed me I could distinctly smell the odor of alcohol on his breath. He's already been drinking someplace else, I realized. On his collar I noticed a reddish spot, a tiny smudged stain—lipstick that he apparently had tried to wash off.

Wow, could the night get any worse?

Cheers went up from the girls. Lisa and Sara had already been working on some martinis. Carly had her second shot of bourbon, along with a beer back. They had all arrived about an hour ago and were past feeling tipsy. Before my ass hit the seat a round of lemon-drop shots arrived at the table. The waitress had an entire pitcher full of them for us over at the bar. "Congratulations to us…another year in the rear view mirror," Lisa heartily toasted, before we shot them down—just as another round came around.

The sneaky sideways glances had started before the appetizers had even arrived. The copious quantities of booze was pulling back the curtains hiding Tom and Sara's lurid desires—placing it all out in the open for all of us to see.

Sara was gorgeous, a blonde-haired, blue-eyed bombshell, with breasts as big as her brain was small. She never needed pom-poms shaking to get attention. As a member of the cheer squad, with her over-the-top perky attitude, she could beguile any man that crossed her path. For tonight, she had squeezed herself into the tightest most revealing outfit ever known to man. Why didn't she just wear pasties on her nipples? It's about the same thing. Either she was going to be stripping at a bachelor party later on, or she was heading for a porn-shoot? It was definitely one or the other.

As dinner progressed, so did their interest in each other. Tom took every opportunity in the conversation to turn the attention on Sara. It was like they were on a blind date the way they carried on. She was oh-so witty and charming—with him flakily chuckling at every little thing her pouty lips vomited out. Of course Tom had to notice her, but hello—right in front of me and my closest friends?

It made me want to puke!

Thomas could see that I was annoyed, by something. After such a long hectic day, it was easy for me to give him the stink-eye. And he had to take it without question for now. He didn't want to dig into whatever was bothering me in front of my friends. The fake smiles stayed plastered on his face and he bit his tongue, probably because he knew where it might take us, and it could get very ugly. "You seem tired," he whispered in my ear, hoping that's all it was. "You've had a very long day, huh? I can remember those excruciatingly long final exam days."

The other girls were engaged in a discussion about something as Tom kissed me on my cheek. It made my skin crawl—wondering what other female lips they had probably just been sucking on. Not giving him a warm reaction, I asked him coldly, "Did you come straight from the office?" The alcohol was getting to my head too, fast, getting my dander up, if you know what I mean?

"Yea, I walked down," Tom answered calmly. "So, I might need a ride back?" He asked, like he was telling me—I have to give him a ride back to the office.

I grabbed another shot and downed it as the others kept on gabbing. The vodka was working on loosening up my tongue, and I didn't want to keep holding it back, so I let it fly. "Why don't you get a ride from whoever that was that dropped you off outside?" My eyes glared at him, waiting for this reaction. He wasn't going to be able to stay so cool and calm now.

"Oh…uh…that was my friend…my friend Roger," He stammered out a response as if he was stumbling around in a pitch black room searching for something to grab onto. "He's a car salesman down at the BMW place…great guy… showing me few options before I buy." A sly smile appeared on his face, with the smug look that he managed to find the way out, in the nick of time.

"You got his card?" I asked skeptically. Tom obviously

forgot who he was up against. "Maybe I should give him my opinion too?" I was not letting Tom get off the hook that easily. Our eyes locked hard in an epic questioning stare-down. He looked stunned to me, even nervous, cornered, since I landed a clean right hook to his jaw. Regaining composure, his hands nervously patted down his pockets. His fingers frantically probed into each pocket, as he mumbled, "I'm pretty sure…I had one someplace….could be I left it in my other suit or my jacket—."

I was about to blurt out something hatefully condemning, when, he almost magically pulled it out of his coat pocket. "Here it is…I knew I had one," he said, sounding extremely relieved. It was a wrinkled-up, coffee-stained, old looking business card that he had obviously been carrying around with him for several weeks now. The name *Ronnie* was printed on it—BMW executive sales division.

"I thought you said his name was Roger?" I snarled, trying to regain the upper hand, after being knocked back by his unexpected uppercut.

Tom stared down at the card. He mashed on it, pressing it out straight on the table top, while coming up with a response. "Well, yea…I knew it was Roger, or Ronnie, Ron, or something like that." He was now squirming like a school boy who got caught cheating on a test. "He's not that good of a friend," he had to point out, after the fact.

I snatched the card from between his fingers and shoved in into my purse. Tom turned away, instantly joining in with the chattering girls. For him it was as if nothing had happened. He was going to ignore it—like he had done with everything else wrong with our relationship up to that point.

Carly put her arm around my waist and leaned over to

whisper in my ear, "everything alright?" She had picked up on all the drama unfolding between us. I slumped down and gave her that look, the one that says—*I'm tired, I'm pissed, and I just want to go home.* Carly grinned and said under her breath, "Sara's such a skank." We fought to stop ourselves from busting out laughing. The others noticed and stopped gabbing long enough to ask us, "What's so funny over there?"

For some reason, right at that moment, an image of David's amazing naked body flashed in my head. Could have been the booze telling me something? Whatever it was, I went with it, announcing, "Lisa, will you join me in the bathroom please?"

"Of course," she squealed happily.

Carly wandered off to the bar to order another round. Sara was more than pleased to get a few moments of *alone* time with Tom.

After checking the stalls inside the ladies room to make certain we were alone, with no co-worker stragglers that may be eavesdropping. I joyfully confided with Lisa. Her eyes stretched as wide as the toilet seats as I quickly let her in on David, and about his offer to take me with him on a wild, impromptu, hopefully incredibly romantic trip to Paris. "Oh yes you have to go," she insisted without even thinking twice. "I'm so jealous," she gushed over and over without letting me get a word in to explain why I was telling her all this.

"Listen Lisa," I forced her to focus, "I'm telling you everything because I need a huge favor from you." She kept smiling while nodding that she was listening, and agreeing. "I need you to cover for me while I'm gone. Obviously I can't tell anyone else, not my father, mother, or anyone else at the office."

Lisa's eyes widened again as she asked, "You need me to say you're going someplace with me for a few days…that it?"

Staring in the mirror, my lips smiled, as I came up with a plan. "I know…we'll say we're going to Florida to stay at your father's condo at the beach…and you invited me… because we're both so stressed out from school and we both need a break."

Lisa smiled big, gushing, "That's absolutely perfect."

We giggled all the way back to the table. I let Lisa make the announcement that we would be departing for Florida the following week—the third weekend of May. Sara tried to invite herself along, but Lisa regrettably informed her that, "there just wouldn't be enough room."

Tom didn't suspect a thing. At least he didn't show it. He even ordered another round of drinks, to toast our little *girl's weekend* in Florida.

"It's getting late…and I've got to get going," Carly finally lisped through her numb lips, having reached her fill. "We've all had too much to drink," she muttered loudly. Pushing herself upright on her wobbly feet, she knocked her chair back on two legs, nearly sending it all the way over. Grasping the edge of the table she steadied herself.

"I've already taken care of the tab…including the tip," Tom announced to everyone. The waitress was busily cleaning off the table as we prepared to depart. With her fingers clenching several empty clinking shot-glasses, she shot Tom a happily satisfied smile-and-a-wink. It seemed that she'd served him many times before.

I've got to get out of here!

"Sorry to be a buzzkill, but I've got to go too," I chimed in as the party started to break up. My head was as light and bubbly as Carly's whenever I stood up. Carly giggled with her hand over her mouth seeing me swaying.

"Don't go…we're going out dancing…it's still early," Lisa pleaded, getting up to hug us goodbye. The second Lisa stood up, Sara slid over into her seat to get closer to Tom. They kept on talking about something as Carly and I staggered toward the exit. Lisa had to give Tom a painful pinch, to remind him that he needed to walk us out.

"Wait up girls…I'll walk you to your cars," Tom half-heartedly requested.

"Don't bother," I snarled back at him, saying, "We'll be fine. I'm going to get Carly a cab and I'm parked right outside."

From behind us I could hear Sara saying, "bye-bye girls," in her oh-so-sweet voice. It made me gag.

The hostess was nice enough to call Carly a cab. It arrived in less than a minute. Carly piled inside, giggling like a happy baby. As I started to close the door, she said, "Oh wait…I almost forgot…to give you this." She rummaged around in her purse, an extra-large variety that doubled as her briefcase, and she pulled out a bottle of champagne. Not just any bottle, it was old, a pricey collector's bottle—very expensive. I knew, because mother had some similar bottles kept in her own collection.

"What's this?" I gasped.

"For you…a gift…for finishing another year of law school," Carly stammered. The smile on her face was sincere, and happy.

"This is far too expensive," I replied, wanting her to know that I really appreciated the gesture. But, it was too much. Carly wasn't close to being on her financial feet yet. Still buried under a mountain of student loan debt, there was no way she could afford such a spendthrift gift like that—not right now.

"Nah," she scoffed, "don't worry about it. That's a gift from a client. He gave it to me for doing such a good job for him…saved him a lot of money…an investment gone-bad… pulled his ass right-out-of-the-fire. So, he thought he'd throw me a tiny bone. I thought about drinking it by myself, but hell, I wouldn't even appreciate it like you, so, please take it, and enjoy." With that, Carly pulled the door shut, loudly barked out her address along with some meager directions to her studio apartment a few blocks away, and they sped away.

28

THERE I WAS, all alone in the dark, standing on the barren sidewalk on Peachtree Street in the middle of midtown Atlanta, staring down at my bottle of champagne. *Whoopee…yay for me*!

It was a nearly elven p.m., and everything was closing up, all except for the late-night dance clubs and bars that were just getting busy. It was shift-changing time, when the business people dispersed, as the drunks, druggies, and vagrants, all wandered back out into their nocturnal domains on the nearly vacant streets. I couldn't help but ask myself, *which one am I? How much of a wino bum do I look like right this second, all staggering down the sidewalk carrying my bottle of booze?* If someone was to approach me right now, I would most likely hiss, cradling my bottle like it was my newborn baby—"get back!" *That's right, they should be very afraid of me*, I snickered, with a hiccup. *Yep, I'm drunk*, came the unsobering reality check.

I stopped on the corner where I needed to turn, to get to my car. Something else was pulling harder at me, turning me in the opposite direction. It was the other me, the more spontaneous side of me, telling me that I didn't want to go home just yet. *Why not? A walk would be nice,* I told myself to keep going straight down Peachtree Street. *Besides I don't have to study or work tomorrow.* So I walked on, taking in the sweet smells of springtime. Or was it pungently sweet rotting garbage? It didn't matter, since before I realized it, I was standing directly in front of the High Museum staring awkwardly up at the white wedding cake building—making my stomach grumble for a late night sugary snack. Then I spied my old friend, *The Shade,* standing guard out on the front lawn. He was looking as sad as ever, all hunched over pointing down to direct me to the entrance of hell. *Thanks, but not tonight,* I snickered as I walked across the lawn over to the granite memorial. I gave him a hug, like an old lost friend, before meandering my way over to the museum's windows.

This is where I first saw him, I recalled, sighing. With a woozy head I leaned against the glass, pressing my entire body up to it, wishing with everything in me; *David should be here with me, right now.* I sighed deeply and closed my eyes, dreaming him to life. With my lips so close up to the window, my warm breaths formed a patch of fog. Something appeared in the mist, where someone had run their finger across the glass. And my heart nearly stopped—seeing letters rubbed onto the glass:

EM

I pulled my face back in disbelief. The misted letters evaporated away within seconds. Opening my blurry eyes wide, I peered inside—half expecting to see David on the other side, gazing lovingly back at me. Only, it was pitch-dark inside. Nobody was there. Everyone was long gone, even the cleaning crew. No one would be back into the museum until after they opened up the next morning.

Or would they?

An electrically charged sinister feeling swept over me as I remembered that I still had a key to the employees back entrance. They never asked for me to give it back whenever I finished my last stint interning. Why would they? They knew I'd be back in the fall. *Oh, please let me still have it*, I got more excited, taking out my keys and shaking them until the right one appeared. *I do!*

Glancing around, seeing no one around, I shuffled across the lawn and around the building to where employees went in and out. Opening the door I quickly punched in the code to deactivate the timed alarm system—it worked—they hadn't changed the code thank goodness.

A pale moonlight lit up the interior, enough for me to see what was in front of me, barely. It was a wall of silhouettes set against the light coming through the huge windows. Shuffling up the stairs I wandered into the main gallery where several marble and various types of metallic sculptures where on display. It was like being inside of a department store with all the lights off, surrounded by mannequins up on pedestals, stiffly standing in their appointed positions—except almost all of these mannequins are naked. And with such little light, I could barely make out any images. It was all black and white until I got up really close. There were some glass pieces arranged close to the walls to help prevent accidents. The walls were lined with paintings, realism mostly, with a few post-modern ones thrown in the mix.

There was no way I could turn on a light. A security guard was always on duty, but as usual, he or she, was most likely down in the employees lounge snacking on chips and drinking stale coffee, while watching television. Every couple of hours they would make some rounds, scanning the room with their flashlight just to make sure everything was in order. As long as I avoided being seen, I was golden. Since I knew the place better than they did, most likely, that would be easy.

Moving through the statues I couldn't help but admire their nude physiques. I could blame it all on the alcohol, but it was a real desire none the less—something that I couldn't ignore. Walking up behind a tall sculpture of a man, carved to look something like Michelangelo's David, a slender, muscular, gorgeous hunk of hard stone—I couldn't control myself any longer. Reaching out to touch his buttocks, it moved as my fingers pressed up against his skin, or so I thought. *Stop playing tricks on me*, I laughed at myself, *you drunk slut*. My thoughts and desires for having David, was making me go insane. Rubbing my hand over him, I grabbed a big handful of that round fleshy man ass and squeezed. It felt so good that I groaned out loud, "Oh—".

The sounds of a man's subdued laughing forced me to drop my hand and spin around. It's the security guard, he saw me, I imagined. Swinging my head around I searched for who was laughing at me. There was no one there. No security guard and no flashlight. "Who's there," I demanded, "I heard you laughing." There was only silence. Moving fast, zigzagging around the pedestals and statues, careening around the corner, I finally jumped out into the hallway hoping to catch the pervert red-handed. For that moment, I had completely forgotten that I was the *real* trespasser. I had jumped into my internship mode without thinking what I was doing—a habit. But there was no one there. "What the hell?" I mumbled.

Carefully walking back into the main exhibition hall, I made my way back over to the hunky statute. I wanted to hang-out with him for a little longer—if you know what I mean?

Instead, I found myself standing in the same spot, staring at empty space. The statute was gone. My mouth dropped open and my eyes became saucers. "*What the hell is going on?*" That piece was way too big, and way too heavy, for anyone to come in and move it that fast. This couldn't be some practical joke being played on me. And it damn sure didn't just disappear. "I'm not that drunk…am I?"

Suddenly my eye caught sight of something, or someone, moving over near the window. "Who's there?" I nearly shouted. It wasn't my imagination this time.

"It's just me," David said softly, as he stepped out of the shadows. He was zipping up his pants. His shirt was pulled on over his shoulders but was left unbuttoned, so that I could see his marble white skin. He was covered in a light coating of off-white body paint. His blonde hair was dusted with marble dust to make him look like one of the statutes.

My knees came close to buckling and I nearly fainted at the site of him appearing out of the shadows. "David… it's just you…thank goodness." But then a surge of angry adrenaline took over, and I laid into him, "what the hell are you doing in here? You scared the living hell out of me… you asshole!"

He smiled, so sweetly, to apologize, "Sorry…I'm so sorry Emma…I didn't expect you to be here too."

"Well what are you doing…how the hell did you get in here?" I groaned as I instantly began to calm down at the sight of him.

"I have my ways," he said coyly, giving me those bad boy eyes.

It was hard pretending to be upset, but I did my best pouty face with a stomp of my foot. Really I was more embarrassed than anything, knowing that I was groping his bare ass a few moments ago. He went on to try and explain why he was here in the middle of the night.

"You know how I pose for photographs up at the barn? Well, I also on occasion, sneak into the museum after hours to get a real perspective on my work. You know, to see how it feels from their point of view."

"Who's…the statute's point of view…but they don't have a view?"

"It's an expression thing…I have to feel the space their going to exist in…to know how they should feel…when I create them. It's something my mother showed me."

"You're such a weirdo," I started to laugh.

"That's exactly what Loretta called me too…amongst other more vulgar things…when she caught me that night," David replied with a smile. "I scared her so bad she almost had a full-on heart attack right there where you're standing."

"So that's why she hates you, huh?"

David meandered around a pedestal, getting closer to me. He started to button-up his shirt—till I reached out and stopped him. "That's one of the reasons," he whispered. "You know I followed you to that restaurant tonight…I wanted to surprise you. But then I saw you with that guy…your boy-friend obviously. So, I decided to sneak in here instead. It can be a real rush getting naked in the museum. In fact, you should give it a try sometime," David implied better sooner than later with a seductive wink.

"Maybe I will…sometime," I toyed with him, "But probably not tonight. Why don't we just relax and hang-out for a while first…see where things take us."

David readily agreed.

We found a small open space over against the wall beneath a large oil painting, situated in a tight space between two pedestals, out of the way, so that if the security guard did pop in and flash his light around, we could ball ourselves up and hide.

"Oh, I almost forgot to tell you," I gushed, "I've thought about it, and I would love to go with you to Paris next week."

"But what about your boyfriend…won't he mind?"

"It's all arranged. Now I just need to get my ticket."

David was so happy, saying, "That's so awesome…you are going to love it." But then his face turned more serious as he said, "there's just one thing though. Could you possibly buy your own plane ticket? I only had enough money left over for my one ticket, and I already bought it.

"Of course," I replied. "I'll use my father's credit card and he'll never notice until he gets the bill…nearly a month later."

David's face lit up. "Well then…why don't we pop open that bottle and let's celebrate."

I forced the cork out slowly until it popped, shooting across the room and bouncing off a porcelain vase—forcing me relive a momentary shocking flashback. The vase didn't budge. *Whew!*

My head was starting to spin a little. Staring at him with silly dizzy eyes, I wanted him bad. Tugging playfully at David's shirt I was doing my inebriated best to get him to give me a taste of his sweet candied lips. But he ignored me, so I believed, waiting for me to take a drink of the bubbly as the bubbling champagne flowed out of the top. Taking a big swig on the bottle and passing it over to David, I gave up on romance for the moment, and said, "Alright, fine, so let's hear this story of why Loretta hates you and your family."

David braced himself, taking the bottle from my hand, tilting it up for a long tug. Spacing off into memories past—he started telling me his parent's story. "First off...I have to tell you that I'm not who you think I am. My real name is not actually Laurent. My father's real last name was Braun—Jonas Braun."

29

I'M SOMEWHAT ASHAMED to say now that I can't remember everything David told me about his parents, since I was starting to black-out. The long exhausting day combined with the excessive drinking was taking its toll. With my head bobbing, I forced my listing eyes to stay opened, as I did my best to stay focused—to listen. Between the black-holes of blotted out memories, this is the best that I can recall—

David's mother, Melissa Meyer, was a bright up-and-coming artist. With a full scholarship to the Sorbonne in Paris, she was a young college student with natural sculpting skills that rivaled any professional artist of her day. An aspiring sculptress, she was living in Paris near the university on the West Bank of the River Seine while studying art history. She was working as an intern at the Louvre Museum, spending nearly every free moment wandering through the halls getting to know every inch of every sculpture, letting each of her senses soak in their very essence. Alone, with no one watching, she would rub her hands over them with her eyes closed, tracing each muscle, bump, vein, and fold, or curl, feeling how the master sculptor must have known them—as they carefully carved them into existence.

It was her inspiration and example, that taught David how to pose, becoming one with the art, letting his body change into a sculpture as it turned to living flesh from within him. His own body would harden into stone, forming the perfect reflection of life. It was up to the artist to discover the life living essence within the marble—and find a way to bring it out—giving it life.

Melissa was a student at the Sorbonne until she was in her final year, preparing to graduate and take a curator position at the Louvre. It was 1939 and the Germans had begun their invasion of Poland. Everyone was leaving, especially the American students. Melissa refused to leave Paris, even as the Germans sent waves of battling soldiers into neighboring countries, Belgium, and the Netherlands. Even as the Nazi blitzkrieg panzer divisions flowed across the French border, Melissa would refuse to cower and run.

Her fierce independent spirit and love of Paris would not let her abandon what she longed to make her permanent home. It had always been her dream to become an art director, or curator, at one of the prestigious museums in France, hopefully Paris. Giving up on that dream now that it was at her doorstep, even in the face of the Nazi aggression, was not something that she could accept. Staying put and finding a way to keep her dreams alive became her sole driving ambition. Until the day she met David's father Jonas Braun, that is. Then, everything changed.

Jonas was a young and vibrant musician and painter from a tiny village in Germany. He grew up along the French border and spoke both German and French fluently. His mother was French and he was well acquainted with both cultures, and he could easily switch from one to the other without nearly any distinction. His father unfortunately was inducted into the ranks of the Nazis.

It wasn't long until this indoctrination caught up to Jonas. As the German forces occupied Poland, he was forced to leave his home and join the ranks forming along the border with Belgium. Given the rank of a low level SS Officer, he was assigned to a military division that would be used to interrogate prisoners for information. This was because of his language abilities and aptitude. It was his skills in detecting soldiers and civilians who attempted to hide their true nationalities that made him extremely valuable to the Nazis. Knowing when someone was lying, or faking, was a rare talent that they would put to horribly thorough use.

Jonas was forced to participate in the most horrendous and gruesome torture sessions, as they pried tidbits of helpful information from the tightly held tongues of prisoners of war. Always reluctant, he eventually complied and participated to a degree, believing the entire time that Hitler would soon be satisfied and the war would end. It never did, and the torture sessions became ever more lengthy and gruesome as the prisoners became ever more resistant.

On the day the invasion of France got underway, was the day Jonas make the fateful determined decision to abandon his homeland for that of another. The Frenchmen were as much his own countrymen as the Germans, and he could not endure torturing them.

Placed up on the front lines Jonas endured the most brutal of the fighting. Mile after bloody mile they trudged, as they slaughtered the helpless French. It felt as though he was killing his own family. Much like stabbing his own heart with a dagger, he starred into the eyes of the dying soldiers. Knowing, that after each battle, as they marched into the streets of every tiny village, he would be summoned to where the prisoners of war were being held captive—to begin their interrogations. If they resisted answering the questions, they would be made to scream in agony, until they talked.

By the time Jonas abandoned his unit, fleeing into the countryside outside of Paris, he had become as hard as stone inside. Leaving himself behind, he forced his emotions, and all of his feelings, to die, there on the battlefield. It was his only way to survive—without going insane.

Coming across a wounded French soldier hiding against a hedgerow, Jonas waited with him until he finally succumbed to his mortal injuries and passed away. They spent the time waiting for fate to do its dirty work by reminiscing about the old days, before the war. Jonas took in as much personal information about the young man as he could. After the soldier died, Jonas removed his tattered and bloody uniform and dressed himself in it. Using his dagger, he inflicted deep wounds on himself, making it appear that he had been injured in the same places. Then, he moved stealthily across the roads and fields in the dead of night he slowly made his way to the outskirts of Paris. Using his German voice when confronted by soldiers, hiding his true identity, he was able to avoid arrest until he was inside the city.

Jonas found papers inside the dead soldier's pockets. There was a hastily scribbled last letter to home, to his wife, in case he perished on the battlefield. There was also a bank register showing his account balance and some other important personal information such as addresses and his employer.

With this paperwork, along with what the dying soldier had revealed, Jonas was able to create a false identity. No one would be the wiser.

Managing to avoid the German occupiers as he moved across the city, Jonas made his way to the American Hospital that was known to be a safe haven for wounded soldiers seeking to escape. The staff immediately removed and burned his French army uniform and rushed him to a bed. Dressing his wounds and providing comfort, they advised him to say that he was merely a wounded farmer who was caught-up in the onslaught, and wounded by shrapnel from a mortar round. It worked, the Germans who came through searching for French soldiers believed him. His perfect French, spoken with his convincing small village dialect, fooled everyone that spoke to him.

As Jonas lay recuperating in his hospital bed, Melissa walked into his life. With the Germans occupying the entire city, restricting peoples travel and access to normal life, she had been kept away from the museums, from everything she loved. Spending time at the hospital helping care for the injured helped her to pass the time. At least she could be doing something productive while being suppressed. Her energy was seemingly boundless and she refused to allow them to slow her down.

Not wanting to let her French language skills get lax, she sought out anyone who could speak fluently to carry on conversations with. Hearing Jonas speaking to a fellow nurse in his perfect French tongue drew her to his bedside. It was magnetic, and magical, an instant connection, that quickly turned romantic. As romantic as a couple can become inside a hospital full of wounded soldiers that is. They inspired passion on one another, even while surrounded by death and destruction.

Melissa's father was of Jewish origin, and was her certain undoing if the Germans found out. It wasn't very long after they occupied Paris that they began searching for Jews. Melissa knew that they were being rounded-up and sent off to internment camps in Germany, or detention centers in other parts of France. The stories she was hearing were unbearable. She and Jonas decided that they should take their chances and try to escape to Spain, where they could find transportation to America.

With the help of the American Hospital staff, and the other resistors, they followed the others that were making their escape, heading across the mountains, and making their way to the Spanish coastline. There, they found passage on a ship that would carry them to Savannah Georgia. Finally out of the raging storm of war, they found refuge and a permanent home up in the foothills outside of Atlanta. Together, they began to build a life together. Melissa set up her art studio in the barn. Jonas, not able to speak English very well, spent his time gardening and raising livestock. Working hard, they eked out a meager living.

Being so afraid that Jonas would be discovered for whom he really was, they never attempted to marry. They didn't want to arouse any suspicions. Everyone was already on edge about Germans hiding inside the United States, war criminals, spies, and saboteurs. If anyone discovered Jonas' true identity he may get arrested or even deported back to Germany or France, to possibly face a tribunal. No one could ever find out that he wasn't really Pierre Laurent, a former business owner from Paris.

Poor Jonas never was able to leave behind the horrible memories that followed him. The war was never far away. Neither was the real Pierre Laurent. He haunted Jonas' dreams, startling him awake at night, or in the daytime, every time something reminded him of him. They smell of the hedgerow, the muddy splatter on his boots, or the blood. And all of the voices, of men pleading for mercy as they were tortured—screaming out for death—became torturous echoes inside his head that would never cease. They never gave him a moment of relief. Slowly, over the passing years, he felt himself dying inside once again, avoiding the painful memories the only way he knew how. He couldn't seek medical help, not without revealing himself as the murderer he used to be. Making himself a stone, someone without feeling, absent emotion, hard as a rock, he built up a wall of resistance.

It wasn't enough. Melissa watched him slipping into madness, and there was nothing she could do to stop it from happening. Her heart and mind went into her passion—into her sculpting. It was her way of escaping from her own agony.

Melissa spent more and more time down in Atlanta. She was almost living at the museum. Joining the Atlanta Arts Association, the Women's Committee, and any other organization that could use her talents, she kept herself busy. Her favorite activity was teaching a small art class in the evenings. That's when she met Loretta.

They became acquaintances, serving together on the various committees, and volunteering to teach art classes. Never really friends, they immediately squared-off as artistic rivals. Loretta was so insanely jealous of Melissa's educational history at the Sorbonne. Not to mention her superior artistic talent. Loretta, even with all of her inherited wealth, was never able to match what that impoverished hillbilly of a woman could do. And it ate at her constantly.

Loretta secretly vowed to find a way to destroy Melissa.

Using her learned skills of nosiness, using flippant gossip like a surgical instrument, Loretta tore deeper into Melissa's hidden life up on the farm. Soon a whispering army of secret agents was on Melissa's tale, constantly watching her, eavesdropping, trying to find out what she was up to up there. Suddenly everyone was taking such an interest in her, and all about her secretive boyfriend; wanting to know what he does for work, where does he come from, who are his friends, and why don't we ever get to meet him? It was starting to feel like the Nazis were looking for him again. The lurid tactics being employed were just as diabolically effective. And they were closing in. With each passing day, with another interrogation, Melissa was running out of answers, and excuses.

There was even a rumor being spread around that she was in fact, a lesbian. No doubt that one was started by Loretta herself. Melissa's getting pregnant with David put that rumor to rest. But the daunting pursuit persisted—even as Jonas slipped deeper into madness.

Jonas eventually gave up fighting the demons in his head, and he surrendered. Falling into a comatose state, there was nothing anyone could do to pull him out again. Melissa reluctantly agreed to have him placed into the Georgia Hospital for the Mentally Insane. As he languished there, Melissa could feel her passions for life dying. She stopped sculpting, locking-up the barn, and leaving her unfinished sculptures to languish in dark silence. All she could do was stay at Jonas' side. David would stay with her older brother.

On certain rare moments, Jonas would break out of his coma, finding a brief spark of lucidness, and they would converse together in French, as they did when they were alone. In those precious moments it was like they were back in Paris, falling in love all over again.

Melissa vowed to regain her passion for sculpting—somehow. She had been working on a special carving—a life-sized sculpture similar to *The Kiss,* by Rodin. It was for Jonas, to immortalize the passion that they once knew. It was nearly completed before Jonas fell into his comatose state. After that, Melissa gave up on it, leaving it covered-up in the barn. It became her desire to finish it—if only she could find the spark, the passion, the desire that was needed, to bring the life out of the stone.

And that's about all I remembered hearing—before I blacked-out.

30

EVER WOKEN UP on a cold tile floor, not really quite sure where you were at, with your head pounding so hard you couldn't think straight? Then you know exactly how I was feeling when two young boys around 9 or 10 started poking at me, snickering, and asking, "you alright lady?"

"Ugh, where am I," I groaned, prying my red-eyes open to see them nervously smiling down at me. Pushing myself upright, my hand knocked over the empty champagne bottle, sending it rolling over the tiles until it hit against a pedestal. The clinking bottle rattled in my ears like banging cymbals. I groaned loudly and put my head into my hands—shielding it from the world.

The boys took a nervous step back unsure of what this strange, crazy looking lady, was about to do.

Luckily these two boys had stumbled across my unconscious body before any adult had. They scampered off in search of their parents as I crawled to my feet like some deranged junkie recovering from a heroin binge. They would be back within seconds. "Oh no, I've got to get out of here," I mumbled, grabbing the bottle I stumbled towards the employees exit. Wanting to vomit with a swimming head, I quickly scanned the area for any signs of David, but he had vanished, leaving me to escape on my own.

My car had managed to not get towed, somehow? It was still parked out on the street waiting for me. Screeching the tires I sped out of there hoping the police weren't on their way. Every inch of me was in pain—especially my head. All I could think was; *I need water, aspirin, and a bed,* in that exact order. My blurring eyes carried me directly home.

My queasy stomach rolled over and I fought back the overwhelming urge to puke right there at the front door. Pushing it open I stepped into the foyer on my wobbling legs. Mother's head spun around to take me in. Her lazy morning eyes went right back to the pages of her Southern Living Magazine, with her saying sarcastically, "Bout-time you got home…you had us worried sick." Her voice didn't sound concerned at all—more put out than worried.

"Sorry to bother you mother," I muttered under my breath. Stomping over to where she was sitting, I plopped down next to her and sank deep into the cushions on the couch. It felt so good to sit, letting my head fall back on the fluffy pillow, staring straight up at the ceiling fan slowly rotating—then I felt sick again—and I closed my eyes. Mother shook her disappointed head and headed off to the kitchen to get me that glass of water and two aspirins. It was like she was reading my mind, or, she was experienced enough with that condition that her reaction was now instinctual. I'm more surprised that she didn't already have the water and aspirin on the coffee table waiting for me.

"Fun night, apparently?" mother suggested with obvious sarcasm. She knew we were out celebrating. But this was the first time I had ever been out all night long, where she had no idea where I was at. "A call would have been nice." She couldn't help but throwing in a sharp jab.

Downing the water in four gulps I rested my head back on the pillow to wait for the aspirin to kick-in. "I ran into someone," I mumbled, wanting to confide in someone.

"Who was it?" Mother asked, turning her attentive eyes to me, lowering the magazine.

That sure got her attention!

Maybe I was still a bit drunk—since I let it all spill out. "David…we met up at the museum."

Mother shut her magazine and tossed onto the coffee table. "But I thought you were meeting Thomas for dinner?"

"I did…that's how it all started. We had dinner and all. Then they started ordering shot after shot until everyone was getting so wasted."

"So, then what happened?" Mother asked seductively, with a naughty little purring in her voice, urging me to go-on.

It came out of me, like the vomit I was holding down, and I revealed that, "I think Tom has been cheating on me."

"Why would you think that dear?"

"He's been running around town with some woman in a blacked-out BMW…I think? And I confronted him about it after dinner and he denied it…making up some stupid lie that wasn't believable at all."

"What did he tell you?"

"Dumb-ass tried to make me believe he was riding around with his car salesman on some extended demo ride… dumb-ass. So then I got angry. All the booze wasn't helping. I stormed out of the restaurant with Carly and left him there."

That really got mother aroused, and she purred excitedly for more, "So that's when you ran into this David fellow. Who's he?"

I turned a suspiciously disturbed eye at her. *Seriously!* Mother's not that senile—not yet. How could she have forgotten who David was so fast? "You don't remember meeting David the other night...up in the hills...out in the barn? That day we went antique hunting. It was just the other day...seriously?"

Her face went blank as she racked her fading memories. "Well, I was pretty drunk that night, remember? I was feeling worse than you do that next morning, that's about all I remember."

I sat up and glared at her angrily. "You groped his ass... remember that? I had to drag you away from him and stuff you into your car."

Mother smiled, giddily, feeling a little ashamed, in a fun way, as she replied, "Well, I do recall finding you out in that dark barn...surrounded by those statutes. And I may have gotten a little too friendly with that one that was a gorgeous naked man, so muscular and sexy. How could you blame me for that? Neither of us could keep our eyes and hands off of him," she snickered, adding, "I may just have to invest in my own nude piece of—"

"Mother, that nude sculpture was David," I huffed, making her stop. "You weren't that drunk. You can't use that as your excuse for everything embarrassing you do."

But mother wouldn't stop, as usual. "Why don't you bring this David over to the house? I would love to meet him again," She giggled suggestively.

It was more than I could handle in my hangover condition,

fuming, with my stomach churning, my pounding head was yelling at her; *you're making me ill!* Forcing my limp body off the couch I stormed up the stairs to barricade myself inside my darkly shuttered room. Tearing off my dirty clothes I flopped into my soothingly soft bed—where I spent most of the day.

Tom never called to check-up on me. Neither did David, for that matter. Ignoring Tom's snub was easy enough since I was still very angry at him. But why would David be so callous? That required an explanation, in person. *I'm going back up there!* I decided, *right now*. My blood alcohol level was still high enough to get me do something so impetuous and unpredictable. *He'd better have a good excuse for leaving me there, passed out on the floor like sum bum out on the street.*

It was nearly sundown by the time I parked outside David's home. It was dark in his house, vacant looking like the other times I was up here. Out in the barn working, I imagined. And I was right. Walking up to the open barn doors, I could hear his chisel busily striking the marble stone. It sounded a little like a woodpecker drilling into a tree trunk—giving me a comforting feeling all over for some reason. My stomach and head were feeling better. Now feeling even better as I peeked inside to see him, the master sculptor, shirtless, covered in marble dust, chipping away at his inspired creation.

On the drive up, I had prepared myself to give him a thorough verbal thrashing. My feelings were hurt terribly and I wanted to get some pay-back—to make him feel some of that same emotional pain. But when I saw him there working—all of those angry vengeful thoughts shyly melted away. "Hello," I called out softly, to not startle him too badly.

He turned and smiled, saying, "Emma, I knew you'd

come back." His hands quickly pulled the blue tarp back over, covering up the large marble block he was working on. It was his mother's piece, the one she never finished. As I walked closer, he took the edge of the tarp and pulled it further down, covering it up completely, so that I couldn't even get a tiny peek. "You look terrible," he snickered, seeing my bloodshot eyes circled by sagging dark lids, on my pale face, surrounded by my straggly pulled back ragged hair.

"Alright, I guess I deserve that?" I replied, blushing with a restrained smile. Letting him know; *I know—but you don't have to point it out!* "But why did you leave me in that condition last night?"

His smile disappeared. "You kept babbling-on about some guy named Tom...saying that you couldn't betray him...that you couldn't get involved with me right now."

I turned away, caught off-guard and completely embarrassed. "I should have told you about him...I know," I murmured. "But I was blacking-out from all the booze. I don't remember saying those things."

David went on to say, "Then the security guard came around flashing his light... and you told me to just leave you there...that you knew everyone there and it would be alright if they found you. Tom would get you off. And then you said that you could get away with anything because of who your father is. But they'd put my sorry nobody ass in jail with the other broke-ass losers. So, I left."

The sick feeling in my stomach came back with a vengeance. *How could I be so stupid...of course I must have said that to him? Sounds just like something I'd say...my feeble attempt at being humorous while sloshed out of my mind...so stupid. Like mother—like daughter!*

"I was out of my head…I didn't mean anything I may have said to you last night," I mournfully explained.

"I understand completely," David replied sweetly, "been there many times myself."

Swinging my blushing gaze up at the carving he was working on, I said, "isn't that your mother's piece you're working on?" I needed to change the subject before I puked—out of disgust with myself.

His eyes filled with a passionate fire as he looked at it. "That's right, so you do remember some of what I told you." A vibrant smile reappeared on his lips. "I've been given a spark of inspiration and I have to start finishing it. There's only one thing left to do before it'll be ready for the finishing touches."

"What's that?"

Gazing deeply into my eyes, he said, "Our trip to Paris of course."

"Why's that so important?"

There was a fire raging in David's eyes as reminded me of what he told me before I passed-out—some important details that I had apparently missed, or forgotten. "My mother did everything she could to find a way to bring my father out of his comatose state. She went over everything they ever did together, every last detail, searching for a memory, a tiny spark, anything that would help him remember her…how they fell in love."

"Yes, so what happened," I mumbled, eagerly urging him to continue.

"They first kissed while admiring the sculpture by Rodin. While admiring *The Kiss,* he stole a kiss from her that stole her heart. It was at that moment that they fell in love. She had taken him to the museum from the hospital, just hoping it would lift his spirits a little, while he was recovering from his injuries. It worked."

I blurted out, "So, she was making this copy of *The Kiss*, hoping that when he saw it, he would remember their first kiss?"

"That's right," David replied solemnly. "But she never was able to complete it."

"She couldn't finish it because she died in the crash…is that why?"

David nodded. "She took Loretta's seat when it came available. She was hoping that going back to Paris and seeing *The Kiss* again in person, would somehow fill her with enough passion to get it done in time. And that she could find a way to make it work…saving him. There was no way she could have afforded to pay for her own trip over there. Loretta donated her ticket to mother to help her out."

"Loretta feels guilty," I whispered, "she feels like she's to blame for your mother's death."

David nodded again. "That guilt has made her angry. She wants nothing to do with me or my family anymore…anything that reminds her of what happened." His eyes dropped to the ground, tearing up as he said, "that's why I have to go to Paris. I have to find the passion she was searching for. It has to be carved out from this stone…to bring it back to life. There's a very nice hotel close to the museums called the Hotel d'Orsay. I've been there a couple of times and I know you'll love it. You should ask for room 212. That's my room."

I could feel myself melting inside as the idea swept over me—us together, all alone in Paris.

David smiled wide, saying, "Meet me inside the Rodin

Museum on the sixteenth day of May. That's on a Saturday I think?" Giving me a weird cockeyed look, he advised me to, "Wear a long raincoat."

I suppose he expected it to rain?

"Alright, I'll be there," I mumbled, wondering what he was planning.

Turning to face the tarp, he was entranced, inspired, in a way that only an artist can be. He needed to get back to work. With a stern voice, David then told me, "We'll only stay two nights so that you can return in time, so that you won't arouse any suspicions. Remember, room 212."

"Alright," I answered softly, but he didn't seem to be listening to me anymore. He remained focused on the stone beneath the tarp. It was as if he had become a part of the statue he was creating. "I'll leave you alone to work," I whispered, letting him go. Sauntering through the open doorway, I glanced back to watch him lifting up the tarp, just high enough to find the spot where he had stopped working.

David merely nodded as I left. Fixated on that spot, he took another blow, chipping away another piece of the rock. He could see something in there that was hidden from me. Something he had to bring out.

"OK, well then, I'm going, and I'll meet you at the Rodin Museum on that Saturday as we planned, right?"

David nodded, before making another exacting strike.

31

BEFORE I KNEW it I was boarding my flight to Paris. It was the most excited I had felt in years. Not because I was on my way to Europe, no, since I had made that trip three times before. Once on a school sponsored trip, the other two with the family. None of the prior trips were eventful or memorable in the least. There was no desire to see anything over there; getting drug around by the nose like some farm animal, caged-up inside tiny hotel rooms with no hot water, forced to trudge for miles through dreary musty old castles, cathedrals, and yes, all the museums. Only, not the ones I wanted to visit. Mother and father set their own agenda and created their own itinerary, without consulting us kids. Nothing could have been more boring—at the time.

This time it was definitely going to be different!

I only packed a small carryon bag, since I would only be gone for three nights. My raincoat was slung over my arm. It was an overnight flight leaving late in the afternoon. As the plane rose into the sky, the sun was already dropping, going down faster as we soared over the Atlantic Ocean. My coach seat was so uncomfortable. Shimmering and squirming for the next nine hours was pure torture—absolutely not a wink of sleep—with a businessman seated right next to me reading his newspaper. His overhead light stayed on the entire time, with his hands rustling the sheets of paper constantly. Even my eye shades were useless. If I did manage to nod-off for a second, he would accidently nudge me with his elbow, or cough, or clear his throat, or have to get up to use the restroom. As the wheels finally touched down in Paris, everyone shuffled in their seats preparing to disembark. I couldn't get off that plane quick enough.

A taxi whisked me from the airport into the city center. It was bleak outside, overcast and gray, and much colder than I expected it to be this time of year. My thin Atlanta skin was no protection. Now I was thankful David told me to bring the long coat. It was dreamlike as we drove along the bustling corridors passing the quaint cafes and shops. We passed the Notre Dame Cathedral, giving me Goosebumps. *I'm really in Paris*. The driver understood a little English— just enough to get me to my Latin Quarter hotel anyways. Abruptly hitting the brakes he jumped out and set my bag on the curb. I stepped out and looked up at the six story white stone building. A doorman suddenly appeared to snatch up my suitcase and hold open the door, waiting for me to walk inside. He directed me over to the check-in desk.

The lobby was small but nicely appointed with Italian marble floors, dark hardwood paneling, Persian rugs, with aristocratic oil paintings on the walls, all illuminated from the dainty light from an enormous antique crystal chandelier. I could inhale the age of the place, with the thick odor of *old* hanging in the air. An irritated clerk with a tiny thin mustache took my passport. A stern, grumpy older gentleman with a balding scalp, gray sideburns, and deep craggy wrinkles making him appear to be even older than the motel itself. Without bothering to use a precious moment to welcome me, he busied himself jotting down my information. Looking up at me somewhat suspiciously, he asked, "You are only staying with us for two nights, Madam Morgan?" He didn't allow me the opportunity to say anything in broken French. It was evident by his demeanor that hearing my vulgar attempt would have disturbed him far too badly.

"That's right," I answer softly, feeling light headed as my drooping eyes took everything in. It all seemed surreal. I was completely out of my element. The clerk didn't seem to hear me, or listen, as he kept scribbling on his guest register. Taking a peek at it, I asked, "Has David Laurent checked into room 212 yet?"

His pen stopped moving, as his cold glaring eyes rolled up at me. "There's no gentleman by that name registered in room 212."

"That's the room he should be staying in," I murmured, "Are you certain he's not here?"

"I'm quite certain madam." His eyes rolled back down, to where he was starting to write once more.

"I would like that room then," I requested boldly—before he could assign *my* room, *for* me.

His pen stopped. There was a long solemn pause, as if he had just heard that someone close to him had perished—a breathless moment. His eyes remained on the page of the register, as he asked me, "How did you learn of our fine hotel madam…not by mere coincidence I imagine?"

"My friend recommended I stay here…in that room."

The old clerk's eyes rolled back up to stare at me. His grizzled face was expressionless, his dark-brown eyes cold.

He took his time, this time, to closely examine my face. Now, I was not just another American tourist that needed to be herded through his lobby. Hardening his gaze on me, he asked me, "why that particular room?"

I wasn't prepared for that question, not at all. It was hard enough to just stay awake. *Is he serious?* I was asking myself, as he glared at me, waiting for my answer. "My friend told me it was his room, whenever he stays here," I tried to explain.

"There are lots of nicer rooms on the upper floors," he suggested, intently. "How about I put you in a top floor suite with a nicer view?" He was already reaching around for the key, without giving me a moment to think. All of the room keys were hanging on the wall besides him, arranged from the first floor, up to the sixth, with twelve rooms on each floor. He was about to remove the key for room 608, before I managed to stop him.

"No…no thanks…I'll take 212…thank you," I blurted out, stammering nervously, boldly insisting on having *my* room.

Turning to face me he slammed his palm down on a bell—summoning the bell-hop. The young man from the door rushed over and retrieved my bag. "212," the clerk told him. Reaching his other hand beneath the front desk in front of him—he slowly pulled out my key. It was a skeleton key, unlike the keys to the other rooms. This key must have come with the original lock, for the original door.

Holding out the key for the bell-hop, he hesitated. The old man nodded at him to take it, and go. Slowly, the bell-hop took the key, before nervously looking over at me. For some reason it took him a moment to remember which way to go. "Please follow me," the bell-hop finally requested. He then scurried-off down a back hallway.

The old clerk stopped me before I walked away, to say, "If you are disturbed for any reason, please let me know. I will assign you to a *nicer* room."

With a loud nerve cringing squeal the bell-hop pushed the door open. Immediately I realized what the old man was trying to warn me about. The room probably hadn't been used in months, maybe even years. Flicking on the light the bell-hop plopped my bag on the bed and rushed out without even considering a tip, leaving me alone inside the barely lit room. Only the sunlight forcing its way through the thick curtains let me see. There was a queen sized bed, covered in a darkly colored duvet. Matching pillow covers with tiny tassels. Older handmade furniture, fashioned from dark imported hardwoods. On the dresser there stood a bust of some French dignitary from another century.

My eyes stopped dead, on the statuette sitting on a pedestal in the far corner. It looked very similar to the one that David's mother had done—the one of her standing over him as a young child. It was a young man and woman, draped in flowing togas, embracing lovingly, with yearning lips that were about to kiss. It made me melt inside, and my heart swooned—realizing how much I missed him.

The bed was calling to me, and I would not disappoint. Just a little nap, I told myself as I undressed and crawled beneath the sheets. And just that fast, out like the lights, I was fast asleep.

The feeling of a hand stroking my arm startled me awake. It was even darker in the room with the sun setting outside. Jostling upright, I saw him. It was David seated on the bed next to me—wearing nothing at all. My head was still blurry, and I was hoping that I wasn't dreaming. Reaching over, I hit him hard on his arm, groaning, "Where the hell have you been?"

With a sweet disarming voice he replied, "My connecting flight got delayed in New York City."

That made perfect sense, and I couldn't fault him for that. Lying back on my pillow, I relaxed and took him all in, as he stood up and meandered across the room. "When did you get in?"

"About an hour ago," he said while staring down at the marble statuette of the man and woman embracing. "Sorry if I scared you…I wanted to let you sleep while I got a shower and shaved."

He must have been as quiet as a church mouse for me to not have heard anything. I'm a light sleeper—or so I thought? I couldn't remember hearing the creaking hinges, squeaking water pipes, or the water running, nothing at all? Must have been overly tired from staying awake all last night? But seeing him standing there in the buff, right in front of me, was all the heart pounding stimulation I needed to get my stalled-out engine jump started. I was plenty awake, and very aroused, now. "Are you ready for bed…or are you wanting to go out?" I asked him shyly, unsure of his intentions.

The way he was standing there, in the low-light, with his eyes fixed on the statuette—it was haunting. *It must hold some very special meaning for him?* "Was that one of your mother's pieces?" I asked softly, not wanting of pull him out from his spell. My eyes moved down the carved stone with him, taking in the delicately carved details. Facing each other, face to face, the man and woman were entwined as lovers, making one person, with nothing separating them—connected not only physically, but emotionally, with lusting eyes that wanted nothing more than to be together, forever. It was mesmerizing. We could share their every emotion. Two people melding themselves together with pure unrelenting passion. A pure love carved in stone.

"It's very beautiful," I moaned. I think he could tell that it was arousing me—giving me warm tickling butterflies all over. That must have been the reason he insisted that we share this room together. He knew that carving would have that effect on me—on us.

"My mother made it for my father, after they met. She was forced to live in this room by the Nazis after they occupied Paris. This was expression of love that she felt for him… back then."

"Why is it still here?" I asked, delicately.

"They had to escape together quickly and couldn't take it with them. They could only take very little, clothes and what they could carry. She intended on taking it back with her to Atlanta on her return flight, but the hotel owner refused to allow her to take it…and she couldn't afford to buy it back since he wanted too much money for it."

Breaking away from his memories David sauntered over to the window. He lifted the curtain a little-bit to peek outside. "Let's stay in tonight," He suggested with a sly grin. Moving slowly back around the edge of the bed, running his fingers up the length of my covered leg, until he touched the top of the duvet. Goosebumps tingled all over. With a slow cascade, he peeled back the bed cover—slowly uncovering my naked body. Standing still, he took me in, with lovely devouring eyes. "What shall we do to entertain ourselves," he smiled sinfully.

"Well, get into bed, and we can try and figure something out, *together*," I suggested playfully. Sliding over I made room for him, next to me. Lying down, he pulled the duvet up over us. Even though his entire body was as hard as stone, he was warm and comforting to touch. My fingers stroked his hair, so I could see his eyes. Over his broad shoulders I began to explore him, moving cautiously down along his bulging muscular arms, until my fingertips felt his rippling abs—causing him to tense up with flexing delight. A spontaneous smile came over him—me too.

Wrapping my arms around his waist I pulled him in to me. The length of our feverish bodies pressed together. His throbbing manhood rubbed over my inner thigh as he became aroused with blood pumping passion. Lifting my leg, I made space for him to fulfill his potential—all the way to my—.

A light rap on the door interrupted us. "Excuse me, madam," the bell-hop called through the closed door.

"Yes, what is it?" I yelled back begrudgingly.

"There is an urgent phone call for you at the front desk, can you take it?"

Glancing around, I couldn't see any phone in the room. *It must be Lisa? No one else knows that I'm here. What the hell could be so important that she would call me now?*

Throwing back the duvet, I called out, "Yes, I'll be right out." Jumping to my feet I threw on the same clothes that I had arrived in. They were piled on the side-chair where I had tossed them. David rolled over to send me off with a look of—*really?* "Don't lose that thought," I said, throwing a squishy-lipped-kiss at his utterly frustrated, disappointed, blushing face. He sent me back a smack with his luscious lips to let me know he'd be waiting for me, *right here.*

Stepping out into the hall I pulled the door shut behind me, making certain it was secure. Didn't want to leave it open for any passing hotel patrons to get a glimpse of David's sublimely naked body—since that was all mine. "This had better be damn important," I murmured as I tore down the hallway to the front desk. The old clerk was waiting for me, holding the phone in his hand. There was no way to judge how bad the news might be, or who was might actually be on the other end of the call, by the looks of the old man's cold dead stare. Taking the receiver I put it to my ear and listened for a moment, hoping to get some clue to who it could be. The line was as cold and silent as the old man's face. "Hello, this is Emma," I reluctantly took the call.

"I thought you were going to Florida for a couple of days?"

Shit—it's Tom!

Wanting to hand the receiver back to the old clerk and run—I fumbled around for a good-enough lie. "Well, there was a change of plans…and I…it seemed like a good time to get away and—

Tom's angry voice cut me off before I could think of anything even somewhat believable, saying, "a friend of mine that works in a shoe store happened to run into Lisa while she was shopping up in Buckhead. Lisa didn't go to Florida, and obviously she isn't even with you is she?"

"No," I whispered sheepishly into the phone. The old man grimaced before turning to walk away. He could overhear Tom's loud voice in the phone.

"Lisa and everyone else are worried about you. You're acting nuts. Who exactly are you with?" Tom demanded, getting even louder.

"I'm fine Tom—," I tried to say as Tom blurted out.

"What the hell have you been doing behind my back? Now tell me who it is. You at least owe me that!"

That was the wrong thing to say!

My heart was pounding out of my chest and I was now seeing red. It didn't matter who was listening to our conversation anymore, as I yelled back at him, "Oh, I owe you!? You're the one sneaking around all the time…tomcatting with every pretty skirt that catches your eye…I owe you…I don't think so…goodbye Tom!" Placing the receiver down on the front desk I walked away, fuming. Tom continued ranting, screaming into the phone at the top of his lungs. I could hear him yelling all the way back down the hallway.

Stupid bastard!

As I got close to the room, I could see that the door was cracked open. The bell-hop was a few feet away, stiffened-up, staring pale faced at the open door. "I must not have closed it good enough," I mumbled to him as I brushed past. *Great, he must have spied David?* I imagined. *And by the way he was staring through the open door at him I would have to guess that he must be gay? And, great taste in men. Have to give him that.*

Pushing the door open I found David out of bed, standing by the dresser, getting dressed. His seductive eyes had vanished. All there was now was disappointment. "You heard us arguing?" I asked solemnly—already knowing the answer.

He sadly nodded his head, *yes.*

Our mood was dashed like the Titanic hitting that

iceberg—he had lilted, and was now giving me the cold shoulder. "I do have a boyfriend that I've been seeing for a couple of years now," I whimpered, knowing David had lost interest, for the moment. "His name is Thomas. And apparently wants to be all overly protective of me right now. He's been acting very jealous lately…for some reason?"

"You love him?" David asked softly.

"Why wouldn't I?" I blurted out defensively, as if reminding myself that; *Tom's perfect for me. He really is. He just hasn't realized it yet, not yet, but he'll want to get married soon, I'm certain.*

David spun his head around to ask, "Then why are you here with me?"

"I, uh, because he's not—," I started to answer before David cut me off.

"Because he's not the one for you—that's why."

I was about to tell him that Thomas was not being faithful to me, and I wanted to give him a dose of his own medicine. But, perhaps what David said was more accurate—maybe he wasn't the right one for me? Even if he wasn't, I couldn't bring myself to say it out loud—not at that moment. I lowered my head in submission, gesturing over to the messy bed, to say, "why don't we just sleep on it tonight…and see where we end up tomorrow?"

David stepped towards me and brushed my cheek with his hand. He leaned in to me, making think he was about to kiss me. I closed my eyes expectantly, with my lips parting, waiting to feel his lips pressing on mine. Instead, he gently kissed my cheek, whispering with his lips into my ear, "you sleep…get some rest…we'll see where we end up tomorrow."

Our devouring eyes melted together. Our breaths were

deep and passionate—feeding our desires. Before our burning flames erupted out of control once more, David opened the door, and left.

Throwing myself into our messy bed, I pulled the warm duvet over me, and floated off into a deep sleep.

32

A BUZZ OF ACTIVITY woke me up. I could hear a jumble of sounds of people talking outside the window out in the plaza, honking horns from cars in stalled traffic and thumps of footsteps passing the door. Along with the tinkling sounds of dishes being ushered around on trays let me know that it was at least lunch-time. I had overslept. Rising off the pillow I scoured the room looking for David. His side of the bed was empty. The bathroom door was wide open and it was dark and silent. He was gone.

But I remembered that he had mentioned that he wanted us to meet at the Rodin Museum. Jumping out of bed I scurried into the bathroom to begin my morning routine. *He's probably there now…brooding…still mad at me. Let him pout…he deserves it…big baby…after leaving me hanging last night.* I thought as the water streaming from the shower head slowly heated up until a refreshing steam rose up to the ceiling. A chill-to-the-bone feeling came up from the tile floor, up my legs, all the way to my head, as I started to shiver. The air around me was just as chilling. It was so cold here, compared to Georgia. Goosebumps swelled-up again, but not the fun sensually erotic kind. *I hate this kind…brrrrr!*

As I opened the hotel room door to depart for the day, I paused to run over a checklist in my head—purse, yep, map, got-it, raincoat, nope. Got the coat and headed for the lobby. All the tourists and business travelers were busy coming and going—going mostly—departing for adventures of their own. A brisk wind hit me as I stepped outside tossing around my *just finished* hair. My Paris city map flapped in the wind getting all tangled-up. The doorman held the door so that it wouldn't hit me. With a painted-on-smile, he inquired politely, "Would you like some assistance madam…a taxi, or, help with some directions perhaps?"

"Can I walk to the Rodin Museum from here?" I asked, fumbling with the map to try and get it under control, to where I could look at it.

"Yes madam…not far…only a few blocks away," He answered, still smiling. "Here, let me show you on the map." His well-trained eyes quickly located the museum on the map and his finger plotted my shortest route. "You see there…is not far at all." He gestured kindly.

I also noticed another museum on the map—one that was very close by, and not far out of the way. Instead of taking a left, I'd take right up ahead, taking the road to the l'Orangerie Museum, at the Place de la Concorde. "Thank you very much," I smiled back. Moving with the wind I walked briskly down the narrow street. Within a few steps the history of Paris was seeping into my veins, making all my juices flow. Feeling the cold midmorning breeze blowing across my face with the soft sunlight warming my delicate skin—every part of me was coming to life.

Reaching a bridge that crossed over the River Seine, I slowed down. The Eifel Tower was sticking-up in the distance surrounded by low-hung gray clouds that were being swept along by a passing cold front coming in off the English Chanel. Wide open spaces with chatting friends sitting leisurely at café tables, sipping coffee, with yapping tiny poodles on leashes at their sides, buzzing scooters and flowers everywhere—it was a living dream. *Why don't I live here?* I pondered while trying desperately to take it all in. Taking a moment of respite from my worries, I forced myself to sit down at one of the tables and ordered a sandwich with coffee and water. *Oh la la…Now this is living.*

All too soon I was back on my feet making a bee-line for the l'Orangerie museum. The inside was even more inspiring than the city outside. Every impressionist artist that I adored was on display—including paintings by Cezanne, Gaughan, and Manet. Not to mention my absolute favorite of them all, Monet, and his ever pleasing water lilies. Walking into the immense rotunda room where it was displayed took my breath away. Taking a seat on the padded bench I stared at the wall where the painting begins, in the morning, with the fresh sunlight just peeking over the trees, lightly springing to life his garden, pond, and lilies. What a spectacular show! Shifting around on the seat I followed as the sun slowly rose, getting brighter as the day progressed, with the light becoming brighter, reflecting a vivid array of colors, causing the water to reflect a shimmering palate of life. Moving over to where the sun crests and starts to make its fall, slowly fading to oranges and pink, deep purples, deepest of blues, fading away to night—where it would start all over again in the morning.

Sauntering through the rest of the museum, not really taking time to devour details, I noticed how every painting, sculpture, or design, had an airy carnival life feel to it, all brightness with smiles and play. Fun, would be my best description. Capturing the king's garden and keeping it alive for everyone to enjoy must have been the curator's intent. My heart was much lighter as I walked out the exit door. Beams of warming daylight gave me some comfort. The cozy and safe feeling I remember having when my mother used to wrap me up in my baby blanked on cold winter nights.

I was feeling so good that I nearly forgot about David—oops!

Racing on foot down the boulevards, I followed the map until reaching the gates to the Rodin Museum. Walking onto the grounds, moving across the manicured lawn, seeing the dark bronze statues arrayed out front—I suddenly felt cold again. *The Shades* were there to greet me, all three of them looking even gloomier than I had ever imagined them to be. The naked men with their straining necks bent over as they peered down into the underworld, where souls of the damned were being delivered up for eternal punishment. The Thinker was there too, apparently pondering his own eternal demise.

Wow, my heart sank low.

Once inside the old mansion that now served as the main museum, I wandered around searching for David. *Don't grab any naked man's ass*, I snickered to myself. *Oh, I'll try not to.* Then I realized that I was standing right in front of Rodin's first signature piece, *The age of Bronze*, a life-sized bronze statue of a completely naked man standing upright with his arms raised up above his head, and I was staring straight down at his—.

"See anything you like?" David whispered in my ear, making me clench-up and squirm.

"You've got to stop doing that," I gushed nervously. Spinning around he gave me a sweet kiss on the cheek to say *I'm sorry*.

"About time you showed up...I was getting worried that you ditched me," He said jokingly with a smile.

"I got distracted by Paris," I snickered.

He stared at me intently as if he understood, and stated, "I'm glad you got to enjoy the l'Orangerie Museum. I know it's your favorite."

With a puppy dog, eyebrow lifted, tilted head look, I asked, "How did you know that?"

"That you love impressionist art, or, that you couldn't resist going there first?"

"Both."

David shifted and moved away from me, like the other art patrons lingering about, speaking in hushed tones, "I've had my eye on you for a very long time now. I know a lot about how you think."

"Oh really....some kind of stalker, huh...so then, who's my favorite artist and what's my absolutely favorite work of art."

David raised an eyebrow of his own, in deep reflection, before answering, "Well, if I had to guess that...I would have to guess Monet...and his *Water Lilies*."

"Good guess," I replied, a little taken-aback. *How the hell does he know that, I wondered? Maybe he has been stalking me?* "Should I be worried about how you could possibly know that about me?"

"It's easy," he said confidently, "you spend so much time down by the lake, most mornings, and often in the after-noon, just sitting and watching. And I know how much you love art, especially paintings. And you seem to linger longest whenever you're looking at the impressionist paintings. You especially seem to like the ones with the brightest palettes of color, or those with less distinctive images. Sometimes I think you go into some kind of mesmerized trance while staring at them."

He really is a stalker!?

"So, do you creepily follow many other girls around the museums?" I half-jokingly had to ask, hoping to reassure myself that I'm safe.

"Only you I'm afraid," he replied with a silly sinister Dracula face. The one where the girl discovers the villains true identity, and now has to be killed, turned, or eaten, or whatever that villain likes to do to women. "There's something else about you I also know," he added, smiling devilishly as someone does when they are holding back a secret.

"Oh really…and what's that pray tell?" We were giving each other wide grinned expectant stares waiting for him to spill it.

"I know that it was you who cracked the back of the head of that marble bust at the High."

My face was stunned—astonished in fact—and I couldn't respond. My bulging-out eyes asked the question my mouth couldn't, "how in the hell could you know that?"

"I've seen you checking on it…to make sure that the super glue was still keeping the broken piece stuck in place… when nobody else is around," he whispered, letting me know that he really had been secretly watching me.

I couldn't even breath—knowing that I had never told anyone about that, ever!

"But I know something even more disturbing about

you," David said softly, as he drifted up very close to me, pressing his hand onto mine, with his face close enough to taste his sweet breath—whispering gently, "You don't care for Rodin's work at all."

Staring into his caring eyes, I swayed my head back and forth, saying silently, *no*, while now knowing, that he understood me, the real me, completely. He could feel me, how I felt, in ways that no other person possibly could. Nothing was hidden from him.

Squeezing on my hand, he said softly, "Too depressing right?"

My head nodded, *yes*, knowing that he was right, once again.

All I had to do was lean forward and our lips would be touching—kissing. But I held back, staying planted, my head still nodding as he spoke the truth to me.

"You hate how real it all is...showing their brash emotions...the anguish and coarseness of real life displayed in sculptured forms. How Rodin was able to peel back the skin on the models and pull out their inner tortured emotions... forcing you to feel their inner pain...right?"

"Yes," I whispered back to him, wanting him so badly. I could feel his soul in mine, with his burning desire, desperately wanting me, so painfully it was hurting him deep inside. *Let it out and kiss me*! I wanted to scream, and then wrap my arms around him to smother him up with my fiery passionate kissing right here in the middle of the museum.

But he stepped away. *Ugh*!

Pulling me by the hand he led me around each of the exhibits. Marble and bronze sculptures, naked men, contorted women, and somber children, perfectly formed hands and faces, all of them sad and depressing, yet, every one of them tantalizingly mesmerizing, each in their own way. "Some people believe that Rodin was able to actually capture the spirit of these lost soles in his sculptures of them," David stated somberly. "I'm one of them."

"You believe that they are somehow alive…that these images have living spirits still inside of them?"

David looked at me sincerely, nodding, *yes*. "Don't see the sculpture, or the metal, or the marble…but see the emotion. Those people are still here. I can see them. Oh yes, they are captured there for sure."

He was getting way too serious for me, and I wanted to lift the mood, saying jokingly, "So then, if you sculpted me…then I would be captured in it forever?"

David nodded, *yes*, and whispered intently, "forever." And then he smiled with a big silly grin, making me feel foolish.

"Oh you idiot…you're such a weirdo," I groaned, smacking him on the arm. He made claws with his fingers, sneering and bearing his knowing fangs, to make me squeal with squishy delight as he chased me around the displays. Everyone close by turned to look—shaking their heads in disgust.

When we finally felt embarrassed enough—noticing the others with their disapproving frowning faces glaring at us— we settled down. Taking a seat to relax, we started in on each other, teasing and tickling each other until our stomachs ached from the fighting off the hard giggling laughter. We could have been two middle-school kids by the way we were cutting-up. A couple of teenagers even gave us the snotty stink-eyed look of a prude. Nice!

The rest of our afternoon was spent gawking at the

distorted images that Rodin created. It was definitely an emotional experience just as David had said. Each of them seemed hopelessly trapped within a perpetual state of unhappiness. All except for one piece—that caught our attention like no other. David squeezed my hand again as we gazed up in lusty wonder at, *The Kiss*. My knees went wobbly as we gazed upon the life-sized marble carving of two naked lovers embracing. The man was supporting the woman with his hand on her back. With her fingers tangled in his hair, she was pulling his face to hers so that she could take what she most desperately wanted—his passionate kiss.

"Getting any good ideas?" I whispered into David's ear. Turning slightly, with a sexily taunting nod, he gave me a look that made me light-headed. My eyes closed down, expecting him to kiss me, I started to pucker-up—but he didn't.

"Come here," he said quietly, pulling me along behind him. Taking me over to a private spot in the back, we leaned against a wall. *Finally, here it comes*, I silently prepared for him to take me. Leaning in close, he whispered to me, "I've got something planned for later…think you can handle it this time?" There was a naughty gleam in his eyes. It wasn't an impromptu sexual rendezvous he was planning, not at all. It was something far more daring. I nodded, *oh yes; I'll do whatever it is you want.*

_33_

"**I**'LL GO GET everything ready," David said with a wink. Rushing away he disappeared into the hidden recesses of the Rodin Museum—back where only the employees are permitted to go.

All alone, I wandered around the morbid carvings, feeling myself connecting with them more than usual. Having plenty of time to take my time, I let myself feel the way they were expressing their tortured emotions. My own emotions flowed to the surface. _What am I doing here? What am I about to do with him? This isn't me...this isn't who I'm supposed to be._ Touching my breast my heartbeat was thumping like a bass drum. It was almost like waking up from a nightmare, feeling unsure of my own surroundings, not sure if I'm even really awake. Wondering if my whole entire life before that was only a bad dream, and now I'm actually finally waking up. _Father will kill me for doing this. He'll disown me. Thomas is going to dump me for sure. I'll probably get thrown out of Law School, lose my internship at the firm, and have to start all over again._

Walking past a mirror on the wall, I couldn't help but notice that my own facial expression was looking unnervingly similar to the carvings surrounding me—appearing helpless, scorned, frail, frightened and lost—showing on the outside, what was remaining of them on the inside, hard, cold, lifeless stone. *Don't let yourself be like them*, I told myself, beating back the urge to slink out the door and return to my hotel room, alone. *Try and be more like David, fearless and fun, living a life of meaning, creating something worthwhile.* Finding a lonely bench to take a rest, I sat down and waited for him to return. *I don't want to turn back this time. I won't.*

After a couple of hours I started getting worried, wondering if David was coming back. It was getting close to closing time without a hint of him being around. The crowds had thinned-out. All the tourists were leaving to get ready for dinner and drinks. A couple of employees were milling about, straightening and sorting, and watching. Only one security officer was over by the exit, watching as the people filed out the door. He wasn't keeping tabs on anyone. He was only there to make sure that no one tried to take anything or cause any sort of ruckus. Frail and tiny me hidden beneath my long black raincoat blended in to the surroundings as if I was wearing camouflage—no one would have noticed me at all.

Moving slowly back to the back of the museum, attempting to stay hidden from view behind the statues—slipping from one to another like some spy—I made my back to where David had disappeared. I found a small hallway that was barely lit by one small ceiling bulb dangling down. At the end of the hall was a wooden door with a black-and-white plaque on it that read: Employees Only. *Where the hell is he!*

"David…you back here?" I whispered. Only silence.

"David…where the hell, did you go to?" I called out softly, with an impatient groan. The doorknob on the Employees door turned. The door slid open. David peeked out.

"C'mon…in here," he called to me in a hushed voice. Looking back and forth nervously between the bright exhibit hall and the darkened doorway, I hesitated. "Now," David barked. Without thinking I rushed inside with him. We were inside of a large office, with a cluttered desk, a phone, piles of papers, envelopes, invoices, and boxes—all the stuff I was used to seeing as an intern at the High. David silently pointed behind me, at a door. I grabbed the knob and pulled it open. It was a very large storage closet, even larger than the office. Even more cluttered, it was stuffed with all sorts of cleaning supplies, mops, floppy brooms, long-handled dusters, rags and rags and more rags, stacks of them up to the ceiling. "For cleaning all the carvings…so much dust," David mumbled.

Gently pushing against my back, he urged me to move past the piles of supplies, back into dark cavern. In the very back we found a couple of large cardboard boxes that contained more cleaning rags. David started taking them out, emptying the boxes. We quickly stacked the rags on the outside until there was enough room for us inside the boxes. Crawling in, we hid beneath the rest of the white cotton cloth like a couple of gophers burrowing into the ground. Only our head and shoulders poked out, so that we could talk—in softly spoken whispers.

"How long do we have to wait in here," I asked.

"A couple of more hours…till everyone is gone for the night."

"What about the security guard?"

David smiled, saying, "He's always eating dinner right after sunset. So, we'll have about twenty minutes alone."

"You brought all the stuff?" I asked.

Glancing over at the walls where painting supplies were lined up on shelves, he nodded, "there's plenty for both of us. Plus, I put some extras in your coat pockets back in the room."

Feeling around in my pockets, I felt the lumps of two slender plastic paint tubes. Inside of them was enough body paint to cover my entire body. An allover tingling spark of excitement swept over me, with the realization that—*this is really happening and we're really doing this!*

David could see the building excitement on my blushing face, and he said, "This is freaking fun, huh princess?"

Wow, he thinks I'm a spoiled rich girl, with no experience with doing anything remotely dangerous or scandalous. *Maybe I didn't want all those jagged scars...did you ever think of that?* Sadly, he was absolutely right. And it hurt, to hear him say it right in my face oh-so smugly. We were complete opposites when it came to living on the edge of life—afraid of nothing, tip-toing along the edge of a mile-high cliff, staring-down the grim reaper that was stalking you and all of those sorts of things. Not for me.

"So how did you become such and thrill-seeking adrenaline junkie?" I asked snidely, now having to know how he became such a hardcore smug punk. The question actually caught him off-guard, biting him a little. Reflecting on the idea, he seemed a little sad. "I shouldn't have—"

"No it's alright," He stopped me, not letting me apologize for going there. "You're right...I have lost it...I am a bit twisted when it comes to how I've lived my life. Losing both of your parents so young can do that to a person."

I slipped my hand through the soft layers of rags, to find his buried hand. Touching his fingers with mine, I thought out loud, "You must have done all those crazy things to hide from your pain…is that it?"

His eyes reddened a little, as he reflected on himself. "Rock climbing, back-country-skiing, racing avalanches, base-jumping, motorcycles, skydiving…I suppose you're right about all that? It gets me out of my head to do dangerous things. Letting the adrenaline take over and push me to the edge. It's like being on a drug sometimes. It helps me to not dwell on things. At least it's better than taking drugs. But I confess…I did those too," he added with a less-than-innocent smile.

"What's the wildest thing you've ever done," I asked with fascinated eyes.

"It would have to be the day I fell—"

"Please don't say in love with me!" I cut him off mid-sentence, "That's not a joking around subject."

David snickered, and replied, "Let's just say it was the day I fell hard, for something…period. I let my guard down for a momentary lapse of reason, and wham!"

It was me…he definitely fell hard in love with me…period.

He glared at me with a skeptical eye, and asked, "So then, what's the craziest thing you've ever done princess?"

Without hesitating for a moment, I gushed, "Coming here with you would have to top my charts…so far. Maybe later tonight we can reach a new level of risky business."

Wow, that came out sounding very slutty. But who cares!

David was pleased with my naughty suggestion, saying, "Sounds like a plan."

It may have been the layers of cotton rags getting me all hot and bothered, with drips of perspiration running down my back, but then again, it could have been being so close to David, finally. It took every scintilla of restraint to stop my hands from slinking like evil serpents beneath the covers over to his hard body. My mind was unbuttoning his shirt, running my fingers beneath his shirt to toy with his rock-hard chest, nipples, bobbing down along his rippling abs—before popping the button of his pants. Oops, I blushed, as I tickled his zipper down—sending the temperature way up past comfortable.

"Are you alright over there?" David muttered, breaking me out of my spell. He was looking concerned at my reddening face, seeing that my hot fantasizing was heating my blood up to a rolling boil. "Maybe you'd better get out for a moment," he suggested.

Just then, a loud bang rang out as someone flung the office door all the way open. It shook the wall it hit so hard. We could hear people talking fast, a jumble of mumbling words, as they talked over each other. They were in a hurry, trying to get everything done for the day, so they could check-out.

"They'll be gone soon," David whispered, while pulling rags up on top of his head, trying to cover up every inch of him. I did the same, and we tossed rags over each other until we were buried out of sight. The office door opened and slammed shut a few more times with people rushing in and out, making calls, shuffling papers, and putting things away. Soon, it quieted down again. After about another twenty minutes or so, we could hear somebody walking around in the office, all alone.

Unexpectedly, the utility closet door creaked as it was being pushed open. Hard soled shoes stepped inside and shuffled towards us, way back in the back. A flash of bright light glowed on the thin covers draped over our eyes. *Stay still*, is all I could think, *don't move.* Anything but calm inside, I was a frightened fawn quivering all over as the wolf sniffed around my hiding bush. *Get ready because he knows you're in here*! I was screaming to myself. Not soon enough, the flashing light turned back towards the door. Shuffling footsteps retreated back out into the office. David and I stayed frozen in place until we believed the security guard had made his way all the way back out into the main exhibit hall.

David took a quick peek out, looking like some silly prairie-dog, and then whispered, "Should be all clear now…we can get out."

Bursting out from underneath the pile of warm tiny blankets it was such a relief to get out of there, like being reborn and getting a first fresh breath. "Oh thank God," I whimpered, "I thought for sure we were totally busted?"

David raised his eyebrows with a hell-raiser look in his eyes. "That was only a warmup," he whispered wickedly, "Now comes the really fun part."

34

STANDING IN THE near pitch-black storage room, with the smells of cleaning supplies, bleach and ammonia, tickling my nose, we searched for a good place to get ourselves *ready*. "Will I need a change of panties after this?" I asked whimsically, to lighten the mood. David's face was mostly hidden in the shadows, along with the rest of him, but I could hear his faint hushed laughter.

"You won't need any panties at all, for what we are going to do next," he muttered under his breath. "Let's get undressed," he told me, sounding so matter-of-factly, as if he was some math teacher or something like that. He had already shed his coat and was unbuttoning his shirt, fast. It was shocking. I hesitated, to rethink this whole thing. "Am I making you uncomfortable," he asked sympathetically, seeing that I wasn't joining right in on the action.

"It's not that—," I started to explain, when he cut me off.

"It's alright...I'll go out into the office to get ready... since it's your first time and all."

Before I could reply he was almost to the door. Vanishing like a vampire he left the room, shutting the door so fast I didn't have a split-second to reconsider. Once he was gone, it did actually feel much more comfortable. I've been naked in front of guys before. Sex wasn't a big deal for me, so it wasn't *that*, that was making me nervous. It was getting naked in front of David that way, so casually, letting my hair down on a dare right out in the open. One of my favorite sexual fantasies is being taken up against a large Oak Tree out in a wide-open field, in broad daylight, for the whole world to watch. But tonight I wanted something completely different—this was special. I wanted for everything to be sexy and sensual of course. It needed to be perfectly endearing. And most of all, the most memorable even of *our* entire lives.

I shed my overcoat, letting it slide down my arms before softly dropping to the floor in a small pile. Unbuttoning my blouse and removing my bra, my fingers unloosened my pants, allowing them to fall down to my ankles. Even though it was very dark I peeked around nervously, making sure that no one else was inside the room—a habit of mine since childhood. Pinching the top of my silk panties I rolled them over my hips, sliding them slowly down along my thighs—wondering the whole time if I was making a huge mistake—until they were all the way down to where I could step out of them.

Too late! There I was, standing bare-ass-naked in a utility storage closet in the Rodin Museum. And it felt awesome!

Taking a tube of body paint from my coat pocket, I bit off the top of the spout like a rabid animal. I squeezed out smooth glops of sticky paint into my hand to make a goopy blob. Not being able to see what it looked like I had to imagine the grayish-white sticky paint coloring my skin as I started to rub it all over. First my legs, in case someone busted in and chased me out. At least it wouldn't be *so strange looking,* if I suddenly had to go running down a crowded Paris street. Up to my waist, over my stomach, across my buns, smoothing it over my warm breasts—it started feeling kind of good, very good, in a sick perverted way, as I smeared the slippery muddy paste all over every inch of me. My nipples raised up, hard and pokey. I couldn't stop myself from wondering, *why didn't I let David paint me with this stuff? That would've been way more pleasurable. This definitely won't be the last time we do this together.*

Arms, shoulders, neck, and face—every inch of me was now painted—all except for my hair. That was asking too much. I struggled with myself, forcing my fingers to rake the sticky goo through my long strands of blonde hairs. All I managed to do was make long messy streaks. Not being able to see what I was doing—it was good enough.

Pulling on my long coat I left the rest of my clothes on the floor. Scooting over to the office door, I called out in a hushed voice, "David I'm all painted and ready to come out." He didn't answer me. Cracking open the door I could not see David anywhere in the office. He was long done and gone, getting finished painting himself way before I even got started. Poking my head out the door I couldn't see anyone down that hallway. Remembering that I was supposed to bring a camera to document our triumphant escapade, I patted-down my coat pockets. It was still in my pocket— patiently waiting—ready to capture our moment of purely unabashed pseudo-pornographic-history.

But I couldn't go any farther. Staring through the open doorway, not wanting to take a step outside—it was like being perched up on the highest diving platform, inching up to where you can look over the edge, all the way down to the rippling pool water below. Feeling the whole time like somebody is sneaking up behind you to push you off—and you suddenly freeze. The thought of going any further was just too frightening. *Don't do it*, I told myself, *there's no going back…once you go out there.*

"Emma. Come on. It's safe," David called to me. His voice was as soft as the air at the lake, as gently soothing as watching a drifting leaf on top of the water. Floating to my ears, he beckoned to me with butterfly wings. "C'mon Emma…come out to me."

I stepped out into the darkened hallway. Moving quickly on pitter-patter feet I rushed out into the main exhibit hall. Surrounded by black and white, dark and light, stone and glass—I was all alone and ready to be placed out on display. David reappeared from out of the shadows. His body a grayish-white marble demi-god figure. Naked, striking a poetic pose, he motioned for me to join-in-with-him, and become like stone. Dropping my cloak I revealed myself—a voluptuously sculpted Aphrodite on the hunt—a living Goddess of love. I gave him all that was real, of me, inside and out. Letting my emotions surface, expressing itself on my canvas of a body, nothing could have been more true to me in that moment. It was so real, so vibrant, so loving.

We moved together, eye to eye, not blinking, without talking, mind in mind, connected on every level of existence. It was magical. Our bodies swirled, arms stretching, leg muscles bulging under the pressure, as we contorted around each other to form our own sculpted masterpiece. Together we became as one—giving, while taking—creating.

David froze, interrupting, to say, "Set up the camera…I don't want to miss out on this moment."

Leaping back over to my coat I gingerly picked through the pockets, getting spots of paint on it. Finding the camera I set it up on a display, pointing the lens in our direction. After setting the timer I hastily rejoined David in our ritualistic dance in the shadows. A soft moonlight from the large windows illuminated us. Our painted skin glowed a pale blue causing us to look just like a couple of spirits floating about the museum floor.

David whirled himself around and flung his heavy body down onto a bench. Pulling me towards him I plopped down next to him. Gazing up into his piercing eyes, my leg instinctively slid up over his leg. Pressing my calf down between his legs, I pried his legs apart, tickling his calf with my toes, running them softly up and down. Running my hand up the back of his neck I plunged my fingers into his thick hair, gently pressing his face closer to mine. Moving in to kiss him—he hesitated and pulled back. Leaning up, I pressed his head down to mine while pinning his leg beneath my squeezing thigh—until our lips touched. A spark of passion swept over me as we pressed together hard, kissing deeply, passionately. We explored one another with every sense of our being. I tasted and inhaled him—consuming his ecstasy—knowing that nothing could ever be sweeter.

It was my most passionate moment ever. My head was swimming. It was hard to concentrate. Everything was surreal. Our kiss seemed to go on forever—till. The lightning bright flash of the camera snatched us out of our dreamy fantasy. Turning to look, we saw another light in the distance. A flashing light was darting back and forth as a security guard came racing into the room.

We jumped up and David tore off, disappearing into the

darkness. "This way," he called back to me in a desperately hushed voice.

I started after him, but then remembered, *my coat!* Spinning around I leapt across the tile floor to snatch up my coat and fling it over my body before fleeing. Dodging the searchlight, I ducked behind a large statue, shaking and scared, feeling like an escaping convict. The second the light turned away, I scampered in the direction that David had gone. Finding an exit door I slammed my body against it as I tried to make a run for it. I hit hard against the glass and my semiconscious body was bounced back onto the floor. Staggering to my feet, I high-tailed-it, stumbling through the darkness, feeling dizzy, disoriented, and lost.

"This way," David called out to me at the last second. The guard was hot on my trail, and coming at me fast. The beam of his flashlight caught the backside of my coat as I fled through an open door. I found myself out in the garden surrounded by looming dark statues. David was gone. Rushing across the lawn I made my final escape, running through the open gate and down the street in the direction of my hotel. "David, where are you?" I called out quietly all the way back, hoping to find him. It was both exhilarating and frightening at the same time—flashing along the lonely dark streets, holding my coat tightly around my naked body as a shield, feeling like everyone who noticed me was staring in my direction, pointing me out.

Fighting back surging feelings of anger at David for leaving me behind, I was simultaneously being overwhelmed with mind-bending giddy hysterical laughter. Clearly it was the ultra-high adrenaline rush bending me emotionally back and forth—in one second wanting to wring his neck, and the next, wanting to rape him. *I had better hear one amazing excuse come out of his sexy mouth!* I made a sincere effort to reserve final judgment, until I could see his face, and then I would either punch him, or kiss him.

Clambering back inside the hotel, rushing past the door-man with my face half-covered, I raced down the long hall-way to my room. The door was still locked. Patting my pockets, I realized that the key was still in my pants pocket—back in the museum!

Thank goodness there was no hotel or room information on the skeleton key. But, I would have to retrieve a spare key from the clerk. Shit!

Pulling my collar up around my neck and face I did my best impression of some shy celebrity that was trying to remain incognito and sauntered slowly up to the front desk. With my face down, paint caked hair dangling all over, I mumbled for some attention, "hello, desk clerk."

The craggy old man suddenly appeared across the desk. His facial expression hadn't changed at all. Still sullen and nasty, he stood there silently glaring at me as if I had dis-turbed him—now more than ever.

Keeping my head bowed hoping that he wouldn't notice the streaks of paint clinging to my face, I muttered, "I'm sorry to bother you with this, but I've somehow lost my key. Can I perhaps get a spare please?"

Clearing his rattling throat, he grumbled back, "there's only one other key to that room. We can't make another. So, I will have to let you in and out from now on. I'll retain the key here for the remainder of your stay."

"Yes," I humbly replied, "that would be helpful, thank you."

Following behind the old man he opened my door and let me inside. It was then that he noticed my dirty bare feet smudging up his floor. With a sickly-sour scrunched-up face he bit his tongue. I could hear him screaming at me from all the way inside of his thick head. He stood right outside glaring at me through the crack in the door, until it was all the way shut. The doorknob rattled as he inserted the key and relocked the door. He grumbled some incoherent words as he shuffled away. Thankfully I couldn't hear him well enough to make it out. It wasn't good-night pleasantries, I'm quite certain of that.

"You made it back. I was getting worried," David said softly. He was standing inside the bathroom doorway, lurking in the dark.

Seeing his face—I was his. Tearing my coat away I pushed my naked body against his, forcing him back into where we stepped into the antique claw-footed bathtub. Turning the spout the shower erupted. We stood kissing as the water streamed down over us like rain. Slowly the water warmed until it became a hot, steamy, misting waterfall. Our wandering lustful hands washed away the paint. Rubbing hands over every inch of our bodies we returned to our fleshy delights—shedding away our painted-on stony facade.

"That was fun," I whispered happily into his ear.

"We're just getting warmed up," his sultry lips whispered back.

Luring me into the bedroom David tossed me seductively onto the bed—where he took me. Over and over again, we made passionate love—with unending, muscle clenching, breath stealing, convulsing orgasms—until my mind was as blurry as one of my favorite impressionist paintings.

Everything was spinning, all bright and vivid, as I was swept away within a frenzied fantastical composition—of my own paradise.

Wow, was David ever forgiven! As my head swooned, turning in slow ecstatic circles, I couldn't even recall why I was mad at him…?

We talked in bed, in soft wilting voices, as our heads drifted back down from the heavens. Playing footsies with him, my hands explored him, in a pleasurable search for hidden muscles. The ones that I hadn't managed to discover yet. My eyes stared creepily at his face, memorizing it. "Too bad we have to leave in the morning," my still quivering lips spoke sadly. Part of me was hoping that he'd tell me that we shouldn't ever leave, stay right here and move to Paris, to live happily ever after.

Of course, he didn't.

His eyes drifted over our feet under the covers, down to the foot of the bed, over to the small statuette that his mother carved. His lips stayed silent as he pondered over something that was lost to me. Finally, he reluctantly asked, "would you mind doing something for me?"

"Of course I will David," I mushily replied, rubbing my hand over his enormous rock hard chest. I gave my answer before finding out what it was he wanted. Big mistake— should have waited till the orgasm wore off—to where I could think straight again. A shimmer of pleasure was lingering between my thighs, keeping me preoccupied, making me wonder if he was perhaps able to *go at it* again. *Please, let him be able.*

Tilting his face to look me straight in the eyes, he asked

me, "would you please take my mother's statuette back home for me?"

Lifting my head with a start, I huffed, "What…you want me to steal that statute for you?"

Looking perplexed, he suggested, "Well it's not exactly stealing since it really belonged to my mother, originally. Hell, she's the one who made it. And besides, the hotel owner is really the one who stole it from *her*, along with those *damn* Nazis who forced her to live here. In all reality, it is mine."

"Why can't you take it with you?"

David seemed genuinely afraid, as he replied, "because they'll be watching me…watching me closely. The old man up at the front desk remembers me. I think he knows that it's my mother's. He'll probably be making certain that I don't try and take it with me? I can't risk getting caught…getting thrown out again."

Getting caught, again?

Glancing nervously over at the small statue I sized it up—about two feet tall, maybe forty to sixty pounds perhaps? "Well what do you expect me to do…carry it out of here with my bare hands? How am I supposed to get that out of here without being noticed and getting caught myself?"

"Your suitcase should do?" David said like an excited boy having a great idea—that is just ridiculously stupid. "It should fit inside there? Nobody would notice."

"What about my clothes David?" I gushed, not believing what I was hearing.

Making that pouty puppy-dog face, he whimpered, "Uh, well, you could leave them behind. All you need is what you'll be wearing on the plane-ride home."

How could I possibly say no to that?

Damn orgasm! Say goodbye to sound judgment.

Draping my soft body across his hard torso, we drifted fast into a deep sleep. It felt easy to rest with him there. David cradling me in his strong arms was the warmest and most safely comforting place I could ever imagine. Nothing could have mattered to me—everything was finally perfect.

35

I AWOKE THE NEXT morning feeling euphoric. Happiness had stayed with me through the long night. The bed was warm still, but David was gone. His covers flipped over as he left. Must be in the bathroom getting ready for our long flight home, I mused. I listened carefully to hear the sounds of shower or sink water splashing as he was washing or shaving. But it was so quiet. The only thing I could hear was the sounds of doorways being shut hard, with a deep rumble as the walls shook all along the hallway, accompanied by the muffled voices of people talking as they departed the hotel. "David…you up?" I called to him softly.

There was no reply. Climbing out of bed the cold air of the room gripped me, waking me completely. It was cold enough to cause my entire body to shiver at once. Skipping inside the bathroom I ran a hot shower and climbed in. All I wanted was to feel David's warm body wrapping around me like a blanket again. *He's gone out to get some coffee and croissant*, I hoped, *he didn't want to disturb my sleep, is all.*

By the time I had finished doing my hair and makeup it was getting late in the morning. No David. Waiting impatiently I studied his mother's statuette, contemplating on how I would fit it inside my suitcase, and manage to get it all the way onto the airplane—without getting caught. Throwing some of my older, less worn clothing onto the bed, I carved out some space in the middle of my bag. Eyeballing the space, I mumbled, "it will be a tight squeeze…but it should fit."

Taking the heavy marble piece with both hands, squeezing like a professional wrestler on steroids, I heaved it up and rested it flat against my chest. My knees nearly buckled as I shifted my feet to step over to the suitcase. Pain shot up my back muscles as I gently squatted-down to where I could lay the statute down on top of a soft layer of thick sweaters, just like it was some tiny infant child being placed inside a crib. "Ugh," I groaned as I let go, "now that's heavy." After stacking another protective layer of pants and sweaters over the statue I closed the top and forced the zipper around. Bulging out all over it looked like I had stuffed the suitcase with souvenirs.

Taking a seat on the mattress I tried to relax. Time seemed to be speeding up as the clock ticked away the last few precious minutes left before I had to depart. I knew that if I didn't leave soon I would miss my flight back to Atlanta. And there was *no way* that could happen! "Where the hell is he?" I fumed, while staring at the clock. Right then, there was a soft knocking on the door. David must have forgotten to take the key, I thought, as I leapt over the suitcase to rip open the door. I couldn't wait to see his beautiful face.

But it wasn't David. Instead of a smile, I was greeted by the front desk clerk's scowling face. His glassy-eyed stare went straight through me. Nothing could have been more foreboding. Morticians envied him. It was downright disturbing.

This guy could even outdo my father in being a morning sourpuss. My heart crashed down to the cold floor. "Yes, what is it now?" I asked somberly, anticipating bad news.

How could it possibly be anything else, coming from this guy?

Clearing his throat, he informed me that, "the Chief Investigator phoned this morning. He is requesting that you speak with him regarding some incident at the Rodin Museum. He has requested that you remain here until he arrives."

"What about David…has he already spoken to him…is David in custody already?" I nervously replied. That would at least explain why David never came back.

The old man looked puzzled, as he told me, "I have no knowledge of what you are speaking about madam."

He could see the growing concern on my face as I explained, "You know, the young man you let into our room…with the spare key…someone from the hotel let him in…didn't you see him…his name is David, or Zachary…he *is* staying in this room?"

"You are the only registered guest staying in this room," The agitated clerk responded. His skeptical eyes reflected his disbelief. "I have not permitted anyone else to enter into this room since your arrival. Only I have the spare key to this room. No one else would have been permitted to use this key." His hand hesitantly held out the single skeleton key.

"But he was here…with me…all night…someone must have noticed seeing him? Someone let him in this room." I muttered.

"I urged you not to take this room, madam," the old clerk replied, his bloodshot eyes and veins bulging out. Suddenly, he took a step back, away from the doorway. He was clearly now concerned about something that was inside the room. "You must checkout now…I will summon you a taxi," he said sternly, before turning and rushing towards the front desk.

"What about the Investigator?" I asked him as he walked away. He pretended not to hear me—walking even faster.

A moment later the bell-hop rushed into my room and hoisted my bag up by the shoulder strap. His face strained beneath the weight. Turning a bright red he grunted as he rushed back out. He was used to carrying extremely heavy suitcases all day long, so he managed it. Grabbing my coat and purse I stayed right on his tail, following him out to a waiting taxi. "Careful," I requested, as he plopped the suitcase in the open trunk. The doorman had the car door open for me, with a friendly smile. "Pleasant travels," he said robotically as he shut the door. Rubber screeched on the pavement as the driver sped away. In what appeared to be one long blurry flash outside my passenger widow, Paris whizzed past us. All too soon I was deposited at my Orly Airport terminal. My bag was handed-off to an airline baggage handler and taken away. Finding my gate, I sat and waited to board my flight—all alone.

Sitting there alone I watched the throng of passing travelers, hoping to catch a glimpse of David coming to meet me. He never did.

I was rushed on board and seated in my coach seat next to the window. A portly businessman wearing and sport coat over a sweater took the seat next to me. Of course, he barely fit, as he squeezed in-between the armrests, with his side-rolls resting on top of them. His overly large arm took-up half my space, forcing me to lean over closer to the window. Clutching the morning paper he was finishing off his bagel, with a sprinkling of crumbs falling over his belly. Squirming for room, he jimmied me in the side, only to give me a piti-ful, *Oh I'm sorry,* glance. That's when I noticed the dusting of dandruff all over his shoulders. *Yuck*, I squirmed, feeling a sick realization coming over me—knowing how long this flight was.

Not soon enough, we taxied down the runway and read-ied for takeoff. Engines roaring the nose lifted and my stom-ach sunk. Rising slowly upward, I looked out the window to see Paris shrinking below us. Instead of the city, something else caught my attention. There on the ground, in a large open field right below us, there were these strange bluish-gray illuminations. They appeared to be hovering over the grassy field. I would call them lights, but they clearly weren't electrical. Not any kind that I had seen before. Nudging the man next to me I said to him, "Hey, check out those weird lights down there." He leaned over to look out our tiny win-dow. I ignored the flakes of dandruff falling my way as the hunched over me to stick his round face right in the hole. "Is that some sort of memorial for today?" I mumbled in his ear. Leaning back up, he gave me a strange look of contempt, and immediately went back to reading his paper—completely ignoring me. "Well, didn't you see it?" I insisted.

After taking another quick peek outside, he looked over at me with a bothered grimace, to reply, "There's nothing down there." His face was yelling; *please just leave me alone!*

Taking another look out, I was able to see them again, hovering in the field, looking like giant bluish fireflies. How could he not see them? They made a magical light show, their pastel hues contrasted by the bright reds, yellow, deep blues, grays, and greens, all of the wildflowers bursting and blooming with life all across the overgrown grassy landscape. *Weird*, I considered, just before losing sight of them as the plane lifted up into a cloud. A fluffy grayish white mist filled the widow, blocking my view of the ground.

All there was to see for the next few hours was blue water and white clouds. Leaning back in my seat, I prepared for the long haul across the Atlantic Ocean. Every second was an agonizing reminder of how much I hated flying—especially in coach.

36

FINALLY TOUCHING DOWN I pushed my way down the crowded isle and gangway. I could barely keep my eyes open after staying awake for so long, with the jetlag starting to kick-in with a vengeance. The last thing I wanted to see was Tom standing at the gate waiting for me to disembark. But of course, there he was, with folded arms and a frown. He had plenty of time to prepare some wretchedly punishing speech to chastise me with. His voice started playing in my head as I walked up to him; *how could you possibly deceive me?*

That way, I could prepare my own nasty retort—to tell him off once and for all.

Then he smiled at me—sneaky bastard! Wow he was smart, making moves on his chessboard two or three steps ahead of me.

"Welcome home Emma," he gushed, with wide-open-arms ready for a warm embrace. Not saying anything, I stood in front of him feeling like a living corpse that needed to be reburied. All I wanted was a hot shower and a bed. Wrapping me up in his arms with a sweet kiss on the neck, he whispered in my ear, "I figured you would need a ride home since Lisa dropped you off."

"What about Lisa…is she with you?" I asked him, glancing around at the streaming by crowds. She had dropped me off, instead of taking me down to Florida. We just didn't quite make it that far—that's all.

Thomas grinned, pretending to be happy to see me home, and replied, "Oh no, I wanted to pick you up myself, so I told Lisa to not worry about it. Besides I have a surprise for you."

Oh great…hear it comes! The devilish glint in his eyes betrayed his true intentions. He definitely was planning something—some surprise. "So what is it?" I asked him cautiously, not being sure if I really wanted to find out?

With a wide smile, he replied, "Let's pick up your suitcase on the way out. I'll show you when we get out to the car."

It was an eternity waiting at the baggage carousel. Watching it churn, slowly spinning as it deposited everyone else's bags but mine. *Where is it?* I nervously wondered. *Hope they didn't find what was inside?* The way Thomas was staring at me with that cheesy grin—it was all unnerving. It was like being poked allover with pins and needles. My heart raced faster the longer we waited, with no suitcase showing up. Glancing around at everyone, I started feeling like everyone was looking at me. At any moment now the police are going to swarm around me, throw me down on the floor, handcuff me, and then drag me off to jail, with Tom laughing uncontrollably in the background.

Then it was there, flopping down onto the conveyor belt. *Whew!* Thomas was kind enough to grab the strap. His head looked like it was going to pop like a red balloon as he hoisted it up. "What the hell did you pack in here?" He groaned under the strain. "I knew you were a big packer, but this is ridiculous." Lucky for him, he parked close by. If it was much farther away he probably would have died.

"So where's this surprise?" I asked when he suddenly stopped walking.

Setting my bag down, Thomas gleefully dug around in his pocket to pull out a set of keys. I thought he was overly happy to get to put the heavy bag down, but then he said, "Its right behind you." I turned to see a black BMW coupe. Sparkling new, it was nearly exactly the same model as the one I saw him riding in. "I bought it," he exclaimed with the biggest smile ever. He was a boy on Christmas morning that found his most wanted toy beneath the tree. "And I wanted you to be the first person to get to ride in it."

Wow, lucky me, I mused, *what a wonderful surprise... for me?*

Thomas gleefully unlocked the doors, popped open the trunk and loaded my bag, before jumping in and firing-up the engine. It did have an invigorating revving engine—with a smooth powerful vibration that made you tingle all over. That's my kind of toy. "It's a very nice car," I said seductively, while feeling the leather seats and breathing in the new-car-smell. I couldn't hold it back, and I finally gave him a reluctant smile. He was so darn cute with his new toy. And, it did feel sexy as we flew down the freeway passing by everyone else. "Thanks for picking me up," I whispered to him, with a soft kiss on his cheek. It was hard to tell what smelled better—the new leather, or his cologne. Both were very erotic.

"Look," he said emphatically, "I realize that I've not been the best boyfriend lately." His eyes focused on the road as he drove us through the heavy Atlanta traffic—but his mind was completely focused on me. "Yes, I've been messing up…doing things that I shouldn't…but that's all in the past." Glancing over at me, his weepy eyes let me know he was serious, and sincere. "We need to work through this and not screw things up."

But he wasn't getting off that easily!

"I'm not the one who's been running around town with whoever it is that you're messing around with," I shot back. "This is how I work through it…by moving on."

"You're moving on with that guy…who is he?" Tom demanded to know. "That guy you met over in Paris…is that who you're moving on with?"

"Maybe I am?" I whimpered, not wanting him to know the whole truth. That David was as much a mystery to me, as he was being. Neither of them was showing me anything even resembling honesty. Neither of them was acting trustworthy. Both of them were leaving me hanging-on, or high-and-dry, with absolutely no feelings of security. I wasn't about to hold back my true feelings, and I told him, "Perhaps, you should show me how you really feel about me, before he does!"

Tom clenched his jaws, as he gnawed on his own teeth—grating them together. Hopefully he was chewing on my words. He needed to swallow them. They needed to stick inside him, and stay there, reminding him over and over again like horrendous indigestion—that he had better treat me better—or I would burn him up inside. "He's no good," he burped up like rancid gas that had been building up inside, and had to get out, "he's a very bad guy and you need to stay away from him…whoever he is?"

Glaring at Tom, I lashed out, "What the hell do you know about him? He's been way better to me than you ever have!"

"I know enough," Tom replied in a low growl. "Mitch looked into his background, and he told me some things about that guy…things that aren't good. You have to trust me on this and just stay away from him."

"What did Mitch tell you?" The real question was—what was Mitch *not* telling *me*?

Tom started to calm down, really thinking about what he was about to say. "Exactly what I've been trying to tell you… that guy is not really who he says he is. He's a fake, a fraud, a Charlatan, and he's trying to trick you into something, for some reason. He's probably trying to swindle you and your family out of money. Maybe he's setting you up to get at your father before he gets nominated for Federal Judge? Whatever he's up to, you are getting set up, trust me."

My mind flew back to the trunk, and my suitcase, remembering the statuette that David had me take from the hotel. *Oh Shit!* I got still and quiet. Tom noticed. It was obvious on my face that something wasn't right. "What is it… what has he done?" He asked concerned.

No, I couldn't tell Tom about the statuette. Not without getting an explanation from David first. He deserved that at least. In a calming, stoic voice, I replied, "Oh, it's nothing…he didn't do anything. I trust you. I'll stay away from him. It was about time Thomas acted like a jealous lover and did something to protect me—at least pretend that he cared. Sure I was sick-to-my-stomach angry at David. But making Thomas mad enough to pay me some sweet attention was at least something I could get out of this whole mess. Now it was time to take full advantage of him—making him pay for all the past neglect. Make him appreciate what he had, and was about to lose if he didn't change his ways. Poking Thomas in the ribs, I snickered, teasing with him, "*And you*, have to promise to be with me…*only me*…from now on, promise?"

Thomas smiled with lips of honey, sending me a reassuringly sexy smooch, saying all lovey-dovey, "Oh, I promise you everything sweetheart. There's no one else but you, *for me.*"

That's all I wanted to hear. "Good answer," I whispered sweetly in his ear, giving his lobe a nibble.

We had started kissing by the time we pulled into my driveway. Luckily nobody else was home. Thomas lugged my bag up to the front door. Then I decided that I had better leave it in the trunk of my car, so that I could deliver it to David as soon as possible. Didn't want that stolen statue in the house for father to find—he'd kill me. "I'm so tired," I yawned big stretching my arms out wide, giving Thomas a not-so-subtle-hint that I wanted him to leave, so that I could get some rest. "I'll see you tomorrow morning at the office sweetheart," he politely excused himself—leaving me with a delicate goodbye kiss, and a seductively spoken, "love you".

Yes! He was already behaving much better.

After Thomas departed, I dragged my suitcase out into the garage to deposit it in my car's trunk. Using my last scintilla of energy left, I managed to hoist the heavy bag up over the bumper. Every muscle was aching and tired. I was more than ready for a long nights sleep.

37

WAKING UP BEFORE the sunrise I got ready and drove into the city center. My mind was so preoccupied with everything I had to stop by the lake, to think. Watching the soft morning rays rising up over the lake, with the birds chirping, flowers blooming, dewdrops falling, life seemed simpler there on my bench. Everything came into better perspective for me in those surroundings. And it did this time as well. Only this time, it wasn't what I expected to become so clear—that I was in love with David. Coming to grips with that was even less easy. It would mean giving up everything I had lived for up until now. And I wasn't even sure about who David really was, or if, he was even worthy of my love?

Was he a fake like Thomas believed? Was I creating a fantasy love out of desperation over the way Thomas was treating me? There was only one way to be certain about my feelings for him. I made a firm resolution on the drive to the office building—that I had to confront him—about everything.

I was feeling better about things until I walked inside my office. A note was waiting for me, on my desk. It was from father. He wanted me to come up to his office—first thing.

Those sticky notes were what he used when he didn't want to use the phone, fearing that someone would overhear him talking on the phone and start spreading rumors around the office. My stomach churned the entire way up the stairs and down the hall. It was the feeling you get when being summoned to the principal's office at school. I had to imagine it because I had never actually experienced it before—not until this moment. His secretary glared at me, disappointed. She obviously was told why I was being summoned. The note was in her handwriting. "Go right in, he's expecting you," she grumbled with a scowl.

Father set down his pen the second I walked in. Tilting back in his chair he motioned for me to sit down in a side chair. He had never looked more serious. But he remained calm, making me even more afraid of what he was about to do. Staying calm was how he acted whenever he was deadly serious about something. Those were his gunslinger eyes, letting you know that he was about to draw, shooting you dead in your tracks before you could even blink. It was better to not move, or to say anything that might set him off. "Did you enjoy your trip?" He asked in a deadpan voice. I nodded, *yes*. There was *really* no reason to answer, since he *really* could've cared less. "Bring back any expensive souvenirs?"

I didn't think my heart could sink any lower—but it did. He knows. I nodded my head again, *yes*, while doing my best to not make any recognizable facial expressions. Not a hint of a smile. Not a gesture of pleasure. Staying stone faced, like he taught me. *Don't tip your hand.* Not until you're cornered, without any moves left on your gaming board.

"This isn't a game we're playing Emma," he stated emphatically, letting me know that he could read my face like an open book. "Now I only expect to hear the truth coming out of those lips."

I nodded compliantly. *Wow, am I that easy to read?*

Piercing me with his truth-detector stare, he asked me bluntly, "Did you remove a statue from the hotel room that you were staying in?"

My eyes dropped down to my wrenching hands, as I nodded the answer, *yes*.

"I'm not going to mince words with you young lady," He laid into me. "Whatever you've gotten mixed-up in, it's got-ta stop. You understand me? Whatever has your head so spun-around it's got-ta end, right now."

My eyes started to melt, but I held back the tears, pleading, "I'll send it back…it's not damaged or anything. It was a mistake. I'm sorry. I don't know what I was thinking?"

Sitting up in his chair, father replied flippantly, "Oh it's too late for that. I spoke directly with the new owner of the hotel. And he made it perfectly clear that he doesn't want that thing back in his hotel. In fact, he was trying to find a way to unload that on somebody, so he could finally remodel that old room. He seemed quite pleased in fact."

A sense of relief swept over me, and I allowed a tiny smile on my lips, as I replied, "Well good, then that matter is resolved…no harm, no foul."

Father tensed up, letting me know that, "Oh, they still expect to be compensated Emma…in full."

My heart immediately hit the floor again. "How much do they want for it?" I whimpered.

His eyes were turning redder, as he imagined thousands of dollar bills flying out the window behind him, scattering in the wind like confetti. His lips trembled as he reluctantly revealed, "Sixty-thousand, or there-a-bouts. Way more than it's worth. And far and away more than you can afford that's for certain. They'll agree to not press criminal charges against you if we pay. Its damn blackmail is what it is…but I don't' have a choice. I can't afford a scandal in the family like that right now. Not right now."

The anguish in his voice almost made me feel sorry for him—but what about me? That was more than a year of tuition for Law School. It would take me years to pay him back—even if I graduated at the top of my class, and then made partner after a few years of working here. I would wind up being his indentured servant for years. Father could live without having his precious judgeship. He would still be successful and rich. What about my life?

Forget about him—I was feeling sorry for me!

"I'll pay you back. I'll find a way." I murmured, afraid to raise my voice, or sound overly optimistic. "This whole thing will blow over and be soon forgotten."

"That's not all Emma," father said, sounding despondent. It was so difficult for him to broach this topic. I could tell by his wavering voice. The last time I heard that voice was when he and mother were having marital problems, and talking about getting divorced. "There's another problem that's come up…something that may have happened on your trip to Paris? Is there something else you want to tell me about?"

"No, not really, nothing really comes to mind," I fidgeted, dodging the question. "The hotel was nice…saw some sights…didn't really get to eat out—"

"What about the Rodin Museum?" Father cut me off. "Spend any time in there?" His pen-pointer-laser-eyes were trained on me again. There was no sense in trying to pretend.

He wouldn't have asked me that, if he didn't already know the answer. Besides, I'm clearly no good at lying.

"Yes, it was very nice," is all I replied. Smiling sweetly at him, I did my best to act like nothing special happened there—absolutely nothing weird or out of the ordinary—nothing at all.

Oh, and apparently, I'm a terrible actress as well.

Father's jaw clenched. "I also received a telephone call from a Police Investigator in Paris. Not about the stolen statue. About something else entirely...want to guess what about?" He was squirming inside. I could read him well-enough to recognize that. He wanted me to come out with it, saving him the embarrassment of having to say it out loud, himself.

I swallowed, keeping my lips sealed. He was going to have to say it—because I wasn't.

It took him a few tense moments, before he could force the words to come out, "They told me...apparently that... they recovered a camera...inside...while they were investigating a break-in at the Rodin museum...on the day you apparently visited." His eyes were bleeding as he sadly asked me, "You want to try and guess what was on the film that they developed?"

The camera...oh shit, I totally forgot to get the camera!

Hard swallow—lips sealed—I emotionally braced for what was coming next. I shook my head, *no*, pretending not to know.

"Well, I'll tell you then," father groaned under the mighty weight of it, as he mumbled, "They discovered a photograph of you...after hours, in the dark....right out in the middle of the museum…bare-ass-naked and kissing on one of them damn statues."

"How can they be so sure it was me? It could have been anyone," I blustered, hoping to find a loophole in the nick of time to save my neck.

In a stern, reserved voice, he went over the cold hard facts, "Well let's see, they found your clothing in the utility closet…with your hotel room key still in the pocket…that is a unique skeleton key that only fits that one particular lock. And, the hotel clerk was more than eager to pinpoint you as the person in the photograph. He was able to describe your clothing, appearance, the time you left and returned that night, exactly. As the cherry on top of all that, you used my credit card to pay for everything, including your ticket for the museum. That's how!"

Instantly it felt like I was falling all fourteen floors of the building—landing flat, with a body crushing splat, on the concrete basement floor. How could I feel any lower? Oh yea, father's forlorn face was pushing me further down, deeper underground, that's how. He was going to be embarrassed beyond belief if that news got out. Not to mention the actual photograph. His entire career could be ruined. Not just his judgeship. How could he ever show his face inside a courtroom again after that?

I felt like a worm. My tight-lipped façade was shattering. Glancing around the room I could feel my eyes watering-up with tears. No amount of money was going to bail-me-out of this situation. Now I was cornered. "What did you tell them?" I asked squeamishly. My desperate reaction revealed my secret for me. He was hoping that I would jump out of my seat yelling at the top of my lungs that, "hell no, that

wasn't me naked in the museum sucking face with a statue…
who would dare accuse me of doing something so disgusting!" Instead, I merely folded my hand, laying my playing
cards out flat for all to see—that it *was* me.

Father bowed his head, as the reality of it all sank in. "I
can't believe my little girl would go and do something like
this?" He sorrowfully mumbled. "How am I going to break
this to your mother? What is Thomas going to do? Can't wait
to have to try and explain this to the other partners. This is
bad…real bad."

"It wasn't my fault," I blurted out, wanting so badly to
stop his grieving. If there was any way I could smooth things
over a little—I was going to do it. Even if that meant throwing David up under the bus with me. But, I wouldn't betray
him *too* eagerly.

"What's that…not your fault? Please tell me you were at
least wasted drunk, or something?" Father shot me an expectant look, wanting to hear—one hell-of-a-great explanation.
I looked away, not able to give him a believable story that
would satisfy him. "Well then if it wasn't your fault…then
who's fault was it Em?" He asked as if he was a bird-dog sniff-
ing out a scented trail. "Did someone put you up to this?"

I nodded head, *yes.*

"Who was it?" Father prodded. He was desperate to find
a way out of this too. "One of those frat girls you've been
hanging around…what's her name, Lisa?"

I shook my head hard, *NO, not her.* It felt a little-bit
wrong covering her ass, after the way she blew my cover; but
hey, true friends were in short supply.

"Then, who was it Emma?" This was the last time he was
going to ask. His fiery eyes were telling me that he'd reached

the end of his chain, and he was about to break free and start chewing me up.

"It was David…Zachary David Laurent…the artist that you forced me to go investigate, for the memorial exhibit at the High." I let him pry it out of me—making it sound almost like it was his fault. Since *he's the one* that forced me to go up there and *investigate* David in the first place. In a way, it was father's fault. "We've become friends…and he convinced me to go to Paris with him and visit the Rodin museum. I had no idea what he had planned…not until we were inside…hiding in the closet…and he pulled out these tubes of body paint…and one thing lead to—

I went on telling father what David and I did inside the museum. How he made me feel safe and secure, and free to be myself. About how it was so exhilarating and amazingly liberating—like nothing I had ever experienced before. How I finally felt like the person that I really was. I was so involved in my story that I didn't notice that—I was smiling.

I suddenly felt so happy, reliving that intense moment when we first kissed. Even if I wasn't saying it out loud—I was feeling it inside, tickling me, making me giddily intoxicated all over again. I was back inside the dark museum, all alone with David, pulling his lips to mine, tasting him all over again. His rock-hard body was pressing against mine. The sweet taste of his breath in my mouth, the feel of his hair brushing through my fingers—with my entire body, heaving, aching, yearning for his.…

When I looked back up at father—he was staring at me wide-eyed and blank-faced—like he didn't even know who I was anymore. After a long silent pause, he said calmly, "Look Emma, I know you have been under an incredible amount of stress lately…with final exams, working long hours, worrying about Thomas and everything—"

Here it comes—the whole you've gone insane speech. He was using that same tone of voice that he uses when mother goes off the deep end, flying into a raging bitch session, to the point where he's exacerbated, unable to reason with her, and thinks that he's run out of options—so he calls her crazy.

"That's not what happened," I blurted out, not letting him go there. "I'm not insane. It happened exactly the way I just told you. And, David is the one who convinced me to take that statue from the hotel. His mother carved it when she was forced to live there by the Nazis during the occupation of Paris in WWII."

Father sprang up straight, asking nervously, "Who told you about all that…about the hotel room, David's mother, and the stuff about the Nazi's?"

"David did," I replied, as if that was a stupid question.

"When and where exactly did he tell you that Em?"

"Up at his family's farmhouse…while we were out in their studio, out in the barn…and while we were together one night at the High Museum…then while we were together in Paris. He's been telling me about it ever since I went up there to investigate him, like you asked me to." I did my best to shift blame back onto him—to leave him some of the guilty feelings.

"I don't want you going back up there to that house. And stay away from that barn too," father grumbled anxiously. His eyes were wandering around, looking lost. "This situation has gotten you into enough trouble…and I'm sorry for getting you involved at all."

"What about David?" I asked, wanting to know if the authorities were coming after him too.

Father locked eyes with me, a matador and a bull, and he replied sternly, "Forget about *him* and move on with *your life*."

He was the rippling muscle-bound two-ton bull, snorting, tossing up clumps of dirt with his hooves—lowering his needle-sharp-horns to charge at me. I wilted, dropped my red cape, and stepped aside, nodding, *yes sir*.

"So where's the statue now?" He snorted again.

"Still in the trunk of my car," I whimpered.

"Don't let it out of your sight, for now. It may be as valuable as they claim. Maybe we can sell it to pay them off."

"Yes sir."

"And before I forget…hand it over," father demanded with his hand stretched out. He didn't have to specify what exactly he wanted. I opened up my purse, plucked-out his credit card, and placed it flat down on his open palm. "Thank you," he murmured, while nodding with his head for me to—*get out*.

Being summarily dismissed from his office—I now know exactly how it feels to be a freshly spanked school-girl leaving the principal's office. Ouch!

38

THAT AFTERNOON AS I was leaving the office for the day, I asked Thomas to help me remove the statuette from my trunk. He cheerfully agreed, knowing that father had tanned my hide good, leaving me with no options other than abandoning David. "I can probably find some art and junk dealer to take it off your hands," he offered snidely. He couldn't hide his jealousy. It was so thick it was oozing out of him.

Art was never in Tom's blood, and he never learned to appreciate the beauty of it. Taking him to the museum with me was like taking a bored infant child that only wanted to find an excuse to cut up and act foolish to get attention. Most often, he would spend the entire time poking fun at the naked images, or making derogatory comments about how cheesy everything appeared. "No talent hacks" as he referred to the artists. To him, every artist was merely an unemployed vagrant peddling kitschy trappings to vapid elitists with more money than good taste. "Most of them should be arrested for thievery," he always implored as we exited.

Popping open the trunk I unzipped my bag to inspect the statuette. It was even more impressively engaging than I remembered it to be. Emotion evoking—it left me breathless for a moment. It was that powerful. My eyes drifted over the entwined lovers, as they embraced, fondly gazing at the other, only wanting to be together—forever. I was wilting with butterflies fluttering. "It's so lovely—", I started to say.

"What a cheesy hunk of junk," Tom chimed in. "You would think they would try and make something more useful with all the time they waste making this crap. Now I'm the one that has to break my back trying to unload it on some unsuspecting sap."

"This is a cherished piece of art," I grumbled, giving him a nasty glance. His smug face was spitting down on it, with utter disdain. "But you wouldn't appreciate something so beautiful," I muttered beneath my breath.

"The artist was obviously a forger, or some gimmicky souvenir vendor. I've seen thousands of these all over the world. We'll be lucky to get twenty bucks for this piece of shit."

I slammed the trunk lid down, nearly cutting off Tom's fingers. He lurched back, snatching his hands away just in time. "Hey, careful," he snapped at me—not even realizing how he angry I was. "Thanks, but I don't need your help anymore," I growled, letting him know that, "I can take care of this myself."

Stepping back, Tom asked, "You sure you don't want some help?" He was holding his hands out pleading with a questioning face as if he was wondering what he did wrong—trying to believe that he was some type of savior coming to my rescue. "I don't mind helping you get rid of that...not at all."

"I'll see you tomorrow," I said coldly, before hopping inside my car and speeding away, leaving him with the sullen face of a spoiled child that didn't get his way again. But I wasn't going home. In that instant that Tom opened up his mouth to belittle David's mother—I made the fateful decision to return Melissa's statuette to the one person who would most appreciate it—her son.

I made the drive up into the northern hills in record time. Traffic even seemed lighter than usual. It felt good to be doing the right thing. But the idea of getting to see David again was even more enticing.

Flying up the driveway I parked the car and skipped up to his front door. Nobody answered my knock. Walking to the back I could hear the wafting sounds of music coming from the barn. He's working, I surmised, and headed that way. The barn door was wide open. The sounds of his striking the chisel with his mallet spiked through the sounds of the stereo. Way in the back of the barn, a soft light illuminated him. Shirtless, his rippling body was beaded with dribbling lines of sweat. The chisel was firmly in his hand, placed on the large marble block like a surgeon's scalpel, making precision cuts. The top half of the large marble block was covered-up by the blue tarp, hiding it from view—until it was finished. Being late in the afternoon, the sunlight was already beginning to fade. I watched him working for a short time, not wanting to disturb him. It was one of those time slowing moments, when you relish each movement, every curving muscle, the toss of his hair—the glorious sight of *him*. That time passed to fast. "David," I called to him, as gently as the warm summer breeze blowing in behind me.

As I said his name, I felt a surge of passion for him. It was like reciting a magic word, placing me under a spell—a love spell. "Emma," he whispered my name back to me, striking my heart. His chisel could have been slicing through me, it was so intense. His voice pierced me to my core, letting me feel his power. "I've been waiting for you." My lips trembled, wanting to reply, but I was overwhelmed. All I wanted to do was run to him and throw myself on top of his body.

David stood and took the edge of the blue tarp in his fingertips. He pulled it down over the stone to hide what he was carving. I could tell that there was a nude man, next to a nude woman—but that was all. Only their hips down to their feet remained uncovered. They seemed to be seated, facing each other. I was not permitted to see their upper torso, or faces.

After covering the statue—David turned to look straight through me.

"I brought you your mother's statuette from the hotel," I managed to say with a swirling head. My heart was pounding hard, my palms wet, lips trembling—wanting to say more.

"I want you to keep it," he replied.

"Why?" It didn't make sense, why he would want me to have it?

"Because you're the only one who will ever know why it is…what it truly is. It's love." David spoke forcefully, cutting deeper into my heart, forcing me to accept what he was saying. I did feel the burning passion, the desire, the undying love—every time I looked at it. "It was carved for someone like you Emma…a loving passionate person, who can appreciate its beauty."

"How can you know that about me?" I gushed, letting my emotions take control. My eyes began to burn as tears flowed. My passions were too strong. My desire for him was more than I could resist. All of *this* was more than I could handle—without understanding—why was he doing this to me?

"How is it that you understand me so well David? You know what I love more than anyone else…more than my so-called friends…my boyfriend…even my family…why is that David? How can that be?"

David slowly walked towards me, glowing softly in the twilight sun. His face was a light-blue haze. Smiling, he replied in a saintly voice, "I've known you for longer than you know. I've watched you from a distance. In the museum, when you lingered after hours in the exhibit hall. I was there, with you."

"That doesn't make any sense," I mumbled, searching memories for something I missed, forgot, or lost. "When were you there in the museum with me? I can't remember ever being alone with you there."

"You wouldn't have known," David said with a smile.

"You're messing with me…aren't you David," I replied, feeling nervous. My mind began racing, searching for answers, going over everything that had happened since we first met. Father's voice started repeating, along with Thomas's, telling me to be careful, to not to trust David, that he was trying to take advantage of me. "Is this some sort of game…are you playing me?" I demanded to know. My emotions were running hot as I retreated to safer ground. The teardrops dried up as I raised-up a shield of self-protection.

"You've been playing yourself Emma," David replied sternly, taking a step towards me. "You've not been honest with yourself for a very long time."

"I've been dishonest?" I shot back. "What about you? You said you'd be paying for that trip to Paris. You promised me that you sold a *fake* statue and you would be using that money to pay me back. Then, you talked me into trespassing in the Rodin Museum, before stealing that statue from the hotel. Now I'm the one getting the blame, maybe arrested, and having to pay for what you tricked me into doing. So, who exactly is being dishonest here David?"

"You are!" David groaned.

"How am I being dishonest David?" I lashed back, perplexed.

With a sincere stare, he stated bluntly, "Let's see…you've been dating a lecherous asshole for a few years…all the while making excuses for him. You have nothing in common with him. He's using you to curry favor with your father until he makes partner. The only reason you're dating him is to make your father happy. On top of all of that…you aren't even in love with him."

My face was a bright red by this point. Well, I wanted to know!

David went on, pointing out that, "You've been trying to please your father by being his lap-dog…drooling at his feet doing every trick he wants you to perform. He gives you treats along the way by paying for everything and promising you more and more…even though you detest going to law school, hate lawyers, despise the sleazy jobs you have to perform, and hate yourself for making yourself do it all. So, who's being dishonest Emma?"

The tears were welling up again. David was the one telling the truth. Looking deeply into his eyes, I begged of him, "Why David? Why do you care so much about me?"

His crystal eyes gleamed with passion, as he replied, "Because I've fallen in love with you Em."

Tears flowed, trickling over my cheeks. "I love you too," I whispered softly back to him.

David stretches out his arms to take me in. Wiping away the tears I move towards him.

The sound of a blaring car horn—stopped me cold. A man's yelling voice sends a freezing shiver up my spine, "Emma...Emma where are you!?" Thomas calls out frantically from the front of the house. There's a brewing storm within his thunderous call. "Emma I know you're here! Where is *this* David?"

He followed me up here! Now what do I do?

David was peaceful, with caring eyes watching over me. Smiling sweetly, he said, "It's time for me to get back to work. I have to finish this piece in time. Everything that's happened to me, my mother, my father, it was all for a reason. You are that reason Em. It's the most important thing I've ever attempted. It may just change everything."

"What is it going to be...how could it be so important?" I asked quickly. Tom was still calling for me outside, getting closer to the barn, with his loud voice rumbling like fast approaching thunder.

"Always remember Em, that everything I said to you was the absolute truth," David spoke softly with a sincerely sweet smile, "Especially the part about loving you. You'll understand when you finally see this piece finished."

Tom's yelling was getting close—very close. He was almost to the barn door.

I rushed to David and pushed my lips hard against his. It was as if we had become one person. Taking one last deep look into his loving eyes before pulling away, David whispered to me, "I have to finish this for you. I love you… the *real* you."

"Emma, are you in there?" Tom bellowed through the open doorway.

Tearing my body away from David, I turned and rushed through the door. Tom was standing there waiting. His chest was heaving, his eyes bulging out of his red-hot face, veins popping and muscles flexing—ready for a fight. "Where is that bastard?" He demanded to know. Rushing inside the barn Tom screamed, "Come on out and face me, you conniving thief!" But David was gone. Tom tore around the barn, searching violently like a raving lunatic, bouncing from one statute to another, throwing away the sheets and tarps—finding no one, growling, "Where's he hiding?"

"Please just leave him alone Tom," I begged for him to stop. Tom was pouring sweat, his face throbbing red. Glaring back at me, he paced towards me with his fist raised high. He stopped with his nose pressed up to mine, breathing fire in my face as a menacing dragon. It had to be the thought of my father throwing him under the jailhouse that stopped him from punching me in the face. "You swore you wouldn't come back here again," he snarled, through grinding teeth.

"I'm sorry…I wanted to return his statue," I whimpered, in submission.

The only thing I was really sorry about was that David didn't leap out from the shadows to protect me. He had vanished altogether, leaving me helpless at Tom's mercy.

Tom calmed down and stepped back. Wandering around the studio, seeing what was there, he talked loudly so that David could hear, saying, "Told you that guy was a spineless loser. Look at this filthy den of thievery. Bunch of fakes and forgeries I imagine?" Blowing some marble dust off one, he added, "How many fools do you think this guy has swindled with this junk?"

Tom stopped in front of where David had placed his mallet and chisel down of his stool. He nimbly snatched the bottom edge of the blue tarp and pulled it up. "It's not finished yet," I said loudly, stopping him for a moment. Shooting me a dismissive sneer, he lifted up the tarp. Spinning around I rushed outside, not wanting to see what was underneath— not yet.

It was quiet for a minute. I could hear the tarp rustling as Tom pulled it completely away from the sculpture. More silence. Then, there was the sound of shuffling feet as Tom rushed towards the doorway. Suddenly he came rushing out—pacing very fast—walking straight past me without even noticing that I was still there. His face had turned clammy and white. His eyes appeared lost and confused. Without looking towards me or uttering another sound—he went directly back to his car, got inside, started it up, and then drove away.

All I could hear was the sound of the tarp rustling again, as it was being slid back into place, covering up the unfinished statue.

I stepped back into the open doorway and peered inside the barn. David was not there. It was eerily calm, and much too quiet. Dust was settling all around. "David, where are you?" I called out. There was no response. It was disturbingly silent. Darkness was filling the cavernous space as the sun dipped below the horizon. Shadows moved over the carved bodies, with their darkened faces watching me. "David," I called to him again. The bottom of the blue tarp covering the sculpture swayed gently in the breeze. A creepy-crawly sensation tickled over my spine, and I knew it was time to leave.

It was a lonely walk back to my car. Turning around, I paused to look for signs of life inside the house. No lights were on—nothing moved in the windows. As my fingers touched the car door handle, a song started playing on the radio back in the barn. I could hear David's mallet striking the chisel, as he went back to work.

I hesitated, wanting to go back to see him. But I didn't. I left.

39

THE NEXT MORNING I walked into my office with the weight of the world resting on my shoulders—pushing me down through the floor. It must have shown on my face since nobody wanted to even say a simple "morning" to me. The word had spread like a briskly blowing wildfire, burning through the offices, sizzling in every interested ear. Everyone glanced my way and smiled, or snickered. *The brat finally got what she deserved.* That's what I could hear them whispering in my head.

An enormous stack of paper-stuffed files was waiting for me on my desk. Father had made sure that I was kept busy—to refocus my mind. Plus, now I was working to pay him back. It was a great way to try and prevent me from thinking about anything else either, especially David. But that didn't work at all. The more I tried to concentrate on the cases, the more my thoughts returned to him. This wasn't right—nothing was right—just as David warned me. The last thing he told me was true, and getting more obvious by each agonizingly passing second. I was slowly dying, buried beneath a mountain-high pile of avalanching paperwork.

This is my life now. *This is my nightmare!*

The very moment I was able to get a free second, I stormed down to Mitch's office. He was standing outside chatting with a secretary when I stepped onto his hallway. Spotting me, he ducked inside his office and tried to shut the door. Slipping my foot in, I caught him. "Mitch, it's me, Emma, got a second to talk," I said firmly as I pressed the door open.

"Sure Emma, come on in," he reluctantly stepped back. Taking his seat behind his large desk, it was as if he was taking refuge behind a wooden barricade. "What can I do for you," he asked. He was fidgety, unable to look me in the eye—very uncharacteristic for such and manly man. Obviously he was already aware of every embarrassing detail about my unfortunate trip to Paris, so I didn't bother to mention it.

Getting right to the point, with an unrelenting stare, I demanded to know, "Exactly what did you find out about Zachary David Laurent? And don't try and feed me another line of BS this time Mitch."

Leaning back in his high leather chair, he studied my face cautiously. With a rigid jaw, to not reveal his intent, his mind was swirling around in all directions in search of some excuse—for some reason to not divulge what he knew. But the more he stared into my *stony-hard-eyes*—the ones inherited from my father—the more he realized the jig was up. "Your father asked me not to tell you this," he grumbled, while reaching down to his bottom desk drawer. Pulling out a large manila envelope, he tossed it up on his desk for me to inspect.

The envelope was empty, with the once taped seal cut open. It was dirty and tattered, looking like it had been sent through the mail over a dozen times, or had been lost in a dusty bin. It was shocking to see David's name printed on the label as the person who mailed the envelope. He had sent it to the High Museum. "What is this?" I mumbled to Mitch.

Mitch swiveled in his chair, clearing his throat, ready to spill the beans, saying, "Apparently your David, mailed that envelope to the High Museum. It contained the submission packet for the memorial exhibit that got us involved in this to begin with."

"So what...we know he sent it to us?" I scoffed.

"Take a look at the date on the postage, there."

A shiver ran up my spine when I saw the date. The envelope had a mailing date that was over five years ago. "This can't be right," I murmured.

"Oh it's right alright," Mitch pointed out, telling me the rest, "David mailed that package a week before he disappeared...vanishing in thin air. I spoke to his uncle that he was living with out in Colorado. This was the last thing David was working on before, he-up-and-vanished without a trace. Nobody's seen or heard from him since."

"Do they know where he went," I gasped, not believing what I was hearing.

"Not a clue," Mitch replied sternly. "So, whoever this guy is that you've been dallying around with...that's telling you that he's David...is some sort of scam artist. The real David has been missing for over five years, and apparently, he's either dead, or just doesn't want to be found."

"That can't be true...he saved me when I was skiing in Breckenridge. I've been with him at his home...in his workshop....we met in Paris last week...none of this makes sense?" I stammered, trying to put the pieces together. "Nobody could know him that well to pull that off…or know so much about me, the way David does Mitch."

"This guy was probable close friends with David, or got to know him on the road someplace, traveling buddies, that kind of thing. He learned enough that he could take his place. Moved into his house, and pretended to be him, faking the whole thing. I've seen this happen before, a thousand times." Leaning forward to give me his best rendition of a trusted friend, Mitch said, "Believe me Emma, this guy is a phony."

"I've got to talk to him face-to-face to be sure," I muttered, barely able to speak, saying, "It's the only way I can be certain."

Mitch reacted bitterly, telling me, "That's not a good idea Emma. This guy could be dangerous. If he knows we're on to him, he may do something nuts. *Stone* wants me to get up there and get the jump on him, get the goods, so we can take him down. That just may be the only way to pull your hind-end out of the fire. Don't go near him for a few days."

"Alright Mitch," I nodded, letting him know that I trusted his good judgment. Leaving the envelope behind, as evidence, I trudged back to my office—to get *back* to *my* work.

It was the same thing, every day, after that. Another pile of cases appeared on my desk every morning. Legal research, writing motions, briefs, running here and there stepping and fetching for father and the team of attorneys he had me slaving for. Not a minute to spare—ever. Even my lunches with Carly were getting cut down to frantic rushes to grab a sandwich, take-out, eating on the way back to the office. With a nonstop line-up of secretaries, clients, witnesses, calling or banging on my office door, all of them impatiently waiting for me to give them what they had to have—right that second.

By that Friday I was completely frazzled. Father had taken away any chance of freedom for me. No more credit. My bank account was drained of funds. Mother, Jon, and anyone else who knew me, was banned from loaning me a single penny. I may as well have been chained-up to my desk. Not only that; now my paycheck was being directly deposited into father's account so that he could be repaid first. All that was left for me was gas money, enough to get me from home to work, and back again.

I was boiling over mad. Nothing was going to scare me away from finding out the truth. If David was a fraud, and had ruined my life, I was going find out—for myself.

There was barely enough gas left in my tank to get me up to David's house and back, barely. Right after work, I drove straight up there to confront him. The house was dark, as usual. Banging on the front door, nobody appeared. Hot as a tin roof on a summer day, I stormed back towards the barn. Adrenaline surging like a prize fighter getting ready for the first round, my heart was thumping. With each step I was mentally preparing. *Either he's the real David, with the most amazing explanation ever, or, I'm going to kill that bastard!*

The barn door was closed. A chain was wrapped through the handles—with a large padlock slinked between the links—holding it shut tight. Tensing-up, shaking the chain wildly, I yanked on the padlock, huffing angrily like a growling mad dog at the end of her leash. I wasn't going to let him lock me out—not this time! But no matter how hard I tried, the lock and chain held on tight.

A low-pitched-rumbling-sound forced me to turn around. That Harley-Davidson motorcycle came rolling up the long driveway. Passing by the house it purred to a stop in the back yard, where I had seen it parked before. A man was riding it—*David?*

He removed his helmet. Long stringy hair fell out into a dangling pony-tail. Swinging his spindly long skinny leg over the saddle, he walked towards me. Scruffy and tall, the skinny man asked suspiciously, "Can I help you?" Walking up closer, he asked me again, "You up here lookin' for someone ma'am?" Beneath the graying whiskers, the rest of his face was dry, cracking, and wrinkled, tanned from the harsh elements. All of his remaining teeth were pitted with black decay. His black leather jacket and torn blue-jeans were as worn and tattered as his face. Crudely drawn tattoos painted his sun-darkened arms.

"I'm looking for David," I replied sharply, wanting to appear bold, in case this turned out to be a nefarious accomplice.

The man thought for a moment, wrinkling-up his forehead, before replying, "You talkin' bout Zach?"

"Yes, that's right; Zachariah David Laurent…is he here?"

With a strange smirk, the man seemed puzzled, saying, "No ma'am, I ain't seen Zach around here in years."

"Well, do you know where he might be?"

With a twitch of his head, he raised-up his eyebrow—as if questioning my question—then he answered, "I'd imagine he'd be out in Colorado, ma'am."

"Who are you and what are you doing here?" I asked timidly, hoping he would be honest, and not too offended.

"Names Earl," he replied, "Zach's uncle pays me to watch

out for his place…till he finally figures out what he wants to do with everything. Guess you might call me his guard dog. Now, who might you be?" With a menacing smirk, he displayed his jagged teeth—the nasty fangs that were about to devour me. "What you been doin' out here is the real question? You been tryin' to get inside the barn again?"

"I told you I'm looking for David." I answered nervously, with my bold façade melting away.

"More like trying to get at my whiskey again more likely," he replied with a sinister smile. "I've seen your car tracks coming and going in and outa here at all hours of the night. You're the one that's been drinkin' up my best bourbon. That's why I had to chain it up. Plus, he's got some expensive fancy art stuff stored-up inside there. Hope you wasn't thinkin' bout stealin' none of it?"

"Of course not," I replied, shocked at the suggestion. "I was with David…he let me inside."

His cracked sun-dried lips stretched wide, as he smiled. "Alright lady, if that's the way you want to play this? Then how bout I call the law out here, and let's just see if they believe your story?" With that, he turned and headed for the house.

"No, please don't call, I'm leaving right now," I pleaded as I followed him up to the house.

Growling at me, he replied, "Get on outa here, and don't ever let me catch you prowling-round-here, ever again."

40

THERE WAS NO way I could go back home, not without some answers. A gray haze enveloped the sky. Droplets of drizzling rain covered my window. A thick fog came over me. I was driving blind, in a way, since I couldn't focus well enough to decide where I was going. Driving down the traffic clogged interstate for what seemed like hours—I eventually swerved off an exit directed by the green airport sign. Then, I found myself parked outside of an airport terminal. Mist matted my hair and started to melt my makeup as I heaved my suitcase out of the trunk. Without really thinking, I walked inside and found what appeared to be the closest airline ticket counter. The glazed-over-tired booking agent stared back at me, blank-faced, as I asked, "Is there any flight leaving for Denver tonight."

"Wrong terminal," he muttered with contempt. "This is commercial shipping, he grumbled as he bent over to pick up and toss a cardboard box onto a conveyor belt.

My heart sank as I looked around to notice that I was the only person with a suitcase. What he said, *wrong terminal*, echoed in my brain, taunting me some more. Looking like a wet rat that had wandered inside, I slumped down, about to cry.

"Emma, is that you?" A man asked as he walked quickly towards me. He was tall and thin and wearing a pilot's uniform. At first sight I thought he was a military officer. There was a silver winged medallion on his lapel. "Emma Morgan, well I'll be, it is you," he gushed with a wide happy smile.

I forced a fake smile, thinking, *I don't have time for this.*

"You don't remember who I am, do you?" the pilot asked whimsically. My eyes drifted down to his engraved metal name tag that read: Ethan Lowry.

"Ethan…is that *really* you?" It slowly donned on me. I couldn't believe my eyes. It was him, my first real boyfriend, and he was now actually a real pilot. His face was the same, but that was about all that was familiar. The awkward shy pudgy teenager was erased by time. His once soft curly brown hair was shaved down, and receding, leaving him with a crescent dome. Much taller, thin muscular build, he was now all-grown-up, handsome, polished, and confident. Ethan was now all man. In a deep, firm, reassuring voice, he said, "I can't believe we ran into each other? It's been so long."

I was somewhat stunned, not knowing what to say. All I could think about was what a mess I must look like right now—yikes! So, I just kept nodding with a cheesy grin, mumbling, "So nice to see you again Ethan."

Then he glanced down at my bag, and asked, "So, what're you doing in here? Come to see me, or, here to ship a package?"

A thought hit me upside the head—a devilishly clever idea. "Well Ethan…I'm actually needing to get this special item delivered out to Colorado right away…problem is that

I have to travel with it...to safeguard it...since it's far too fragile and valuable," I muttered awkwardly, making it up as I went along.

"Oh, it's something for the museum?" Ethan guessed, knowing that I worked there. He also knew who father was, that he was on the Board, and how involved we all were with the museum. "Can I take a peek at it?" He asked sweetly.

Unzipping the bag I flipped back the top flap to let him see the statuette inside. We both stared at it in stunned silence for a moment, in awe. "I see what you mean, amazing," Ethan whispered reverently.

Staring into Ethan's eyes passionately, I told him, "But they won't let me fly with it here. I can't get a ticket tonight. And it has to be there by in the morning." My voice was oh so desperate. "Father would do anything to repay someone, if they could help me get this delivered."

Ethan glanced around nervously, thinking, seriously considering his options. Turning back with an intent stare, he replied, "I have an idea."

I smiled oh so sweetly, encouraging him on with my gooiest lovey-eyes. *My hero*!

He went on, saying, "I'm flying my West Coast leg tonight...leaving in about an hour. I have two delivery stops on the way, Memphis and Vegas. I can divert to Aspen for a short stop...due to some malfunction or weather or something." I grabbed him in the biggest bear-hug squeeze ever— leaving him breathless. "I only ask for one thing in return however," he let me know.

"Anything," I giddily replied.

"You'll have to agree to go out on a date with me...when you get back into town."

I noticed that he was stealing a look at my ring finger, to see it barren. "Of course I will...that would be lovely," I accepted his proposal.

Ethan zipped up the bag and lugged it like a gentleman all the way across the terminal to his gate. He had me quickly board and get situated in a jump-seat. My suitcase was secured in a luggage compartment next to me. Soon the engines roared and we were off to Colorado. I fell asleep, only waking up for a few minutes as they unloaded and reloaded shipments in Memphis. A bracingly cold air greeted me as I stepped off the plane in Aspen—even for late May. The sun was starting to rise-up over the tops of the mountain peaks. Ethan was kind enough to arrange for a shuttle-bus to take me down to Breckenridge. He even paid the fare in advance, along with a tip for the driver. "Now, don't try and forget about our deal," he snickered as the driver secured my bag. "Never," I breathed into his ear, leaving him with a softly placed wet kiss, letting him know that, "nothing would make me happier."

"What's the destination?" The driver asked, his eyes peering at me in the rearview mirror. Then, I suddenly realized that I wasn't really sure where I was going. David mentioned that his uncle owned a Bed and Breakfast in Breckenridge—so that was my destination. "Do you know where a Breckenridge B&B is...that is owned by the Meyer family?" He had to think for a few moments, before replying, "Yea, I think I know where that place is?" We sped off down the freeway. After a few minutes we exited onto a winding two-way road that zigzagged up a long winding canyon. Pulling up to an enormous log cabin building that looked like it had been transplanted out of an old western movie, the driver hopped out and deposited my suitcase on the front steps.

I pulled the heavy bag inside to the lobby area and slammed the door. A large burly man with a thick beard appeared from out of the back room. "Checking in?" He asked kindly. I didn't know what to say. "Are you Mr. Meyer...brother of Melissa Meyer?" I asked with trembling lips. "Yes, that's right...Benjamin Meyer," he replied cautiously. After that, we stood there, staring at each other, both wondering what the other was thinking. How could I come right out and tell him about how I knew David? He might think I'm a nut, or worse, get angry and throw me back out into the cold.

Just then, a gray-haired lady walked out to stand next to him, to say, "Hello I'm Lyn." She had to be Ben's wife. With a soft motherly face, she asked, "Are you all alone dear?"

For some reason her question made me well-up, with teardrops forming in my eyes. I was all alone. And I didn't want to be. All I could imagine was David standing beside me, urging me on. "I'm a friend of David's...I mean Zachary's," I mumbled, fighting back my emotions, to say, "And I've brought something for him. It's something special. It once belonged to his mother."

Lyn stepped closer, taking my hand, to ask, "What is it dear?" I motioned down to my suitcase. She quickly knelt down and unzipped the top. Burly Ben walked up behind her, to peer down over her shoulder. As she flipped back the flap—they both gasped. "It can't be true...it is real?" They started to mutter. Ben spun-round and yelled towards the back room—where an enormous warm fireplace was crackling. "Jonas, come in here...Jonas come quick!" The darkened silhouette of an old man appeared in front of the orange flames. Shuffling down the hallway, he made his way towards us. Bent with fragile bones he could barely walk. Ben and Lyn hastily lifted the statuette, setting it upright on the floor for him to see.

Jonas walked out into the light of the lobby. He was now a time-worn frail elderly man. With a hunched back and age-spotted skin, his sagging eyes gazed down at the marble carving on the floor. The sight of it overwhelmed him and his tired eyes opened wide. Moving a little faster his old decrepit body seemed to surge with youthful adrenaline. His lips twitched and trembled as fond memories filled his tired mind. Fumbling for words he was trying desperately to say something. Only a groaning moan came up from his dry tender throat. Thick tears filled-up his grateful eyes. Soon, flowing rivers traced down his wrinkled cheeks. Falling to his knees on the hard wood floor—his quivering hands reached out to touch her face. "My beauty," he whispered so softly we could barely hear him, "My Melissa…you've come home." Wrapping his arms around the carving, he sobbed as he gently kissed her marble face, repeating, "My sweet Melissa… you've finally come home—

When I looked up—David's uncle and aunt were embracing, with tears running down their own cheeks. They were enraptured—as this miracle unfolded in front of them. The uncle glanced over, saying through his sniffling, "He hasn't uttered a single word…in over twenty years."

Lyn silently took me by the hand and led me down the hallway. We sat by the blazing fire, drying our tears. Ben hoisted the statuette up in one arm, cradling it like a baby. Jonas clung to his other arm. Together, they shuffled back to Jonas' bedroom. The statuette was placed on a table at the edge of his bed. Ben then joined us by the fire. Over the crackling burning embers we could hear Jonas speaking sweet words to his long-lost love. Ben wiped the last tear away, as he said, "That's the last thing in the world he has to remember her by. None of us believed that we would ever see it again."

"What's your name dear," Lyn asked. In all of the excitement, she had forgotten to ask who I was.

"Emma Morgan," I replied softly.

Ben and Lyn turned as white as ghosts—staring at me wide-eyed. "The Emma Morgan," Ben asked suspiciously, "The one Zach was always going-on about? You work at the High Museum, right?"

"Yes, that would be me," I blushed with a sensitive smile, "I call him David."

Lyn patted my hand, saying, "David was in love with you...so he thought. He would go on-and-on telling us all about you whenever he would come back from Atlanta. He was just too afraid to ever talk to you, in person." Ben smiled knowingly, nodding his head in agreement.

"What could he have been so afraid of?" I gasped with disappointment.

"You come from high-society, that's what," Lyn replied stubbornly. "He was afraid of your father and what he might do to him if he found out about the two of you. And David never believed that you would want to be around him. He was such a scoundrel," she snickered, remembering him. "He stayed up in the mountains, did a lot of drinking, drugs, bad-boy stuff...staying on the run and in trouble. But he was a good person. Had such a good heart...but didn't know how to show it to anyone…especially to pretty rich girls like you. David had finally gotten up the courage to ask you for a date when that old crony bitch from the museum…Loretta I think is her name…she threw him out and got him banned from going in again. After that, he was certain that you'd have nothing else to do with him."

Needless to say, I didn't mention that I had recently been hanging-out with him, getting naked in museums, running from the law, stealing from motels, and generally being a bad girl myself.

And then it finally donned on me—why were they refer-ring to David in the past-tense? "So, where is David right now…isn't he here?" I asked curtly, expecting a joyful, "oh he'll be home anytime now". Instead, Ben and Lyn clammed-up, getting stiff, sullen, with far-off glazed-over eyes. They were a thousand miles away from me in that terribly long lasting moment of reflection. "Is everything alright?" I asked softly.

Ben looked over at me and forced a weak smile on his lips. He started to say something, but had to stop as his lips trembled—as if his thoughts couldn't be spoken of. "Why don't you take Emma up to meet Dalton," Lyn suggested as a kind gesture, letting Ben of the hook. "Who's Dalton?" I inquired. Lyn told me that, "Dalton was David's best friend growing up."

She did it again—*was his best friend?*

Ben drove me up the road a few miles before parking out front of the E.M.S. station. "Dalton and David worked here together," he let me know as we walked up the stairs to go inside. Dalton came out and greeted us in the lobby. A shorter stocky man with a thick reddish beard, he could be mistaken for a grizzly bear up in the mountains. His face lit up as if he was recognizing an old friend. "Hello Ben…it's been awhile," he cheerfully handled us with his pudgy paws, shaking hands, and giving hugs. After a quick introduction, he stared intently at my face, before asking, "Where have I seen your face before?" It took a couple of seconds before I realized that he looked very much like the fellow that rescued me when I had my skiing accident. Then he smiled big, with rosy blushing fat cheeks, he asked me, "Didn't I give you mouth to mouth?"

My face turned a bright red too, as I replied, "I think that was me…yes how embarrassing. It was you that pulled me out of the snow…you saved my life, right?" We all laughed, with Dalton beaming with pride, adding, "You were my first resuscitation. We never thought we'd find you in time. You must have slid over a hundred feet down that ravine. You were completely buried by a small avalanche that covered all the tracks. We couldn't see nothing of you at all…it was all white. It was over thirty-minutes before we even got up there."

"How did you manage to locate me at all then," I asked, giggling out my words.

Dalton reflected on the moment, before replying mystically, "I'll never forget it. We got up there and couldn't find any tracks. We started searching up top, making our way down, going in the wrong direction away from where you ended up. Something caught my eye…a bluish hazy light hovering up over the snowpack…like nothing I've ever seen anywhere else, ever before, or since. It must have been a reflection off of something you had on, or dropped. But

I just had this gut feeling we should search that spot. And there you were…a miracle."

My mouth was hanging open at that point. I could see the hazy bluish lights in my head—the ones outside my window at the Orly airport. It wasn't my imagination. "And I called you David," I recalled, remembering how he reacted.

Dalton's face became serious, "That's right…you did," he replied, "I had forgotten that part."

Ben chimed in, saying, "That's why I brought Emma up here to meet you Dalton. She wants to know about David… about what happened to him."

41

"ARE YOU UP for a hike?" Dalton asked me to join him. "Certainly," I replied hardily, ready for anything that would provide some answers.

Ben departed to return home. Dalton drove me in his truck up a winding dirt road up to near the tree-line. He had fitted me with some sturdy hiking boots back at his office. They came in handy as we trekked up a thin rocky trail that is covered by snow most of the year. Breathing became more difficult as we ascended up into the thin air at the crest of the mountain. Dalton stopped in front of a large granite boulder. "Here we are," he gasped, leaning against it for a badly needed rest.

Carved into the face of the boulder was the amazingly detailed image of the Greek God Zeus, sitting atop his mount Olympus, reigning fire down on the hapless humans. It was obvious that David had inherited his mother's incredible talent for sculpting. "This was his absolute favorite spot," Dalton let me know. "He spent so many hours up here working on that. He just wanted to leave his mark on the world. But I think he was trying to hide from it."

"What do you mean by that?" I asked.

"David had a hard time after his mother died in that crash

so suddenly. His father was no good to him…losing his mind and being stuffed in that nut-house in Georgia. All that messed him up inside and he started hating people, life, everything really. The older he got, the more he started acting out. I probably didn't help matters since I instigated a lot of it. Anyway, his only escape was doing stuff like carving that right there."

"You still haven't told me where he is," I blurted out, venting my frustrations. "Why won't anyone just tell me where he is right now?"

Dalton stared off into the vast mountainous wilderness stretching out before us for hundreds of miles. Crest after mountain top crest, bald granite spires poked up as far as we could see. "Because none of us know," he mumbled remorsefully. The sound of his voice let me know that I had torn open a closed wound, one that was very painful.

He went on, recalling that, "David was so young and headstrong. He could outrun, out-ski, outdrink, out-do any of us up here in the mountains. Sometimes he was more like a mountain goat, than a man." Dalton smiled a little bit. "About five years back, some novice hikers came up here from California, wanting an adventure to end all. Well they got it, alright. It was late November and the resorts were getting ready for ski season. Not sticking to the trail, they headed into deep country where the rocks are loose and unsteady. Any wrong step would send them crashing down to be buried beneath a rock slide. After a couple of days of them disappearing, we got the call to go up after them, all of us. We got suited up, ready to go up, when we got another call, to call off the search before we even got started. An early storm was blowing in fast from the West. They didn't want to risk going up on foot, so they sent up some spotter planes to scour the area in the air."

"David went up anyway," I mumbled, knowing what he was about to say.

Dalton continued, saying, "That's right. David wouldn't wait for the storm to pass. He took off on foot and never came back down. That storm dumped several feet of snow up where he would've been searching. It didn't thaw until the next summer. We never found him, or those stupid-ass hikers. They just up and disappeared out there someplace."

I wanted to tell him that David was back in Georgia—that we had been together just the other day. But I couldn't. It was all so crazy. It felt like the side of the mountain was falling away beneath my feet sending me careening down tumbling head-over-feet. Getting woozy-headed, I leaned back against the cold granite boulder to prop myself up. My face turned white and I could barely breathe. With a shivering mouth I tried to say something back, but couldn't find the right words. What the hell could I say that would sound rational?

Dalton was staring at me, seeing my pain. "He talked about you all the time," he said reassuringly, before I could mutter anything. "Look over there," he told me, pointing to the other side of the boulder. Shifting around the large rock, I could see where letters had been chiseled deeply into the hard glittering stone.

EM

As I ran my fingers along the lines, Dalton revealed that, "You were the only thing David was truly afraid of. And, probably the only person he ever truly loved."

My eyes burned as tears welled-up. A single tear fell, washing over my dry skin. "Why didn't he let me know…why?"

Dalton patted me on the back, with the comforting words, "David had deeply carved scars on the inside as much on the outside. Other people, bad relationships, getting hurt emotion-ally, are about the only things he ever had a weakness for. I think it was because of how he lost his mother and father. He just kind of got lost inside. Seemed like in a way, he put all that pain into trying to save people all the time, even if it meant risking his own neck. I believe that David couldn't handle you rejecting him. So, in his own weird way, he came up with a way to win you over. He said that your one true love, your passion, was art. So, he was going to sculpt something so beautiful that you couldn't help but fall in love with him, whenever you first saw it."

"That's why he's been working so feverishly on that sculp-ture out in the barn," I mumbled to myself. "That must be what he's been hiding from me, until it's finished."

"What's that...he's doing what?" Dalton asked squea-mishly, hoping that he somehow heard me wrong, with my lips trembling causing me to mumble.

"Nothing...it's nothing, just the thin air making me light-headed," I replied, rolling my eyes and acting all dizzy. "Can you take me back to Ben's place, please?" Right then, all I wanted to do was get someplace safe and warm. Someplace I could focus long enough to try and wrap my head around everything.

Dalton guided me back down the mountain and depos-ited me safely back on the doorsteps of the B&B. I thanked him profusely—over and over again until he was sick of hear-ing it—for saving me, and for saying what I needed to hear. His response was that he was only doing his job, like David had done.

Ben and Lyn were so grateful for my returning the statuette to Jonas, that they put me up for the rest of the weekend in their best room, for free. They even purchased a flight home

for me on Monday morning—first class. I never mentioned
that the hotel was demanding to be compensated an exorbi-
tant amount for it. I'm certain that they would have insisted
on paying the ransom for me. Best left unmentioned. I never
mentioned seeing David, not once. None of my story about
him was rational—even to me. They only would have believed
that I was delusional. And I wouldn't have blamed them at all.

As I was getting ready to board the flight home, Ben mentioned, "I plum forgot to tell you that some lady called from
the High Museum the other day, before you arrived. She mentioned that she knew you. Her name was Lorraine or something like that. Turns out the museum you work for is interested in those carvings out in the barn."

"What did they want Ben?" I asked, thinking that it was
father wanting to keep tabs on me.

He was puzzled, not able to remember exactly, replying,
"I know she mentioned something about that Orly memorial
exhibit for one thing. We didn't have much time to talk much.
She asked me to call her back today to work things out. I'll
have to return her call as soon as I get back home."

I smiled and gave him a kiss goodbye, "You make sure you
do that, first thing." This was good news. The Board must have
changed their vote, and now they wanted to display Melissa's
other statue for the memorial exhibit after all.

By the time my flight touched down back in Atlanta I
had firmly decided to never mention David to anyone again.
Not unless he was standing next to me in the flesh. It would
be social suicide to have everyone think I was seeing ghosts,
or something worse, mad delusions. Father was already thinking that I had lost my mind completely. Saying something like
that would only cement the idea in his head. It was going to be

difficult enough getting out of the trouble I had created up to now. Nothing could be gained from saying anything—about anything. Paris, getting naked and making out with statues, all of that could be easily explained away as stress related. A momentary snapping out of reality, brought on by the enormous weight of final exams and finding out that my boyfriend was cheating on me for the umpteenth-time. Throw in a good dose of alcohol induced, mind erasing blacked-out freaking-out, and *voila*, I'll have the perfect unimpeachable defense.

42

THERE WAS AN eerily strange calm when I arrived home. The entire family seemed to be intentionally avoiding me, for some reason. That was fine with me since that is what I wanted to accomplish myself. Avoiding meaningful contact with anyone let me hide my feelings. Bottling-up my emotions was the best way of not-slipping-up, saying something stupid, blowing my cover, getting caught-up in my own meandering sloppy lies. The longer they treated me like some mental ward patient, the better off I'd be. There is nothing better than the dull passing of time to help dull the memories of others. And they don't have to forgive for what they can't remember.

Even the entire office staff was playing along. Keeping their eyes down when I strolled past. Turning in the other direction in the middle of the hallway, or breaking off conversations mid-sentence to scatter, pretending to be doing something else, anything else, in order to avoid me. It was all too perfect. No questions—no embarrassing problems.

Carly was my only base of support. She was the only person that I had actually confided with. Blabbing to her every detail about David and what happened to us—back when I believed he was a real living person. A friend like her never doubts you to your face. Her way of keeping you focused on reality was to prick you with pointed questions, to make you think. The way she learned to be critical without getting an ass-whooping from one of her many older brothers at home. It never occurred to me that she was trying to give me some good advice along the way.

By the way everyone was looking at me—I realized that Carly couldn't keep her big mouth shut. But I couldn't blame her for that. I'm the most interesting gossip this office ever produced. *Let them think whatever they want to about me… it'll roll right off my back*, is what I pretended. Inside I was mortified beyond belief. It was bad enough being the boss's daughter. But now, I was the boss's *crazy* daughter.

Tom played his role in the whole *don't do anything that may be upsetting to Emma*. He danced around our awkward conversations to the point it was getting funny. No one had more practice at lying to me than Tom. But seeing him squirm so hard, bending over backwards to avoid mentioning certain things, to the point that his back was breaking, made me snicker inside. I was *still* his boss's daughter. And he *still* had to make partner. So, he *did* what he *had* to do. Just like me.

Tom's final test was coming up. We had dinner plans for our exclusively dating anniversary. Enough time had passed that we had reached that most important of milestones. That point in time where it was time to either put-up, or shut-up. When a woman needs to hear him say one of two things; *I love you*, or, *I think we should remain friends*. If he couldn't say the first option with a heartfelt passion—then at least I would know that he was thinking of the second. And the jealous spat over David, real or not, should have been plenty enough incentive for him to close this deal, and finally put a ring on my finger. If he felt like I was worth catching, he had better set the hook, fast. It was now, or never.

Life didn't slow down however, just because no one wanted to be associated with me. Work was piling up on my desk faster than I could clear it away. Paper-stuffed-files stacked up so high they were spilling over. Messages were coming in non-stop from irate clients that wanted answers, and something done, by yesterday. Every time I glanced down at my calendar there were more things penciled in—depositions to attend, client meetings, court hearings, legal research, motion and briefs to prepare, phone calls coming in and even more calls to go out. The more I got done—there was even more that suddenly had to get done.

While nothing was actually getting done—nothing!

One file went out as another one was plopped down on my desk. The week was dragging by, so slowly. All the while, in the back of my mind, I was thinking about David's unfinished sculpture hidden beneath the tarp. *Why was he hiding it from me? Was it really all just my imagination running wild? I'm not insane…he was there…and so was that sculpture he was working on. I felt it when I struck the chisel. My own hands helped to sculpt it.*

As the endless stream of work built up, so did my stress. And I could feel myself changing, hardening, building up a protective shell. Feeling a bit like some sea creature forming a rock-hard protective shell—I was crusting over. A few unrelentingly rough days went by as I silently toiled, doing the work I inwardly despised. Waiting for an emotional payday that I was beginning to realize would never ever materialize.

Letting others spin me around like some hapless manipulated marionette. Retreating inside my emotional cocoon seemed like the only option I had left. Soon, my memories of David became the only things *real* in my life—since I was turning to stone.

By the end of that week I was hardened and numb. Seeing my life with Tom, this job, every day for the rest of my life, was all too much. *There had to be something more for me?* I pondered as I walked to my car. If only David was here with me. Then I had the thought; *if he's not here, at least his sculpture could be. It would be like having a small part of him with me always…something I could touch and feel.* I remembered how Jonas wept at the sight of Melissa's creation, knowing that once again he could have something of her, with him, always.

Racing along the freeway with the rush-hour-traffic I sped up into the smoky foothills. My adrenaline was surging. I was feeling refreshed. Like the night in the museum with David, naked, lusty and free. My scaly-hard dragon skin was sloughing off the closer I got to the farmhouse. All the colors of the flowers and trees were more brilliant, more vivid—alive.

Running down the trail through the trees I caught sight of the barn doors. The large wooden doors were dangling, swinging in the breeze, left slightly open. The padlock and chain were missing. A pitch-black hole filled the space between them. "What's going on?" I gasped, pulling open the doorway. Inside it was empty and dark, as barren and foreboding as a raided tomb. A cold sensation swept over me seeing that the blue tarp covered sculpture was now gone. Nothing was left. The lighting, the camera, the coverings chisel mallet and stools—all gone. White marble dust dotted the dirt floor. Wheel tracks were pressed into the dirt where the heavy sculptures had been wheeled out. I fell onto my knees and sobbed, having lost every part of David. Nothing was left for me.

⮞

Another long week passed, landing me on today, where this story first started. Nothing about my life had changed. I was only halfway through another tediously long workday, already dreading the start of my third year of law school. Tom continued to withhold his love, along with a wedding ring. Nothing magical or romantic spark erupted during our anniversary dinner—not too unexpectedly. Lingering a little longer each morning down by the lake, I would sulk on my bench wondering if Ethan would remember our agreement, and give me a call. Mother remained inebriated and aloof. Father was as gruff and demanding as ever. Jon stayed hidden within his own world entirely. And to top it all off, apparently—David never really existed at all.

My life was now a still-life portrait, stiff and unrelentingly predictable. Sadly, I accepted my plight, hardening in my resolve. I'll finish law school. Become a partner in father's firm. Maybe I'll even marry Tom someday? A loveless unfaithful marriage is all that should be expected. Besides, appearance and reputation is more important than substance. Suck it up girl. You'll buy a big house in Buckhead. Hire lots of servants. Drive the fanciest cars—work, golf, booze it up to dull the pain, while doing all those other things that high-society people do.

Before leaving for lunch with father, I had finally forced

myself to accept that I could survive this life of mine—if I became as hard as stone.

As it turned out, David wouldn't let that happen to me. Somehow he had found a way to reach across the void to save me—yet again. When I walked inside the High Museum today to find his sculpture on display, with everyone crowded around staring up at it in awe. There I was, carved into that large white block of marble. Holding David in my arms, pulling him to me, as our lips first met, for a deep passionate kiss—our kiss that would now go on forever.

Now I was sobbing, with my tears dripping onto the floor of the Orly memorial exhibit, wilting beneath the blistering summer sun—knowing that David was real in every way. And with his final sculpture completed, he had sealed our love completely—eternally. *Our kiss* was undeniably real, resonating with a living passion that could not be tempered. Anyone who looked upon the marble stone kiss would feel our undying desire, and know for certain, how true love felt.

Looking up at *The Shade*, he was gloomily staring down at me, with his drooping hand pointing down towards a life of eternal damnation. David was right—I could feel him in his anguished despair. *No, I won't submit!* I screamed inside, wiping away my tears. He was real to me now, not molten metal, not imagined, he was my emotion, wanting to take away my soul.

I resolved right then and there that I wouldn't be bowed down in submission like Rodin's statue looming over my shoulder as a condemned man. Hell was waiting for me back at the office, with an endless torment of shuffling piles of paperwork for miserably demonically demanding clients.

David showed me my fate, and that I had a choice. And I decided right then and there to make a different life.

A fighting anger filled my blood, hot enough to melt my metal mold. No, I would not be cast in bronze, not controlled, contorted or bent in directions that I did not wish to go. I would remain flesh and bone inside and out. I would not be locked up inside a false reality, or forced into a miserable state of mind. I would not be hardened. Not be turned to stone.

EPILOGUE

OUR KISS CHANGED my life completely that day, over twenty years ago. Looking back now, I wouldn't change a single thing.

A few days later father let me in on a few things that I didn't know about. He had received a copy of the photograph snapped in the Rodin Museum from the French Investigator—the one showing me and David posing naked as we kissed. Of course he was shocked and disgusted at the time. But then Mitch came to him with an incredible story. When Mitch went up to David's place to investigate what was going on, he discovered all the sculptures out in the barn—along with *Our Kiss*, as it was soon to be called. Mitch described how the likeness captured in the photograph had been somehow miraculously carved into a marble statue, down to the fine facial features.

Father and Mitch dropped everything and drove straight back up to see what was inside the barn. Finding the amazing trove of precious carvings, they immediately notified the High Museum Board of Directors about what they had found. They showed them pictures of each piece.

Father laughed whenever he told me how Loretta's face

went white, as if she had seen a ghost. She was being haunted alright, just not how she imagined it. Loretta was so moved, or frightened, by the photos that she instantly brought forth a motion to purchase the entire lot for the museum. She was so insistent that no one dared to vote against the measure. That's when she took it upon herself to contact David's uncle to arrange the purchase. The museum bought everything, including the statuette that I lifted from the hotel room. Loretta, being the forceful person that she is, managed to get the hotel to accept far less than they were demanding.

Father convinced the Board to put the pieces out on display, along with the other Orly Memorial Exhibits. This set the stage for my fateful encounter with *Our Kiss*.

When I first saw it, David was there too, with me, guiding me toward a better place. It was undeniable and exactly how he told me it would be. And I could feel him there with me. He was not cold marble. He was hot-blooded emotion that touched my heart.

I dropped out of law school and never even started my final year. It was a horrible nightmare coming true for father at the time. But he eventually softened to the idea. Once he could see how much happier I was. Instead, I changed my major and pursued a master's degree in art. Eventually I finished my formal education by earning a Doctorate in Art History. While pursuing my doctoral thesis I continued to work at the High Museum. With my doctorate completed I was offered a curator position—my dream job.

Father never got the nomination for the Federal bench. He made plenty of money with his firm and took an early retirement. After a minor heart attack scare he decided to finally slow down, try to mellow out a bit, before it killed

him. I like to believe that him seeing how much happier I
was with life, being something different, helped him choose
to turn on that fork in the road. Nowadays you will find
him holding court out on the golf course, where he still wins
every argument. Or so he tells himself.

I bump into Thomas every now and again whenever
he stops by the museum. He is usually with another new
bimbo girlfriend, trying to impress her with his sophisticated
insightfully intimate knowledge of art. It was fun eavesdropping on them as he discussed his impressions of the pieces
on display. Of course he learned it all from me. Getting fed-
up with waiting around for father to make him a partner,
he decided to move on and open up his own law office. His
ego wouldn't allow him to work beneath anyone else anyway. Flitting about as a socialite butterfly, hobnobbing with
the elitist folks, he constantly flitted from one pet project to
the next, trying to climb up the tall Atlanta social ladder.
He even served a short stint on the Board of Directors after
father stepped down as the Director. But once Tom got his
fill after only a few months, he naturally got bored. Checking
that off his list, he moved on to other more interesting pur-
suits—just like he did with most everything else in his life.

Jon opened a men's clothing boutique downtown. It was
overwhelming successful. Before we knew it he had opened
up other stores in L.A. and Frisco. Now he's become such a
snobby bitch! We hardly ever talk or see each other. But I
know that he is happy, and that's all that matters.

Carly scratched her way up the office floors, all the way to
the top floor. She was actually made a partner ahead of Tom.
That had to bruise his tender ego. That is most likely the
reason he decided to move on. We still have lunch together.

To this day, she is the only person that I can talk to about certain things—namely David. No one else would believe me anyhow.

Ethan did call about a week later—at just the right time. We went on that date as I promised him. And a couple of years later, we got married. After a few years of flying freight Ethan became a senior pilot with a major airline based in Atlanta. This is perfect for us both. Since every now and then we leave our two children with mother and father and fly off to New York City, Paris, London, or Rome—anyplace with an incredible art museum.

Finally, I must confess something about myself. Sometimes, when I'm all alone in the High Museum, after everyone has gone home, late at night with all of the lights turned off—I do something naughty. I take off all of my clothes inside of my office. After peeking out to make sure that the security guard is not around, I slink like a cat down the darkened hallways. Then, I nimbly slip out into the cavernous exhibit hall, where, the soft moonlight flowing through the large windows causes my body to glow a soft hazy blue. Striking a sultry pose, I wait. Then, when David comes to me, we embrace—for our kiss.

www.ingramcontent.com/pod-product-compliance
Lightning Source LLC
Chambersburg PA
CBHW031148120726
47905CB00006B/1856